Praise for Celia Brayfield's no

For *Harvest*

'A good read but far from trivial. *Harvest* is a brilliantly textured "proper" novel about the women who surround and love, ever so painfully, a manipulative media man. A literary romance featuring the sophisticated English abroad in France' Fay Weldon, *Mail on Sunday*

'Cunningly plotted, extremely well written and compulsively readable' Beryl Bainbridge

'The authentic tang of human emotion at every level' Claire Rayner

'A cleverly plotted, witty black comedy, modern storytelling at its most enjoyable. Packed with insights – some acid, others poignant, all with the ring of truth. The throwaway observations made me laugh out loud' *Literary Review*

'Grand guignol in a gîte – shockingly readable' *New Statesman*

For *Pearls*

'Long, absorbing, its grammar impeccable, its theme the sufferings and eventual triumphs of a pair of beautiful sisters. Ms Brayfield knows what she is doing and what she does she does well. Her Malaya is exactly rendered, her women sound and act like real women' Anthony Burgess, *Independent*

'A triumph – Celia Brayfield's first novel is a complex and delicious amalgamation of glamour and sensitivity, sensuality and betrayal, sweeping from war-torn Malaysia through the England of the Beatles. A rich, multi-faceted story, her plot is a masterpiece of construction, her prose literate, insightful and frequently witty' *Rave Reviews*

'From a sudden crop of British bestsellers with feminist undertones – sisterhood is powerful in this passionate page-turner' *Time*

'A great adventure of our time' *Le Meridional*

For *Getting Home*

'Deliciously comic – lightning flashes of wit and scalpel-sharp observation. Highlight of an excellent cast of larger-than-life characters is Brayfield's terrific comic creation, Allie Parsons, queen of daytime TV' *Daily Mail*

'With a sharp wit and snappy dialogue Brayfield has produced a very funny, cleverly plotted novel that displays Fay Weldon's understanding of the pleasure to be derived from seeing the bad get their just deserts' *Daily Telegraph*

'At once a biting social satire and a passionate denouncement of mindless environmental vandalism. Definitely Brayfield's best yet' *Good Housekeeping*

'Funny, fast and very enlightening – should be read by everyone who lives in a house' *Ireland on Sunday*

Celia Brayfield is the author of six novels, *Pearls*, *The Prince*, *White Ice*, *Getting Home*, *Sunset* and *Heartswap* as well as *Bestseller*, a non-fiction book about writing. As a journalist she has written for a wide range of publications, including *The Times*, where she was a television critic for five years, and London's *Evening Standard.*

Celia Brayfield was born in London and educated at St Paul's Girls' School and at university in France. She now lives in west London with her daughter.

Also by Celia Brayfield

FICTION

Pearls
The Prince
White Ice
Getting Home
Sunset

NON-FICTION

Glitter: The Truth About Fame
Bestseller: Secrets of Successful Writing

Harvest

CELIA BRAYFIELD

A *Warner* Book

First published in 1995 by Viking
This edition published by Warner Books in 1999

All characters in this publication are fictitious and any resemblance to real persons, living or dead, is purely coincidental.

A CIP catalogue record for this book is available from the British Library.

ISBN 0 7515 2902 8

Typeset in Garamond 3 by M Rules
Printed and bound in Great Britain by Clays Ltd, St Ives plc

Warner Books
A Division of
Little, Brown and Company (UK)
Brettenham House
Lancaster Place
London WC2E 7EN

ACKNOWLEDGEMENTS

My thanks are due to many friends and colleagues who were generous with their advice during the writing of this book, particularly Henrietta Green, who shared half her library with me and patiently answered innumerable questions about food and foodies. I am also grateful to Tim Hodlin and Tony Schulte for giving me the benefits of their mind-expanding experiences, and to Jonathan and Lindsay Acton Davis, David Harrison and Barry and Mary Turner, for the beautiful interludes in Gascony which were consequent on their invitations or hospitality.

The care with which Allegra Huston edited the manuscript was a renewed inspiration. The support of Bernard Nyman and enthusiasm of Dotti Irving have been invaluable. As ever, I am more grateful than I can say to Andrew and Margaret Hewson, whose advice was peerless and whose patience and understanding extraordinary; their friendship, and that of Willow and Tony Schulte, sustained me from the events which inspired this book through to the end of the writing process.

For Willow and Tony Schulte

PROLOGUE

Thirteen Years Before

When was it, the moment when Grace lost her own life? She was sure that there was a moment, a turning point at which she could have made a different decision and saved herself, but when she rewound the tape of her memory and searched for the frame that held that fraction of time there was nothing. Her love for Michael had appeared instantaneously, from nowhere, and knocked her existence off its axis.

One picture of him was crystal clear: she had been walking down a corridor towards the studio, and he approached in the opposite direction, a tall man with an aquiline stoop in his shoulders, flanked by a group of subordinates – secretary, researcher, vision mixer. They passed each other amicably. Nothing was said. He looked at her, she looked at him. She knew him; that was no surprise, the network political editor, the whole country knew him. In the centre of the group he was walking in silence, as if caught up in his own thoughts. That inner concentration drew out something from her.

No spark passed at that moment which she would have remembered if they had never met again, but by the time she was turning the corner at the end of the corridor it had happened; they were connected. She looked back, and so did he. You. You and I. Soon.

A sexy environment, a newsroom. All those days being seized, all the climactic deadlines, the general culture of intrepid opportunism. 'The political editor is having a preliminary meeting to discuss the election; perhaps you'd like to come along and then you can meet Michael . . .' Grace had resented the way the secretary had phrased that invitation, as if Michael were one of the world's major must-sees, like dawn over the Pyramids. Double presumption, since the election date had not been announced and the subtext of the message was that the political staff had a leak.

Even setting aside the magnificence of that prize, his manner was very simple. Laying the whole thing out in plain words, brushing the astonished congratulations aside, inviting cooperation in the happy task of wiping the opposition off the air, there was an honest, nonconformist modesty in all of it, although in running the meeting he was annexing the producer's territory.

With a young woman's handed-down cynicism she had been more than ready to despise him, as all the production staff despised reporters, teeth and smiles, autocuties. 'Grace, we'd like you to produce the midday bulletins.' Guilt for that readiness made her freeze in the searchlight of his enquiring stare. 'Fine,' was all she could manage to say. The next day she returned to earth, assessed the fearsome responsibility she had accepted and called his office. 'If Michael can manage it before the election, I think we need a little making-acquaintance time.'

He had a heavy schedule; it was necessary for him to come to her house on a Saturday evening, and she was glad to welcome him. There was no rigmarole of polite appreciation for her interior decoration, although nothing material in the world delighted him as much as a single woman's kitchen, that exquisite sampler of domestic life, displaying in miniature her skill in the crafts of comfort.

He sat familiarly on her kitchen table and said, 'Does it worry you that we broadcast the news four times a day and all it amounts to is an incoherent menu of the world's problems? Because I worry about that, more and more.'

'Yes.' He had voiced her own misgiving so exactly that she felt almost tricked. 'That worries me. But it's an incorrect thought and you'll be sent away for re-education.'

'I have other incorrect thoughts. I think it's no job for a man, wearing a different tie every day to deliver the top three world events in not less than fifteen hackneyed phrases.'

'Don't put yourself down.'

'I suppose there are enough people doing that already.' Again, that clean, almost boyish modesty. Putting coffee on the table, she caught the light, aromatic scent of his breath.

'People admire you,' she told him, annoyed that the

statement undiplomatically betrayed her own previous indifference. He was certainly the most admired broadcaster of his time, but Grace never ran with packs.

'You don't need to flatter me.'

'I wasn't.'

'No. No, you weren't.' He looked at her from the clear brown depth of his eyes. 'You are quite addicted to truth, aren't you?'

'I've never thought of myself as addicted, I think it's important, that's all.'

So he hinted at it. In time, he seemed to promise, he would present her with her true self, perfect as a flower, perfect as his own true self which appeared so admirably uncompromised. He offered her the freedom to peel away all the accommodations she had made with her own character for the sake of the roles she had to play in life, the producer, the lover, the student, the daughter. I have the power to be just as I am, he promised, and I will give it to you.

She had pinned to the wall a child's portrait of herself, drawn by the son of her closest friend, a misshapen, highly coloured figure which somehow expressed her essence in square shoulders and curling dark hair. He looked at it and asked, 'Do you want to have children?'

'Very much. My friend's son drew that, I'm passionately jealous of him.'

Then he introduced Jane, saying, 'My wife has doubts. She worries that having a child will restrict her life.'

'Well it will, but it will be worth it, don't you think?'

'And I have a daughter from my first marriage,' he

continued, as if it was unreasonable to expect him to be content with that. 'Imogen. She's only four. Quite demanding. Jane thinks she needs to have us to herself for a while longer.' There were dark rumours about his first marriage, a general recognition that it had been troubled, an idea that the child had been abandoned.

Then he said, 'Tell me what you think about this.' His confidence was thrilling; he took her up to his high place and showed her the world, the brilliant ambition that would in time become NewsConnect. She would cross some deserts with him in pursuing that golden mirage.

'It's difficult for my wife,' he said, 'for Jane. She isn't from our world, which in some ways is a . . . stabilizing thing.' He seemed to be too loyal to say that Jane did not understand.

He made a formal enquiry into her own status. 'Is there someone in your life?'

'Not now,' she said, with regret but also with anticipation. 'There was, we had been together since university, but he went abroad last year.'

'Did you live here together?'

'Yes.'

'You must miss him.'

'I do.' Especially at weekends. Working side by side, they had been patient with each other, and affectionate, and at about this time on a Saturday taken a break from their separate heaps of paper to exchange back rubs and plates of pasta before knuckling down for the final three hours.

They had felt too ordinary to talk about love. He had been offered a research grant to study in Mexico City, and they had patiently and affectionately agreed that neither of them was ready for a lifetime commitment at that point. All the same, she felt bereft. Occasionally they scribbled cards to each other. Sometimes he telephoned, but the line was bad and the time difference insurmountable.

Michael left, and there was emptiness at the heart of her home. The old pine table, on which over the years she had written essays, served meals and made love, appeared bare in spite of the litter of paper and pens, the bowl of red apples and the white lily in a vase. Her chairs seemed blatantly unoccupied, her saucepans conspicuously unused. Without him, already, she was less. She had to turn on the radio to fill his space.

The election began, long adrenalin-crazed days and short blank nights of exhaustion, and she was astonished at the sheer depth of his memory for political facts, and his ability to retrieve them, smiling in front of a camera, fluent and authoritative and inexhaustible. Then when it was over and he had made them feel, individually and together, that they were the true victors, he took her away from the party and asked, 'Can I come home with you?'

There was ecstasy, in the beginning. It was more spiritual than physical; he gave her joy and a blissful optimism about their union in which she trusted, mistakenly, that the physical satisfaction would develop. After a while she realized that he felt secure while he could be cerebral, but his emotions scared him and he would not venture far into eroticism.

She was the first to feel guilty, and he saw it and swiftly stepped in to retrieve her. 'I believe that love is *the* most important thing in life. It ought to be – the centre, everything else that we do should flow from it. The best that a man can do . . . is love. The most precious thing we can do, we ought to live for it – I mean tend it, sacrifice whatever we have to.' After weeks of listening to his beautiful voice and flawless delivery, it was strange to hear him stumbling over his own thoughts.

'Maybe that needs another read-through,' she said, protecting herself with cynicism. Her experience had been of not talking of love until, for her, it was too late because her own emotion was long dead of insecurity. It was alarming to be with a man who used the word freely.

'I like that,' he protested. 'I open up the bottomless depth of my soul and all you can do is be sarcastic.'

'I'm not used to people getting real on me.'

'Real,' he repeated, quite bitterly. 'You're the real one around here. Sometimes when I go into the washroom at the end of the day and walk past the mirror I'm surprised to see my own face, surprised I'm there at all. If I am real, it is only because that's what you make me. I love you for you, but I need you for that.'

It was never about sex. He was unaware of what there might be for them to explore together and afraid to make discoveries. He offered her love, and truth, and her best self. She thought he was the most honest person she had ever met; he seemed to be struggling continuously to balance on the sharpest edge of reality. It was many years before she was able to correct the picture.

CHAPTER ONE

Thursday

He looked well-fed, like a family man; she noticed that when he rested his elbow on the bar and his jacket gaped open there was a small mound of belly in his shirt. She encouraged him to move close, tilting her head back, flexing her throat, gazing intently beneath thick eyelashes as if their conversation concerned the deep mysteries of life, when it was really nothing more than the neutral interchanges of two people who might later wish to pretend that they had no interest in each other.

She saw that he was looking at her, not only her face but all of her. He found her tallness was almost shocking. As the kids said she was in his face – but literally; her eyes were level with his eyes, it was disconcerting, quite a thrill. Leaning back against the bar, resting on one elbow, her limbs were so slender that the knees and elbows were their widest points. She moved around slowly, as if choosing exactly where to place her feet and hands. With her glossy black hair and soft black clothes, she made him think of a beautiful big bird from Africa, a flamingo, a crowned crane.

'It's a nice little place, this, isn't it?' A smile creased his cheeks. Round, smooth cheeks, he had shaved again before leaving his office. 'I often drop in here for a drink on my way home.'

'I've never been here before.' You must lie, she reminded herself. Lying gives you the power. She had tried this place earlier in the week, scored well and decided to try it again. These little bars were all the same, clattery wooden floor, bizarre metal lamps, syrupy Semillon Chardonnay, the well-fed men not hurrying on their way home. 'I used to work in a place like this. Actually they made me the manager. A very responsible job, and the money was good. But I had to give it up. Too much pressure, I was totally stressed out. No energy, nothing. My work was suffering, I couldn't keep up with my course.'

'What course is that?' For an instant he was confused. Something about the girl announced wealth; it was not quite confidence, she seemed fragile, partly because she was so thin, but she looked around her with a muzzy expectation that her wants would be fulfilled. Spoiled rich girls did that, but they did not work in bars. Her smoky eyes were roaming his face and his doubts drifted away.

'Design. I'm a student. It's hard, you know. A lot of work. Coming up to the second year, that's the hardest. By the end of term I was working all night. I don't go out in the evening much . . .' A cough and a vague gesture around the convivial room with her cigarette.

'I thought I hadn't seen you in here. I would have remembered you.'

Her wide nostrils twitched. She smiled. 'It's busy, yeah? Is it always as busy as this?'

'About now, yes. Happy hour, half-price drinks. It's a good idea, people like it.' Definitely a family man, to be so excited by saving money. He was rich enough, though, you could see from the cufflinks and the fine white shirt. Rich and mean. It's time to pay up, sir, I'm going to give you the bill.

'You work near here? Where, in an office?'

'Western Oil, just across the street there.' She leaned forward to look out under the canopy of the bar, the point of her shoulder almost touching his chest. Magnificent shoulders, she had, perfectly square, the clean lines of a young body. And all that grace expended just to see the place where he worked.

'The big bronze doors?'

'No, the next one along. The seventh floor.'

Now she looked around at him, smiling again, pulling at the feathery tufts of her black hair. It had been hacked unevenly, in some places almost to the root, but he did not notice. 'The lights are on.'

'People are working late.'

'That's a pity. I was thinking that later on maybe you could have shown me around. I like your tie. Does it mean something, a club or something?'

'A shooting club.' He felt short of breath.

'What do you shoot?' Look away quickly, you're reacting and he must not see. Prepare yourself. You must not be distracted from the purpose. After all, the worse he is, the more he deserves what's coming.

'Just targets.'

'Really?'

'Yes. I like hunting, but I can never get away, and my . . . I mean, people complain if I do, so . . .' She made herself reach out and finger the edge of his tie. Raw fingertips, nails bitten to the quick and white, rough skin around the knuckles, but he was looking at her face. Where her hand had brushed his chest, under the shirt cotton, his skin tingled.

Women today, they knew what they wanted and they were not afraid to ask for it. He liked that. Honest, simple, no stupid games; that's how things ought to be between a man and a woman. When you both want the same thing, why not say so?

'I'm not from Paris,' she continued, speaking as if he had asked a ridiculous question. 'My accent's disgusting – I know you can tell.'

'I was thinking perhaps Australian.'

'My mother was Swedish. Then she was American. Is American. I must remember not to kill her off. But she ran off and left me so I was brought up by my father, so I have to be what he is. No choice in the matter.' She shrugged, sharp collarbones showing under her sleeveless black polo. 'So where is it that you live?'

'Out of town. Just beyond St Germain-en-Laye. Quiet, clean air. A very nice area.'

She nodded. She knew it. Way out of town, big houses, big gardens, big trees. In places like that nothing moving outside commuting hours except gardeners in the morning and children in the afternoon. 'It must be nice, if you live there. Wow, that is a *long* way out. What time do you get home?'

'Oh, not too late.'

'What about your wife, doesn't she complain?' There was an empty bar stool and she took it, twining her long legs around each other, keeping her eyes on his face. Confess. Tell me how guilty you are, before I punish you. Her knee was almost in his crotch. Her brown leather rucksack lay collapsed on the floor, taking up an inconvenient amount of space in the crowded bar. She made no effort to move it so he bent down and folded it more neatly, anxious because this was the flashpoint, it was here that women could turn cold and leave. Still, no sense in evading the question; silence answered it just as well.

'I suppose I must look married.'

'Yes, you do.' She was smiling again, and eating olives one after the other, very fast.

'My wife has nothing to complain about. I'm a good husband, she has everything she wants. Right now she's in Normandy with the children, relaxing by the seaside while I'm back here in Paris in August, sweating my guts out.' He checked himself, aware that he was almost babbling with nerves. 'You've eaten all the olives.'

'I'm hungry. I'd really like a big steak, and ice cream.' She was still with him and still smiling. His heart beat hard with relief. There was a good moon up tonight.

Such a sweet girl, not beautiful, you could not say that, but striking, yes; too tall and too thin, these students never ate properly. It would be a pleasure just to walk into the brasserie with her. He asked her name.

'Imogen.'

He had a classic, Burberry-style mackintosh. They all did, it was like a uniform. She took his arm as they left the bar, gloomily anticipating the steak. It would be necessary to eat at least some of it. One of them got so mad when she wouldn't eat that he had stood up and walked out, throwing money for the bill on the table. She had wasted a whole night. It was important to learn to compromise if you wanted to achieve what you desired, to learn to give in order to get.

Her father always lectured her about compromise. She would not go to his extremes, though. There was a difference between compromising and being compromised, the way he was. To get what he wanted he gave away so much of himself that in the end there was nothing left, not even the remains of a personality, only that ravenous will which had made the first compromise necessary. Greed in a suit, that was all that remained of Daddy.

The victim was holding open the restaurant door. They were so easy, these family men. This one was the easiest yet. Perhaps they got panicky towards the end of the holidays, worrying that the pussy season was ending and they hadn't got their share. He looked so clean and pompous in his fine white shirt and his suit. He commanded waiters like a dictator, his chest swelling. Such a display of power. She thought of how he would be in a couple of hours, so eager to shuck off the carapace and humiliate himself.

'Grace. It's good to see you.' The kiss on both cheeks from the friend, then the friend transformed herself into a gynaecologist. 'Sit down, please. How are you today?' The worst thing about being sterile was having to be treated by someone you'd had to dinner.

'Lousy, thank you.' No response. How could it be that a woman gynaecologist was actually colder, less comprehending than a man? Every time Marie-Laure's name appeared in her diary she was bad-tempered for a week; it was almost as good as PMT, which she had never had. Grace had once been on good terms with her body, proud of her health and delighted with physical pleasures. Now she thought of her body as an enemy.

She sat on her hands because she had an impulse to get hold of Marie-Laure by the shoulders and say, listen, you little cow, you have a womb too, that at least we have in common. Your biology is my biology, your hormones are my hormones, and in addition you've eaten at my table, so quit pretending you're not reading up my file and give me some goddamn empathy here. It's been three years, I could use a kind word. She tried again.

'I'm tired all the time, I can't concentrate, I feel like I've got a hangover.'

'Have you been drinking more than usual?'

'You know I don't drink, Marie-Laure. Not even wine with lunch. You need a clear head in our business.'

'Yes but perhaps . . . in your business . . .' There it was, the you-media-people brush all ready to paint out her identity, wielded with the I'm-not-being-judgemental professional hand. Just because once, just once, I cancelled an appointment when I had to cover the Rwanda crisis. Grace asked herself if she was being paranoid. It was difficult to maintain friendships outside the business. Everybody mistrusted journalists. Everybody thought their own stress load was special but yours was just an excuse.

'So, how is your work going?'

'Like it goes in August. Silly season. Air traffic strike called off, farmers complain of drought, oldest duck in France killed in road accident, foreign news editor dies of boredom.'

'So stress management is not a problem for you right now?' In Marie-Laure, this passed for humour.

'Not that kind of stress. Maybe it's this situation that's getting me down.' Every time her period started she felt less of a woman, more of a failure.

'It's never an easy process, investigating problems of conception. How are you and Nick?'

'Nick and I are fine. We are following instructions and keeping our good feelings for each other in our minds and hearts.' That had to be in some textbook somewhere; every doctor they had seen signed off with exactly the same words, try to keep your good feelings for each other in your minds and hearts. Nick was also a doctor, so most of them were his friends, and sometimes she caught them monitoring their marriage, looking for the good feelings, curious to see a living specimen of a relationship strained by unexplained infertility. Even so, they had absolutely no idea what hell it was to feel a normal desire grow into a monstrous obsession, to live out the brutal paradox which demanded that to make a baby they must sacrifice all the pleasures of love. And for Grace and Nick, those pleasures were considerable.

And then, the personal stuff. Marie-Laure was one of those perky, gamine women who get lost in crowds and have a hard time looking authoritative. Grace was a goddess with cheekbones who was always noticed and had a hard time looking vulnerable. She made Marie-Laure uneasy and if she tried to be nice to her it came out patronizing. On the other hand, in the past three years Marie-Laure, with her miniature pelvis and triple-A-cup breasts, had popped out two ten-pound babies. The doctor–patient relationship had acquired a certain caustic informality.

It was all right for Nick, he'd been a doctor all his life, he didn't need all the reassuring bullshit, the white coat and the impersonal manner, but Grace did. They'd argued about it, the three of them, and Marie-Laure voted with Nick for wearing ordinary clothes in non-clinical situations. So here she was in a Hawaiian shirt and safari shorts, sitting on a sofa. Grace would have been quite happy with Dr Kildare.

Marie-Laure was saying, 'You performed very well in the interaction tests for your husband's sperm and your cervical mucus.'

'Maybe we should take it up professionally.'

'And your husband's semen analysis is excellent.'

'That's reassuring.'

'Yes it is.' Not a smile, not even a flicker of amusement. Please. 'So now, in this second phase of investigating your continuing sub-fertility, we are entering the area of looking for one of the very subtle but important biological anomalies which could account, in a healthy couple such as you obviously are, for the absence of conception in your case. Then, when we have identified the condition, the challenge for us will be to discover how it can be treated, and for you, for a little longer, the challenge will be to be patient.'

God, the *jargon.* Three years they'd been going through this. They never said 'treatment'; they said 'management'. This was the management of sub-fertility. 'I wish you'd stop managing me, Marie-Laure. Why don't you just lay it on the line? Just level with me. What's the next thing? What are our chances?'

'In any couple, the chances for future childbearing are always imprecise. Fifteen per cent of couples in the Western world are clinically sub-fertile. There is no line to lay it on right now, Grace. We are still finding out about you two.'

They had had some fun, having this problem managed for three years. Lying still for an hour after intercourse with a pillow under her bottom had been a good laugh, especially when she'd only just trained Nick for the post-coital cuddle. Then that riotous farce in the consulting room when Nick had to produce a sperm sample and decided he needed her help, thereby scandalizing the nurse but inspiring the man with the same problem in the cubicle next door.

You had to laugh because you'd cry otherwise. The temperature-taking, the red-ringing of Big O (for ovulation) day, the tiptoeing around each other on eggshells trying not to have a row, slip a disc, overeat, overwork or get drunk for two days either side of the Big O, a real gas. And, at the same time, praying for no news story to break anywhere in Europe – just hilarious. She had actually lit a candle. She had called up her mother for help to figure out the appropriate saint.

Using condoms for three months in case she was allergic to Nick's sperm had been a thrill; his own clinic dispensed them and he said the experience gave him many useful insights. And Marie-Laure giving them the results of the intercourse evaluation test – an act not to miss. Fascinating to find that you got a pain in your shoulder if someone blew carbon dioxide through your cervix; the marvels of the sympathetic nervous system. More fun than the fibre-optic safari up her fallopian tubes with a D and C for luck. And that was just phase one.

'But it's down to me now, isn't it?'

'It is important in these cases not to look around for implications of fault or guilt in either partner. Subfertility is a problem of the couple as a unit, not of the man or woman exclusively . . .'

'But you're out of tests for Nick, aren't you? You know all you need to know about him, he's got sperm, megamillions of them, they're normal, they're speedy and they're making it through to the right place. You've checked him out, he's all OK. This *is* my problem, isn't it?'

'We now need to investigate your ovulation process a little more closely.'

'So it's down to me. Come on, Marie-Laure, hit me.'

'Ideally, you should have an ovarian ultrasound scan every day so we can review your follicle normality, with a daily blood test to see what's happening with your pituitary function and your luteinizing hormone.'

'Ultrasound every day? Not this month, sorry.'

Marie-Laure sighed, and Grace interpreted it as another you-media-people sigh that meant you were an overstressed, overpaid social parasite bringing all this on yourself with your terrible lifestyle, a sigh asking what kind of mother would you be anyway if you were still putting your career before having a family at this stage. 'I know it's very demanding working for newspapers . . .'

'Which is why I'm going on holiday tonight.'

'Ah.' That had thrown her. 'It's Thursday.'

'Yes, it's Thursday. I'm taking an extra day off. I want to miss the weekend traffic.'

'You're going to your place down – where is it?' Marie-Laure knew it was somewhere remote, bizarre, unfashionable, somewhere only you-media-people would choose for a second home.

'Gascony. You must come some time.'

Grace knew she was quite safe. Gascony was just about as far away from Paris as you could go before you hit the Spanish border. Marie-Laure always took her family to Switzerland; she said she could relax better in a country where the people were better off than they were back home; peasants gave her a bad conscience.

'In that case, we can arrange the ultrasound when you return, and in the meantime perhaps we could try something else to start filling in the picture of your hormone function.' She got up and went to search the drawers of her desk. 'It's a daily saliva test you can do yourself, with technology dipsticks which change colour and the chart ready printed to fill in.'

'Goody-goody. I love charts.'

'More pleasant than blood tests, anyway.' The personal stuff again. Grace was a veteran blood donor, star of the A-positive vault, no problem with needles, but Marie-Laure had eventually confessed that she hated taking blood. 'Then we can begin the ultrasound in September. I would like to do three months.'

'And suppose after that everything is still normal?'

'Why don't we wait and see before . . .?'

'Come on, I am an adult.'

Marie-Laure was annoyed, but she swallowed it. 'If your ovulation cycle is normal after these tests then, in my opinion, it would be biologically sensible to attempt IVF.'

'What does biologically sensible mean?'

'It means . . .' She shrugged, struggled but could not come up with a translation. '. . . biologically sensible. But you know, Grace, that is a possibility only, and a long way ahead. We need more data first.'

She explained the use of the testing kit in detail, put the components back in their shiny white plastic box, handed it over in one of the clinic's tactful white plastic bags, and turned back into a friend.

'Enjoy your holiday – and give my love to Nick.' Kiss, kiss.

'I'll tell him his sperm are still performing well.'

'Where is he today? Normally I see you together.'

'On holiday already. He left last week – there was some course in Basque cookery he wanted to take.'

'Oh yes, he likes to cook, I forgot. I'd find that very difficult, I'm so territorial about my kitchen.'

'Well, I'm not. It's nice to come home from work and have dinner on the table.' We-media-people, we know what hard work is. With an unworthy smile, Grace said goodbye to Marie-Laure.

She needed a coffee. Nuts to optimum nutrition, her metabolism was screaming for a large espresso. And not on the same street as the clinic, because there was this adorable little baby shop right across the road, flaunting its pink and blue *broderie anglaise*-trimmed crib sheets and Babar the Elephant night-lights.

Poor Marie-Laure; only being herself and doing her job, she didn't deserve all that sarcasm and ill-will. For a moment, Grace considered going back to apologize, but then again the poor earnest creature might feel even more threatened by an emotion out of place.

The street was crowded. Men hurried past and she felt their glances linger momentarily, approving, aroused. What did they know? She had always caught men's eyes, whatever beauty she had was bold and arresting. Her body suggested vitality, health, good appetites. Who was to know that when the chips were down it was useless?

Today, she felt tense, but that was probably the idea of

Marie-Laure inducing an emotional crisis. Perhaps she would have been able to accept this problem better if she had been more accustomed to ill-health. Pulse, blood pressure, cholesterol, iron count – everything was always A1. She had perfect teeth, straight toes, a complexion like oyster satin, the eyesight of a twenty-year-old at the age of thirty-eight and periods you could set a clock by. Her physiology ate toxins for breakfast with a double order of stress on the side – no colds, no allergies, no indigestion, not so much as a hangover in her life. She ate well, slept well and had orgasms. No drugs, except the coffee. The only flaw in her body was the scar on her forehead, more or less self-inflicted in a car crash, and even then the doctors had said they'd never seen a fractured skull heal so fast. Her flesh had always done everything nature intended.

Call it superstition, but Grace knew this was not a physical thing. She didn't just want a baby. She yearned specifically for the state of pregnancy. She needed to give birth, in order that she herself could be reborn. She would surrender her body to an inevitable process of transformation; the old broken Grace would conceive a new whole Grace. But what was stopping her was an abnormality of her heart, a dysfunction of love. So she was up against God's own Catch-22.

It was a long drive to Gascony, ten hours flat out in her old English MGB, taking hideous risks overtaking the long-haul container trucks and stopping only once to top up the caffeine. The last two hours were on the *département* road, running south through pine woods.

Their resin scented the hot night air and she stopped again to fold down the roof. Gradually the land began to rise, hills swelling up towards the distant Pyrenees, and she turned into the snaking lane leading to their village. This was an old pilgrim route to Santiago de Compostela; the squat church tower could be seen for miles, even by starlight.

She arrived at the magic hour just before the dawn, when the bats came swooping back to the village like fighter planes returning from a raid, flickering through their palm tree and over the old tiled roof, disappearing into the ancient walls. Their house had been the village cinema; Nick had named it the Alhambra. Inside the cavernous auditorium the local carpenter had built them an oak staircase and a gallery leading to the bedrooms. The old foyer was the kitchen. Nick would arrive tomorrow but someone was already waiting for her, the white wild cat with half a tail who came and went as she pleased through holes in the massive walls.

'Who told you, puss?' The animal sat still, wary and expectant, her mutilated tail tucked around her paws. Grace looked in the freezer, found milk, thawed it in the microwave and poured some into a bowl. She put the bowl on the floor and retreated to the far side of the room, and when the cat saw she was safe she ran forward and lapped up the offering at once. Pink teats showed through her belly fur. 'More kittens, huh?'

The road was still roaring in her ears; she was too tired to be emotional now. She refilled the bowl. 'All right, puss – how come a scabby undernourished alley cat like you can pop 'em out like shelling peas?' For a second only the cat lifted its nose and blinked at her with affection. 'What do you know that we don't, eh? Come on, why don't you let me and Marie-Laure in on the big secret?'

In the instant of awakening a drop of self-pity permeated her consciousness: I am married, I should not have to wake up by myself in the bed. Resentfully Jane curled into her own warmth, but in a few more seconds she was fully awake and reining in her imagination before it reached her husband. She was in France. Michael was at home, in theory. Checking up by telephone was for wives with no self-respect. She was alone, he probably wasn't but thinking about him could not do her any good, so she turned her mind away; it was automatic, a habit of survival.

Anyway, she lectured herself, you are not alone, you have your children and your friends. You're just alone in your bed at this moment, that's all.

Another habit was filling the first hour of the day instantly. Jane woke up now the way cats could, fully conscious in a nano-second With one bound she leapt to her own rescue, slapping ideas and projects together to dam the flood of misery which had built up overnight. Once she imagined the picture of this unhappiness, a welling black pool, silent, evil-smelling, all kinds of debris in its filthy depths – dead branches of resentment, twigs of weakness, great logs of hatred and leaves of deceit at the bottom rotting down to an oozing mud. She was the beaver, working like crazy to keep all that vile stuff behind her dam, so that the forest could be sweet and green and sun-dappled and aromatic all day.

Most people thought that Jane Knight's life was wholly sun-dappled, and marvelled as to where she got the energy to be so perfect. All those children, a new book every year, the TV series, a famous husband, two homes – they saw her face on her cookbooks and were awestruck. Miraculous to achieve so much and still give dinner parties. (Of course she gave dinner parties, they had been featured in *House and Garden*: 'Media Czar Michael Knight Entertains'. Her husband would do things for journalists. Her revenge had been the jellied borscht; all men hate cold soup.)

Most people added: and she's still such a pretty woman. Jane had the looks of a Noel Coward ingenue – small-featured and fine-boned. Her hair was the colour of ripe oats, a silver blonde, not thick but disposed to fall obediently in a bob to the base of her neck. Although her profession ensured a sturdy shape, her appearance was always delicate. Her eyes were deep-set, her skin seemed very thin and her mouth made people think of the flowers called 'bunny mouths' by children because of their soft, downy lips. She had been waiting since sixteen for maturity to do something with what she considered an idiotically sweet face and a nothing of a body. Goddammit, she would exclaim at the mirror, I am grown up, why can't I look it? Then somebody would tell her she was lucky. All round, people thought she was lucky. She accepted their opinion, although it did not fit the facts as she knew them.

I am lucky that my thoughts are so docile and my head so neatly arranged that I do not have to think about Michael if I choose not to. I am lucky that I have been able to create a life so full of interest and incident that there is always something to do to distract me when I need to distract myself. Sunday, I have the lunch. Tomorrow there will be the preparation, the caterers, the marketing. And right now at five o'clock on Friday morning, I can think about mushrooms.

Outside the shutters she heard the faint hiss of rain. It was gentle, hardly more than a heavy dew. It would be swirling in clouds across the fields, leaving a sheen on the windward side of the roof and tiny droplets hanging along the spiders' webs. She could hear occasional drips falling from the leaves of the cherry tree outside the bedroom window. Moisture without destruction, perfect rain for mushrooms; there would be thousands of them under the oak trees. She sat up, threw back the quilt and reached for her jeans.

The farmhouse, when it was full of sleeping people, seemed like a huge pregnant animal. She imagined it breathing, the old stone walls expanding rhythmically, the beams rising and falling like ribs. Houses had been built the same way in this region for centuries, the same features appeared in village houses that were five hundred years old and in the new ticky-tacky boxes in Saint-Victor's industrial zone. Impossible to say how old their house might be, or guess how many lives had been lived in it before them, how many souls had flown into the roof, how many spirits watched from the walls.

It was handsomely large for a farmhouse, but the vast sky miniaturized it and made the whole assembly of huge timbers and massive stones look as simple as a house made of baby bricks. The main building was square, sited just below the shoulder of a hill on an outcrop of limestone rock, looking westward down a shallow valley, with outbuildings in proportion scattered around it. On the level ground before the rise of hill was a generous walled courtyard, while the west wall ended in three stone arches enclosing a terrace, and below that a garden planted among the rocks led down to the pool. It had been a *grand domaine* in its heyday.

The house was never full, but Jane had no feeling of isolation in it. On the ground floor she had ordered interior walls to be removed and small chambers made into bigger ones, creating rooms of baronial proportions now appropriately filled with massive French country furniture and draped with long, heavy curtains. Upstairs there were rooms which were never used, where the beds lay shrouded and cold, waiting for the guests who never came. Jane said she did not like to overwhelm the marriage with her own friends; Michael said he was never there long enough to make invitations worthwhile. People stay away from couples in trouble; they do not visit intimately or share holidays, afraid of exposing the rotting interior of the marriage.

Her bare feet fell soundlessly on the staircase, shrinking from the cold stone. There was a light under the kitchen door.

'Oh, hello. I didn't think you would be up yet.' The

kitchen smelled of wood-smoke and coffee. At the stove stood Louisa Fields, tugging around her abundant body a grimy white towelling robe with collar and cuffs of quilted satin, patting back her thick auburn hair.

'Something woke me. I thought it might have been an *owl*? Or one of the *children*?' To Louisa, regretfully single and born to tread no further than the lush carpeted corridors of luxury city apartments, owls and children were thrilling exotica.

'The owls aren't very noisy. If something wakes me, it's usually Emma. I was going to look in on her, but I don't think you would have heard her upstairs.' She loved Louisa, even if she was incapable of making coffee without strewing grounds, spoons and tin-lids over the kitchen with the viciousness of an anti-personnel mine.

'Poor mite – is she a *bad* sleeper?' And even if she patronized the children.

'I wouldn't call what Emma does sleep. She makes more noise asleep than some children do when they're awake.' Preemptive self-criticism was necessary on the score of her children. Nothing cut more deeply than the tactful silence of friends too sensitive to acknowledge that she had at least two troubled offspring. Emma was a tense, unthriving child who muttered to herself all night, shouting in her dreams, spasms of her limbs pitching covers, pillows, and toys to the floor.

'I forget, which one *is* Emma?'

'The eldest. She's eleven.'

'Of course. Coffee?' Louisa approached the oak refectory table with the red-hot percolator and Jane slipped the spare tile she used as a trivet under it in the nick of time. 'I used the ready-ground, I couldn't find the beans.' In her own kitchen, Louisa would no more use stale ground coffee than use margarine. Like Jane, she called herself a cook, but she framed her interests far more ambitiously and wrote a column for *Gourmet* magazine. 'What are you doing up at this hour?'

'I was going out for mushrooms.'

'Oh, good-*y*! I'll get my boots, shall I?' She set down her mug, splashing coffee over her satin cuffs, and bustled joyfully upstairs.

While she waited, Jane scribbled a note for the children: 'Gone mushrooming – back for breakfast.'

'Do you need to do that?' Louisa said on her return, her eyes round in wonder. 'Surely if they wake up the nanny'll look after them?'

'She will if she wakes up. Debbie's a better sleeper than they are.'

'Won't they just play?'

'Sam will. He'll just plug himself in. Actually I think Sam is really a new secret component genetically engineered into my womb by the Sega corporation. It's Xanthe I'm worried about, she's only two and Emma's tossing and turning wakes her up.'

'So why put them in a bedroom together?'

'Because Emma will take care of Xanthe if she does wake her up.'

'Oh, I see. Golly. The things you have to think of. What about Antony? Wouldn't he . . .'

'Mnuh.' Antony, her other guest, was Louisa's

travelling companion; it was not quite fair to call him a lover, since she groused that he was seldom capable of fulfilling the role. Antony imported wine, and was a creature so urban that Jane would not have left him in charge of a mint plant. She reached for her coat, debating the question of the children. The house stood by itself in the rolling fields, several miles from any other building. It was charming by daylight but Jane knew the children found it frightening at night, with its creaks and cobwebs and unknown corners. Eliminating the rats was a task she always soft-heartedly promised herself she would take on next year, so there were nocturnal scufflings in the wall cavities and scuttlings across the roof beams.

If little Xanthe woke, she reassured herself, Emma could be trusted, so it was safe to leave them alone. Twelve years of motherhood meant twelve years of never leaving a house without computing the possible hazard to the children. 'It's so refreshing to be with you, Louisa. I need people who can just walk out of houses around.'

'Does this mean you're thinking of walking out of this one?' Louisa halted expectantly in the act of putting on her boots.

'No. no. I hate to disappoint you but – no change.'

'*Pity*.'

'For God's sake don't lecture me, Louisa. It's too early in the morning.'

'OK, OK – silly question, sorry I asked.' Their friendship predated Jane's marriage, the only one of its vintage she had left. They had been friends so long that offence had become very hard to take.

Her favourite knife was in its special slot in the knife block. Jane pulled it out with a twinge of satisfaction. She liked rituals. The same tasks, the same actions done over and over, the same tools kept in the same places, gave her work a reassuring sense of archetypal correctness. She felt she belonged in the real scheme of life, that she was connected to the farm women who had used the old bread oven, and the cavewoman she imagined squatting by her hearth-stone.

It was the best knife for mushrooms, and for most other purposes. It was small and sharp, and special because she had found it in the house, in the kitchen, it belonged to the property. It was comforting to build these primitive little superstitions into her life.

While her own kitchen knives had gleaming triangular blades of stainless steel, the old knife was of iron, mottled with corrosion. its cutting edge honed down to a curve. The wooden handle was scarred with small burns and bound with packing thread where it had split towards the end. It was a vicious, sturdy implement with a long career in the day-to-day butchery of the farm behind it. Jane decreed that the knife had to be wiped, never washed, oiled if it was to be left unused for a while and kept in the lowest hole of the knife block, where by chance it fitted exactly. She had a constant, lingering sense that her world was under siege, and observing these customs was like drilling the garrison, a ceremony which affirmed that the situation was not hopeless, that one could at least die with self-respect.

She recalled her own advice to her readers and

sharpened the knife against the carver, pleased that she could make the two blades flicker together in a fast, practised rhythm. 'A good mushroom knife must be exquisitely sharp, to cut the fungus cleanly, without any crushing.' Exquisitely sharp. 'Sharp enough to cut into the ball of your finger if you press it flat against the tip.' The sub-editor had wanted to take out that addition, being offended by the notion of drawing blood. Odd how people liked cookery to be absolutely bland, as if eating and killing were nothing to do with each other.

Her own boots were neatly placed together beside the door. Louisa was still in her bathrobe, now worn with heavy green stockman's boots and an Hermès scarf tying back her hair. Jane made no comment. but handed her friend a basket.

They strolled out into the courtyard in the half-light, their destination the wood which began a hundred yards down the valley. The air was fresh and damp; in the sky the grey cloud was lifting and a streak of illumination the colour of egg yolk announced the dawn. Beyond the mown grass and cedar spires of the garden, the landscape rose and fell in patches of grey and fawn, the hedges casting no shadows. It was breadbasket country, mantled with crops as far as the eye could see curving and undulating like the body of a nubile woman stretched out in sleep. In the valley bottom, a veil of thick white mist hung motionless over the stream bed.

'I won't lecture, I promise.' Louisa considered tough love a duty of old friendship.

'Please, it's 5 a.m., the sun's not up. I don't want to

hear about foolish choices or loving too much or feeling the fear and doing things or getting the love you need or any more of that fuzzy-brained New Woman crap. The people who wrote that stuff couldn't imagine a man like Michael if they did creative visualization for the rest of their lives.'

'All right, all right. Let's drop it.' She was panting to keep up now, Jane had accelerated in her annoyance.

They were all that moved in the early-morning landscape. The cool, humid air was still, and the tiny spiders whose cobwebs as fine as chiffon rags draped the undergrowth were invisible. The edge of the sun was above the horizon, but muffled in a ribbon of low cloud.

Despite the rain, the ground was parched and hard on the feet, even in the depths of the wood, where soft darkness lingered under the trees. Louisa squatted to examine the forest floor, collecting dew along the hem of her robe. Jane could find the mushrooms almost by instinct after gathering them for so many years. They sprang up coyly in different places each season, their shapes beloved to her mind's eye. The sheer abundance of them was cheering, it was hard not to be gratified by it, as if they crowded up out of the earth because they knew they were welcomed. She took care always to leave some of the finest to mature and decay, scattering spores for the next year.

'Chanterelles!' she called, pointing to a cluster of overlapping curds showing pale against the dark litter of leaves; in full daylight they would be a rich apricot colour. She crouched and began to cut them in clumps, enjoying their light, meaty resilience. Louisa joined her and held a bunch to her nose as if they were flowers.

'Wonderful smell! Like sherry, don't you think?'

'Uh.' To Jane's nose, they smelled nothing like sherry, but she never liked to offend anyone. 'These are the best eating. People rave on about the *pieds de mouton* because they're rarer, but I think they're tasteless.'

'Mnyeah.' This equivocal grunt was Louisa's signal for mild disagreement. 'Actually, I think the *pieds de mouton* are my favourites, so sort of thick and *crusty*, creamy-white, dear little spines underneath, so soft . . .'

'I expect we'll find some.' Although the *pieds de mouton* grew only in ones or twos they were conspicuous, and they gathered a good number.

'Tickly!' Louisa stroked her cheek with a particularly spiny specimen, then bit off a corner. 'Myum! Try a piece.'

Jane nibbled as bidden. 'I can see you're not impressed.'

'I'm thinking – I've got to do a column next week. Another year, another August, another mushroom story . . .' She shrugged and sighed.

'Yeah.' Louisa suddenly fell silent. Her own meditation on autumn mushrooms had already gone to press.

With a fallen twig Jane explored the carpet of leaves, considering the options. There was the famous gastronomic argument, should mushrooms be cooked in oil or butter? Or both, as the nineteenth-century master August Colombie had advised? Or goose fat, as the locals did? Or served raw, dressed with oil and lemon, as modern palates preferred?

There was a new editor, a nasty, brisk woman who scribbled 'Readers are always asking for low-fat recipes' or 'Remember we have many vegetarian readers' over her faxes. Low-fat and vegetarian were difficult concepts to apply to peasant cooking, in which the possibilities of the pig were central.

'Do you know,' she marvelled, half to herself, 'there's a Landais recipe for stewed ceps in Cahors wine with duck fat, marrow bones, pork skin *and* pig's trotters?'

'Do you have ceps?' Louisa demanded, feeling she should break the silence before her friend realized she was holding back her secrets.

'Do we have ceps! How could I forget – they're usually down there . . .' She led the way onwards, to a slight depression in the ground, the muddy course of a stream so small it was little more than a damp area sprouting greener, coarser grass. Here a few pine trees grew among the oaks, awkward, angular old trees with many broken branches, and it was around their roots that the ceps were most plentiful. Swelling up from the ground in glossy chestnut-brown humps they were easy to find, but insects loved them and there was no point in harvesting a handsome cap to find that the spongy yellow interior was riddled with grubs.

Recipes, the editor thought she was just a machine for recipes. Maybe she could try out the local *daube de cèpes*, casseroling the caps in red wine with some Bayonne ham – no, remember the vegetarians. *A la grècque?* Too banal. A warm salad of wild mushrooms with rocket, or young spinach? Too much like restaurant food. Perhaps *cèpes à la bordelaise* – so simple, just mushrooms, oil, garlic and parsley, the dish which had outraged Paris with its country simplicity when the Café Anglais had introduced it in 1880; that, of course, was a historic moment in the history of gastronomy, when the smart world first fell in love with peasant cooking.

'Look at this big fat perfect thing!' Louisa held up a huge brown cap. 'How nice to be an early worm, or whatever.'

'Do be sure, look at it in the light,' Jane advised, trimming the earthy base from a bulbous white stem. 'Those big ones usually do get infested. Here, take the knife – cut it in half to make sure.'

'Nothing's been near this baby, I pr . . . ugh!' As she spoke a grub wriggled indignantly from the mushroom's gills and fell between the satin lapels of the bathrobe.

Louisa's scream reverberated from the hills, loud enough to wake the roosting pigeons in the treetops and send them tumbling and shrieking into the sky. Breakfasting rabbits bolted from the field and every clump of undergrowth rustled as tiny animals leaped in terror. There was an instant of quiet, in which the echo of her voice rolled back and forth among the trees, and then a commotion of thrashing branches and snapping twigs directly beside them. A young deer, eyes white with fright, scrambled from a hidden wallow in the stream bed and leaped between the two women. Louisa stumbled backwards, screamed again, flung up her arms and overbalanced.

'Holy shit! Fucking hell!'

'Are you all right?' Jane was at her side, torn between concern, irritation at the histrionics and watching the magical creature escape, its white scut bobbing in the leafy shadows.

'Yuck, yuck, *yuck!* The mud!'

The deer was gone. Louisa sprawled half-naked on the forest floor, flailing her dimpled limbs. Her mushroom basket was six feet away in a clump of butcher's broom, upside down with most of the fungi scattered. In the cleft of a root Jane saw the fallen cep, a big brown ball which split into two halves as she retrieved it.

'Are you hurt?' She had enough experience of Louisa, and of accidental falls, to be sure the main injury was to the bathrobe, which had sustained a ripped armhole. People with broken bones usually screamed in a more purposeful tone.

'Ugh. Oh God. My back.' At last she struggled into a sitting position and began to pick the pine needles and dead leaves from her sleeves.

'Does it hurt?'

'I *think* it's just a bang.' She wriggled her hams experimentally. 'I can move – ooh, it hurts.' Jane waited until her guest felt restored enough to stand, then helped her lumber to her feet. With curses and caution because of the broom's sharp leaves, they gathered up the scattered mushrooms.

The fall had knocked out Louisa's enthusiasm and she began to groan and talk about breakfast and other plans for the day, pulling the bathrobe around her in order to look wretched and in need of sustenance. Jane was unwilling to let her friend give up before their task was finished. 'We can't go back yet,' she said, trying to infuse her voice with enthusiasm. 'The best ones are always over by the railway.'

'Do we . . .'

'I need a lot – there are fifty people coming on Sunday.' Louisa looked so pathetically deflated that she continued, 'If you're tired, just sit and watch me.'

Slowly, they made for the far side of the wood, where a railway line marked the border of their land. It was invisible from the house. The single track ran imperceptibly downhill in a cutting towards the white stone bridge which carried the road. Trees had been felled to leave a shoulder of open ground, and more chanterelles grew there, fluted orange caps clustered on top of each other like fallen petals.

Louisa sat heavily down on the embankment. 'It looks awfully rusty, the railway. Are there any trains?'

'One a day at this time of year. It comes down from Paris at about six every evening, goes to the cooperative outside Saint-Victor, loads up with wheat and comes back at midnight.'

Jane pulled a bag from her pocket and began to fill it, while Louisa lay back on one elbow and desultorily picked a few blades of grass out of her basket. 'I'm sorry I nag you about Michael,' she said after a while, looking genuinely contrite.

'Oh well – I can't blame you, I always dump on you about him, I know.'

'I only do it because I love you.'

Jane sighed, feeling racked between sympathy, gratitude, embarrassment and shame because she was unhappy and unable to help herself. 'You realize that's Michael's best line?'

'Oh God, I might have known.'

'That's one of the reasons why I always end up feeling I can't win. But I have done something. Something that'll bring him up short. It may not work, but I might as well tell you and then you'll get off my case for the weekend.'

'Well, good for you. I promise I won't tell . . .'

Jane hesitated, aware that whatever she might promise, gossip, scandal and confrontation were meat and drink to her friend. But then, her tiny gesture of defiance would not be a secret for long. 'You know the first one – at least, the first one I was sure about?'

'The woman he worked with, his director or something?'

'Grace Evans, she was. She's Grace Nichols now. I met her husband this week.'

'*No!* I didn't know she was married. He doesn't usually leave much on their bones, does he?'

'She's the one who got away, it seems. She went back to newspapers and moved to Paris. He's a nice man, her husband. I liked him. It was at this Basque cuisine seminar. So – I've asked them for Sunday. See how Michael likes them apples.'

There were no more chanterelles in sight, and she stood idly beside her friend, suddenly afraid of what Michael might do. He was furiously secretive. Very seldom had she dared any defensive manoeuvre against him, and his response had always been inordinate rage. 'Go on,' she prompted Louisa with anxiety. 'What do you think?'

'What do you mean, what do I think?'

'What do you think he'll do?'

Louisa was biting her tongue on the opinion that Michael had beaten better challenges than that. 'Whatever he usually does, I suppose.'

'He hates intrusions. you know.'

'What do you think you'll achieve?'

'I don't know . . . I just thought . . .' Suddenly it seemed that her bold move was only an idiotic, ineffectual gesture. 'She is the only one I'm absolutely sure about, that I've got the chapter and verse on. And Andy Moynihan will be there, and Andy told me what was going on, and so I've got a witness.'

'So you want to confront him again?'

'No. There's no point. He always denies everything and I just feel I'm going crazy.'

Louisa scrambled to her feet and picked up her basket. 'Can we go back now, have you got enough?'

'Yes. But tell me, what do you think?'

'Let me ask you one more question. Just one.' Revived by the rest, Louisa waded through the undergrowth, careless of the briars which snagged her bedraggled skirts. 'Jane – do you love him?'

Jane swallowed, a child taking medicine. 'Louisa, must you? I'm not going to do anything else. There is nothing I can do anyway.'

Her friend gave a satisfied cluck and nodded, having heard the answer she had expected. 'Then – *why?*'

'Because I've had enough, Louisa. You are right, I do want to end it, I can't live like this, it's killing me. And I've tried before, you know I have, but he is stronger than I am, and he always wins. I need something, someone on my side.'

'And one of Michael's mistresses is the right person to have on your side?' One eyebrow arched in contempt.

'I don't care, I don't care.' Jane turned her face away, afraid she might have tears in her eyes. 'You don't understand, he isn't an ordinary man. I just want to end it, I don't care how or with whom or how awful it is. I can't do it alone, that's all I know.'

'You mean you think I wouldn't help you?' Now she was approaching anger, her bosom swelling with indignation.

'Of course you would, I don't mean that. But she knows him like I do – do you understand?'

Louisa was hurt and said nothing. Then she saw new mushrooms, fairy-like pure white things speckling the grass. She bent down and picked a single ghostly parasol.

'What's this? It's so pretty. Look at the little ones, they're like bird's eggs. It can't be any good, can it? Too charming.'

Amused, Jane made her turn the mushroom over so she could investigate the colour of the gills, which were milk-white. Ruffles of white flesh at the top and bottom of the stem made the fungus look as if it wore a frilled shirt.

'Good for what? That's the question. It's an *oronge*. Every farm seems to have them round here. Nothing charming about them except the way they look. It's the most poisonous mushroom in Europe.'

'Fancy!' Louisa examined her find with new respect.

'It's easy to identify, you can't make a mistake, no other summer mushroom is this pure white colour underneath.'

'And it's really poisonous?'

'Deadly. More than one toxin, no antidote.'

'But there are a whole bunch of them down there. Shouldn't we do something? The children might eat them, mightn't they. If we pick them all won't they die out?'

'Perhaps. They are a mystery, mushrooms. One year they're everywhere, next year – nothing. But Madame Montaud was quite proud of having these.' She remembered the old woman stabbing the ground with her walking stick as if to punish the mushroom for its wickedness, and then walking violently away from it, rolling at every step on her bowed, arthritic legs. Despite her warnings, Jane had retained the impression that the deadly *oronge* was deliberately included in the harvest.

Over the years, she observed that in late summer and early autumn, when the entire province became obsessed with mushrooms, occasional deaths were reported in the local newspaper. Since every countryman around Saint-Victor possessed an encyclopaedic knowledge of food, Jane came to regard these fatalities with amused scepticism. It tickled her fancy to think that the prudent farmer would grow a few poisonous fungi in case there should, one day, be a need of them.

Louisa placed the white parasol on top of Jane's wholesome basketload. 'There you are, my dear. Just give that to Michael for his breakfast and all your troubles will be over.'

'Give it a rest, Louisa. Let me deal with my troubles my way.' Annoyed, Jane threw the *oronge* away and walked off in the direction of the house. She was ashamed of her childish anger. To her horror there was a strong urge to go back for the evil thing, under cover of an apology. The notion of having one in her possession, hung up to dry from the beams in the kitchen, was desperately attractive. No one would notice; she would have the power of life and death right there, and Michael would sit under it at the head of their big farmhouse table in all ignorance.

He never noticed what he ate. In fact, she had often suspected that he made a point of not enjoying her food, as if to emphasize that what the rest of the world praised her for meant nothing to him. No more Michael, no more lies, no more agony, no more pitying discretion from her distanced friends. And she would be able at last to tell the truth about him; that would be the real victory, to wipe out his image of himself with her own. Michael Knight exposed. Non-father, non-husband, selfish, cruel, a liar. Intoxicating, wicked vision. The force of her fascination horrified her. What was she becoming in this marriage, what was Michael making of her?

She accelerated her steps, trying to put the scenario

behind her. Louisa panted to keep up, congratulating herself for provoking her friend a little closer to the level of assertion proper for a woman at the end of the second millennium.

When he was finally asleep she slid out of the bed, gathered her clothes in her arms and took them to the bathroom. More than anything at that moment she wanted a shower, but the noise often woke them and then there was more trouble. She washed herself thoroughly at the bidet, despising the peach-coloured porcelain and the rose-scented soap. The steak, what she had eaten of it, was lying heavy in her stomach, obscene meat, poisoning her with its hormones and its great big selfish indigestible proteins. Still, it was cover; if ever they came after her they would never think of looking for a vegetarian.

Between her legs felt wooden, just a groove carved in a block, not registering the touch of her hands as they spread the lather. With no feeling, it was impossible to judge if she was bruised. He had put on a great display of virility, which was excellent because he had been tiring himself out and getting ready for a good long sleep, but she had so little flesh that she was easily hurt.

Snoring began in the bedroom, a reassuring noise. She was methodical. She found her gloves in a side pocket of her backpack. Her socks she put on, boots she left downstairs by the front door, unlaced and ready to step into. One of the nannies used to do that for her. It was suffocatingly hot so she laid her jacket ready beside the boots, smiling, remembering her father. 'We're still waiting to find out what exactly it is that my daughter can do.' This was something she could do. This she did expertly, in fact, beyond anyone's criticism. Nearly six months now and she hadn't been caught. These assholes never went to the police, they were too guilty. They just told their wives another lie. Not very significant, after so many. One more corpse tossed on the pile.

The bedroom first, or the dressing room if that was how the house worked. Once the man had woken up as soon as she opened a drawer; she had pretended to be looking for body lotion and let herself in for another hour of horror. Now she was extremely quiet. There wasn't much, there never was, the men were too mean, but no sensible wife took all her jewellery on holiday so there was always something.

She found gold chains, absolutely vulgar but so easy to sell, and two eternity rings, in their boxes, cheap boxes. Probably one for each child. One box had an inscription embossed in the satin lining: 'The Symbol of Everlasting Love'. Maybe he started fucking around when she was pregnant. Everlasting love for her and their two children, here in the outer suburbs, immured behind the cupressus hedge, and he never hurried home. Everlasting love, another big fat lie.

Downstairs, his jacket was on the kitchen floor where she had dropped it, a new refinement of her strategy. The jacket was the goldmine, not only for the money; jackets gave you your victim in three dimensions. She loved getting all those personal things, the driving licence with his traffic crimes logged in it, the business cards telling you who he had met, the little scribbled notes, the credit card slips witnessing his shopping and his restaurants. A good jacket was an afternoon's entertainment, but they were such noisy things, flapping with wallets, clanking with keys, and the men seemed to be umbilically attached to them and often stirred in their sleep as soon as she reached for the collar. Not this one, he was still snoring. No doubt his wife had to put up with that every night as well. Sometimes she got so frightened that she nearly threw up when she got to the jacket, and then the fear of throwing up, of that noise and disturbance, made it worse, so it felt like a string of pain around her throat, as if she was being strangled.

Then, when he had made the lunge across the kitchen and pushed her back against the pinboard with the children's drawings and the school timetable, it had occurred to her. How neat, how simple, during the kissing, just push the thing off his shoulders and there it would be when you were ready, waiting for you by itself in an empty room.

Flipping open the wallet, she saw that he had plenty of cash. Men always did, they liked to have money lying over their hearts to protect them from feeling. Good credit cards, gold ones. Someone at college knew a man who would buy credit cards. Now, what else? The steak felt like a pool of slurry in her stomach, seeping out, polluting her blood. The early dawn showed above the high suburban cupressus hedge. Little birds were awake, fluttering between the treetops and the telegraph poles.

The lamps were still on in the sitting room. Selective now, she turned over a photograph frame, appraising the faded velvet backing. Maybe they were antiques, some of them. She put half a dozen in her rucksack. These houses were always the same, too feminine, stuffed with cosy trinkets, padded with excessive furnishings, trying to fill up the space where the man should have been. The wife was pretending that the family was real, but real families had emptier houses, with things lying around where they were used, instead of all this self-conscious arrangement. One day maybe she would do a painting of a room like this.

The dining room was the usual trophy display, silver candlesticks and coasters, nice linen napkins to wrap them in and stop them rattling. So professional, she was becoming. Sometimes when she went to sell things like this the dealers were suspicious. Last time a man had joked that she was too young to be selling the family silver. 'You can't do it unless you're young,' she told him. 'It's when people get older that they get sentimental.'

The rucksack was full and heavy. She took off her gloves, laced her boots, pulled a note out of the wallet for fares and slipped out of the door into the dewy small hours of an August morning. The air smelled very clean, like the breath of children. A fox ran rapidly across the road and she blew it a kiss, one predator to another in the suburbs.

CHAPTER TWO

Friday

'Mr Knight, the concern of this committee is that if your news agency becomes part of the Altmark media group, a situation will arise that might be considered incompatible with the ideals of a freedom of information which this country has upheld before the whole world.'

The committee table was stacked with depositions, reference books, piles of notes. The room was windowless and felt airless, the table lamps creating a pool of light in the Rembrandt gloom. The faces of the nine men and two women forming the committee were tense with the effort of concentration in the enervating heat. It was August 2, the last day before the summer recess, the day Michael Knight had chosen for his appearance before them. 'I want them to think about these issues, really think about them. If I get to them before recess, they'll have the whole of August to give their minds to the question.' People only needed to think, he believed, to realize that he was right.

He was the finale, the star turn, but his manner dismissed ego considerations. After all, his reputation preceded him. Michael Knight made nation speak peace unto nation. He had dedicated his life to NewsConnect, the news agency of record, a concept not a company. NewsConnect was about more than live pictures and interviews with telegenic English-speaking people; NewsConnect told the whole truth, including the overview, the context, the world leaders who did not speak English respectfully translated, and because it got the best pictures fastest it still grabbed audiences. NewsConnect was a national treasure. Michael Knight had invented it, he owned most of it, he was its guiding spirit and its guru, and now he wanted to sell it to a brash multinational media conglomerate spreading round the world like a virus, owned by a South African and financed God knew how.

Michael Knight was taller and broader in life than on television, with a noble forehead and an intense gaze; in speaking he had a habit of leaning forward and pulling up his shoulders, a posture that appeared either protective or predatory, according to his listener's attitude.

He chose a soft opening. 'Forgive me, was that a question?'

His interrogator was better than that, she ate it up. 'Let me rephrase. This merger is one step nearer a global news consensus – how do you feel about that?'

'Let me explain the view which we at NewsConnect

take of the changes in the landscape of our industry. News-gathering today is a global business. There is a manifest need for international cooperation.' He was trying to infect the committee with his own sense of mission. These were second-rate politicians trying to work up the juice for one more attempt at recognition. They saw the control of the girdle of communications satellites around the earth as a glamorous, easily assimilated field in which to deploy their overlooked talents. Michael saw it as the most crucial issue facing the world, and it frightened him that they might be stupid and ill-informed enough to screw up and make the wrong decision. The right decision favoured his own interest, but that was beside the point.

'As a company within the Altmark group,' he continued, 'our editorial commitment will not change, but we will be better resourced, with better access to the essential technology, and able to be on top of the new developments which are going to make news-gathering a faster and more effective process in the future.'

His delivery was magnificent. Pens flew over paper. The committee loved evidence like this, packed with ready-crafted, gift-wrapped nostrums which would leap eagerly into their own policy speeches and spawn good opinions among their party chiefs.

The interrogator was in terrier mode; the only committee member with a legal background, she was also the only one instinctively suspicious of men who equated the public interest with their own interest. Her hands, fast-moving, kept fluttering to her lapels, feeling for the edges of a gown. Bright-eyed and sharp-suited, she bowed and bobbed to her colleagues as if to a jury.

'Be that as it may, Mr Knight, how can you reconcile the public interest with a network of strategic alliances between all the major news agencies?'

'We can only function at our best if we have strong links with our co-suppliers.' Now Knight spoke rapidly, without much inflection, as if running through an item which had already been agreed. 'It cannot be other than in the public interest for us to be able to provide the public with high-quality news coverage obtained at a sensible cost to us. It is our overriding imperative.'

'NewsConnect already has as shareholders companies such as Reuters, News International, CNN, companies with interests virtually *identical* to yours.'

She had made a mistake. 'We only have a two-way supply deal with CNN, there is no involvement beyond that.' Regretful, almost chivalrous, he glanced in admonition towards the clerk recording the session. At that point, the interrogator lost the support of the committee.

'But your company, and these others, have *exchanged* non-executive directors.'

'Isn't that normal in any field of business?'

'But we aren't talking about *any* field of business, Mr Knight. We're talking about public information. Your stock in trade, to extend your analogy, your stock in trade is the truth. What are you doing to guarantee the purity of your product?' Little sighs of irritation; the pens had stopped moving.

Knight made a helpless gesture, implying the futility

of answering an irrelevant question. 'Everything we can. Naturally, everything we can.'

They sagged a little in their seats, embarrassed that one of their number had overstepped the brief. Knight glanced behind him at the public benches. A man who liked to be accompanied, he had arrived with a team of five who had come into the room discreetly just before his appearance and sat in the front row in a line. First was a familiar figure, NewsConnect's Head of Corporate Affairs, William Greenstreet, who had already made his own appearance before the committee, stocky, amiable, sitting with his hands on his knees. Stewart Molfetto, the Finance Director, was beside him, sleek, dark, contained. They were both in their thirties; NewsConnect was a young company. The man next to them looked twenty years older, much grey in his thinning hair and close-trimmed beard: Graham Moynihan, Professor of Media Studies at a northwestern university, the leading voice in his field and due to appear before the committee in the autumn. Finally there were two women, one taking flowing shorthand, clearly Knight's PA, and the other merely listening with intense interest, her fingers running through her sleek straight hair. In the rest of the public area there was only a couple of students and a scattering of corporate loafers further towards the back. A robot camera registered the scene for the day's news bulletins.

'Michael.' It was the chairman speaking; the first questioner had sat down. 'I think what my colleague is really interested in is the issue of editorial control.'

'Of course, naturally we appreciate that.' Never I,

always we, not an unwarranted assumption of a royal we, but a way of including everyone listening in his opinion. The chairman was Morris Donaldson, a freckled chunk of blubber hunched in shirtsleeves over his papers. He had listened to Michael employing the universal 'we' since they had started out together as young reporters on a two-bit small-town teatime news show, raw from university, the housewife's heart throbs. Donaldson had gone directly from TV to politics, losing his looks and much of his intelligence in years of late-night bar sessions; he looked on Knight with wistful envy and Michael, who hated any degree of dislike, viewed him with fraternal sentimentality.

'At NewsConnect, we consider ourselves observers of world events, not participants. Our mission is to inform to the best of our ability and after that it's up to the viewers what to do with the news they have seen.' Knight sat forward again, resolved to flatter them with his concern for their good opinion. He had to win them. Above all else, Alan Stern of Altmark was counting on it. Stern was new on the scene, and he had no illusions about his image. Knight's skin prickled with shame at the mere idea of getting fucked by a bunch of mediocrities because he had been unable to win their understanding. 'But we are well aware of who our viewers are. Our reports have reached eight hundred million screens, in two hundred countries. They reach a mass audience, and they reach world leaders, governments, armies, industries, the United Nations. All these viewers trust NewsConnect as a reliable source of information. We are an international presence, and we feel a sense of international responsibility.'

He was inspiring. The committee seized their pens again. They thought about directorships, about being interviewed, about being filmed in flak jackets on fact-finding missions at flashpoints. They thought about their futures and reminded themselves why they were there. Much to gain and nothing to lose. Media ownership was a question in which both political parties were equally uninterested, so they were not in danger of setting a contentious course, blundering into a politician's Bermuda triangle.

They even admired his clothes. You could not accuse the man of vanity: why, before NewsConnect he had been the most admired political interviewer of his time, and had set aside celebrity for the higher good. Some of the earlier witnesses had been disgraceful hustlers, wearing satin bomber jackets embroidered with slogans, but Knight, like the committee, wore a lightweight grey suit, a white shirt and a tie; unlike them he looked fresh, tailored, trim. He had long legs which he crossed and recrossed to punctuate his speech, just as a more hesitant personality might cough or light a cigarette. Knight never appeared hesitant in public, he projected certainty as flawless as a halo.

'In short' – he was winding up now, feeling them all nestled docilely in the palm of his hand – 'we are aware that our reports affect the substance of decision-making processes at the highest level. Without it being our intention, we have become the channel for a new form of diplomacy. That being the situation, editorial independence is the central requirement from Altmark. There will be no deal unless that is guaranteed. Ownership and ethics are different things. You have my word on that.'

It was over. Solemn and spellbound, the committee had no more to say. They were his. Then, at Donaldson's side, a florid right-winger leaned in to put his stamp on the decision. 'Our concern was only to do with information becoming a commodity . . .'

'Information always has been a commodity.'

'Our point is that the value of news product . . .'

'That is not a phrase I would use myself.' The words were carefully expressionless; I am not patronizing this sweaty, politically incorrect fool, although he deserves it.

'The value of information must surely determine the judgements made about its dissemination . . .'

'My people make their judgements objectively. They are first-class journalists.' The captain on the bridge to the last, the officer defending his men; there was a ripple of appreciation from the public benches. Donaldson looked at his watch, gathered up his papers, asked if there were further questions, then thanked Knight emphatically and declared the hearing finished. They shared a quality of voice, a gritty northern burr; in Donaldson it was a broad accent, in Knight merely a tang in the vowels.

For all he had succeeded in his purpose, Michael left the room in a backdraught of anxiety, running the questions and answers over in his memory, feeling sick with the fear of having betrayed himself. A drink would be good. He wished he smoked. He was rubbing the fingers and thumb of his right hand together, a nervous mannerism. For all he felt it proper to show modesty in public, no one was more conscious of his high position. Normally he cruised in a cloudless stratosphere of achievement, his sights fixed higher. Episodes like this were gut-wringing turbulence, in which he imagined himself out of control, plunging earthwards to annihilation.

'All right, Michael?' Donaldson caught up with him, struggling into his jacket.

'Sure. Fine. What did you think?'

'Great show, they loved you.'

'Do you think they really grasped it?'

'Oh sure. They're not specialists, any of them. There's a limit to the amount of background you can absorb . . .'

In the lounge, the video report of his submission to the committee was running already on the early evening news, included across the channels by editors who knew the man might give them a job one day. The team from the public gallery watched him on a large, old-fashioned television in the corner of the House bar.

The men were nodding, satisfied. The taller of the two women said, 'He looks so calm.' Her suit was dark blue with faint white stripes, a loose cut made baggy with long wearing.

'You must tell him. He gets really strung out about these things.' Knight's secretary was checking the next day's engagements on her electronic organizer.

'Does he really? I can't believe that.'

'Oh yes, you'd be surprised. Do tell him. There they are now.' She snapped the diary shut and turned around to watch Knight and Donaldson making their way towards them.

As they approached, and the men weighed in with their congratulations, sexual alchemy transmuted Knight's anxiety. He responded to Greenstreet's criticism of the initial questioning, but his attention was on the women. His gaze focused on the taller one, and in the hesitant poise of her head and the softness of her smile he saw an irresistible allure. He could not distinguish between the pleasure he took in a woman's beauty and her intention to please him. Unconsciously, his eyes flickered over her entire figure, finding the ripe high curve of her buttocks, the faintest impression of a nipple under her white vest, almost hidden in the shadow of her jacket.

Coffee was brought. Moynihan took him aside for a few points about the committee's amendments, then said, 'Until Sunday, Michael,' and left early to catch a plane. A couple more committee members appeared; Greenstreet, radiating good-fellowship, swept them into the group and a loud discussion of the opposition evidence began.

Michael was able to move aside and concentrate on the women. 'Morris.' He took Donaldson by the shoulder. 'Can I introduce you – Serena Larsen from ChildAid, and you know my assistant, Marianne Walsh. This is Morris Donaldson, we started out together.'

'Another member of the Knight mafia. How do you do.' Serena's thin silver bangles tinkled as she shook hands.

'He's from Ilkley, just down the railway from you. You're from Grassington originally, Serena, isn't that right? And your father still lives there and you had to take the train to school in Ilkley.' He was blatantly at pains to charm her, and seemed to enjoy his freedom to be obvious. They had a trivial conversation two weeks ago in which they had exchanged backgrounds; she was now astonished that Michael Knight remembered the name of her home town and that her father still lived there and the names of the stations on her railway branch line. He himself came from further south, the son of a small-town librarian, but everyone remembered that, it was part of the Michael Knight mythology. The librarian's son who heads the NewsConnect media empire.

There was an exchange of praise, hers for his performance, his for her suit. 'Becoming,' he called it, an old-fashioned word.

'I got it in a charity shop,' she told them, a slight flush on her very white skin. 'I was pleased to find it, they're supposed to be coming back, these stripes.'

She looked from Michael to Morris, and compared them. Fifteen years ago they must both have been handsome. Drink and compromise had overwhelmed Morris, so his face was coarse and a substantial belly hung over his belt. He smiled at her, intending to convey friendliness but achieving only a blurred leer.

Donaldson's uppermost concern was deciding which woman Michael was sleeping with. After the second child of his second marriage, he had a lot of unallocated libido and little possibility of satisfying it. Michael held a special fascination for him. Of all the creeds the man could profess when he had to, feminism was the least close to his instincts; when the acolyte in attendance was female, there was only ever one reason for her presence. But he was not your common-or-garden philanderer, Michael. Not a skirt-chaser or a secretary-screwer or even a man who scored junior researchers. Michael's women were always quality.

The scent of lust was in the air, like the smoke of the first hearth-fire of winter. Serena felt uncomfortable. Apart from Donaldson, the other men were beginning to give her questioning looks. Michael had never behaved as if he had any sexual interest in her, there had been no flirting, no compliments. She found him attractive, as most women did. He talked about his family a lot, in fact, more than most men. She had an instinct about him, but put it down to her own vanity. Had she been wrong?

The atmosphere of the House intimidated her. The entire edifice was gloomy, oppressive, dirty, old-fashioned, a place where rituals and regulations masked impotence. The gothic decoration was bogus and the lighting meanly low. The bar contained only men, pompous in manner, loud, assembled in conspiratorial groups, with ugly women servants moving among them dealing with the ashtrays and dirty glasses.

'Do you work for Michael?' Donaldson was eventually able to begin a conversation with her.

'No. I work for ChildAid, an international relief agency. We are helping NewsConnect with a report on the war orphans in the former Yugoslavia.' Odd that he had not registered her introduction.

'So what's your interest here today?'

'Michael suggested I should sit in on the rough cut of the programme later, I'd get a better idea than from the script. Since he had to do this first, he asked me if I'd care to see a committee in session. I've never even been inside the building before, so I jumped at the chance.' She looked past him, seeking Michael. Over Donaldson's well-padded shoulder he was just in view, with a group at the far side of the room. His presence energized them, the conversation had accelerated and there was frequent laughter.

'He's right, the rough cut will give you a better idea.' She wondered why Donaldson was nodding over her, as if he had just made an important discovery.

They left for the NewsConnect offices in two cars, both women travelling with Michael, who turned to Serena at once. 'What did you make of Morris?'

'He seemed very proud that you'd been friends for so long.' Donaldson's envy had been blatant, but it was Serena's instinct to show the significant facts in the most flattering light.

'Twenty years, it must be. He was a great reporter. Really rigorous, persistent, never let go. Excellent interviewer. Mind like a computer, always way ahead of the argument, figuring the angles. Very fine-looking man, great on camera.'

Such loyalty. Serena admired it. She noticed that Michael used the word 'heart' a lot, also the word 'guts'. An honest, simple, conventional man, she thought, but comfortable with emotions.

'Difficult, that committee. I thought I covered everything.' He left a questioning silence at the end of the statement.

'I don't really know enough about broadcasting to give you a useful opinion.'

'People tend to think media issues are just sexy, don't they? Then they get to the nitty-gritty, find it's technical and they're bored. I could feel their eyes glazing – do you think they managed to grasp anything?'

'Oh, sure. They were making notes all the time – especially when you were talking about ownership and ethics.'

'And you could follow, yes?'

'Well, yes. I could. It seemed quite simple to me. I felt they were lost for good lines of argument; you made everything so clear they were casting around for loose ends to question you on.' She was flattered to have her opinion asked. It was quite a novelty in her life. At ChildAid, as in the office where she had worked before, people never asked the opinion of the public relations officer until it was too late.

'The committee seemed pretty satisfied in the end.' By instinct, he was testing her softness. Michael was drawn to what he called a kind woman, meaning one with a strong instinct to soothe, reassure, even flatter away a man's fears.

'They were impressed. They were right with you, I could see that.' She tried not to say any more for fear of betraying how little she herself had considered what went on behind the day's news bulletins.

'Good. Good. Marianne, what have I got this evening?' The question was unnecessary; he always knew his schedule. Marianne consulted the organizer and confirmed that the night was free, finishing with a prim compression of her lips.

'Good,' said Michael, and looked out of the window, tapping his long fingers on the arm-rest. Suddenly he made the car stop and disappeared into a sports shop, coming out with a purchase. 'Shin pads. My son is starting to get serious about football.' She was impressed that in the midst of such important affairs he would remember a minor deficiency in his son's sports kit.

When they arrived at their destination he sent Marianne to his office to make some calls and turned to Serena as they walked down the corridor. 'This is likely to take some time – would you like dinner afterwards? Or is there someone you need to get home to?'

'There's no one at home,' she told him, feeling as if someone else were saying the words. 'Dinner would be fine – how kind of you.'

'Good.' He managed to make the word embrace both counts. Had Michael been asked, at that moment, if he had any sexual intention towards Serena, he would have said no. He was running on instinct. Had Serena been asked, she would have said probably, and that only because she had been brought up to be modest. She would have meant definitely. Sad because of his wife, flattering but nothing she intended to get into. Serena had heard the stories, although no one had mentioned his warmth, the way he got involved in his programmes, as if he really cared. He was a good man, and good to be with, but that was all.

'I'll never be really sophisticated, I still think it's glamorous, telephoning by the swimming pool.' Half-comatose in the heat, Grace lay on her stomach and watched the bees working her lavender hedge. The energetic morning sun was frying her shoulders agreeably. 'Marie-Laure wants to put you in for the Iron Man Triathlon. What you lose on the running, your sperm will make up on the swimming.'

Her husband chuckled in the handset. 'What else did she have to say?'

'I'm in the hop, spit and jump. Every day I have to spit into a plastic tube and test it with a dipstick.'

'Never seems to run out of ideas, does she, Marie-Laure?'

'Nope. I tried spitting this morning but my mouth was dry.' She rolled onto her back, but the sun reflected from the surface of the pool glared in her eyes, so she sat up and looked for her hat.

'You need something to get the juices flowing. I've got some fantastic sausages, and some trout for lunch.'

'Haven't you done enough cooking for one week?'

'Never. Anyway, it'll save you shopping.'

'What about tomorrow? And Sunday?'

'Oh, yes . . . we have an invitation for Sunday.'

'Who?'

'Surprise.'

'Don't tease, who?'

'I'll tell you when I see you. Got to go now, no more points on the card.' The line was cut with a decisive whine. She smiled, picturing Nick's large form in his pink polo shirt and too-new jeans, his face already reddened from the southern sun, climbing awkwardly into his car in the stinking heat haze of a gas station in high summer.

Afterwards she recalled the merest shadow of misgiving, because Nick never held back anything, but at the time she dismissed the doubt, starving it in favour of the fondness she felt for him. Marriage seemed to be a question of cultivating the right emotions.

A low cloud, the only one in the entire sky, cut out the sun for a few minutes. The Alhambra was a village house, and the village occupied the highest hill in a spine of smaller peaks, almost a thousand feet above sea level. Banks of cloud rolled in from the distant Atlantic, broke up over the Pyrenees and did not reform until past these foothills. The altitude saved them from the stifling air of the low-lying land, but without the sun the air had an alpine crispness, even in August. Grace shivered and switched off the phone.

Nick was the most lovable of men, and yet she did not love him. Precisely, Grace did not know if she loved her husband. Her judgements were stern, and harsher of herself than others; she felt that if you had to ask if what you felt was love, then it was not, it was something less.

This was affection. This was respect, and trust. It was liking, but perhaps not more than that, it was too quiet. She had mistrusted it, and expected it to sour quickly once the first flush was over, but instead it had endured, becoming a smooth, broad emotion which sweetened her life but had no power to overwhelm it. Sometimes, she felt ashamed of having married him. Because she had been thirty-four years old and wistful for children, she had done it. She was afraid that love was finished for her; she was also afraid that it was not, and would find her out one day and force her to hurt this blameless soul. Her best hope was that now she had loved enough, and had earned at least some years of peace.

They had bought this house for the sake of peace. The deep peace of rural decay – Grace joked about it, as she joked about everything, but it had lulled her very well. They had wanted a summer retreat; she wanted Nick to restore himself after the long months at his work.

In her own work the deadline guillotined each day; if she had been careless there was a point, every twenty-four hours, after which nothing more could be done and the next day all mistakes would be forgotten. Nick's work had no deadlines. Of course, his patients died. Attached to a paediatric HIV clinic, he saw babies and children face death every day. His field was research – not caring for these tragic infants or smoothing their journey to the next world, merely observing them. Much of his day passed in abstract thought, much of it in tedious laboratory procedures. It astonished her that he was never careless, never permitted himself a mistake, but acted always as if every patient could be saved. He gave too much of himself, and by the summer he was pale and drained.

Grace had planned to escape from her newspaper. After Michael the daily fever of news had subjected her life to a healing madness. Once she was with Nick, being called at any time, in any place, to follow a story which nine times out of ten was of no significance seemed futile, and when she broke arrangements with Nick he was incapable of understanding. Her editor was a resentful man who felt his life lacked pleasure; he presumed foreign correspondents to be sitting on some shady plaza with a leisurely drink while their colleagues sweated, and liked to keep them on their toes.

Anywhere else in France a holiday would inevitably have been spoiled by the office, calling to demand a report on flash floods, forest fires or a blighted vintage, but nothing ever happened in Gascony, not even natural disasters. It was a blank tract on the newsroom map, where the farmers had better things to do than demonstrate and there was not so much as one fascist mayor capable of making a speech fit for a headline.

In the roasting silence of midday, she heard the purr of her husband's Peugeot, and the crunch of its tyres as he turned into the lane to leave the car in the shade of the church tower. With his suitcase in one hand and an assortment of shopping bags in the other, he squeezed through the side gate, eyes bright with mischief.

'Stay there – don't get up.' He dropped the case and most of the bags, bringing one with him to her side. 'I brought you a present – here, you have to try this . . .'

'What have you got in there?' She sat up on one elbow, dizzy with the heat; he was rummaging among the ice packs in the eskimo bag. Other men bought such equipment to take beer to football matches; Nick kept his in the car to bring pâté and cream cakes home in perfect condition.

'The best thing we learned all week – all week – was what to do with a pomegranate. Watch.' Out of the bag, he produced a round red fruit and a small knife. 'You make a tiny cut in the skin, like this, then you crush it . . .' His strong fingers pinched the rosy globe all over. 'Then you suck it – here, try . . .' He held the fruit out to her and obediently she put her hand over his, closed her mouth around the cut in the skin and felt the cool juice spurt into her mouth. It was sweet but fresh-tasting. 'Isn't that delicious? The most refreshing taste you could possibly imagine, isn't it? And so neat, no drips, none of that bitter pith, nature's own juice box . . .'

'Mmmh,' was all she could manage to reply while he steadily squeezed out more juice for her. Eventually he let her hold the fruit herself. 'Delicious,' she agreed. 'I always wondered if you were really meant to fiddle around with all those pips.'

'Say hello properly.'

'Hello properly.' She reached up and kissed him, her

lips now cool, his warm and dried in the sun. 'I'll come in with you, it's too hot out here.'

Sitting in the kitchen, enjoying the pomegranate and the cold tiles under her feet, she watched him energetically stowing new-bought treasures in the cupboards and drawers.

'I found this Galician cheese . . .' It must have weighed at least two kilos, a hard yellow round wrapped in newspaper. 'And some quince paste to go with it . . .' Flat dark red packets were stacked beside the cheese. 'And the best *chorizo* I've ever tasted, quite mild but very spicy . . .' Tall as he was, he had to fetch a chair to hang the sausage from a hook in the ceiling. 'And these extraordinary black peppers . . .' Temporarily at least, these were hung around his neck. 'And a pot of savory because nobody watered the last one . . .' The aromatic plant was installed outside the door, next to the tarragon and marjoram. 'Now, will trout be all right for you? Steamed in lettuce leaves? It looks pretty, pink and green . . . Can you see a lettuce, I know I had one somewhere . . .'

Still half-asleep from sunbathing, she let her head rest on her arms on the table and watched him fondly. Cooking relaxed him like nothing else; he bustled around the kitchen in a world of his own, inviting her to admire the fish and advise him on the precise state of her appetite, but in fact wrapped up completely in the delight of making a meal. He was not the most fastidious of cooks, but as he cleared up the debris he scattered all around him and always forbade her to wash up she had no complaints.

When the trout were a luscious memory and they had agreed that a translucent slice of quince paste was the perfect addition to a slice of hard mountain cheese, when the dishes were stacked in a workmanlike pile and Nick had brewed coffee, when they had decided that it was still too hot to go outside and were moving into the sitting room, she remembered the question of Sunday.

'So tell me, what is this surprise you've planned?'

'Ah.' He had been about to sink into his favourite seat, a brocade wing chair, lumpy and worn, an early junk-shop extravagance which had loyally accompanied her throughout most of her life. Instead, he stood in front of the cavernous fireplace.

'Lunch on Sunday, you said someone had invited us.'

'Yes. Look – ah – you'll never guess who I met at this thing. It was marvellous, she was just as I'd imagined, exactly . . .' The words tumbled out in a nervous rush.

Foreboding squeezed her stomach, curdling the comforting after-lunch glow, making her throat feel obstructed. 'Yes,' she encouraged him.

'You know who it was, don't you?' Now he was trying to be playful, hoping against the cold warning of her face that she would be able to share his delight. 'It was Jane Knight.'

She turned away from him, shocked, wanting to hide her face, wishing the name back into his mouth, the meeting back into the future. Too late. They were facts, events, they were lying there in the present, irreversible.

'We don't have to go, of course we don't have to go. I know how you feel about her husband.' Nick stood swaying from one foot to another in sudden misery, like a wretched circus bear. The words were in her mouth to tell him he knew nothing of the kind. Early on, she had tried to explain to him, wanting him to understand the great scar that lay across her life, but he could not really hear her. His own feelings were not complex. All he retained was the idea that she was somehow opposed to Michael Knight.

She kept her back to him, watching their reflection on the far wall in a spotted old mirror which she had bought for its fantastic gothic frame.

'It was just a casual invitation. She gave me their number, I can always call and say we've got something else on.'

How can I look so strong when I am so weak? Her face, a blurred reflection in the old glass, was heroic. She carried herself proudly and her eyes were always steady. Her dark hair curled strongly away from her forehead, setting off its breadth, and the width of her cheekbones, the long firm sweep of her jaw. She looked like a patrician Roman wife, a heroic matriarch defending her honour, when she felt like howling with panic and crawling under something to hide.

It was difficult to turn around. She had a subliminal vision of a chasm behind her, a huge fissure opened in the ground in seconds by an earthquake; if she turned around she would look into it, lose her balance and fall in. 'Nobody has anything on around here in August. We chose this place for the peace and quiet.'

'So, if she doesn't believe me, that isn't the end of the

world. She's a nice woman, she'll just think . . . well . . .' His sandy eyebrows peaked with distress. 'Well, it doesn't matter what Jane Knight thinks. Perhaps she's thought better of inviting us by now. Oh, I'm sorry, it's all my fault, my love, I ought to have realized how you'd feel. We'd got along famously over our salt cod casserole, like people do on these foodie things, and I was flattered, I really was.'

'You really rate her, don't you?'

'I was surprised she was there, I thought it was just for amateurs. I mean, I read her every week in the Sunday paper right from the beginning, I've got all her cookbooks. After I got divorced, the first thing I ever cooked was Jane Knight's *omelette paysanne.* My life isn't like yours, I don't meet famous people every day . . .'

'You know I hate you saying things like that.' She turned towards him at last, anger giving her the strength, and folded her arms around her body, feeling cold. She had furnished the room in cool blue linen, a good colour with sunlight, and the massive walls and small windows kept out the summer heat. The room was always dusky, with lamps throwing deep shadows on the whitewash, leaving the corners dark.

They were standing a wary distance apart. 'It annoys me that you think my life is so important,' she said. 'You know all I do is turn in whatever trivia the editor requires. If I go to a press conference and see a junior minister in the distance, that's the biggest thrill of the week.'

'All I mean is that I was too bowled over to think.

We'd been getting along famously and she was just carried away by the enthusiasm of the moment, and invited us. It wasn't a big thought-out thing.'

My husband and my former lover's wife got along famously. Even in her distress, Grace was moved to smile. The passion of the moment was forever carrying Nick away. In Paris, he was a different man, silent and intense, profoundly caring of his infant patients. Her memory was forever imprinted with the picture of his great red hands around a newborn baby, his fingers as thick as its arms. Once that intimate contact with life and death ceased, and he was at leisure, he became an eruption of good nature and crashed about like a young gun dog, ever alert to pleasure and careless of where he put his great paws. His absolute loyalty was yours; in return he would gratefully accept an occasional thump in the ribs as a token of your love.

He was running on. 'We were just swapping stories of how we found our houses, we realized how close we were, she said she'd like to see you again . . .'

'We aren't close to the Knights, how can we be close?' Why wasn't he angry? The situation threatened them, challenged their bond, but Nick never defended himself as harder men did. She heard the pitch of her voice rise, felt the resurrection of the old Grace, the woman she had left behind when she left Michael. 'Their place must be hundreds of miles, hours away at least, half a day . . .' She checked herself, she was protesting too much. If now she revealed that Michael Knight had been her lover it would appear as a long-established deception.

'Look, don't worry. I'll just tell her it's too far, too far just for lunch.'

'Suppose she asks us to stay?'

'Then we can always say no. Honestly, it isn't a big deal. I left it open, I didn't know how you'd feel.' Now his shoulders drooped and his back bowed under the weight of regret for the pain he was causing.

'I don't know how I feel, either. Can we talk about it tomorrow?'

Relief lightened his eyes and his smile returned. She prayed that he would not try to touch her at that moment. Nick was a great man for hugs, pulling smaller people right off their feet, but when she was distressed she never wanted anyone to touch her. Now she wanted to be alone, searched for a pretext and went outside to find her sun hat by the poolside.

Five dragonflies were hovering in formation over the surface of the pool. All the village was dozing after lunch; the calm was profound. The gold of thousands of acres of sunflowers and wheat gleamed in the sunshine. The roof tiles burned red, the white stone walls shone, and when wind rippled the crops and stirred the hazel and blackthorn in the hedges, the fields appeared to wash up around the mound of ancient buildings like seas around a lighthouse.

Just when I thought I was safe. In her mind, Grace repeated the phrase to herself. Just when you thought it was safe to go back in the water. She smiled, then wiped her hand over her face, imposing seriousness. She was feeling fear, a special fear, an old, painstakingly forgotten sensation she had never wanted to have again, the fear that was part of loving Michael Knight. Humour had been her anaesthetic – her humour covered up too much.

Over the palms and oleanders of the neighbouring garden, the back of the house looked south, towards the distant mountains. Even on hazy days like this one there was a sense of the backdrop of dark, snow-topped peaks. Today there were storms down there, so distant the thunder could not be heard, but even in the brightness the lightning flared silently like fireworks far away.

Grace collected the cushions, smart in striped Basque linen, and put them under cover at the end of the outdoor dining table. It was a big table, enough for ten people; they had bought it in anticipation of their children, picturing their extended family gathered around it. Time was cheating them of that vision. Nick's mother had died the previous year, and hers was becoming too arthritic to travel. She had failed to get pregnant.

The cat had appeared silently through the wall, hoping for fish-heads. Above, she heard Nick closing the shutters of their bedroom against the afternoon sun. He was hurt, and it annoyed her, although he had responded only to her pain and taken no thought for his own. Nick liked to stand on firm ground, he was always questioning her, asking her things about herself she could not answer. Michael had never been like that; Michael was as sensitive as a sea anemone, always withdrawing into wounded silences. Nick wanted everything in the open, whether he understood it or not. Every day, Grace pledged herself not to compare them, and every day she did it.

The butcher across the road was running up his shutters and the stall-holders of the street market were setting up their trestles by the time she reached home. With relief she ran to the bathroom and got rid of the steak. The smell of vomit pleased her, it was familiar and an honest stink, not some lying fragrance brewed in a laboratory from chemical roses. The meat was still in lumps, brown islands in the white ice cream. She decided to leave the stuff in the basin for a while, let its good ugly smell soothe her.

Outside the window the pigeons jostled each other on the ledge. They were her friends, she gave them crumbs and the close noises of their scratching feet and cooing conversation went on all day. Although her room was high up, the window was very small and awkwardly set under the eaves, not at all conducive to throwing yourself out. She had taken the room because she liked those little cramped windows; she could be sensible about things like that.

She slept for a few hours, then woke up in a rush of nervous energy, anxious to dispose of what she had stolen as fast as possible. She turned the bag out on the bed and began to divide up the haul. It was bad to have talismans of deceit in her space longer than necessary; they could spread infection. The photograph frames were really quite pretty, too decorative to sell just for the weight of the silver. Maybe she would keep them until Sunday and try that woman with the kind face who sold old silver at Saint Sulpice. She ought to be knocked out by them, they were definitely antique.

Damn, Sunday. She had promised her father, his party. Well, this year they could do it without her. This was business, it was more important. He'd get that, he couldn't miss, the principle on which he'd based his life. Business is more important. She could get Jane to tell him. Or try. Jane was only strong when you didn't want her to be; when you needed her to stand firm she had a way of oozing away with that wispy half-smile of hers, as if it was something she couldn't help and was anyway no more important than burning the toast. But Jane would be pleased if she stayed away, that was something you could always do right by Jane.

Stephen was coming, hadn't he said that? Adorable Stephen, he always did what he said. Yes, she was sure of it. How lovely. He'd sort everything, he always did. There's nothing in the world Stephen can't take care of, even me. Had he said when? Shit. He wouldn't like this game; if he knew, he'd get judgemental. Have to work fast.

Having no fingernails long enough, she used a nail file to open the backs of the photograph frames and take out the pictures. Father in uniform and mother in a fox wrap and orchids. A young woman with very soft eyes and long blonde hair, the bride, for here she was again in the wedding photograph, wearing a silly white dress with a peplum and puffed sleeves. Two blobs of babies in cradles, then the mum, dad and the kids all together, not that recent for he looked thinner. Already the boy had that blank look, a little man, a little android, fascia fitted and programme running, standing beside his mother and facing the world with a set jaw. The girl was grinning like an idiot in her father's embrace.

That asshole ought to have a memento of this night, she decided. Indeed, he had said so at one point, some slushy line about how he would always remember it. God, why did they always lie so much? Was it an instinct in them, like wanting sex? Was it the same instinct, was there a place on that pathetic little chromosome where the genes for lust and lying slotted together? Perhaps if she was HIV he would already have a souvenir. The notion seemed perversely romantic. No dilemmas then, no need for all these escape plans, the way out was straight ahead. She was not HIV, or they would have told her when they did the blood test. Perhaps they didn't test for that without your permission. No, that was for ordinary people, if you were pregnant now they checked you out for everything. Still, even if she was, and even if she had given it to him, it would be years before he knew.

What to do now, to make him remember, rub his nose in it, what could she do? His address was on his driving licence in the wallet. She had a good thick envelope, and a stamp. In the kitchen bin there was a plastic bag. She took the photographs into the bathroom, dipped them, one at a time, into the bowl of vomit, dropped them into bag, put the bag in the envelope, sealed and stamped it.

Stephen was coming. She remembered, he had said Friday and now it was Friday. How nice. She was always all right with Stephen, whatever came down he handled it. Why should he have to, though? He was sweet, and she gave him so much grief. He ought to be getting on with his own things, with his important business, not mothering a useless creature like her.

Guiltily she looked around the room. Everything was tidy. Tuesday, Monday, whenever it was when she last dropped a tab, she had gone mad tidying up. Amazing how orderly you could get when you were tripping. No clothes even on the floor, she was still wearing the same things. In the bathroom there was just the shelf, a mess of dust and makeup, and the shower tray was grimy. She could leave them; such a housewife, old Stephen, he tidied and cleaned because he enjoyed it and he would need something to get into.

He was a policeman too, always looking for her drugs. Well, that was OK, there weren't any now. Two temazepam in the little mother-of-pearl box, but temazepam was straight, you could shoot as much as you liked if you were really that fucked. A good insurance policy, Mr T. He would bring you down if things turned nasty. It was good to be careful, there were things around now they said turned people into animals.

All the same, if Stephen was going to be around she wouldn't be able to get hold of anything. He was coming for a week. A long time. Maybe she could catch up with Marc somewhere before Stephen arrived.

The envelope was still behind the tap, needing to be

posted, so she ran downstairs with it. In the street the market stalls were all set up hopefully, polished apples and plump tomatoes, bunches of carrots and onions. She stayed on the vegetable side of the road, avoiding the disgusting butcher with his bowls of bloody liver and cow's tongues like great white slugs. Suckling pigs looked like dead babies. The postbox was at the end of the street and she slipped the envelope into it. Letting it fall felt good. It felt like dropping a heavy weight which she had been carrying too long. She walked away, imagining that she could float like a ghost.

Marc was always in the Café Brésil in the afternoons. It was off the Beaubourg, one of those crammed studenty places where you couldn't hear yourself speak. She was still tired, the missed sleep was catching up. All cities were revolting in August, even Paris; sticky heat, dust, bad-tempered people, nothing in the shops but the end-of-season tat that no one wanted to buy. For a while she drifted along Saint Germain looking in shop windows, then settled on a bench in a little park and let the drone of the traffic and the bustle of people lull her into a doze.

She came back to consciousness slowly and began to focus on Marc. He did not take American Express. A cashpoint, then a taxi. The streets were already clogged with traffic, weekenders getting away early.

The café was crammed, people were packed in, eight or nine around every tiny table, yelling at each other through the din. Marc was in his usual place, behind the pillar at the back with a couple of friends, looking like he always looked, thin and blond with a little sharp smile.

He was pleased to see her, naturally; one of my best customers, let me get you a cappuccino. He had those little ways of making the business elegant, behaving like a high-class purveyor of luxury goods to a discerning clientele.

'Looking forward to the weekend?'

'A friend's coming over.' Across the heads of the crowd, the barman put down her coffee; she scraped off the chocolate powder and stirred in the froth.

'Boyfriend?'

'Sort of.'

'Going out?'

'No. He's not a party animal. My father's having a thing for his birthday but I'm going to miss it.'

'Yeah?'

'At his place down in the south. Too far to go.'

'It's a long way then?'

'Oh, yeah.'

It sounded like casual chat, but he was figuring out what to offer her.

Another good thing about Marc, he was really creative about the business, always looking for new things, like he really wanted to give you exactly the experience you were in the mood for, even though you wouldn't know what you wanted until he gave it to you. 'You had snowballs?' he asked eventually.

'What are they?'

'Acid and E and jam on it. They're good.'

She pulled a face, unimpressed.

'Gates of Heaven?' he offered.

'Gates of Heaven's really nice,' one of the friends contributed.

She agreed with him, but felt a little manipulated. 'Straight acid would be OK.'

'Certainly. I've got strawbs, Martians . . .'

'Give me some strawbs.'

A very organized man, too. Everything in little plastic envelopes in an old tobacco tin with green and gold decoration on the lid; she picked it up and admired it while he sorted out her stuff.

'I suppose I'm going to have to get grass off someone else?'

He nodded his head; Marc considered grass juvenile and beneath him. 'I'll give you a present,' he said as if to make it up to her, sifting through the envelopes with his delicate small fingers. From the bottom of the tin he pulled out a packet with some scraps of white card in it, carefully shook one out to add to the pink square of strawbs.

'One of your free samples? What is it?' He was very reliable, but she liked to appear cautious. You had to keep people at a distance or they started thinking they could take you over.

'Microdot. They're new, I've just got them. Good, they last you. It's a trip but there's gotta be something quite whizzy in them, people tell me they keep you up, keep you going. Try it, tell me how you like it.'

'Supposed to be quite heavy. I wouldn't do them on your own,' the friend warned, looking at her as if she was some idiot girl who couldn't take care of herself.

'Thanks. Aren't you kind, giving me presents?' She picked the notes out of her wallet and pushed them across the table. Nothing furtive about Marc, he was in good standing with the management and valued by the clientele. The plastic envelope went into her makeup purse, under the old tissues and the eyeshadow that had lost its lid and put purple powder over everything. There was so much junk in there Stephen would never find it.

Her street was closed because of the market, so she had the taxi drop her back on Saint Germain and walked the last block. There he was, Stephen, walking out of her hallway and looking up, trying to see her windows. He must have run up to her room while she was away, got no answer. His hair had grown, how cute the way it sprang up and fell forward all shaggy like a pony's mane. Oh, the loveliness of seeing him, it poured in the way bright sunshine did when you pulled the curtains at midday.

'Imi! I thought you'd forgotten.' Lovely to run into him, big and solid, his thick heavy clothes smelling of silly aftershave.

'You smell of silly aftershave.'

'But you gave it me.'

'Did I? When did I?'

'Last birthday.' Such terribly red lips. All that healthy red blood, manly red blood.

'Are you sure?'

'Absolutely. I was touched you even remembered.'

'I must have decided it would be a real Keith and Linda thing to do.'

'Keith and Linda?' Oh God, that puppy face. She hated it when he looked that way.

'Fabulously naff, like you giving me chocolates.'

'But I'd never, you hate them.'

She pulled away violently and sat down on a vacant barrow. 'Leave it alone, can't you? I think you are a Keith really, deep in the marrow of your bones. You need radiation to burn it out of you.' Where had it all gone, the joy of seeing him? Now she felt sour and weak, and the putrefying hopelessness that was forever eating away at the corners of her life suddenly multiplied and advanced towards her core.

'Come on, let's go for something. Coffee, something. Come on.' His hand, picking up one of hers, was hard and his fingers were cold. Stephen's fingers were always cold, even now in high summer. When they used to make love, she had liked them, his cold hands.

She let him lead her towards the coffee shop at the crossroads, only twenty yards further down the street. The woman with the fruit stall outside her door was grinning, showing all her teeth. 'That woman thinks I'm your sister – she told me after you were here last. I suppose because we're both tall and we've got black hair. Maybe because I'm so awful to you.'

'At least you said that.' Sensing that she was under discussion, the stall-holder picked out an apple, flourished it, polished its matt golden shoulders and gave it to Stephen, then found another for her. There were thanks, smiles, polite bows, a little conversation. Not my brother, my friend. My special friend. My mate. He is

Stephen, I am Imogen. No, not my fiancé. He was last year, now he's my mate.

'You've confused her now.'

'So what. She's a stupid woman.'

'It's a good apple.'

'Always look on the bright side, Keith.'

'That's what I always say. It's good to be here, Imi.'

'Don't talk crap.'

Louisa lay in the sun by the pool, frowning at the girls, Emma and Xanthe, splashing in and out of the water. Antony read a book, sharing the shade of one of the white umbrellas with Jane, who spread a large sheet of paper on a table and was trying to work out a seating plan.

'Would you mind terribly if I put you near Michael?' she asked.

'Yes.' They had been friends much too long to fight, and by now also too long for there to be any need to explain their differences. Louisa loathed Michael and despised Jane for tolerating him.

'Please, Louisa, for me. He likes you.'

'I don't want to sit next to your husband.'

'I don't mean next to him – just near him. You're a wonderful conversationalist, you can hold your own with Berenice Stern . . . How about next to Stuart Devlin?' NewsConnect's war reporter, monosyllabic and mentally never out of a camouflage shirt, was the only unattached man on the guest list.

'Oh, all right.' Jane wrote in the name, telling herself that her friend was still single after thirty-nine years of wanting passionately to be married because she had no understanding of love, or of men, motherhood or family dynamics. These unspeakables had been aired years earlier; now it was only necessary to touch base with them occasionally. Originally there had been anger, then distance in its place. Now there was resignation, slightly bitter but familiar and comfortable.

'Mummy, Debbie's teaching me to dive. Are you watching?' Emma ran up, dripping with water which splashed over Louisa's feet and caused her to recoil with an exclamation of annoyance.

'Yes dear. Be careful.' Jane was preoccupied, wondering where she would seat Grace Evans and her husband – if they came. She was beginning to hope for an apologetic telephone call from the husband, making their excuses.

The child ran away, watched with distaste by Louisa. 'Are those red patches her eczema?'

'Yes. When she's in the water she gets cold and it looks worse than it is.'

'Poor thing. She looks hideous.'

'Not so loud, she'll hear you.' Jane was always defensive on the score of Emma, partly from pity for her afflicted daughter, partly from the ineradicable feeling that every problem her children had was her own fault. 'The sun's good for it and the water seems to make it itch less.'

Louisa sniffed. The shock of the cold water had roused her, but she had no desire to share the pool, ample as it was, with two screaming brats. She pushed her sunglasses up on her forehead and peered into the distance at the lacy silhouette of oak trees.

The wood began with a border of saplings standing diffidently apart from each other, their light foliage hardly shading the ground. 'Why are those trees all the same size? Surely it can't be forestry? Not with oaks. But they're such even distances apart.'

Jane welcomed the change of subject. 'Oh yes, that is planting, I know it is. The whole wood was planted centuries ago and managed ever afterwards on purpose for the mushrooms.'

'Gosh. *Gosh.* Serious menu planning.'

'When we bought the place, Madame Montaud put the price up for it. *Terrain à cèpes.* Michael was furious.'

'They really do *think* about food, don't they?' Louisa was awed, and regarded the trees the way architectural tourists look at Chartres cathedral.

Almost joyous now that the scrutiny of her family had been dropped, Jane began an oblique appeal for understanding. 'The wood was what started me learning about French food. I remember trying to tell Michael that it must have been planned for mushrooms, and he wouldn't believe me.'

The conversation, idle at the time, had been a fulcrum in her life. It had taken place out there, among the young trees, when they were in the first stage of their marriage and any days away from the infant demands of Imogen were precious. She had been charmed to discover a corner of the world where Michael was not a household face; he said he was delighted also on that score. They had only just bought this tumbledown heap of building and neglected corner of land, and she still believed that they would all be happy if she could get her husband away from his work, so he could relax and spend more time with his daughter; she was beginning to be able to hold a conversation, and Jane was sure that if he could only be with the child a bond would form.

Imogen was just beginning to trouble her. Although Jane gave the child the same punctilious care her own parents had given her, she was not responding. Hollow-eyed and listless, she did as she was told and nothing more. It was impossible to make her happy.

Already Imogen was revealing a conspicuous gift for snuffing out hope. Jane felt a constant sense of failure in the little girl's presence; when she was away from her, that burden was lifted, but then she felt guilty. Intimidated by becoming a stepmother at an age which she felt was too young for any kind of parenthood, Jane had insisted that her own children would have to wait; now, in the first excitement of finding the farmhouse, she was drawn to the notion that a child of her own would bring back the promise of their marriage.

Michael had led the way to the wood at the end of a spring afternoon, when the sun was foundering among black cloud banks in the raw red sky. He had been striding between the saplings, his long legs eating up the uneven ground while she hurried after him, and her intention in asking the question had at first been only to get him to slow down and wait for her.

'Do you think they planted this wood for the mushrooms?'

He had halted and turned to look at her with no

understanding at all. Michael had a characteristic, piercing gaze; his irises, light brown at rest, seemed to darken to black when he was gathering intelligence. Now he looked almost alarmed, as if he feared the unknown hazards of alien territory.

'I was thinking – why's this wood here? It's not a logical place. The mushrooms could be the whole point of them, all those wonderful old trees over there.' She ignored his reaction. 'Three hundred years old, the very big ones, the *notaire* said. Oaks, beeches and pines, perfect for mushrooms.'

'Surely it's just a wood?' The grass was shorter then, recently grazed by Madame's last remaining pair of cows.

'No, no – look at the whole landscape around here. Only the worthless corners are left as woodland. Everything is planted for a reason. They even use the marshy corners to raise their young trees for windbreaks. The only natural woods left are where the ground is so poor it's got no value for crops. And we haven't seen a concentration of oaks like this anywhere else, have we?' Shortness of breath forced her to pause. It should have been a romantic thing, an evening stroll across the field, but Michael had again set off impatiently towards their goal, leaving her behind. Obstinate to make her point, she ran a few steps to catch up with him. 'Look – this is good land, prime land, flat, easy to plough. No sensible farmer would have allowed it to go to waste.'

'My goodness, what extraordinary things you think about. Old Madame Montaud is far too doddery to get out here and as mad as a hatter.' With a fond chuckle he put his arm around her shoulders. This gesture never comforted her, only made her feel physically overwhelmed. 'Why would anyone bother planting a wood just for mushrooms when they could buy them in the market?'

Exasperated, she let herself stumble over a fallen branch to break out of his embrace. 'Nobody round here would pay good money for mushrooms when he could grow enough to sell. And see how there are lots of young trees here, just a few really old ones . . . I'm sure they planted this wood to raise the mushrooms.'

The implications of the pig-killing shed and the duck-fattening barn, buildings destined to become their pool house and the children's wing, had already signalled that natural heirs to this ripe countryside were confined to an unmerciful existence. She was passing her first summer in Gascony in awed discovery of the absolute dedication of peasant life to the production of food. The property even took its name, Les Palombières, from a pair of hides for shooting wild pigeons, great status symbols in earlier times, reduced now to twin heaps of mossy rubble under a tangle of brambles at the margin of the wood.

'This is your Marie Antoinette thing, is it, playing at being a peasant farmer's wife? They wouldn't bother. Mushrooms just grow anywhere. Look, they're all over the place.' He pointed disdainfully at a great bed of fungi rising out of the meadow grass in open ground, the young ones penis-shaped, thumb-sized and an unearthly violet colour, the mature caps ragged and greyish.

Confidently, she had embarked on the final explanation. 'Not the good eating mushrooms. Those things are ink caps, you can eat them but they just cook down to mush, they're pretty worthless. The best are the really meaty mushrooms, the ceps and the chanterelles, they make a really good meal, people can bottle them or dry them – but they only grow in woods, they need special chemical conditions which you get under old oaks and pines. That's why dishes with mushrooms are called *forestière* . . . What's the matter?'

'Nothing.' He ought to have been charmed by her enthusiasm. Instead, Michael's eyes had again narrowed in concentration and a black frown flickered over his face, to be wiped away with a conscious effort and replaced now with a look of bland interest. 'I'm sure you're right. I didn't know you knew about things like this.'

She was gratified to have a genuine reaction from him. 'It's just a little thing, hardly important.'

'Is it something you've just found out?'

'I suppose so, talking to people about the house and so on.' At her office in the Department of Agriculture, she saw European Community papers on fungi. Mushrooms had been part of the fairy-tale interludes in her childhood when she and her brothers had been sent for holidays with their Scottish grandmother, who lived on the edge of woodland. She had forgotten their forays until now, but was reluctant to tell Michael too much.

Much as she wanted him to be proud of her, she knew already that to her husband knowledge was power.

Expertise of her own could be annexed to his greater mastery. She saw that soon he would be showing the bounty of the wood to their friends and guests, saying 'Let me explain how it is about these mushrooms . . .'

'Let me explain' was Michael's little bit of conjurer's business, the distraction while he performed the trick. The trick was to make you wrong. 'Let me explain how it is with a man,' he would offer when at last she had enough evidence to accuse him of having an affair. A few years later he would set aside her insistence that his conscious presence in the home was necessary to her and their children, saying, 'Let me explain how it is in a marriage.' These explanations came from such a lofty perspective that they could not be refuted; they elevated Michael's personal will to the position of a universal law.

She had shrugged again, looking sidelong at him from behind the golden curtain of her hair, hardly able to believe that she had found a corner of creation that her husband could not invade. 'Maybe it's just a woman's thing to pick up these little scraps of information. I remember my grandmother used to talk about looking for mushrooms during the war. Madame Montaud was so anxious to show me the wood when we first came to look over the place – don't you remember?'

'No, no, I don't remember at all. I'm sure you're right, it's a woman's thing. Feminine mystique, cycles of nature, seasons . . .' When he felt that he had to defend himself against a woman, Michael had a way of making a showy concession to feminism; presuming that she was his opponent, he also presumed that this would disarm her.

'You mean, women are closer to the earth.'

'Oh, come on, J, stop sending me up.'

'I'm not sending you up.'

'Yes, you are, you're making fun of me because I can't express my admiration for you without sounding like a chauvinist.' He pulled a wounded face, kicked up the leaves in mock despondency. It was one of his most appealing turns, this downcast schoolboy act, and more effective as he cut his swathe in the world. Michael Knight, *the* Michael Knight, the *great* Michael Knight is hurt and I am the cause of it – Jane's heart swelled to a more generous volume at the thought, for a short while obscuring the uneasy atmosphere of this conversation, which stored itself away in the memory bank of her feelings.

It would be another year before she arrived at the opinion that nothing could hurt Michael, which was why he could easily pretend sensitivity. He put his arm around her shoulders again and then, as if to show that there were no hard feelings, wanted to make love in the shade of the oak trees.

The wood proved to be the most coveted mushroom bed in the area. Only a few days after that conversation they had woken at dawn to see a stealthy procession of cars without lights driving along the little road that crossed the railway on the far side of their new domain. The occupants climbed out, provided with baskets, bags and old melon crates, and began to raid the wood, their torches flickering between the tree trunks.

Michael had at once protested to the farmer who

owned the adjoining land, who agreed to close the lane with a chain at night during the mushroom season. With amusement, they noted that this action, far from being considered a mean, dog-in-the-manger move, won them looks of respect in Saint-Victor, the nearest small town. The joiner and the plumber employed to renovate the house began to submit their estimates more hesitantly, explaining that of course the building regulations required this or that but it was not absolutely necessary in this case and if they were not too concerned . . . well, why not choose the cheaper option?

It was another proof that she needed him, that every woman needed a man, because the world was made for men and you needed manly strength to tame it and make its energy flow freely. Jane saw that if Michael had not leaped up to protect his territory they would instead have lost respect, been cheated and despised in consequence and never entered into a real acquaintanceship with their neighbours, one of the many mundane human pleasures that she enjoyed keenly in France because it had disappeared from their city life. It was also proof of the injustice of life, because Michael had no interest in the mushrooms, only in defending his own.

Jane had been moved to investigate the precious fungi now in her possession, to consult old Madame Montaud, and Marius, her energetic son who worked as an engineer in the regional capital. She eagerly walked the woods with them, making notes in her new pocket mushroom directory. Marius dropped wistful remarks about the quality of the shooting over the land and she willingly allowed the old woman to manoeuvre her into granting him the rights in exchange for a proportion of his bag. Faced with birds she could not even recognize, she asked for guidance in cooking them.

She compared the Montauds' advice with that of the farmer whose much larger holding of land enclosed their own, and with the wisdom of the market traders and shopkeepers in Saint-Victor. In due time, poking around in the dusty bowels of a secondhand-furniture shop, among the horsehair mattresses and holed enamel milk churns, she discovered old books of cookery and household management, some of them handwritten, faded copperplate on browned pages tied together with a rust-spotted satin ribbon. 'Your pig should be killed when the moon is waning.' She read one sentence and bought the whole pile.

The next year, when she was pregnant with Emma, Jane gave up her job at the Department and began a book, *Food from a French Farmhouse.* It was a pastime, until the day Andrea Moynihan knocked on her door and announced that Michael was having an affair with a woman at his office named Grace. The news had hit her like a blow in the face, but Jane had considered her swelling belly and what she had been told of the ways of the world, and decided to keep the secret. This would pass. She had not then realized that just as Michael was an extraordinary man, he would be capable of extraordinary betrayal.

Without much calculation, in a dreamy ecstasy of fertility, she retired to Les Palombières and poured into the book all her fascination with the house and land as it had operated for centuries before their occupation, an enterprise dedicated to the production not merely of food but of a sophisticated abundance of nourishment. *Food from a French Farmhouse* was a great success.

Michael began to talk proudly about 'our little house in France – where I can be at home with my family and my wife writes her books'. He never shared any of her joys; she had taken joy in their baby, although Emma was irritable and sleepless from the start. Whatever she had done wrong by Imogen, Jane felt she was doing it again. When Emma developed eczema it seemed like her own guilt manifesting in the child's distress.

There were always reasons why Michael could not spend more than two or three days in France, reasons of the calibre in which he always dealt: meetings, ministers, deadlines, emergencies – cast-iron, indisputable reasons. Other women succeeded Grace, other messengers brought bad news to her door. Jane confronted him, and the lying began. He wanted a son; she had Sam. Nothing changed. The children were wretched, Michael was mostly absent, and when he was present he lied. Proudly, she refused to be a *kaffee kvetch* wife, bitching about her husband and her kids in her neighbours' kitchens. Perhaps it was her own fault, perhaps she was unrealistic, too attached to her sentimental woman's vision of a family. She had her work, and she had Les Palombières, and as the years went on and days came when her pain was overwhelming, she clung to these two.

*

'Impressive. Really impressive. Serena, I don't know anyone else, man or woman, who could have done this in the time. Let me know if you ever want a job doing this. Let's see how it plays.' Serena sat down, feeling awkward at his praise, and the editor ran the tape again while Michael read her words as the pictures flickered on the small screen. '. . . and so,' he concluded, in the soft, heavy voice that she remembered from her student years, when you could believe a world disaster was inevitable if Michael Knight assured you it was, 'at least half the children we have met during the making of this film will be enjoying their last summer here in the former Yugoslavia. Conditions in this camp, like many others in this tragic country, are so desperate that unless help reaches them before winter sets in, these children will die.' On the last word his own voice sank to a whisper.

He paused, then went on in a sombre tone to make the appeal over the ChildAid pledge line numbers. 'Is that too fast? Nine digits, it's long. Here, see if you can get a number written down in the time.' A pencil tumbled into Serena's lap, further embarrassing her by falling between her thighs to the floor.

It was almost 2 a.m. For six hours in the flickering claustrophobia of the edit suite five of them had laboured to perfect a film which to her had seemed slickly assembled at the outset. Michael had ridden the producer and researcher unmercifully; to back him up he had called in Stuart Devlin, NewsConnect's most respected reporter, whose awards covered ten feet of the reception wall, who stood patiently at his back with his heavy-lidded eyes on the tiny screen, tipping the arguments this way or that with a few mumbled words.

Out went interviews Michael judged irrelevant, montages that bored him or arguments he condemned as side-issues which weakened the script. Devlin did not always support him, and Michael deferred to his opinion. Taking confidence from that, Serena had crossed him a couple of times, which he had accepted. All the same, she saw that he liked doing this; ripping apart months of work by subordinates was a gratifying power play, but he was also right. What had begun as a sound report little different from many others was now a dazzling emotive dispatch, the kind of film only NewsConnect distributed. She already admired him, and this final small thoroughness with the telephone numbers, this care for the lumpen audience fumbling with their ballpoints, was the cherry on top. Silently, Devlin picked up the pencil for her. He was slight and quiet, with short fleecy fair hair and pale lashes, a face unremarkable in life but on camera the image of a daring war correspondent.

'Take the end one more time please,' Michael ordered, staying the editor as he rose wearily from his seat. 'I want to make sure it marries in smoothly.'

'We can fade in the title music . . .'

'I don't like ending with a fade. Ending with a statement works best.'

Michael Knight's voice was rich and embracing, full of propriety, wisdom and kindness. It was the voice of a much older and bigger man, a man of great consequence, one with a well-earned place in history. His very first job had been as a radio news reporter, where his voice had been the foundation of his fortune. When people said that Michael Knight was a great loss to the screen, what they meant was that no other voice had the same blend of emotionalism and power. The suggestion had never been made that he chose still to narrate NewsConnect's keynote documentaries out of vanity or egotism. No one could have done it better.

His voice was his Orpheus lute, and the first listener to be charmed by its power was always Michael himself. When he was reading a script, he lost himself. The act of speaking words occupied all of his unquiet mind. He became his voice, feeling Godlike in his rightness. When he was speaking he knew that he had total authority, that whatever he said people would be persuaded, and he felt also that this power, whose source was not in himself, was something wholly benevolent, always for the best, never to be defied. At a very deep level, Michael believed the truth of whatever he was saying.

The illusion was not perfect when he spoke his own words, and so early in life Michael had acquired a habit of repeating himself. The necessity to pause and think, to focus on the meaning of what he was saying, let loose demons of doubt in his mind. Worse was the need to struggle with his emotions to know what he meant. The huge, primitive surges of his heart were uncontrollable. When he sensed their chaotic force he fell into familiar forms of words, formulaic announcements which left him with a matching inner serenity.

'Well, I think we've cracked it, don't you?'

'It's good.' Devlin gave his blessing. There was a weary murmur of assent from the editor. The producer, scowling at the massacre of her own original script, said nothing. Michael patted her shoulder. 'It was good. You did a very good job, you went into a chaotic situation, analysed it, did everything you needed to do, thought it all through, got the whole issue on the screen. And the pictures told the story, that was the best. All of you' – he commanded the last shreds of their attention with a brief gesture – 'I want you to remember this film, this is how it should be. All in the visuals. People understand with their eyes. Never forget that.' Now the exhausted, humiliated woman was smiling. Michael put his arm around her shoulders. 'It just needed a little bit more punch, that's all. Don't hate me.'

'Michael, I don't hate you.'

'Yes, you do. You wouldn't be human if you didn't. Come on, I'll buy you dinner. Everybody. Let's eat.' He sprawled back in his chair, folding his arms behind his head. The researcher and editor rose and began to slam drawers shut and shovel paper into waste bins. 'Anyone for the greasy spoon?'

'No thanks, Michael. I need to catch some Zs.'

'Me too. Goodnight all.'

'Be seeing you Sunday.' Devlin was already out of the door.

'Serena? Please. I'm hungry, I must eat something. It's just a little Greek place around the corner that taxi-drivers use.' He made it sound as if to refuse would be some kind of a condemnation.

'I'd love to.'

'You're not too tired?'

She shook her head and smoothed back her hair, suddenly beyond fatigue in a lake of cool white anticipation. Michael turned finally to the producer, who looked from him to Serena, hardened her face and muttered, 'Sorry, Michael. Early start tomorrow.'

Michael watched Serena rise from her chair, remarking her grace. Even now she stood up in one easy movement and all her clothes, crumpled though they were, fell into elegant folds around her body. Effects such as that seemed almost like sorcery. It fascinated him that a woman could think and talk – as he saw it – like a man, and yet have arcane instincts of attraction.

As they left the building a new night shift was arriving, soles squeaking on the white marble floor. The awards covered one wall, the photographs of the award-winners, reporters and presenters, covered another. Michael's picture was no larger than the others, and their order was alphabetical, beginning with Amina Bhatia, glamorous in red with gold earrings, the host of their new early evening magazine.

NewsConnect's studio complex was on the river in the old centre of the city, in the no-man's-land of industrial depots and high-rises built for bankers. A striking postmodern temple faced in white and grey marble, it was in many people's estimation the only beautiful building raised since industrial decay created space for modern architecture. Around it were few constructions on human scale, only some amputated Victorian terraces with odd grimy shops on what had once been street-corners. One of these was the café. It was blessed with a tree, a surreal spectacle in such a place, and under the branches the proprietor, bred in a kinder climate, set flimsy metal tables in the summer.

'I believe,' Michael confided, 'that this is the only full-grown tree on this side of the river between the eastern city limit and the park. Eh? Do you think I'm right?'

'You could be.'

'You're laughing at me.'

'I'm not.'

'I would care if you were, you know.' There it was, the Zen-like movement so full of purpose that it had become that purpose itself. He had talked over the film again, once more anxious, once more seeking reassurance, which she had given. He had relaxed, exchanged jovial conversation with the owner about their children, told her to trust him and ordered barbecued lamb and a plate of salads, and wine, although the café supposedly had no licence. And now, without losing a step or missing a beat, while she was still drawing breath and marvelling that the god of the NewsConnect temple could be comfortable in this mortal hash-house, he reached out to seize her.

She gave him a quick, startled look, unable to say anything. He noticed her eyes, a very light speckled green, and the lashes, fair and fine. Dryad's eyes, delicate, modest, meant for sidelong looks and shady clearings. There was a sheen on her skin, the bloom of starlight.

'I would care what you thought of me. You – don't be

insulted, I mean this as a compliment – but you remind me of my mother. A very beautiful woman, she was. Always beautifully dressed, in very plain clothes, but what she really had was beauty of the soul. She knew what was right and wrong and it always just shone out of her. She didn't judge people, that wasn't her way, she was too good a person ever to think herself better than anybody else. She just had this very pure, sweet look about her. I suppose all small boys adore their mothers, but when I was about eight I thought she was more lovely than any of the film stars. I'd get into fights at school over it.' He was looking at her intently, searching for the tender softening reactions, for encouragement.

'And is she still alive?' Uneasy, Serena retreated into formality.

He shook his head. 'No. We lost her when I was twenty. I think that was when my life went wrong, to tell the truth.'

'Wrong? There doesn't seem to be much wrong about it to me. I'm sorry, that's cynical . . .'

He shook his head. 'Most people would agree with you. But, after she died – I was bereft, really. It was cancer, and it happened so quickly. One week she was ill, the next she went into hospital and never came home. My father was broken by it. And soon afterwards I got married, too soon.' Now he had dropped his eyes and was turning the cork from the wine bottle over and over between his fingers. 'I don't know how much you know about me.'

'You could tell me anyway, if you want to.'

'I want you to understand this. As much as I understand it.' He threw the cork on the table and leaned forward, his hands now a few inches from hers. 'My first wife had some problems . . . I had no idea, librarian's son from a small town, me. I adored her, thought she was the most thrilling person I'd ever met. Swedish, but not Nordic to look at, dark. A musician, a pianist. Should have had a wonderful career, but she couldn't take the pressures. She got depressed, used all kinds of drugs, legal and illegal. I wouldn't say she was addicted, but she wasn't in her right mind a lot of the time. Our life was bizarre. Ghastly, sometimes.'

Drained of his normal humour and vitality, all the lines of his face fell into a haggard mesh. To hear, she had to lean towards him, because his voice had sunk almost to nothing. He caught the almond scent of her breath.

'We had a baby, she wanted it, I thought it would settle her down, which it didn't, then at six months old, it died. A cot death. I was happy for it to be called that, anyway.'

'How terrible.' In the soft summer night tragedy had come down like a cold cloud, blotting out everything but the two of them and their pocket of sympathy. 'I can't imagine what that must be like.'

'In a sense, I was relieved. It wasn't often she was in any state to care for a child. The kind of thing I mean – we were going to take a holiday, to see her parents in Sweden. I was filming in Norway; she had to fly out with the baby and join me. Well, she left the baby at the airport. At the check-in desk.'

Serena proffered something appropriate, words of commiseration, trying to hide her shock. Much of the emotional toll of her work arose from being compelled to use the death of children as a selling point. That was too tough, however much for the greatest good. She was aware of ripening anxiety at her own childlessness, awkwardly conscious that she had a weapon whose force she could not understand. The notion of a woman forgetting a child as if it were a duty-free luxury was obscene.

The tender convulsion of her mouth gave Michael comfort. 'Then she got pregnant again, and once Imogen was born she seemed better. Then one day she just left. Walked out. At first I waited, because she'd had episodes before when she'd disappeared. Then her aunt called. She had an aunt in Seattle. She'd arrived at their place, overdosed . . . they wanted her to stay in hospital, have treatment. I never saw her again.'

'You keep in touch? I mean, she is alive?'

'Oh yes, in a sort of way.' He felt cold and weak, and he snatched at the hot, thin night air of the city, a deep breath that was almost a sigh. Every time he raked this story over, the landmarks of his emotional life seemed like a sequence of despair whose next progression would inevitably crush him. 'And then, you see, when Jane came along, she was so normal, so straight and down-to-earth. Her people were Scottish, a plain, ordinary family. She coped with Imogen, they seemed to take to each other. I was just . . . grateful.'

He fell silent, while Serena stared wondering at the ruined, helpless man who had taken the place of the all-powerful deity whose stardust was even now holding the café proprietor in respectful attendance, although it was dawn and they were his only customers. Her vibrant sympathy, fairly blazing after he had blown upon it, supplied the missing words. I thought I loved her, I was mistaken. She can't fulfil me. I can't help her. She weighs me down. I intimidate her. We have grown apart. I am unhappy.

The moon was a round wafer in the sky, and the river, reflecting, was the milk-blue of spring flowers. One or two tiny birds darted through the free air. The tide was high, and the water lapped contentedly at the stone embankment. They were walking towards a bridge where Michael had promised there would be taxis, when he allowed his feelings to swell like a wave. He had the impression of being picked up and hurled towards her by the force of his obsession, which would sweep the two of them helplessly away.

CHAPTER THREE

Saturday

'The day gapes before us.' Nick put down Grace's coffee at her side of the bed. Bars of light through the half-open shutters announced the blazing morning outside.

A fretful squeak, like a disturbed kitten, indicated that his wife was awake. Grace was not at her best in the morning. She stretched; his side of the mattress was cool now. He had been out of bed for some time.

'*What* did you say?'

'I said, "The day gapes before us."'

'That's what I thought you said.' She wriggled upright and reached for her coffee.

'Is it an awful thing to say, then?'

'Absolutely ghastly. I ought to hate you for saying something like that at any time, let alone before breakfast.' She shook her head and screwed up her eyes, drowsily watching him walk to and fro across the half-lit room. He had put on crumpled chinos and a fresh dark blue shirt, clothes that were kind to his large body.

'But you don't hate me.'

'No, I don't. I might if you apologized, though.' She abandoned the cup and rubbed her eyes.

'Oh, I shan't apologize. I know my place. Do you know you look like a newborn owl when you've just woken up?'

'No I don't. Why did we buy this bed when it's so uncomfortable to sit up in?' Crossing her legs under the light quilt she pulled her spine straight, tossed her dark hair and massaged her scalp with languid movements of her long, rounded arms. The question did not expect an answer. Sitting was not the bed's purpose; they had bought it to make love in. It was a wrought-iron four-post fantasy draped in muslin, discovered at an exhibition of student designs where they had agreed, immediately, completely and in spite of its price, that it was the perfect venue for the unfolding wonder of their erotic life.

'I'm glad we bought it. It's kept us going, hasn't it? It's a presence. Eight feet high.' He looked up at the canopy, where the four posts were twirled together into a point. 'Ridiculous curly bits on the ends. All those times when every time we did it we were thinking is this it, are we going to make a baby tonight? We couldn't get too brought down by it all, not in this creation.'

'Yes,' she agreed, hurt by her own memories, immediately wary of a probing conversation and anxious to return to neutral ground. 'Aren't you tired? Do you realize you slept appallingly?'

'Did I keep you awake? I'm not unwound yet.'

'You weren't keeping me awake.'

'I must have been or you wouldn't be able to tell me I was sleeping badly.' Now he was pacing the far edges of the room, his hands clasped around his cup, gazing restlessly around as if expecting the day's timetable to light up in a dark corner. The smell of the morning, grassy and spiced, trickled in through the shutters, freshening the air.

'I must have slept, I was dreaming.'

'Sweet dream?'

'No. Frightening. But it was a classic. Something was chasing me, a bear or a pterodactyl or something.'

'You didn't get a good look at it, then.'

'I was afraid to look at it. I ran away. In the end I had to jump down a well to get away from it.' She recalled hallucinatory fragments of the night; she had been aware of him breathing violently, talking to himself and turning over again and again. His pillow was beside her, crushed into a ball.

Every night in the city Nick lay still and heavy in their bed, conscientiously restoring his faculties for the day ahead. Here at the Alhambra he was often restless; what agitated him in the nights here was desire. Even now he was still aroused: she could tell by the nervous edge to all his movements and a glitter in his eyes. The turbulence of the night had been because he had wanted sex but held away from her, knowing she was distressed and that comfort sex was not her favourite.

Grace fell back on her pillow, feeling her emotions

stripped. She was nothing but a heap of vulnerabilities, raw to the corrosion of guilt, weak annoyance and gratitude. Below these was a monster, a ravening anxiety searching for meat. Her heartbeat felt uneven.

She shook out his pillow. They had seen many dawns warm the walls of the bedroom from the sweaty wreck of the bed, holding each other close, trembling, tearful, half-terrified at what they had done together in the darkness. After a day or two in the warmth of the south their blood would begin to heat and the pretences and accommodations of their city life melted away. They both had huge appetites, and the rich land fed them. Sometimes, she thought that this extraordinary sex was all that held them together. Sometimes, she thought that only two profoundly connected people could create this extraordinary sex. She put the riddle to herself several times a year, but could never solve it.

Making love ceased to be a polite city convention and became a ritual of abundance and beauty, one of the silent, eternal processes of nature. At their highest moments Grace felt herself united with all the energy of the earth and even her barrenness was only part of the pattern.

Before they met, all their lives, Grace and Nick had been well-mannered lovers who had tempered their desires to what their previous partners had considered normal. Overwork, travel and fantasy absorbed some of the vast energies left unchannelled; some had leached out in rage; they had not always been faithful partners. When at last they discovered each other, they were sophisticated, confident athletes, perfectly matched. The beauty of it was shocking.

All that was needed then was the courage to confess. They had begun together with the same old pretence of restraint, then slowly picked up the hints that here was a libido equally deep and rich, and a soul as bold in exploration. Words escaped, halting requests, startled urging; poses became rehearsed, perfected; in time they released their dreams, joined hands and set off for the subterranean inferno.

A few years passed, and instead of the dying-away to which they had secretly resigned themselves, patterns appeared, cycles of fusion and withdrawal, craving and calm, one pursuing, the other retreating, one tempted, one accommodating. Summer at the Alhambra was one of these cycles, the season of excess.

Grace stared at the cracks in the ceiling, trying to throw off the sickness of her spirit. She had to find peace. 'What time is it?'

'Nine. We could go into town for the market.' He sounded almost childlike in his eagerness. Nick enjoyed marketing almost as much as cooking.

'We don't need much if we're going to the Knights tomorrow.'

She breathed easier. So – it was time to slay the dragon. Merely making the decision had revived her strength.

'We don't have to go if it will upset you, darling . . .'

'I feel OK about it, I really do. That was all so long ago.'

'You're sure . . .'

'Yes. Honestly and absolutely. I want to go. Now call Jane, tell her we'll come. Then we can go to the *brocante* in Castillon.' Suddenly, she shook herself, shaking off powerlessness. Burrowing into her marriage, staying in the safety of the Alhambra, editing Michael out of her new life, negating Jane as she had always done, these were coward's refuges. Part of the disaster of Michael was the atrophy of her will. Always *his* timetable, *his* needs, *his* imperatives – impossible to defend her tiny, selfish preferences against the future of world broadcasting and the happiness of his children. Even now she hardly knew what she wanted. It was time to challenge the past and free herself. 'Go on, Nick. She's probably going to leave for a market herself any minute.'

'You really are sure?'

'Oh, for heaven's sake!' Irritation finally overcame her. 'I've decided, I want to do it. It'll be fine, I promise. Go on. And make me some more coffee. Go on. Please. Now.' As soon as he left the room she threw back the quilt and quit the bed. She frowned, passing the mirror, seeing an unnatural sheen of perspiration on her body. Ruefully she cupped her breasts, passed a hand over her belly; at present they were too full for her own liking, although Nick enjoyed her extra flesh.

The heat of the morning was already in the room. Such a perverse season, summer, the sun provoking lust then the heat enervating it. Sticky silk, sweaty lace – all her lingerie was useless in this climate. At the back she found something that was mostly black ribbon; then, in an attempt to soothe her spirits, she went to the wardrobe and picked out a new dress, a loose voile shift, almost ankle-length, dark violet blue speckled with cream, and tossed the two together on to the bed.

The distant noise of the telephone told her that he had made the call; when he came back she was in the shower. A wisp of scented steam floated on the still air. The petal of chiffon, lurid against the crumpled white bedlinen, caught his eye. He felt a tension at the back of his neck, spreading down his spine, a crawling, tightening warmth.

'All done,' he called, and she heard the roughening of his voice which betrayed the preoccupation of his body. He added, 'Jane sounded pleased.'

'Perhaps she likes new faces. It must be lonely, out here all summer long.' Even as she made this bland reply, annoyance at hearing the name of Michael's wife in her husband's mouth blasted the buds of her desire. For a while she retreated to silence and her aura of displeasure pushed Nick right out of the house. But in the act of dressing her body the wave of anger began to break, and the glimpse in the mirror of the black ribbon around her hips aroused her, so that when he came upstairs again and found her seated, pinning up her hair, there was a charge in the atmosphere.

'I like your hair like that.' He was standing behind her, fingers moving involuntarily as he considered touching her shoulders, weighing her mood.

She leaned her back against his thigh, his heat like sunshine beating down on her cheek. Turning her head, cat-like, she brushed her cheek against him, feeling him grow through the thin fabric. Light, smooth chinos, colourless, textureless – her lipstick was fresh; she printed her mouth on him.

'Now look what you've done.'

All at once she needed to be sure – of him, of them, of her life as it was now, of the past as the past, finished, an irrelevance. If she could take him inside her now she would know she was safe, completely and forever, but even as she was reaching up and opening her mouth their unity dissolved and their desires fell out of step.

He pulled her up by her shoulders and moved her back to the wall, turning her to face him, pulling up the hem of her skirt. The ribbon chafed her hips as his fingers pulled it away. After the shower her skin was tingling, alive, craving to be touched. She reached for him, but he was holding her at arm's length, saying, 'Please, darling, let me just see you like this, let me look at you . . .'

More than anything, she did not want an argument at that moment. When he pulled her dress off, the rough stone wall grazed her back. Then he was kneeling, his fingers holding her, parting, pleading. The sweetness of being overcome offered itself. Of its own volition her spine was sinking into a feral arch. Grace moved her feet apart and gave herself to his mouth.

In a while he surrendered to her; she fell on him on the floor, dragged off half his clothes and got what she wanted, the precious sense of being full of him and safe, and free of the past. Afterwards she felt drained. It was tempting to lie still on the boards where they had fallen.

She did not get up until he finished showering, then set about hiding her tension in activity. She dressed again, made the bed, and finding the kitchen immaculate went outside to water the garden in spite of the sun. Her limbs trembled slightly with post-coital exhaustion; she was physically relaxed and in places agreeably sore, but the certainty she had wanted to feel was not there. Physical pleasure was too feeble a remedy for the fever of anxiety taking hold of her mind.

Was it love he was afraid of, or guilt? He was afraid, watching her face on the pillow, the eyes shut as if she were dead and the spray of hair lying precisely in the hollow of her cheek. So much of him already was anchored here. Her lips closed with such confidence, his pride folded in their forgiving bow. The high, clean arch of her brows, he thought, made a diptych where her eyes would write his destiny.

The smell of her hair was comforting to him. He inhaled deeply, feeling that he wanted to draw her whole being into his body with the scent. 'My love. My love.' The word did not hurt to say. Lightning did not tear open the sky. 'My love.'

Her answer was a short breath, a protest stifled – by courtesy perhaps, or only tiredness. His new-blown world of happiness shuddered on its axis. 'Don't, don't. Never do that, make fun of me for loving you. Serena, my love, I will call you that, you must let me.'

At her hairline the skin was salt where her sweat had dried, for the night had never sunk into coolness and there had been no interlude for the prudent opening of windows or peeling off the quilt. Reliving his violent impulsion towards her bed in this following tenderness, he felt ashamed.

Was she offended, even perhaps physically hurt? Here he had made errors with other women, acting from the feeling of possession he had with Jane. Women who lived free lives did not know the language and told him he assumed too much. She had caressed him, gently, he could feel the sweep of her fingers up his spine, and his ears remembered her chaotic breath and the faint repeated cries of her final pleasure, but now Michael could feel her body straining unconsciously away from him. He moved to fold his arm around her and although she consented she was tense, the cat who hates to be held but hates more to offend his owner. He imagined that he could even hear the turmoil of her feelings roaring inside the thin wall of her chest. Under his fingers polished skin lay evenly over flesh. Her back was muscular, evenly ridged like a beach marked by retreating waves; the breasts, half-liquid, poured against his own body, stirring with each breath.

'I want to sleep now. Hold you and sleep with you, like this.' He knew that he would have to leave her soon; what would she do when he was gone? Reflect with sadness, give way to her conscience, leave him when he had only just found her?

She answered him at last. 'You must be tired.'

Her voice was almost without expression. If she was taking refuge in concern for him, what thoughts were troubling her?

'No, I'm not tired. I want to sleep to be with you, that's all. It's strange, I want to feel completely close to you. Don't you think you feel closest to someone when you sleep with them? It's sharing something that's more than intimate, being unconscious together. Lying down to release your souls. Does that sound daft?'

'No.' Neutral. Wary, disturbing.

The idea that she might retreat from him now, get up with a snappy comment perhaps and follow with good-mannered talk of her day's obligations and a firm goodbye, was horrible. He imagined himself standing on the pavement outside with a great haemorrhaging wound in his spirit.

'You aren't saying anything.'

Her sigh was hesitant. 'Is there anything to say?'

'Yes. Yes. Oh, my love.'

She would not cry, or turn away from him. Instead she lay in his arms without moving, hoping he would sleep or leave her so she could restore herself. The enchantment of the night had gone. The wholeness of her life, the still perfection which had resonated like a country church bell in the early morning, had been cracked. Her sense of him now was threatening; besides, what they had done was wrong. It occurred to her that never before had she broken one of the ten commandments, except forgetting the Sabbath in working on Sunday. Her best hope now was that this all meant nothing to him.

'Yes. Yes, you know there is. Let me make you something, coffee, tea, whatever you have. Where's the kitchen? Come on, we must have a proper talk and I need a cup of tea for proper talking. You stay there. Tell me what you need. Stay there, I'll bring it in.'

She picked at a fold of the sheet, troubled, wishing he would cease to be the tormented man who had reached out for her beside the river and appear in the daylight as an unfeeling shit temporarily diverted by lust from his all-devouring ambition. Easy to have mistaken him, but this was not the way an unfeeling shit behaved. She had some experience of them, and their style was to leave swiftly with cheerful promises, avoiding conversation at all costs.

He pulled back the quilt and reached behind her head to arrange her pillows. Feeling childish, she settled herself against them. 'I usually have a tea. Whatever's there, camomile, whatever. The kitchen is that door on the right as you come in.'

He had no deliberate intention of leaving her naked in the bed they had shared while he resumed most of his clothes and went out into the daylight. It seemed romantic to him, to make their tea on a Saturday morning, part of the glamour of their life which was to come.

Serena's kitchen was as beguiling as he would have desired, a tiny galley made from the corridor. He registered no details, could not analyse the appeal of her modest collection of household equipment, neatly arrayed on blue-painted shelves with paper lace edges, or the strings of dried chillies and bunches of herbs hanging from high hooks. The necessary was his focus, a pair of bright modern ceramic cups, an eccentric old kettle on the gas cooker, teas and coffee in an old biscuit tin with a thatched cottage painted on the lid. The window looked out into blue morning sky; a half-length white cotton crochet curtain, of the kind photographed as typical at rural French casements, blocked out the lower view of a potholed city side-street.

He took the tea back to the bedroom. She had found something to wear, a crumpled blue shirt. 'What do you think about love?' he asked, when she had taken her mug from him.

A fearful look through the steam, and no smile. 'What do you mean, what do I think about it?'

'Do you think it's important, I mean?'

'Of course it's important.'

'I think that love is *the* most important thing in life. I do, I really do. I think you have to make it the centre of your life, let everything else that you do flow from that.' He sat on the bed, facing her. 'Not sentimental, lyric-writer's muck, real love, the love that's God or whatever living in us.' At last she looked at him. It was strange to hear Michael Knight's glorious voice become hesitant. 'The best that a man can do is love. The most precious thing we can do, we ought to live for it, tend it, sacrifice whatever we have to, not deny it or make fun of it. I hate it when people use swear words for making love, don't you?'

'Fucking awful thing to do.' Animation, laughter at

last. She was not hating him, thank God.

'I do truly believe love is the best in us. You have to just live for it. That's it for me.'

'That's a very grand thought.'

'Perhaps I'm feeling very grand just now.' They withdrew to their own tender silences. Down on the street fire engine sirens sounded from far off, approached closer, then died away again.

'I'm not used to people saying things like that,' she broke in a few moments later. 'People are just practical in my world. Why aren't the visas through, why hasn't the photocopier been fixed, why isn't this trust giving this year . . .?'

He nodded, taking the empty cup from her. 'We're full of shit in the media.'

'I didn't mean that . . .'

'I know you didn't. I did. We are full of shit. Everything that happens in the world is just a prioritizing exercise to us, nothing's real. People don't mean very much – even if they have been raped and speak English; then they're a story for a day, might make the year-end compilation if it was a very good picture. And everyone who isn't a victim is just trying to get you over to their point of view. You have to cut off, emotionally, or you couldn't do it. And you couldn't do it if you had no feelings to start with. So you have this strange life, moral deprivation and solitary confinement in a building with five hundred people working in it. Sometimes when I go into the washroom at the end of the day and walk past the mirror I'm surprised to see my own face, surprised

I'm still there, because I *feel* unreal. So to find someone like you is so precious.'

In his mind's ear he heard Grace tell him it could stand another read-through. His mind's eye saw her thick eyebrows rise in affectionate cynicism. He thought of Grace often, she was like a second conscience to him.

Serena was stricken now, he knew the look, that very gentle, fearful, yielding look of surrender. The tension had left her body, she was invitingly relaxed. Was there time to make love to her again?

Curious that at this point he was immune to guilt. It would kick in later, in a big way. The load grew exponentially with every affair but, however heavy, it was never unbearable, he always needed the new love more. Guilt is your thing, isn't it, Grace had accused him once. You without guilt would be like Saint Sebastian without arrows, lacking his reason for existence. You're alive only when you're being stabbed through with the knowledge of what you've done wrong. It's agony, you love it. Her insight was still a loss to him. She was good, very good, far too good for that self-righteous right-wing newspaper. Maybe, when the Altmark thing was through . . .

Michael felt his energy flow freely, aligned with divine purpose, a surge of power. There was a later flight. He could telephone Jane, and Imogen in Paris, and later from Les Palombières he could phone Serena. He put his hand under the quilt, found her warm thigh and swept it towards him.

*

Sunflowers almost hid the track that led off the main road to Les Palombières. It curved around the brow of the hill like a loving arm around plump shoulders, nearly invisible between the swathes of joyous yellow sweeping to the blue horizon. Thousand upon thousand, the great dish-shaped blooms faced the house, their colour flaming in the full midday sun. The little cloud of white dust announcing a vehicle was hardly visible.

Louisa and Antony occasionally looked up from their books to admire the view. They had retreated from the scorching poolside to the shade of the side terrace, a structure which was more than a pergola but less than a verandah, formed by knocking out the stones of old barn walls but leaving the timbers and the roof beams. It was the best arrangement in a climate where it was warm enough to eat outside much of the year, hot enough to be unbearable in high summer but liable to a violent storm at any time.

The year he founded NewsConnect, Michael had announced that there was at last money to restore Les Palombières; Jane, in love with its semi-ruined romanticism, questioned the need, but was unheard. Tamara Lady Aylesham arrived the next day; Michael was a fool for titles, hers was an unjustified hangover from her first marriage. She was amusing company and a competent decorator, unembarrassed by the filthy looks the workmen gave her every time she changed her mind mid-project. Tamara had created the terrace, renovated the cellar, landscaped the pool garden, paved the courtyard and festooned the whole with wisteria, honeysuckle and roses.

Apart from the flycatchers squabbling in the holes in the wall, every noise was swallowed up in the deep vegetable calm of the land. It was too hot for the skylark. Emma and Xanthe were playing around the pool but their shrieks and splashes were barely audible, and the car engine was a distant hum until the last moment. When the vehicle appeared in the courtyard it was as if it had materialized from nowhere.

'Good heavens. How extraordinary.' Antony said this twenty times a day. It was getting on Louisa's nerves.

The ancient grey Renault van rocked on its springs as the driver emerged. For an instant it seemed to be a skinny, black-haired young man, but in the swaggering stance there was a significant suppleness which identified her as a woman. Over her chest flapped a checked shirt and a cheap huntsman's waistcoat, new from the hypermarket, dark green and much embellished with pockets, flaps, studs, zippers, D-rings and loops. Her face and arms were a weatherbeaten walnut tan. On her feet were tattered trainers which, like her jeans and the vehicle's tyres, were extremely muddy.

'I'll see what she wants.' Louisa approached the visitor, swishing pink pleated voile, and issued a greeting in her exquisitely inflected finishing-school French. The young woman nodded, businesslike, and growled a few words. She had a broad Gascon accent. Opening up the rear doors of the van, she hauled out a newspaper parcel, more than a metre long, rounded, stiff and damp, and dumped it in Louisa's arms. Then she shut the doors with a tinny slam and, again looking around with a mixture of defiance and stealth, got back behind the wheel and drove quickly away over the potholes.

'What on earth . . .? Ugh! It's wet.'

'Actually, it looks as if it's bleeding,' Antony informed her without stirring a limb. Louisa's ability to get her clothes stained, and her inability to get them washed, was beginning to irritate him.

'It's the salmon lady.' Emma pattered towards them, wet from the pool. Louisa looked at the child with distaste. Emma had never been a good advertisement for childhood. She was small for her age, with long hair of a lifeless brown which hung in snarled curls on either side of her small face. Her teeth looked too big for her little mouth and were newly disfigured with orthodontist's train tracks. Her eczema spared only the parts of her body that were always covered with clothes. At present she had a livid red weal down one side of her nose, and red patches of inflammation around her neck and elbows.

The child ignored Louisa and yelled into the house. 'Mummy! The salmon lady's been. Mummy!'

'She's on the phone. Is this a *salmon*? Surely not . . .'

'Yes it is,' the child asserted, scratching the back of her neck as she turned to hop away back to the swimming pool. 'She always brings it when it's Daddy's birthday. She steals it, or something.'

'Don't scratch, Em.' Jane said it automatically as she appeared from the house. 'Have you put your cream on?'

'Yes, Mummy. I'm a greasy French fry, just like the doctor said.'

'Good girl.'

'When is Daddy coming?'

'Not till lunchtime at the earliest.' Jane's voice was weary, begging Louisa not to begin another interrogation. The child pouted and came to cling to her mother. Jane had a general appearance of tiredness; she was wearing one of her favourite dresses, a cotton wrapover in faded Madras check, which gave her the air of a work-worn prairie wife.

'Why not, Mummy? I thought he was coming this morning. I thought we could have a picnic.'

'I know, darling. That was what he said yesterday, but you know how it is with his work, things come up.'

'It's his company, isn't it? He doesn't work for anyone else. If a thing comes up he can give it to somebody else. It's deli-something. Delicatessen?' With her bare foot she was kicking at the table leg, obviously disappointed. A scratching hand was wandering towards a patch of rash on her elbow. Gently, Jane took the hand and held it.

'Delegation. Don't look at me, Em. That's exactly what I think but your father says some things are too important to delegate. Are you going back in the water?'

'I don't know. I'm hungry. Are there any cookies?'

'There are some of your special cookies in the kitchen.'

'Can't I have chocolate chip? Just one? Just one cookie? Please, Mummy.'

Jane sighed, but stood firm. 'You know chocolate makes it worse. Better have one of your special cookies, eh? And put a T-shirt on before you get sunburnt.'

The nanny stepped into the picture, a self-contained

Australian girl who held the struggling toddler in her arms. Xanthe had been born with bright red hair growing upwards in a coconut tuft. Somehow it had instantly stamped her as different from Emma and Sam. Jane had chosen her name, finding that it came from the Greek word to describe that red-gold colour and feeling that this child deserved something better than the false-modest plain labels Michael had fixed on the others.

Xanthe's topknot was now tied with a blue ribbon. She had the classic redhead's complexion, very pale and prone to sunburn, and much of Debbie's energy that summer was diverted into schemes to keep her out of the sun. 'Em, why don't you come inside with me?' The nanny held out her hand. 'We'll get you a cookie and make your Chinese medicine? And Xanthe's about ready for her rest, maybe you can help me get her down?'

'Oh well.' The child responded with a show of almost adult fortitude. 'If I must I must, I suppose. That Chinese medicine is totally disgusting. It's even more disgusting than ordinary medicine, which you would think was impossible, wouldn't you?'

The nanny exchanged looks with Jane and hitched the toddler higher on her hip. 'Be worth it if it makes you better, eh?'

Pointedly waiting until the child was out of earshot, Louisa turned around, saying, 'Chinese herbs – is she *really* getting better?'

Jane shrugged and dismissed the subject, saying brightly, 'Who knows? I'll try anything – she woke up five times last night. What's this? Did the salmon lady come? I'm so sorry, Louisa, I should have told you she was expected. Here, let me have it. My, it's a big one this year . . . We must get it cooked at once . . .'

Louisa yawned and stretched, brandishing her unshaven armpits with what she intended to be hoydenish sensuality. 'I love coming to stay with you, Jane. It makes me so glad I haven't got any children.'

There was no point in trying to make Louisa understand. At the bottom of what she called her heart, she was sure that if an afflicted child woke up five times in the night all a sensible mother needed to do was roll over in her sleep to let the demanding brat know that the scam wasn't working. Opulently selfish herself, she attributed all distressing behaviour in children to the same motive and regarded maternal selfishness as the only cure.

The first rashes had appeared when Emma was eight months old. By her first birthday she was diagnosed, and affected over most of her body. For two years bedtime became a ritual of wet-wrap bandages and tiny cotton gloves. Jane felt she was torturing the child. She was relieved that at least there was a good reason why her baby never slept for more than half an hour at a time, and embarked on a long trial of foods and household chemicals; for a while the hunt for domestic toxins dominated her life.

Louisa knew Jane had felt robbed of carefree youth when she accepted the infant Imogen with Michael; with Emma, the anticipated joys of motherhood turned sour. Comforting the child was hopeless; most treats had to be denied her and, worst of all, she was alone with it. Jane's mother retreated, helpless, and attached herself to her sister, whose children were dull and healthy and whose husband was not only devoted but working part-time on invalidity benefit, and therefore often present to validate the household with his masculine presence. Jane's leisure time disappeared. So did many of her friends – a diminished company since her marriage in any case; Michael intimidated them. The company of other new mothers was almost as painful as the child's distress; they reacted badly when the little girl scratched herself to bleeding.

She felt blamed. Michael never implied that she had failed him, but all the same she reproached herself with it, and assumed that he would be overjoyed with another baby, a baby without problems, and a son. A mistake, she knew that now. Only in her work was she able to do things right. She solaced herself with writing. Xanthe had been an accidental conception, and an unexpected, untainted joy to her at last. Whatever reserve of strength she had tapped to draw Grace Nichols to their home, she felt obscurely that her determined red-haired child, growing up so defiantly different, had opened it.

The Bar du Marche must once have been a refuge for the traders, a place where they could take the weight off their feet, check the racing results and pass a few minutes in conversation away from the din of the market. The Left Bank got smarter every year now, the houses were hotels, the baker had become an internationally promoted centre of farinaceous culture where they ground their own flour and pulled the peasant-shaped loaves from a traditional wood-fired oven; the market was no longer a necessity to the neighbourhood. Its true purpose was street theatre.

As this tract of the city had become a canyon of pretension littered with glass-walled boutiques and antiquarian bookshops, the bar had also raised its ambitions, acquired red-and-yellow wicker chairs and planted fringed umbrellas on the pavement. Well-dressed young couples idled their precious time together over coffee, and the stall-holders had leisure to sit on their crates between customers.

'Bloody cliché we are, young lovers in Paris. At least it's not spring any more. You look well, you know.'

Imi looked at him down her nose. It was a nose sculpted ideally for contempt, strong, slightly flattened, scorn carved in the wide nostrils. 'You mean I've put on weight.'

'No, I mean you look well. Your skin's good.'

'Oh yeah?'

Stephen was expecting to feel joyful. Even when she was in a witch-out, being with Imi had always made him happy, in the mindless wriggling way puppies are happy. Now it was not happening. He leaned back on his chair.

'You've lost that sort of look you had in London at Christmas.'

'Yeah, well . . . we don't want to talk about Christmas, do we?'

Of course, she had gained weight, but he knew better

than to say it, and she looked older, more focused, more of a woman maybe. She was not quite the unearthly girl he had loved so long. There was something watchful, baleful about her but she was in control now, she was OK. All that drama at Christmas had just been a reaction to the stress of the time, having to be together with her family.

'Your arm healed OK.'

'Oh yeah.' Automatically, she stroked the inside of her wrist, her hand lying on the table. The skin was almost perfectly smooth now, evenly white, snow in the sunshine, the scars no more than threads. 'It wasn't too bad, you know. Under all the blood.'

'There was a lot of blood.' Eight months ago, and the memory still frightened him, the way a long ribbon of it ran down to her elbow, the leading edge pulsing, getting thick enough to drip.

'I didn't cut very deep. I couldn't. I remember trying to, but it wouldn't go in, the blade. I don't think it was very sharp, actually. Jane had been using it.'

'Her face when you asked about the gravy.' They laughed together but he felt guilty, worried that he was corrupting her with his sympathy, indulging her blackness. 'I like your hair that way. Who cut it?'

'I cut it, dickhead. Can't you tell? I just got sick of it all around my ears and stuff.' Self-consciously, she ran a hand over her forehead, then cradled her thin arms around her head, monkey-like, pulling up tufts with her fingertips.

'Your Dad and Jane will have something to say about it.'

'Jane won't, she's given up on me. I'm sure Dad'll have something to say, he always does, doesn't he? If I see him, he'll have something to say.' No smile. He had the expectation of the little cruel smile that was specially reserved for the idea of wounding her father, but Imi kept her blank, pouting expression and gazed into the middle distance.

'You're thinking of blowing the party, then?'

'I mean he might not see me. He never really *sees* me, does he? Or hears me. Being with him . . . it's the great special treat, special for birthdays and holidays, but he's not with you even when you're with him.'

'I don't mind, we can stay here. I'm here for you, you know that.' He was never quite sure of his position with her family. In his plain, petit-bourgeois world parents were not glamorous public figures, nor did they have nervous breakdowns or neurotic children. A second marriage was a rare, barely excusable phenomenon. Stephen aspired to the status of Michael and Jane, censured their morality and wondered if he did so because they intimidated him.

'Don't look like that, I hate it. You look like a stupid animal in a field, waiting to be turned into hamburgers.'

He was hurt; she always said nasty things, it was part of the testing process, he was used to it, but there was more weight in her words. Today he was surprised to feel that he had been tested enough. 'Imi, I do know what a bitch you can be. It's OK, you don't need to go on proving it.'

'You don't need to go on proving that you can take it, either.'

'I hate not being with you, you know. I hate this having to see you in the holidays and us being different.'

'You gotta study, Stephen. Gotta get your exams, get your degree, be an architect, get a job. You've gotta do it, haven't you?'

Was she accusing him? Her tone was bitter and her face was hard, but she was still staring into the centre of the street, arms and legs crossed, weaving her shoulders slightly from side to side.

'We talked about all this, we agreed. I want to take care of you, you know I do, but I've got to have a job or I can't do it. You're life itself to me, Imi, I'd do anything for you. But we haven't got anywhere to live, haven't got any money – what else can we do? I know it's hard for you to be patient . . .'

'Oh no. Oh no. It isn't hard for me to be patient, don't think that.' At last she turned to look at him, an odd animation galvanizing her features, her eyes digging spitefully into his face. 'I can be really, really patient, Stephen. You don't know how patient I can be. We're going to be together in a place, we are. And soon, really soon. You wait.' He wondered what drugs she had been doing. In the smack phase she'd talked that way a lot, vague, mysterious, threats and promises.

'In case you're wondering, I am straight. I've been straight for months. I know you are wondering, oh yes, I know you, Stephen. I'm chemically pure. Nothing wicked has passed my lips for days. Or my nostrils or my veins or my cunt or my ears or my asshole or any other way into me, nothing. I had dinner last night, you'd have been proud of me, given me a good mark for that.'

'Yes, I would.'

'Yes, you would. I said to myself, if old Stephen were here, he'd be proud of me. I almost ate meat. I thought about cutting the flesh of an animal. What do you think of that then?'

He never knew how to respond when she was like this. Sometimes every sentence was just a mine, waiting for him to take an innocent step forward to detonate the blast. There was a repellent knowingness about her in these moods, she would tease him out of their own bond, their own coupledness, picking out exactly the thing he cared about most to make him stumble over his own high feelings.

'But don't you worry,' she continued, unfolding her limbs and stretching out on the hard chair. 'I'm still all square – no errors there. Come on, let's go home, I'm tired. I didn't get enough sleep last night.'

The vegetarian thing had started when she was twelve, at the end of her first year at school. Sitting together on the summer grass, the bell had rung for assembly but Imi had not moved; he had scrambled to his feet – he remembered himself as a chunky boy always off-balance and lost for words – and stood awkwardly for a few seconds, awed at her disobedience. After he sat down again she pulled up a little green leaf, held it against the sunlight and rambled through an oath, something like, 'I, Imogen Melissa Knight, reject forever any food which will make any animal unhappy or cause any animal pain or suffering and I swear I will never cut the flesh of any animal.' Then she had looked at him, a harsh challenge diffused by the black veil of her hair, and held out the leaf, saying, 'You can swear too, if you like. You like animals, don't you?' That was how they had started out together.

Up in the apartment she lay down on the bed and let him take her boots off, then rolled over and fell asleep without saying another word, zapped by whatever she was feeling. Imi and her emotions, she was like a toy sailboat on a windswept pond, blown over at the first gust.

The sleeping business was one of her habits with him. When they were older, and holding fiercely together through the tyranny of his exams and the escalation of her outrages, she used to drift into his study and go unconscious on the floor. It frightened him at first, he would try to wake her, get her to go back to the girls' house; there were penalties for being out of bounds, after all. She was right out, unconscious, nothing would bring her round. Then, after an hour or so, she'd sit up and say she felt better. He got used to it. He would go on writing an essay and in an hour or so she'd wake up, and quite often eat something, so he liked her sleeping with him because it was good for her. In time the housemaster knew, but never took any action. Stephen was good for people, the school had picked him out for it; all those things teachers approve of, solid, responsible, trustworthy, and because he cared, not because he was just another one of those whose good citizenship was only political.

He looked around the room, reassured by its order

and cleanliness, agreeing with his earlier opinion: Imi was OK now, it was going to be all right. Her books were stacked up, her brushes clean, pencils sharpened, paper all arranged on the desk. A bank statement and a letter from the landlord about rent arrears were under the bottle of white spirit – not so good. There was a whole portfolio of new work, quick sketches mostly. God, she was so talented.

The bathroom let her down. A faint smell of vomit lingered, but he decided to say nothing; probably nerves on his account. This wasn't another bulimic phase; when she'd been doing that she'd covered up by cleaning the bathroom. And she had gained weight. No drugs to be found; all the little hiding places, the filigree boxes and the soapstone bowls, were empty. There were two green capsules in the mother-of-pearl box; he left them, being obviously prescribed stuff. He found the bleach and cleaned the shower tray, dusted the shelf and her makeup.

The kitchen had been used, another good sign. There were toast crumbs and a half-empty bottle of ketchup. It was quiet. The bustling of the pigeons through the open window was the loudest noise, louder than the market chatter from the street far below. Stephen found he was hungry, but knew better than to waste energy opening the fridge. They could eat when she woke up; she would enjoy that, going out to choose their lunch.

Returning to the sitting room he saw one item out of place, her big brown rucksack on the floor, half under the bed. When he pulled it out, intending to hang it up, it was heavy and made metal noises. Inside were five photograph frames, two salt pots, two sweet dishes, two modern silver spoons with elongated handles, a silver Empire-style candlestick and a silk scarf wrapped around some rings and small jewellery.

'What are you doing? Where's my bag? Come on, Stephen, I heard you take it. Where is it? Hand it over.' She was sitting up unsteadily, pulling imaginary clothes around her as if she was cold.

'It's here.' He held it up to show her. 'I was going to hang it up.'

'Leave it alone, can't you? Stop tidying me, Stephen. You know there's no point.'

'What's all this stuff in here?'

'It's none of your business. Give it to me.' She coiled up from the bed and grabbed at the bag, but he stepped back and held it out of her reach. Kneeling, she glared at him. 'That stuff's for us.'

'What do you mean, for us? It's all silver – you didn't buy this . . .'

'No, I nicked it, stupid. And I'm going to sell it. And then I'll have money, and with the money we can get out of this fucking mess. Got that?' She was biting her nails furiously, raising blood at her fingertips.

'Imi, you can't steal things . . .'

'Well, I am. And don't tell me I'll get caught, please. Give me some credit, Stephen. I've been at this for months and I don't get caught. The people I steal from deserve it, they know they deserve it and they don't give me any hassle. And don't you give me any hassle either,

OK? I've had enough in my life.' Again, she lashed out with an arm and this time was quick enough to snatch the bag from him. 'Now fuck off, if you can't give me any peace.'

He sighed, and sat down on the chair by the table, wondering what strategy he could adopt to get out of the fight. A fight was what she was going to work up to. She always attacked when she was in the wrong, and the rhythm was always the same, a cycle of mounting aggression.

'I've got it sorted, Stephen. Everything. We're gonna go to New Zealand, because that's the furthest away. Look, I've got everything here . . .' She grabbed a large envelope off the table and tipped it out on the bed. Travel brochures fell in a lurid pile, shiny pictures of pine trees and beaches. 'You can do your bloody degree there, look if you don't believe me, I checked it out . . .' She threw something at him, a booklet that had no photographs. It fell short, fluttering its pages to his feet, a university prospectus. 'I think of you sometimes, you see. This is it. This is our future together.'

'Imi, what is all this? What's it about . . .' Her tone was whining but still aggressive, she was gathering grievances to fuel her attack. He tried to decide whether to believe her. Imi told fantastic lies, and enjoyed them for their own sake. She had that glittery edge she always got when she was lying.

'It's about us, isn't it? You and me and what we're doing with our lives. We're getting out, that's what we're doing. Fucking getting out.'

'You never said . . . we never talked about this.'

'Why do we have to talk about everything?' Another serpentine convulsion and she was standing in front of him, prodding his chest with stiff fingers. 'It's what we want to do, isn't it? Isn't it? Answer me, Stephen, don't just stand there. You make me crazy just standing there.'

'I . . .' The telephone rang. She rolled her eyes in rage, but went to the table to pick up the receiver.

'What?' she yelled into it, then, 'Nah. This is me, Dad. Don't you know my voice?'

Half-way across the room the characteristic resonance of Michael Knight's delivery was still recognizable. Imi had her own voice for talking to her father, a low, intimate mumble, and within a few exchanges she fell into it, hiding the mouthpiece behind the fingers of her free hand as if the gesture would keep the conversation secret. Stephen watched her, noticing how the pride in her body drained away and her strident posture collapsed, so that her shoulders started to round and her spine curve and she began to shrink down into a cowed, foetal thing ready to curl up, suck its thumb and die. The covering hand was artificially relaxed, skeletal.

'I know it's your birthday but I don't want to come. Don't ask me for reasons, I haven't got reasons for you, I just don't want to, that's all. I've got things to do here.'

She listened awhile and then replied, almost whispering into the mouthpiece. 'Nobody's here, only Stephen.' Then she held out the receiver to him. 'He wants to talk to you.'

'Stephen. Good to hear you. Everything all right?'

Brisk, confident, powerful. There was background noise, he was in a public place.

'I think so.' There was always an impulse to call Michael 'sir', out of respect for that national treasure of a voice, but Stephen had some practice in resisting without sounding ill-mannered. He prided himself that although he loathed this man, he always behaved well towards him. In fact, the more generous and chivalrous his actions, the more Stephen felt superior to his enemy.

'Good, good. I'm glad you're there, Stephen. Imogen is always better when you're with her. I want her to come down for our little party tomorrow. I think it's important that she be there. You'll let me know if you need anything, won't you?'

'Yes, of course I will.' It was not what he wanted to say.

'Good, good. Will you be taking the train? We must get someone to meet you . . .' Now there was no alternative plan, no staying in Paris. The voice had dissolved their options.

What Stephen wanted to do was open his mouth and have an aria of accusation pour out, a huge raging indictment taking in all the years – why did you cheat this child, why have you destroyed her, all this beauty and talent and human worth laid waste, why did you do it? The words were not there. Instead he said, 'I was thinking of the one that gets in at twelve, or five past.'

'Good, I'll get something arranged. And Imogen, how do you find her?'

'Much better, I think.'

'Yes, I think so too. She's been sounding much, much better. I'm really looking forward to seeing you both. Really. Can you put me back to her now, if you please.'

Imogen took the receiver with a listless flourish of disdain. Another murmuring exchange and then she screamed and hurled the telephone across the room, knocking down the TV aerial and cracking a pane of glass in the window. 'The shit! The fucking shit!' The whine of a cut connection sounded from the receiver. She picked up one of her boots and began to batter the apparatus, working up dry sobs and small screams like an infuriated bird. Then she started to cry, and curled up on the floor. He went to kneel beside her and hold her.

'It's money, all the time, money. It's all down to money. Now do you see? See why I've got to get away from that man? The games he plays with me. With us. We have to leave. I'll go mad, I know I will.'

'You don't have to do what he says.'

'I do if I want my rent and my food and next term's tuition fees . . .'

'He wouldn't stop your allowance . . .'

'He would. He has before, remember? I lived a whole month on what the market people threw away. The landlord wanted me to sleep with him. Little creep. I said I'd rather he threw me out.'

'You told me.' She told him everything, but so much of it was fantasy.

'I've got this money now. I don't have to be some wanky bit of the Michael Knight PR initiative any more, thank you. You see now, don't you? The money is for saving our lives.' Her anger was returning, he could feel it as a positive tension in her body. 'You do understand, don't you?' She was wheedling him, tugging her hair. 'I know you think it's like stealing but they're not innocent men. I'm really, really clever, Stephen. I just get away with it, I do. Most of them have got such big houses, so much stuff in there.'

'Imi, for God's sake, whatever you've been doing, you've got to stop it. You know whatever this is, it's wrong. No more, promise?'

'Well, I can't do much if we've got to go all the way to bloody Gascony tomorrow.' She smiled up at him, her lashes spidery against her cheeks, and the glory of her clear dark eyes made him shiver. Imogen's beauty was the frightening kind. She was unreal, she was terrifying. But she was OK, it was going to be all right.

He had a dream of how their life would be, like a video he could run in his mind. She looked the way she did the summer she got her exam results, that quiet, cat-in-the-sun face she had sometimes. It didn't suit her, that look, the whole Imi thing was black and smouldering, that's when he found her extremely beautiful. Ordinary-looking was not for her; when she was happy she looked unexceptional. Her face was unoccupied, animal in a way, because she went inside herself and was OK there. That face was a very clear memory for him, although she was only like that a few days before Michael came back; Michael had not remembered the exams. When she told him he just said the grades were crap and she hadn't worked hard enough.

Stephen saw them living in a house he had designed, probably an old building reclaimed. Abroad perhaps. The work he intended to do would take him to the developing world, like Eastern Europe, or even China. Wherever, as long as they were together. He would work in the home a lot, and Imogen would have a studio. It was always a very light house.

There was always a lot of green in the picture, plants or a garden. He was sure that when she was well, making things grow would give her real satisfaction. He saw her giving the plants water and stroking their leaves, moving around easily, like she used to do when he first knew her, before her walk acquired its strange, puppet-like stiffness. She wore old clothes, everything splashed with paint; her hair was long and tied up at the nape of her neck with a scarf. Her skin had colour from the sun and she did not wear makeup, she did not need her mask any more.

He pictured her standing back from her easel, looking at something she had done from a distance. One of the most exciting things about her work was that it was instinctive; she would paint something working a normal distance away, and then have to step back to see what it was. He thought of himself as Mr Precision, the measured drawing king. What you saw was what you got with him; with Imi, you got everything you didn't know was there until she showed it to you. She would be incredibly successful, several galleries after her, but she would hesitate, and not decide who to go with until she had a whole exhibition finished. It was important to her to be understood.

Sometimes there was a baby in the picture, but most often they were waiting a few more years. She would get the sex thing together; it would take time but he had no problem there. Things were getting settled and they would be happy being together.

He did not kid himself it would be good all the time. She would have setbacks, people would upset her. You can't divorce your family, can you? They would just work it out. He would support her, of course, but she would do it, she would keep it together. She had the strength. He told himself that each time he thought of the future.

'Jane?' Grace had once picked him up on that. Married all those years and you don't recognize your wife's voice? That quality in her speech, true words spoken in jest, tart words sprinkled with sugar, sent shivers down his spine. Who else do you expect to answer the telephone in your own home? In Grace's time his home had not been such an institution. Now it seemed there were always several females there to answer his call. The fact was that Jane answered, always. He did wonder about that.

'Michael.'

'How are you?'

'Fine, thank you.'

'Good, good. I'm at the airport.'

'Yes, I can hear that.'

'I've missed the 10.40. We were editing this morning. I'm OK for the 2.15.'

'Good. I'll see you this evening then.'

'Yes. I've spoken to Imogen, Stephen's bringing her. Everything with you all right?'

'Yes, everything's fine. It's hot now, not a cloud in the sky. Emma's taken Xanthe off to catch frogs. I've been to the market in Saint-Victor with Louisa. We're all set for tomorrow.'

'Good. Everything's under control then?'

'Everything's fine. See you later.'

In the dullness of the exchange and the lack of incident reported, he pictured the harmonious landscape of his home. In his mind he stood before his family establishment like a Gainsborough nobleman before his rolling acres; wife and children, the two houses, the neighbours, friends, and relatives, the furniture and his quite celebrated collection of reportage photography were all details blended into the painted background that signified his status. He had introduced a new figure to perfect the composition. There was the space for her in the middle distance; Serena would be a slender maid with a muslin fichu and shyly inclined head stepping forward into the frame. Her leading foot would be accomplished in one tiny brushstroke, whole, pure and perfect, just like her.

A hostess brought him coffee; lesser business-class passengers, those who were not household faces, had to get their own. Michael relaxed a little. Tomorrow was his birthday, the day in each year when a man would judge his own portrait; tomorrow he would regard himself and wish he was a better man.

He had never intended to become what he was. He

had left his mother's house with his university scholarship, emotionally if not technically a virgin, aspiring only to a plain life of hard work and monogamy. (Curious that he always referred to it as his mother's house. His father lived there still, but he felt no connection with the man except duty.)

Immediately accidents of fate had piled on each other; first Pia, then their children, then her problems, then her leaving – that had cut him to the heart, he could not recover from her leaving. The emotions were devastating, he fought desperately for control of his life. Jane had saved him and imprisoned him at the same time. Affairs became a habit, a way to restore his independence. Grace had given him hope of breaking the pattern, but he had driven her away, then after her another, and another, every regretful parting increasing his loneliness. Now his life was packed with women – warm, affectionate, forgiving but leaving. His wounds grew deeper each year and he had surrendered all hope of healing. At least now there was Serena.

Equilibrium returning, he drew a deep breath. The Imogen thing was all right, really. She had been in a bad mood, maybe that boy had upset her. Michael's blood raced whenever the heavy, shock-haired figure of Stephen appeared in his daughter's life. Jane might describe him as kind, or even caring, but for Michael the right word was weak. Was he really such a good thing? He took Imogen off their hands, she obviously liked him, in as much as Imogen was capable of such a positive emotion as liking, but look at the record: Stephen had been on the scene since the two of them were kids, and the fact was that in all that time she'd been a nightmare. Stephen gave her too much ground. Imogen needed a man who could stand up to her, not take any shit from her.

He was jealous, of course. He could name that demon. 'I don't dislike the boy really, I'm just an old stag seeing a young buck stalking his herd,' he would say. 'I want to get down and clash antlers with him, that's all it is.' Thus he claimed to have tamed the animal in himself, the animal which in truth had tamed him. There was a darker element too. He did not understand the boy. Stephen lived with moral certainty. Michael craved that like an atheist craving faith. Stephen had always given the impression of being outside his control, of playing under a different set of rules. Under Stephen's rules, Michael knew he was not acknowledged as a superior being.

Cued automatically by his empty cup, the hostess poured more coffee and informed him that the incoming flight from Toulouse had just arrived on time. She had a faint accent and a corn-fed country complexion. Her blonde hair lay obediently under its clips and she walked with an energetic motion which made her pleated skirt dance around her knees. It was a new uniform; he remembered the rewards of charm and complimented her on it. The thought of Stephen faded, his anger subsided to an irritable shadow.

Outside there was glaring sunlight; the window framed shining ugliness, a utilitarian geometry of lurid aircraft and drab buildings. He felt his tender recollections of the morning withering in the light. Serena would have dressed by now, perhaps she would be outside, with the sun shining down on her head, drying up her indulgence, hardening the soft instincts which had admitted him to her heart. Her telephone number was on his memo pad. It rang a long time; he was about to abandon the call when her voice answered, breathless.

'It's me. I thought you would be out by now.' What did she do on Saturdays? Dinners at which her friends matched her with other men, games of tennis, expeditions to the cinema, parties, weddings, trips to the country, with other men? If there was one day in the week inherently dangerous for an unguarded woman, this was it.

'I was out, almost.'

He wanted information. 'I don't want to keep you if you've got things to do . . .'

'Only shopping. The library. There's plenty of time.' Beautiful honest woman; he needed to know that she was all his.

'I've been thinking about you. Are you all right?' His voiced was infused with intimacy.

'I feel strange. You . . . I . . . this . . . things like this . . . I don't know, I don't know what I feel. Different. Something's happened.'

Now he was anxious. Could she be slipping away? 'I feel it, too. We've travelled, haven't we? We are in another place now, both of us. Our country. Can't go back. Don't know what's ahead. It's new, strange, frightening. I don't regret anything.' He left the statement floating in the air, waiting for her response, but all that came was a soft, swallowing noise. Was she crying? 'Serena?'

'I'm here. I'm sorry, I don't know what to say.'

'Oh God, I've hurt you. Oh God. If there's one thing I'd never have wished . . .' His mind computed the possibility of a desperate run back to secure her, but there was no time and he was already on the last flight. As if to confirm the inevitability of it, the information monitor flashed up the call for his departure. 'Talk to me, please, my love, please, I don't mind what you say, I want to hear your voice.'

'I'm sorry, I don't know why I feel like this. I've just run up the stairs, I can't get my breath. It's nothing, just a mood, it'll go away.'

'My love. I wish I was with you.'

'Your family are waiting for you.' Ominous, mechanical delivery. She was trying to talk him out of it.

'Yes, they will be soon; but I wish I was with you, now. It feels so bad to have to leave you like that. I felt so connected while we were together, so alive. You must have felt the same – didn't you?' And there he let his voice falter. The earth gaped, the veil of the temple tore, Michael Knight's voice cracked.

'Yes.' It was almost a whisper.

'I'm so relieved you said that, so relieved. If you could hear my heart beating now . . .'

All at once her tone was calm and light. 'Where are you? Aren't people listening?'

'No. I'm by myself. They've called my flight, everyone else has gone down to the gate.'

'You must go too, then.'

'I had to speak to you. I just had to. But you're right, I must go in a second. What about tomorrow? I mean, if I can get away to call you at some point – where will you be?'

With only slight hesitation, she said she would be working at home and his mood soared. In his mind's eye he saw himself making the call standing in the room in Les Palombières designated his office, although he was seldom there long enough to work. His friends would be a distant convivial noise, Jane a faint presence in the background highlighting the significance of his action.

He put down the telephone, swept up his case and walked without haste towards the boarding gate. There was still plenty of time, but urgency was essential to Michael when his emotions were engaged, and so, without knowing what he did, he had pretended it.

Serena looked down at the telephone, the friend who had betrayed her. It had rung when she had been at the front door, on the point of stepping into the sunlight, into the world, into freedom, into reality. She had hesitated to answer it, knowing by instinct that it was him. The hard voice of common sense had argued against her: he screws around, this man, fuck 'em and forget 'em, that's his style, not the pretty sentimental stuff true lovers do. And the telephone had rung insistently, persuading her that it was her mother calling, her office, the friend she had half-promised to meet later, and so, betrayed by reason and probability, she had run up the stairs and back into the jaws of destruction.

Now she felt a piercing longing. She was on the edge of tears. It was nothing significant, she was tired, they had had no sleep, but her instinct was to go out now, not stay in the same space, breathing in his breath. The right thing to do now was to obliterate him, scour him out of her memory. Two incidents of sex, awkward and unsatisfying, should not be hard to forget. The sheets were already churning in the washing machine. From her body she had scrubbed off his touch in the shower. Resolutely, she ran out into the street again, telling herself that there was no destiny cast here, it was just an episode, it would mean nothing.

CHAPTER FOUR

Saturday Afternoon

'Let me drive,' she asked as they were leaving. She wanted Nick to be able to enjoy the scenery, because the road to Castillon was as pretty as a fairy tale but he hated going there for the bric-a-brac market.

There was a short delay while five huge, creamy Gascony cows ambled past the village war memorial. The farmer saw no reason to do his milking at uncivilized hours; he strolled after his beasts, advising them not to wander to the end of the field since it was far too hot to go chasing after them again at the end of the day.

The lane left the village and ran down the spine of the rising hills, yellow sunflowers to one side, violet-blue alfalfa on the other, a succession of sharp bends with a new vista at every corner. Outside Plaisance, the market town, they took a wider road across the valley bottom, at first in full sunlight and flanked by ditches choked with bulrushes, then dappled under the dancing leaves of young lime trees. The river Adour, running slow, deep and clear, swirled across the meadows to meet the road at right angles.

'Beautiful,' Nick murmured as they approached the handsome white stone bridge.

'River's high.' She let the car stop and ran down her window to hear the rushing water. The sun blazed on the beaches of speckled pebbles and the lush tall grass at the waterside. Rings of ripples spread where fish rose in leisurely succession. Above the surface the air hummed with insects.

'Nobody about.' She smiled at him. In their first summer they had discovered that this lovely grove was deserted only during working hours; at lunchtime it became suddenly populated by pleasure-seekers. Lone fishermen and pairs of lovers trampled their bivouacs among the wild mint, courteously keeping their distances in order not to spoil each other's sport.

The far side of the valley was wooded, and beyond that lay open country. Castillon, like all the ancient villages of the region, was on a hilltop; flowering trees, trimly pollarded, girdled it on both sides. At its approach it seemed too decorated to be a survivor of the lawless centuries which had left other settlements with immense fortifications, now picturesquely ruined. Saint-Victor had its ramparts, Saint-Mère the watchtower, Bassous a massive gatehouse, but outwardly Castillon tried to pretend its heritage amounted to nothing but jacarandas.

The village houses were handsome square stone mansions. Between the limestone walls a crooked street the width of a *deux chevaux* led into the square, recommending such traffic as there might be to follow the tree line around the crown of the hill. Today the street was choked with cars; the *brocante* attracted crowds, dealers and buyers from half the *département* and many holiday residents. Grace parked in the shade at the far end of the *boules* pitch.

They had half-furnished the Alhambra here and a pilgrimage was necessary each summer. The noise of the fair, an intense murmur, met them half-way up the alley leading to the village square. It was one of Castillon's hidden treasures, a generous space bordered by broad stone arches, each pillar decorated with a climbing rose. The village had two regular shops only, a baker and a general store, both tucked into narrow sidestreets, but on the first Saturday of every month the shuttered façades of the square opened up and the whole village gave itself to the business of trading defunct household goods.

Grace set off eagerly into the crowd. Between troughs of geraniums, the senior stall-holders took the best positions under the broad, low arcades while the less fortunate filled the centre with bright-coloured awnings and umbrellas.

'I suppose we ought to take Jane Knight a present,' she called to him as she stepped over a bathtub crammed with old black gramophone records, at the same time running her eye over a jumble of kitchen implements.

'Will we find anything here?' Nick was looking anxious. He was bemused at the process by which his wife could pick up a piece of junk from a market stall, breathe on it and transform it into a stylish object which all their acquaintances would admire.

'Well, I know what you mean. What do you give the couple who have everything? I know she goes for picturesque kitchenalia though. They're always using them to dress up the pictures in her books. Maybe one of those little enamel salt tins?'

'It's his birthday, isn't it? I was thinking about wine . . . Oh God, you're right. I suppose those foodie people know a lot about wine.'

'Yes, but it's always nice to find something new. What was that knockout stuff you bought in the Landes last year? I'd rather choose something special for her. Oh, there she is, the button lady. We need some more of those white linen ones for the pillowcases . . .' Like a hound on the scent, she loped away from him. Grace had a particular affection for the button dealer, a tiny, coquettish old woman with a black straw hat decorated with cerise velvet roses pulled down over her sharp nose. Her stall was a mere card table, stacked with shoeboxes rattling with buttons of every imaginable material: plastic, horn, jet, bone, mother-of-pearl, mosaic, beads, crystal, brass, silk.

Frustration took a firm hold of Nick. It was hot. The allure of rusting iron bedsteads, unstable chairs and blistered yellow jars in which generations of farmer's wives had crammed portions of preserved goose had faded.

Grace was not edgy any more, she was absorbed and happy, the threat of the following day forgotten.

'Darling, can I leave it to you? I'll see you in the café.' He strolled away to the narrowest alley where two tables and eight chairs stood hopefully in the shade of the old stone archway. A door between the tables led to a gloomy bar, and beyond a flowering courtyard set with tables laid for lunch.

Swallows had nests in the carved coping of the archway, and he watched them feeding their young, whose gaping beaks were just visible at the nest holes. The arch was another relic of the turbulent era that began in 1154, when Henry, Duke of Aquitaine, inherited the crown of England. This event left the English with the delusion that Gascony belonged to them, a fantasy they maintained despite the impossibility of making one dominion out of two countries that were a thousand miles apart. Four hundred years of war ensued, endured by the Gascons in addition to the routine scrapping of their own local rulers. Even today, schoolchildren would solemnly explain that their own one-shop hamlet had once heroically resisted a siege, or had been brutally sacked, or had been the site of a daring kidnapping for love. Castillon was a typical *bastide*, a town fortified in those turbulent years so life could carry on within strong walls in the protective shadow of a hilltop castle.

It was an hour before Grace appeared, finding her husband restored to good temper. Nick was on his third beer, pink-cheeked and dreamy with history. On the table she proudly put a loose parcel of newspaper.

'Is that all you've bought? I thought you'd be haggling over Henry IV's bed, the time you took.'

'I couldn't find anything that was right. Then just as people were starting to pack up I saw these . . .' She opened the package and spilled over the table a set of old butcher's labels, elaborately lettered and decorated with pictures of jauntily posed livestock. 'Aren't they wonderful? Look at this silly chicken. And this one, "Beautiful breast, 3 francs a kilo". Aren't they perfect?'

'If you say so.'

His idle remark, intended to convey nothing more than his trust in her taste, stabbed through her fragile equilibrium. 'What's that supposed to mean?' Her eyes were suddenly thunderous.

'Nothing, nothing . . . I just meant I'm sure you're right.'

'Did you?' With offended gestures, she gathered up the labels and folded the paper around them.

'Of course I did. What else could I have meant?'

'Lots of things. Anything.' In an instant, the sunshine and enjoyment of the morning were poisoned. How easy to shrink down into one of those vicious women who curbed their men with sneers and rectitude and sighing implications of guilt. Without warning the desolation of life without Nick presented itself, an icy wasteland scoured by bitter winds of remorse.

She put her hands to her head as if in pain, but he pulled them away and held them on the tabletop. 'This is all my fault. I should never have been so stupid and insensitive. Let me cry off, tell her we can't come.'

'No, no. I've made my mind up. I've got to face it.'

'No, you don't need to face anything. Why? What will it change? You never liked the man, so why . . .'

She struggled with her conscience. She was longing to confess, to get Michael out of the shadows and on the table between them to be exorcized. Years ago, she had confessed to a priest and got nothing but what she expected, uncomprehending platitudes. And then he had asked if her husband knew, and advised her to look well in her heart when she wanted to tell him, and ask herself for whose benefit it would be. Trite as the thought was, it echoed.

Above them, high in the coping of the arch, a swallow dived from its nest and flew low past them and out into the bright sun at the end of the alley. 'Because of us. I'm afraid it will change us.'

'It won't, why should it? We're good as we are, we don't need to change.' That pitiful, open look, so like a child who had innocently caused a catastrophe.

'This isn't really the past, Nick. I'm not . . .' She put her fingers to his lips to stop his question. '*Not* telling you everything. I don't want to. It was long ago and it won't do us any good now. Do you trust me?'

'Yes. OK. Of course.'

'But there is something unfinished. You did me a favour, meeting Jane. I didn't realize, I couldn't understand it. There is something I'm carrying round from that time, I just feel weighed down with it. I am frightened, of course I am. But I really, really want to be free of it. For us, for our sake. So we're going.'

'I understand.' Of course, he did not. He took her hands again and squeezed them, sealing the bargain. There was more to say, but she left it and kissed him on his forehead where tiny beads of sweat had appeared, forced out by high emotion in the noon heat.

Comforted by lunch, they journeyed homewards through the golden afternoon, with Nick driving. Grace meditated on her marriage, the image of love generated by their need for it, three-dimensional and with all the desired features and functions, but still of their own imagining. Other people told her that they were happy, but she felt that she was trapped in a mime-artist's cage, a prison of her own mind, terrifying but invisible to all but herself.

As they crossed the bridge and drank in the loveliness of the river, he turned to her and said, 'Do you mind that I'll never be rich, Grace?'

It tore open her heart and she found tears stinging her eyes. 'No,' she told him. 'No. This isn't about money. Do you know what it costs, to be rich? Isn't what we have something money could never buy?' She reached across and put her arms around him. 'Don't ever make money, Nick, please. Just be you. I love you.'

'Salmon is a great, great luxury round here, of course.' In her kitchen, Jane stripped away the wet newspaper and showed Louisa the huge silver fish, smeared with blood around the head, mouth and gills agape. Antony had weighed the allure of his book against the advantage of knowing what was proposed for the *fête champêtre* and followed them; he was standing warily at a distance, as if doubting that the monstrous fish was safe to approach.

'It looks very fresh.' Delicately, Louisa poked one of the gelatinous eyes.

'Caught this morning. Feel, it's still quite rigid. The *rigor mortis* takes a few hours to wear off. But she lays them out nice and straight so there's no trouble fitting them in the pot.'

The major part of Michael's birthday feast was being prepared by caterers from the regional capital, but Jane liked to cook something herself, and the guests expected it. Heaps of vegetables lay on the red tiled floor awaiting attention.

'But where on earth did she catch it? Not in the Gers, surely.' Antony had observed that the nearest local river was a vicious muddy torrent on whose banks fishermen were conspicuously absent.

'No, no!' Jane was looking for something, pulling drawers in and out, puzzled. 'Have you seen where I put my little knife? It's just the thing for this . . . No, no, there's nothing in the Gers, it's polluted to hell with fertilizers and whatever. And it runs into a bigger river before it gets to the Atlantic. You couldn't catch a cold in the Gers.' She pulled a small steel knife from the block and felt its edge. 'This'll have to do. The Adour is where they catch salmon, when they can, nowadays, not many left. South from here, a nice clean run down from the Pyrenees to the Atlantic. She is amazing, she always seems to get one for Michael's birthday.'

'You mean that girl caught it?' Antony normally lived

in a trance of well-bred lack of interest, which showed a brief sign of breaking.

'Uh-huh.' Jane looked up from slitting the creature's belly with a small, malicious smile.

'Good heavens. How extraordinary.'

'Women always catch the biggest salmon, you know. The big cocks. If they're fly-caught. It's pheromones. When she ties the fly some pheromone scent is left on it and the great fools can't resist.'

'Don't watch this, Antony.' Louisa hoisted one hip on to the corner of a table and held out a bowl to catch the dark red entrails as they tumbled out of the body cavity. 'The old Eve, eh? I wonder if some women smell sexier than others – to a salmon.'

'That girl must smell like Sharon Stone, if they do. The size of this thing – it must be twenty pounds at least.' At the sink, Jane washed the fish and patted it dry as tenderly as if it had been a baby. Her face, almost wizened with the tension of worrying about Emma, was serene once more.

'She didn't ask for any money or anything. At least, I don't think she did – frightfully strong accent.'

'Oh, she'll be round later, or tomorrow. People trust each other in the country. She's a Basque. There's a lot of them round here. Nobody would dream of cheating a Basque, they're worse than the Mafia.' Jane pulled up a chair to get the fish kettle down from its hook on a ceiling beam, while Antony, who had obediently retired to the edge of the room, shuffled a few steps forward to indicate that he would have helped her if not pre-empted.

'I suppose she's a poacher, she looked kind of furtive.' Boldness in women disturbed Antony, but he never liked to hold controversial opinions.

'Well, illegal, yes. She won't apply for a fishing permit because she thinks that's collaborating with the stinking French. And then everyone would know where she's fishing.'

'But she is right about that, isn't she? Everybody else would get there first.' Louisa fetched a cloth to wipe twelve months of dust from the pan.

'Probably. But the Basques live on secrets, their code of silence . . .' And as the kingly catch was oiled and seasoned and laid out upon its rack, and onions and carrots peeled for its poaching liquor, and herbs picked and wine poured, Jane told her tales of extracting recipes from the close-mouthed Basques. Forty-eight mountain herbs in the liqueur they called *Izarra*, and every one, and where it grew in the inaccessible mountains, an ancient secret; the herbs were processed in a separate plant and sent to the distillery identified only by labels written in code.

'What's it taste like?' Antony interrupted.

'Cough mixture.'

'Oh.'

The Basques, she continued, had their own species of chilli, which would grow nowhere else, and secret ways to dry it. Earnestly, with wondering eyes, she related the miracle that the Basques alone could make cornmeal porridge without stirring.

'It's a universal peasant dish, cornmeal porridge. And it's an incredible sweat to make. You have to stir it continuously for about an hour. Century after century women all over the world stirring until their arms ache . . . sweating into the fire . . .' Jane was in a trance. She loved the idea of women cooking the same food the world over, in every country wherever the corn would grow high as an elephant's eye, preparing it to be eaten hot or cold, savoury or sweet, *polenta* in Italy, *grits* in America, *gofio* in Spain and all over France where the Landais called it *cruchade*, or the Bearnais *broye*, the Périgordiens *las pous.* Even now, she emphasized with delight, when this humble food appeared on the smartest restaurant menus, enhanced by high-tech industrial processing, a gastronomic cliché, the old Basque shepherds still kept the secret of making it without stirring, throwing the grain into the boiling liquid at the right moment so that a bubble formed in the pot and the meal swelled within, and all that was necessary, at another precisely judged instant, was to prick the magic bubble and scoop out the tender porridge.

'No stirring, no burning, no sweat, no need for technology. I was told about – and they boasted of him – an old man who had never married, in case his wife found out the secret.'

'Goll-*y*.'

'Good heavens, how extraordinary.'

'Because the men cook, among the Basques. Not just the peasants, all of them, businessmen, doctors, millionaires . . . They have dining clubs, men only, cooking for each other, and rather than eat their wives' food at home the men eat with each other every night, even if they have to drive miles to do it. And then the husband and wife have terrible fights . . .'

'They are a rebellious bunch, aren't they?' Louisa seized the vegetables in her short, fat fingers and threw them untidily into the pan. Jane lifted the fish; the notion crossed her mind that she had somehow absorbed the fighting spirit of the mountain race with their cuisine. Her ears were straining for the telephone, waiting for Nick Nichols to call back and explain that he and his wife Grace would not after all be coming to lunch on Sunday. Her courage was failing, she was hoping to be saved from her recklessness before Michael's anger was let loose.

As if cued by the conversation, the salmon lady appeared in the doorway, darting anxious glances right and left, her hands thrust into her jeans pockets, boyishly uneasy. Jane dried her hands, praised the fish and went to find money.

'We were talking' – in no circumstances would Louisa display the ill-manners of excluding a newcomer from a conversation – 'about men and women arguing about doing the cooking in your country.'

Amusement ignited the young woman's black eyes. 'Not only about the cooking. And not just in *my* country.' They all laughed. She held out a casual hand for the notes Jane was counting. 'But not in my house. I promise you.' Tucking the money into a breast pocket, she turned on her heel and returned to her old grey Renault with a spring in her strides.

'Do you suppose she's a lesbian?' Antony, leaning

against the sink, folded his thin arms and wondered if it was too early to ask for a Scotch.

'I'd say she was *happy*,' was Louisa's provocative reply. Absorbed in the tranquillizing business of preparing food, Jane barely heard her.

'I was wondering if it was too early for a Scotch.'

'Antony, you poor man, of course not.' Jane assembled glasses, ice, a decanter and a tempting little dish of olives and goat-cheese morsels rolled in chopped walnuts, and installed him on the terrace again. He accepted her kindness readily and reached out for his glass with movements that betrayed very long practice.

Acceptance was what Antony did best. He accepted invitations, a constant stream of them, with perfectly-phrased notes on expensive personal stationery. He accepted food and drink and amusement and women's compliments with a tight polite smile and a donnish inclination of his head. He accepted girlfriends as he accepted the weather, seldom ideal but inevitable. From his family he had accepted a small private income, considerable intelligence, a superb education and an immense, influential acquaintance pledged to support him in his chosen profession of wine merchant.

He did not quite accept his long-drawn-out failure in this business, his inability to extend his clients' vocabulary of taste, their depressing obsession with varieties of grape which were merely fashionable, the steady loss of customers, the elusiveness of big orders, the need to relocate to cheaper and cheaper premises. Antony felt no needs. He felt nothing. He could react but not act. Jane imagined – indeed, knew – that every night Antony sat down in his tiny, sour-smelling bachelor apartment to pickle lightly in whisky everything in his life which he found unacceptable in its fresh condition.

Every two or three years, Louisa fell in love with a man like Antony. They were usually charming, clever, gifted, well groomed and dressed. Nothing much ever seemed to interest them, not business, not sport, and certainly not other people. Radiating sensual warmth, she fascinated them over dinner and issued a bulletin about her need for a committed relationship. What she meant was love, but the Antonys were so patently incapable of any emotion that it was absurd to contract a liaison on such terms.

After six or nine months of extensive socializing and acceptable sex the more active Antonys implemented their escape plans – neglect, infidelity, perhaps an intrusive ex-wife. From the more passive Louisa would request the committed relationship; incapable of actual refusal, they would mumble, misunderstand or disappear, leaving her furiously condemning another dickhead who had wasted valuable months of her life. When Jane considered leaving Michael, as she did much more often than she admitted to anyone, the vision of a future full of Antonys deterred her.

'Was this room always the kitchen?' Louisa was checking out the *batterie de cuisine* displayed on hooks and shelves, keeping an eye on the poaching liquor in the fish kettle as it approached simmering point. She and Jane were in purist agreement about salmon. The ideal method was to take the pot off the stove as the liquid came to boiling point and leave the fish to cook slowly in the residual heat, then cool overnight before serving in all its moist, pink, meaty splendour.

'Oh yes. All fitted out with one of those huge electric stainless steel ranges the French always have. The builders thought I was mad when I threw it out and put this old thing in.' Jane had brought from England a cast-iron stove with three ovens and blue-and-white tiles, originally intended to burn coal and now skilfully adapted for bottled gas. 'The building inspector was all ready to condemn it, but Michael had a drink with him and won him over somehow. Shall we shell the peas?'

'So Michael is some use around the house.'

'I couldn't possibly live like this on my own money, Louisa.'

'Yes you could, you earn enough now, surely?'

'Well . . .' Jane paused in the act of clearing bowls from the long oak table to make space for the work ahead. 'I don't know. Perhaps – the television pays telephone numbers. Our accountant just sorts us out, Michael sees him every now and then. I can't do figures, my mind goes blank.'

'Why didn't Michael make it this morning?' Louisa tipped out a basketful of pea pods and the two women sat down on opposite sides of the table.

'He was phoning from the airport, he missed the morning flight. They were editing until four. He's getting the afternoon plane.'

'Uh-huh.'

'I'll send Debbie to meet him.'

'Uh?'

'Debbie. Our nanny, remember?' Nothing to do with children ever registered with Louisa.

'Oh, yes.' Jane picked up a pea pod, split it with her thumb, scraped the peas out into the colander, ate the smallest one, dropped the pod into a basket, reached for the next. A satisfying noise, the pop of the pea pods. Their fresh green perfume was delicious. One pod after another, the peas at first ringing and bouncing in the empty pan, then piling upon each other slowly and quietly.

The only part of the house from which Tamara Lady Aylesham had been banned was this kitchen. Jane had ignored plans for built-in units and hand-stencilled walls, and kept the room as much as possible as it had been for generations. The shelf formed by the fireplace beam was edged with cotton lace and carried wooden candelabra, a jar of pens and a small row of books to be read by the fireside on quiet evenings. The furniture was rough and massive, made of oak and fruitwoods from the countryside.

She thought of the kitchen feeding an army of workers at the harvest or the *vendage*, when all the men in the region banded together for the gruelling labour of the day, migrant workers flocked in from the countryside and the women worked at full stretch to feed them. The great hearth, under its twelve-foot beam, would be crowded with singing pots, belching aromas of sizzling fat and stewed onions. Women and children would bustle in and out, carrying loaded dishes to the long trestle tables set up in the shade of the trees near the house, boys darting around their skirts with stolen snacks, the men themselves fetching the heavy flagons of wine. In the little rooms leading off the kitchen, one of which she had made her office, the abundance of the summer would be stored, fruit in jars of Armagnac, duck preserved in its own fat in the yellow-painted crocks, beans laid out to dry in the cool, dry *chambre obscure.*

Jane loved these visions, and loved the house because it conjured them up so readily. Her kitchen connected her to the real life, the right life, the life of a true family in the heart of a living community. She imagined that in all the gaiety and companionable commotion of a harvest supper the necessary tasks would be shared without question and there would be no quarrelling, and no deception, and people would sit down together and eat, knowing each other entirely. If a child was miserable there would be a score of hands to soothe her; if a man had faults there would be but one opinion of him, the general opinion, and he would not be able to slip away on some excuse of international magnitude and pretend he was not what he was.

'So do you believe him?' Louisa threw the last pod into the basket.

'Who, Michael?'

'Yes. Editing until four this morning.'

'He often has to.' There was a lid for the saucepan of peas, and then the fiddly business of skinning baby onions. Well, fuck it, the onions were going to make her cry anyway.

'But – no. No, I don't. I can't tell any more, I used to think I knew when he was screwing around, but it's been so many years, so many women, so many excuses. I don't believe anything he says at all, wouldn't I be a fool if I did?' She cut into the first onion, awkward with distress, and the knife slipped and gashed her finger. 'Oh damn! Damn! This bloody knife's too big.' At the sink she wrapped the corner of a cloth around the cut. The blood oozed through it at once. 'But I know all the same. I wish I didn't, I wish I could stop myself knowing and go on living in fool's paradise – he wants me to, I know, and by now that's all I want. Just not to know. But I do. He gets transparent. He just isn't there when he's speaking to me. He's like a ghost or a hologram or a shadow. Not there.' She lifted up her head and Louisa saw far more tears than could be blamed on a button onion welling in her eyes.

'What about this woman you invited?'

'They're coming. Her husband called earlier.' The thought brought Jane back from the edge of weeping. 'What have I done, Louisa? I'm so worried.'

'What can he do? Come on, if he denies he had an affair with her he can't protest that you're stirring things up by inviting her. They worked together, didn't they?'

'You're right. He'll just treat her like anyone else. You've seen him, Louisa, you know. He acts it out, the perfect husband. That's what makes it impossible for me. If he was a lovable redblooded rake or a hopeless philanderer, I could tolerate it . . .' Louisa pursed her lips in disagreement. 'I could. I did love him. He can make himself irresistible, he still tries. I could be the loyal little woman if I had the right encouragement. But he's never admitted anything. So what can I do?'

Apart from the exuberant steel-cladded design, the arrival hall at Toulouse airport was like a London cocktail party. In fact, Michael reflected as he caught fragments of conversations, the atmosphere was better; there was less posturing, more genuine amiability.

'Didn't we meet at Brian Guinness's?'

'I do believe we did.'

'I heard he just got married . . .'

'Yes, so did I. Who was it? I didn't hear.'

'The same one, I think. Nice woman.'

Ninety per cent of the passengers seemed to know each other and they also recognized Michael instantly but, not knowing him and not wishing to commit the appalling crime of scraping acquaintance with a celebrity, they ignored him. He felt excluded, and it was awkward. In fact, it was humiliating. The same thing happened whenever he stepped outside his own territory. He was hurled back to the age of seven, a playground outcast; he knew why, even then. He was better than they were. The truth was that he had cast himself out of the company of the other kids.

When lessons ended, it had been a lonely childhood. His mother and father were both librarians, and one would always be working an evening shift. In addition, his father was secretary of the local history society, and detained by its business several nights a week. As a couple they were sufficient company to each other, and Michael was their only child. They had a small suburban house with brown wallpaper embossed with leaves. It was deadly quiet; the ticking clocks were often the only sound. The silence echoed in his head as he grew older; by the time he left the house roared with it.

Other children had noisy, messy homes with siblings, pets, friends and relatives, fights and arguments. Most of the time he had only his books, and his mother in the kitchen cooking without speaking. His parents seldom had a conversation, never had physical contact; they were content, but their son did not know what he was. He came into the adult world with a hunger for human connection that was unlimited, and a terror of emotional imprisonment. He also felt perpetual anxiety on the score of acting like a normal person, not a refugee from the silent suburban ghetto of the heart. In time, he formulated a good dinner-party thesis on the emotional deracination of the intellectual class.

Now, in the alienating airport, he needed a connection to take away the discomfort and looked in vain for a telephone. They were all on the far side of the glass wall of the baggage hall. His eye fell instead upon Debbie, head and shoulders above the small crowd of people waving to friends through the glass, and more conspicuous among them because she was still and dutiful, showing no positive sign of pleasure. To gain the time to telephone, he asked her to fetch the car to the door from the short-term car park. Serena was not at home; the discovery increased his discomfort.

The late afternoon heat was blistering. He did not drive. He had never learned, a peculiar lapse in so dominating a man, but the service of being driven pleased him too much. In the car Debbie was already playing a tape, which offended him; the noise was alien, and he knew she was playing it to avoid having to talk to him. This girl ran the household efficiently and so he tolerated her, but her attitude offended him. As soon as she crossed his threshhold, before he had even made up his mind whether he found her attractive, she had silently marked him down as a sexual predator and brought into play a repertoire of evasive behaviour. This was the first occasion on which they had been alone together.

'Can we kill the music?'

'Sure.' One word only. She had presumed he would try to engage her in a personal conversation, which was insulting.

At that time of day, when the trees cast long shadows across the fields, the drive across country from Toulouse was exquisite. Suspicious of leisure all his life, Michael was an amateur in small pleasures, but when forced he could appreciate this kind of beauty. There were two magnificent *bastide* towns to drive through, half-timbered and arcaded, swallows plying above the central squares. Approaching Les Palombières the drama of the landscape heightened; the hills grew steep and craggy, the patchwork of crops varied with blue flax, yellow sunflowers and late wheat gleaming in the heat.

Close to his house they picked up the old Roman road which ran dead straight for five miles. Overlooking a melon field stood the ruin of an immense medieval watchtower, stark and rectangular, angled so that at this time the sun struck it squarely and gilded the white stones. Here and there a small turreted chateau stood behind ancient mounds of clipped box, or a long gloomy avenue of spruces indicated that where they ended lay an old *manoir*.

Each time he arrived he had a moment of regret that his house was merely a farmhouse, not something more imposing. Tamara Aylesham had transformed it in all but spirit. The courtyard was expensively paved and adorned with pots gushing pink geraniums, but the atmosphere of a farmyard hung about it; four centuries of mud and chicken-shit had branded the place with humility. The great double gates had plainly been built to admit haycarts, not carriages. How would it be to arrive by helicopter, like the Belgian chemicals millionaire whose spruce avenue formed his northern skyline? Or to sweep up a semicircular drive edged with topiary? The fact of Jane and her career then arose, grounded in this humble old building, and he remembered that he was not the kind of man who resented his wife's success.

It was early in the evening when he entered through the kitchen. Debbie, under cover of parking the car, contrived to go around the back of the house to the children's rooms. The kitchen was cool, protected by its thick walls and tiny windows from the raging heat outside, and full of pleasant smells. The table was laid for the children's meal. Michael noted the preparations for the next day with approval. He hung his jacket on the back of the carver chair at the table head, opened the fridge, broke off a piece of ham and picked a tomato from a dish.

'Hi, Dad.' His son stood in the doorway.

'Oh, *hi*, Sam.' He remembered that he was the kind of father who hugged his children, bent down a little and opened his arms. The boy seemed not to notice and homed in on the fridge.

'Is there any Coke in there?' He looked expertly around the abundant interior and found none. 'It'll be in the drinks fridge, right?'

'I don't know where your mother keeps it.'

'It's OK. I'll get Debbie to get me some.' After tearing away a piece of ham in his turn, the boy walked out of the room. Michael watched his high, fat backside without pleasure.

'I'm through to the fifth level, Dad. It's brilliant.'

'Oh – that's great.' The words said one thing, the voice another. Sam was known as a big boy. He was technically obese, but only just. He had a big belly, a chest fleshy enough to look like breasts and fat round cheeks above red cherub lips. He was white-skinned and needed spectacles because his sight was poor. This was not Michael's notion of a boy. Fleetingly, he wondered what kind of child Serena might bear. Michael saw a boy romantically as the boy he had never been himself, a skinny, grubby, cheeky creature with dirty knees and holey socks, who longed to run wild and be free. Sam longed only for food, drink and uninterrupted hours with his computer. It was not too late for him to turn out to be bright, but he was taking his time about it.

Voices sounded from the pool terrace; it was Jane, angry, and her fat friend, alarmed. He followed the sound, projecting himself into the role of the work-weary but still caring partner as he went.

To shelter the pool from wind, Tamara Aylesham had decreed that it should be situated downhill from the house, with the natural arms of limestone rock on each side artificially extended by boulders so that the water appeared half-encircled in a natural basin. As he followed the shallow steps down towards the water, Michael saw that Emma had scrambled out on to one of these man-made cliffs and was threatening to hurl herself twenty feet down into the pool.

'Emma, you must get down!' Jane called helplessly.

'Don't be stupid, Em, that's the shallow end.' Debbie was occupied with the toddler.

'I'm coming down, I'm going to dive. Watch me, everybody!' Emma had scared herself, her eyes were huge and her thin limbs shaking, but she swayed determinedly back and forth over the water.

'No!' Jane nearly screamed. 'It's too shallow there, you'll hurt yourself.'

'Jump, don't dive!' called Louisa.

'Don't be stupid, Em, come down. Quit showing off.'

'Daddy! Daddy! Watch me dive, Daddy! Watch me!' At the sight of her father, the child became almost incoherent with excitement.

'Emma! Emma! Get down from there this . . .'

It was too late. Skinny limbs flailing, Emma hurled

herself off the rock and fell into the water, hitting it with a smack. Jane screamed. The impact sent splashes over the entire terrace and a wave of water washed up the pool and hit the far end. In the midst of this tumult, Emma rose to the surface, red-faced and spluttering, demanding, 'Did you see me? Did you see my dive? Daddy, did you see me?'

Debbie pulled the child from the water and tried to wrap her in a towel, but she was too bent on capturing Michael's attention and refused to be held. As Michael approached she ran and jumped at him like a monkey, leaving wet marks all over his grey suit. Laughing, he caught her by the arms and swung her around him until he could safely redeliver her to the nanny's arms.

'Wasn't it brilliant, Daddy?' she demanded, finally accepting the towel. The front of her body was red from the impact of the water.

'Thrilling, darling.' He caught Jane's sulphurous eye. 'Too thrilling. Don't let me ever see you doing that again, it's extremely dangerous. Next time you want to show me a dive I'd like to see a proper racing dive from the side and hold your breath until you touch the far end.'

'Oh, pooh. That's boring.' Emma kicked his leg in annoyance and sulked away to the far end of the pool. Michael kissed Jane, kissed Louisa and shook hands with Antony. All three now in pale summer linens, they made an attractive group under the white sun umbrella. He accepted a glass of cold, aromatic Tursan wine before taking the seat left for him. Xanthe trailed hesitantly forward and he pulled her on to his lap; for all Jane had sprung this last one on him, she was a child to be proud of, at least, a little Joshua Reynolds cherub.

Louisa was observing Michael intensely, no doubt hoping to find the stigmata of infidelity as they had been described to her. Jane saw it and smiled to herself, telling over the signs, the guilty edge of excess in his laughter, the dimension of conscientious application in the way he allowed the girls to climb on him and make his clothes wet. Most infuriating to her was the element of display in the way he was sitting among them creating the impression that this affectionate scene was a normal daily occurrence. Normal it might be, but it occurred perhaps twice a year, and there was nothing authentic about it.

And one more thing, which Louisa would never detect because Jane felt it inside herself: her loneliness. She had felt alone for years, but mostly at a level she could tolerate; this black, howling desolation was an instinctive reaction which only came over her when Michael's body was there and his heart was with another woman.

'Many happy returns for tomorrow.' Louisa raised her glass to him, cocking her head on one side.

'Oh, please – at my time of life birthdays are best forgotten.'

'Don't say that when we've been cooking all day.' She pouted. 'I thought you had a party every year.'

'We do.' 'We always do.' Embarrassingly, Jane and Michael spoke together.

Antony had a good instinct for social lubrication. 'Such a generous thing to do, marvellous for all your friends around here.'

'That's kind, Antony. I just did it once and it seemed to work.' Jane was looking out across the golden fields, an expression of tranquil irony on her face.

'It was a plot to get me out of the office.' Nobody could head off criticism at the pass quicker than Michael. Knowing he spoke the truth, he reached for Jane's hand.

'So I did it again and then we found that people had come to expect it.'

'Shall I take Xanthe in for her tea, Jane?' Debbie had been moving unobtrusively around, collecting scattered toys and clothes.

'I think all the children can have tea . . .'

'No!' Emma shrieked. She had pointed incisors and for an instant looked as if she really intended to bite the nanny's hand. 'I want to eat with Daddy!'

'Darling, you're very tired . . .'

'I'm not!'

Jane was too weary to argue. 'All right, but put some clothes on because you know the eczema gets worse if you catch a chill.' The child slunk after her sister, scowling. 'I'm sorry, she gets so hyper when Michael arrives . . .'

The other three had continued their conversation almost unchecked. Michael was saying, 'I should explain, we don't entertain at home very much.'

'*You* don't entertain. I do.' Jane folded her soft lips over the rim of her glass and sipped, still declining to look at her husband.

'But that's your professional commitment, isn't it?'

'Is it? I do like to see my friends, you know.' She drank

again, enjoying the fact that the topic was difficult for him, that he was inept at faking the affectionate banter of a genuine couple. He had jestingly spoken the truth; as far as she was concerned, the success of that first birthday party was that it had obliged him to attend. She had conceived it in desperation hoping only to secure his attention for a day – by then she had lost all hope of what she really wanted from him, which was anything she could recognize as an expression of love.

The birthday party was the only victory she could claim in the entire marriage, the only occasion – apart from Christmas, and even Christmas had occasionally been in danger – for which he could not find any excuse to be away.

'I'm no good to a hostess.' Shamelessly, he was trying to entertain her friends with the fact. 'No man in the media can be. You have to respond to stories as they're breaking . . .'

'But of course, as your guests, we'd expect that.' Antony was reaching for the bottle to refill glasses. At this, he was proficient and effective. 'Just as if you go to dinner with a surgeon, you expect him to be on call to his patients.'

'One year I'm sure we'll have to carry on without Michael.' Jane allowed Antony to refill her glass, now aware that Louisa was watching her with reproach. 'Media men aren't much use to wives and mothers either, are they?'

'For the same reason, I suppose? Louisa – a splash more?'

Marvellous the way men supported each other, even men who were strangers and had nothing in common but their balls. Jane kept her tone light and asked, 'Where were you when the children were born, darling – Sam was Eritrea, wasn't he? And for Xanthe it was New York.'

'I made it for Emma, though.' The child returned in shorts and a sweatshirt, and leaned against his knee, fidgeting as she started to itch. Awkwardly, he patted her thigh. Emma stood up straight, picked a biscuit from the bowl of snacks and ran away towards the house.

'You did not. You were still in the edit suite when she was born.'

'But they hadn't cut the cord by the time I got there.'

'Only because they'd run out of clamps.' Jane's expression was now sour and the softness was running out of her voice. Antony, feeling awkward, brushed imaginary cigarette ash from his linen slacks.

Satisfied that she had screwed the emotional pitch of the evening a little higher, Louisa tossed her rusty curls and changed the subject. 'So you're expecting fifty people tomorrow?'

'It's not a big thing.' Almost falling over his own words, so grateful was Michael for the escape. 'I'm fortunate that some of my old friends have got places not too far away . . . my finance director, Stewart Molfetto, quite a young man, and his wife, a lawyer in her own right . . .'

'And Graham Moynihan, who was Michael's partner when they started NewsConnect.' Jane knew that Michael now tolerated the Moynihans principally to prove his own loyalty to old friends. 'His children are about the same age as Imogen. They have a house about two miles away.' She thought of Andrea, Graham's wife, three hundred pounds if she was an ounce. Such blatant contentment they had in each other, but Graham was not like Michael, none of the charismatic carnivore about him, bearded, rotund, contemplative, serving the unfashionable god of film documentary. He had quietly peeled away to academia.

'Morris Donaldson, another old friend . . .' Antony knew him and said so; a keen viewer of political television, Antony. Louisa knew Morris, but said nothing; some years ago, during the infancy of his younger child, they had shared a few eventful beds. 'And then Alan Stern. They've got a huge place up at Villeneuve.' Stern last, named with respect in his voice; respect for the wealth, scrupulously purged of all traces of envy.

'Alan Stern of Altmark? The man who's taking you over?' A keen collector of millionaires, Louisa – even tacky technocrats like Stern.

'That's the one.' Her eyebrows remained raised in enquiry. 'The group has a telecommunications research company, I'm one of the directors. It's not a hostile takeover. We need each other. For some time our two operations have had quite a relationship. Their research is taking Altmark towards three new satellites by the end of the decade, and I want NewsConnect's name on one of them.' He was holding back. Stern had the ability to drain his confidence. He was obviously a bigger man but Michael feared he might also be a better man. With his

Calvinist corporate philosophy and ruthless control, he had built Altmark from nothing. Twenty years ago, all Stern had was a handful of chemical companies and a bankrupt African television studio.

'Uh-*huh*.' Louisa fluffed her curls to indicate thought. 'I'd have thought they were more the Riviera type.'

'They are. Actually Berenice is the Saint-Paul-de-Vence type. They have a villa there too.' Jane could see Berenice Stern now, stalking over the grass in high-heeled sandals and gold-buckled cruisewear, lolling back with her desiccated bosoms squeezed half out of a bustier, saying, 'Alan can't afford to divorce me, I know where too many bodies are buried.'

'And then Jane always likes to have houseguests,' Michael concluded, as if this was something which evened their score. Then he got up and walked behind Jane's chair and stroked her shoulders and down her arms where they were bare outside her sleeveless shirt. She had a preference for boyish clothes which irritated him.

'*What* a party; I'm *so* looking forward to it.' Louisa stretched luxuriously, thrusting her breasts skywards. 'And a *heavenly* evening.'

Michael pulled Jane's hair aside and kissed the back of her neck. Her guts shrivelled at the touch. Please God don't make him feel he has to fuck me tonight. She muttered something about dinner and got up to head for the kitchen. There was a splash as she reached the house. Louisa had pulled off her white linen dress and dived into the pool. She was absolutely naked. Antony poured more wine for Michael.

Drinking was another arena in which Michael was an amateur, but he was hurting in more and more places. His guilt was brewing hard, relaxation was irritating, the slights of the journey would not be forgotten. Antony held no interest for him, but was treacherously adept at filling his glass. Under cover of taking his bag upstairs he telephoned Serena again and got no answer.

He identified another source of unease. Jane was behaving strangely. Her mood was impossible to read. Sometimes she approached him with open affection; when she was suspicious or hurt she sank into a resentful docility. Tonight her manner was oddly elated, and above all evasive. She must be feeling that she had something on him. Michael was not very much concerned. His wife had so little leverage in his life that the idea of her trying to wield any advantage was faintly ridiculous. Nevertheless, instinct told him that Jane was keeping a secret.

'Come out for a walk.'

'What for?' Imogen was flinging herself back and forth across the room like a caged tiger, picking things up and putting them down, abusing her father, half-smoking cigarettes, glaring out of the window, throwing off Stephen's hand if he tried to touch her.

'It'll be dark soon. I know you live here, but I don't. We can walk along the river.'

'I don't want to walk along the fucking river.'

It was not beyond her to disappear if he went alone. 'Up to the corner then. You're out of milk and we can get bread or something.'

'Yeah, Keith, we can, that's *right*.' She stood still to light a cigarette. It was her last. 'OK. But I'm not going to that poxy place on the corner. I found this new Italian deli the other side of Saint Germain.'

As he hoped, the walk calmed her. She mistook the route and muddled through the narrow streets until the Seine embankment appeared inevitably ahead. 'You see,' she said, 'who's really being manipulative here? Who's the one who always gets his way?'

The bustling crowds had vanished; the traffic was heavy with Saturday shoppers heading home, but they had the narrow pavement to themselves. Grey mist blotted out the sky and an unseasonably cold wind funnelled down the river flapped the wares of the few print-sellers who were still closing up. Rain was not impossible. It was later than they had imagined but when they did at last arrive at their destination, a cobbled arcade of smartly painted shopfronts, the Italian grocer was still open, manned by a whole family who burrowed among shelves stacked to the ceiling, dispensing home-made pasta and sauces, marinated salads and almond cakes.

The rain began as they left, great lashing sheets of it gusting across the river and splashing on the pavements. She had her mad moments with rain, times when she insisted they get wet to the skin for the hell of it, but this was not one of them. They took shelter in a café. 'This isn't really rain, though, is it?' She watched the drops falling from the awning. 'We know all about rain after last summer, don't we? We know a lot of things, really, considering we're not very old yet.'

The window quickly misted with condensation. Last summer they had travelled together, thousands of miles from Argentina to the Canadian border. It had not been his original purpose to take Imogen to find her mother; one event after another had drawn them towards her, then compelled them to the point where the meeting became inevitable.

'I know you set that up, you know.' She was mixing in the creamy scum on her black coffee, making spiral patterns. 'Trekking off to find my mother.'

'You're wrong,' he told her. 'It just happened.'

'Yeah. Like we just happened to be passing within a thousand miles or so, so we dropped in.'

'Isn't that how it was?'

'I suppose. I reckon you planned it, all the same. You always liked her pictures.'

The first manifestation of her mother had been the drawings which arrived at school, sometimes several a week, sometimes none for ten days, spidery lines on flimsy paper, vivacious and funny, pictograms of imagined events in Imi's life. 'Here you are in chemistry class – phew! Hydrogen sulphide stinks!' Imi was drawn as a cherubic figure with pigtails, most unlike the sullen, etiolated adolescent she was. All she said to Stephen was: 'My father says she's probably mad. She did a lot of drugs when they were married. I send her Christmas cards and things. I mean, I don't remember her. She ran away when I was a baby.'

Throughout the time of putting away childish things, she taped every one of these drawings on the wall above her bed and at the end of term, when the wall was covered to the ceiling and custom required dormitories to be cleared of all personal possessions, she would not take them down. 'I can't keep them, my father doesn't like it.' The way she said this made it clear that the logic of her father's preference overrode all other considerations.

Later, Michael took Stephen aside. 'I think I ought to explain what happened when Imogen was a baby. I expect you know that her mother left us. She was what you might call unstable, mentally. During our marriage she was using drugs as well. I located her in Washington – State, the west coast. We keep in touch now but I don't encourage any contact with her – I was advised that was the best thing, to let her bond with Jane without any interference. But I've always been honest with Imogen about her mother. Everyone has the right to know their origins, don't you agree?'

In awe of Imi's famous father as he was, Stephen smelled deceit. The drawings were naïve but not bizarre; they were asking, in very simple terms, for love, and there was a tender intelligence in them. They did not arrive at the Knights' home. His own mother never said goodbye to him without emotion, although she rigidly suppressed it, and he was home every weekend. He was certain that in some respects all parents were the same, even in the exalted world of the Knight family.

He took a year out of education, half to earn money and the rest to spend it travelling, intending to study the vernacular building of primitive cultures. Imi went down to the school bakery with a bag of grass and tipped it into the mixer processing the dough for the muesli loaves, thus succeeding in her long-held ambition to be expelled. He was surprised that Michael allowed her to accompany him, and astonished that his sole provision for the trip was an American Express card. No advice, no friendly telephone numbers, no state-of-the-art backpack or manual on travelling for ten dollars a day, just unlimited credit.

They travelled northwards, up the American continent, from Patagonia to Rio de Janeiro, across to Peru and up to Mexico, looking at cave-dwellings, slum shacks, turf huts, shelters of palm thatch and villages of mud brick, filling up his notebooks while she filled her head with wonders. 'Why can't we live like this forever?' she asked him, several times a day. Her white skin acquired a smoky, yellowish tan, her hair became long and tangled; she took on a gipsy look. She sang songs on the bus and people smiled at them.

From Mexico they went to Texas, left behind the trains, buses and boats, and needed to hire a car. 'I think we should get whatever's most expensive,' she told him as they looked around the airport for the Hertz desk, 'because we've only got a month more and my father won't get the bill until we get back, so we can spend whatever we want, can't we?' Her tone was ridiculously conspiratorial. He had the impression that now they were in familiar surroundings, the months of being away from her father, and therefore unable to raise his anger, had suddenly become uncomfortable.

'But I don't want more than what we need,' he argued.

'Yes but I do. And I've got the card. And I have to sign it.'

'Your father will think I'm exploiting you.'

'He won't. He'll think I'm exploiting him and he'll be dead right. So what?' She left him and stalked towards the desk alone, littering tattered documents from her purse as she searched for her licence.

She went on a spending spree. After the car she insisted on good hotels. She bought new clothes, and some good meals with wine which, after their diet of street food and fruit, made her bilious. Fretfully, she insisted on flying to their next destination, and bought them a month's pass ticket because it cost more.

Concern for her, curiosity and shame at participating in this aggressive extravagance all combined to motivate him. He began to plant the idea in her mind. 'This is an amazing ticket, you know. We could travel anywhere we wanted on it.' Then a few days later, 'All these plains tribes are pretty much the same. I'd love to see how coastal Indians lived – how they coped with the climate up north.'

She asked him where the study centres were and he mentioned a reservation outside Seattle. 'Well, why don't we go? It's only four hours. Then we can get a direct flight to New York or something.'

When they were airborne over the city she looked out into the impenetrable grey cloud for a long time. Then, in the same sly tone as she used to propose charging up luxuries on the card, she said, 'My mother must be down there somewhere. Why don't we get her number and just drop in? Wouldn't that be something?'

'Suppose your father found out?'

'Well, suppose he did? Haven't you ever thought it was strange that he never fixed for us to meet or anything? In seventeen years? He was pretty pissed off with her for leaving, that's for sure. I mean, nobody's supposed to leave my father, are they?'

Her courage failed later and Stephen had to make the calls. Pia Franklin was her name, and the address was East Point. A man answered, a light, resonant, friendly voice. 'My wife is teaching right now. Can I have her call you?' The colossal significance of the conversation made them all, even Imogen, excessively calm and polite.

Within a few hours it was arranged. In steady rain they took a ferry across the green-grey water of the Sound, a journey of an hour or so. At the dock a man in denims and worn-down boots, young with long light brown hair, came towards them with an open smile, and drove them into the forest. Huge conifers stood straight and uniform like columns, the downpour dripping from their spines. The car needed lights at midday, so little light reached the ferny floor under the trees, yet even in the gloom the green was brilliant. They breathed in the resinous scent, mingled with wet earth and decaying wood.

She was almost as tall as her daughter, finer-featured and very lined, with round blue eyes which gave her face a childlike cast. As a young woman she must have been a dazzling beauty and now, Stephen felt with astonishment, she was the most purely seductive woman he had ever encountered. Her manner was gentle and nervous, but it was impossible to feel awkward with her; she had a way of drawing back which lured you forward. Within minutes she was talking quite naturally of how she had left her daughter.

'I was a mess, quite frankly. Every morning I woke up and I thought I was going to kill myself. You know, don't you, you would have had a sister, but the first child I had with Michael just died and when I look back I can see now I was going through terrible grief. My mother was desperate for me to come to her. Somehow I convinced myself you didn't deserve to suffer because of my suffering, and so when at last I went to my family I left you with Michael. And then of course when I was better and I sent for you he fought me.'

'Yeah, he would do that.' Imogen went through the whole thing as if it was another trip, extremely withdrawn. She had never really spoken of her feelings.

Michael's wrath, when they returned, was based on the Amex bill. He was lofty, eloquent, contemptuous and, Stephen thought, delighted to have a legitimate focus for his feelings. The bill was certainly huge, but, as Imogen coolly pointed out, a speck compared to NewsConnect's profits and his own salary.

In private, Michael turned different weapons on Stephen. 'Do you realize you have done that girl irreparable emotional damage? Have you any idea what a trauma it is for her to even think about her mother, let alone have contact with her? Don't you see that always, in the back of her mind, she carries the stigma of what her mother is, and the fear that she will be the same?

Taking her out there – and let's talk like men, shall we? I doubt very much that it was her idea – that was the most destructive action I have ever seen one person take against another. Whatever happens now, I shall hold you responsible. You have undone everything I've ever done for Imogen.'

Stephen took it all in silence, saying only, 'I thought it was a successful visit. They were good together.'

He rose in Imogen's estimation for making her father so profoundly angry. She was beginning a new mode, in which she would turn her violence in on herself, but in its early stages it looked promising to both men. There was a sense of purpose about her, and within a few weeks she advanced a proposal to study in Paris, supported by a letter of acceptance from a private college issued on the strength of her portfolio and the recommendation of her former teacher.

Beside her sleeping husband, Grace thought about Jane Knight. What was she planning? What did she know? They had danced together for eight years. Jane stepped forward, Grace stepped back, then Grace stepped forward, and Jane stepped back, blindly, neither wanting to see the other or know the other, intimately separated by Michael.

First came the idyllic era, before Jane was pregnant, when Michael had talked about their marriage as an error of judgement which he would soon correct, regrettable, forgivable, a reaction to the trauma of his first marriage. 'I thought it was the right thing to do for Imogen, I thought she needed a woman's care as well as mine. It's hard to explain to a tiny child that her mother has just – well, run off and dumped her. She was showing signs . . . she was difficult. Still is.' And he sighed, holding back from accusing Jane.

Soaked, saturated, macerated in the wonder of their love, Grace asked no questions. She had felt no jealousy. She evaluated her lover's wife as a nice, intelligent woman, a touch overcontrolled perhaps, but supremely pretty, sure to be remarried immediately Michael left her.

Then Jane got pregnant, and Michael, having made much of how his wife had no sympathy for his yearning for more children, particularly a son, announced the fact by complaining of it to Grace, over the studio internal telephone. 'I can't come over today, Jane's pregnant which apparently means she can't deal with the architect this evening.'

After a dumbstruck minute, which Michael did not register because the studio director was talking to him, Grace managed to say, 'Do you know what you've just told me, Michael?'

'I'm sorry,' he said. 'We're having to extend the house for the baby. It's a real drag, I was looking forward to seeing you . . .' Irritation, of quite a high order; almost on the scale of getting a car clamped.

'*Michael.*' She remembered shivering, trying to pull the cuffs of her jacket over her hands because they were suddenly cold.

'What? Is something the matter?' Now moving into

contrition. A man's place is in the wrong. Whatever I've done I'm sorry, now can we get on with the real business of things?

'What did you say about Jane?'

'Oh. Of course. Of *course.* Listen, stay there, I'm coming over, I must see you . . .'

To avoid him, she left the building, got in her car and set off for home. Her house was five minutes away from the studios, and somewhere on the journey she lost consciousness. The car had hit a brick wall, mercifully not a well-built one. Grace joked afterwards that she owed her life to the decline of craftsmanship. The wall collapsed, but Grace was in hospital for a month with a fractured skull. Flowers arrived from Michael, and he visited every day, sometimes twice; curious that he had more time when sex was not involved. He looked tortured, and strangely, powerfully fascinated by her in a new way. The injury he had done her seemed to open more paths between them. Her scars welded them together.

Soon it became apparent that he was boiling with resentment that Jane had taken an initiative and tied him to her, at least for the next few years. When she gave up her job and spent the summer in France, both these actions angered him further. 'I don't know what she wants of me,' he said repeatedly. 'She's unhappy but she won't talk to me. She just folds everything inside herself and goes away.'

Grace spent the summer at Jane and Michael's house, at Michael's insistence. 'It's my home,' he said, 'I want you in my home.' When the baby was born, Grace could hardly breathe for jealousy. She took action, gave up news, gave up producing and took a researcher's job with a Boston-based company making religious documentaries. There was a lot of travelling. By chance, she met Jane in a restaurant. 'Michael is always saying how he misses you,' Jane had told her, girlish and timid beside the famous chef. 'His new producer panics, he always says how calm you were.' What do you say to your lover's wife when she tells you he misses you. 'How kind of him.' Out in Nepal, Grace began an affair with the director.

Jane wrote a book, and it was a hit. Grace, who had nothing but a journalist's apprenticeship on a suburban newspaper behind her, had felt personally disappointed. A woman with a first in philosophy ought to be above the domestic arts; the woman whose intellect Michael always said he respected ought not to become a professional housewife.

Michael founded NewsConnect, ceased to be a sleek television star and became a desperate, needy creature who had to talk over every decision eight times a day with Grace and begged her not to desert him. He generated a storm of emotion which blew away her attachment to the director like dust. She listened, advised, soothed, complimented, despaired and began to resent Jane because she was not taking care of Michael.

Jane had another baby, a son. Michael was enraged, moved into Grace's house for two days, then took a business trip to New York and returned to Jane. 'You were here, Michael,' Grace insisted.

'I know I was. I can always come and see you when I have to go to the airport.'

'No, you'd left home, that was why.'

'Jane's got her hands full with the new baby. I shouldn't stay away longer than necessary, love.' That horrible, clipped way of speaking, meaning I must get off the phone, I haven't time for these guilt-trip conversations.

'No, listen to me. Michael, *listen.* You had left, you said you had left, you said you were angry, that it was all a trick, that you couldn't bear to be there . . .'

'Yes, I know. But you see I can't leave her, don't you? I need you, Grace, I love you, you must believe that. But I have to stick this out. Be patient.' She grew to hate the telephone, it was impossible to understand anything over it. Because she forced herself, Grace had another affair, this time in the Solomon Islands. When she got home, Jane had made a television series, *Farmhouse Kitchen*, and Michael had taken up all the tape on her answering machine. There were postcards from all over America. NewsConnect business had taken him to New York, Chicago, St Louis, Los Angeles. He called half an hour after she walked into the house, so hesitant, so humble that she was actually overwhelmed with guilt, until he came to her house and made love to her in a completely different way. He called her 'honey' and 'baby'. Grace now felt superior to Jane, because at least she herself knew the truth, and because she was, as she considered it, cheating on Michael.

Her own pregnancy was unintentional, despite the

advice of friends, and on a low-dose pill. If it had been a boy she would have had to abort him for risk of feminization. She did not know until the morning of her thirty-second birthday, when she woke up in pain in a clammy, sticky, blood-soaked bed. Very difficult to know whose child it would have been. She was shocked at that; that was for illiterate alcoholic underclass mothers, not a professional woman like herself with a shining career path and extra pages in her passport. Jane Knight's face was on the cover of a magazine at the doctor's surgery. Recipes for autumn fruits.

Round and round each other their lives had twined. Now clearly Michael denied each to the other, interpreted their feelings and reworked their actions according to his own imperatives. A minuet in a haunted ballroom.

She had lost many friends. The affair had been impossible to discuss. He was too much of an icon, too admired, too envied, too publicly married, and the glamour of his achievements overcame judgement. If ever she opened the subject, people reacted to Michael's status, not to her emotions. Even her mother had been dazzled.

Irina was Polish, a teacher of arithmetic to small children during the week. On Saturday she taught the language to the community's children at the Polish Centre, and on Sunday she taught Sunday school at St Michael's church hall. Plump and lazy, never inclined to any kind of grooming, she viewed Grace as a vexing, incomprehensible girl sent to test her faith. Her home was a flat with a winding dark corridor where smells lingered, two cheerful mongrel dogs sleeping in warm corners and a dusty crucifix over every door. When Michael first telephoned Grace at her mother's home, twenty-seven years of moral authority evaporated.

'Gracie-john, it is Michael Knight on the telephone. Your Michael Knight.' She gave a little giggle, black-rimmed eyes round with wonder, hips rolling as she weaved between the cluttering kitchen chairs. 'Gracie-john' was because Irina added the name of her husband to the names of her children and dogs, although he had abandoned them all before Grace's memory began, to go to Canada and die by falling drunk off a railway bridge.

Grace had wanted her mother to protect her from Michael, to fly into a rage, scream about sin and damnation, accuse him of ruining her daughter, but instead she was announcing the call with almost servile pleasure. 'Hurry, hurry, don't keep the man waiting for you! Leave washing the dishes, I do it, go! go!' Grace had felt utterly abandoned at that moment.

Michael's women did not fare well. By the end of the affair, Grace knew most of her predecessors, and the rivals who had accounted for the odd lacunae in their love. Most of these women had barely crawled from the wreckage. Some had found sanctuaries; one was more or less an alcoholic, another espoused Nichiren Shoshu Buddhism. They withered quickly, getting the same hard look around their eyes that went so ill with their gentle natures. None was married. Grace became thirty-two. She had propelled her career into a backwater and it had halted. Finally the opportunity in Paris had appeared; a change of medium, but by now the entire establishment of television was tainted and she left it gladly. Grace heard of the job the day after the miscarriage; made reckless, she had actually telephoned the editor and sold herself to him in five minutes, followed by a lunch.

'Good,' Michael steeled himself to say when she told him. 'It's just the sort of challenge you'll enjoy.' She remembered the wounded look in his eyes, the almost hysterical regret in his voice.

'I'm not doing this to book myself off your conscience,' she said tartly. 'This is the end for me, Michael. I shan't come back. I don't like to say goodbye on the . . .'

'Say *au revoir*, then.'

'That's not what I mean.'

'I see.' Very sober, his last words to her, but incorrect. She knew he could not understand. If he had known how he was destroying her, he would never have begun the process.

When Grace ran away to Paris she immediately understood that she had entered a refugee camp. They were charming people, her new colleagues, working for the international news media, and they were also fleeing disaster. They had left behind in the past the results of their defects of character – their stalled careers, failed marriages and debts – and decamped to the forgiving arena of foreign assignments where they could offer the special lure of the exotic as a rationale for their choice. For a while, they were the true companions of her despair.

Their society comforted her. Here were others who

had suffered and kept their own secrets. At the end of each day, when their deadlines had passed and their telephones were quiet, they met up in cafés and told each other how much they adored France, how terrible things were back home. No stigma attached to loneliness, for they were all alone and deracinated, and so there was an automatic bond between them, and a warm convention of companionship which took care of birthdays, illness and New Year's Eve. She had been happy to adopt their company, drink too much for a while and let her wounds close.

It was a comfortable existence. Her new companions did not ask questions. Like her, they were witty and comfortably supplied with company cars, apartments and credit cards, although their futures were uncertain. Away from the heated turmoil of their newsrooms they knew they could not follow the moves in the corporate games. It was the nature of the medium that editors would come and go, policies lurch violently to the political right or left, the economic up or down. In London, heads would roll, desks be cleared, men fall overboard, and all it would signify in the Paris offices was an alien voice on the telephone, an unfamiliar hieroglyph on the fax. Some were freelances already, and the others noted their precarious existence with anxiety, because permanent foreign staff were becoming a luxury.

They kept up their spirits by recycling old gossip, which was fresh to Grace since she was new to the medium of print, and by recounting the nightmares that they had escaped – but not the worst, those atrocities which were too horrific to speak of. They talked only about the little things they were glad to have escaped, the muggings, parking restrictions, the rotting hospital service. Then the conversation would turn to the pleasures of their exile and so, comforted, they would stroll away into the soft evening to find their favourite little restaurants.

The gentle bravado corresponded perfectly with the strategy Grace had evolved to dull the pain of loving Michael. At first she was afraid that he would follow her, but months went by and she heard nothing. A few more years and she recognized that she had made progress in her rehabilitation; most days she could be optimistic and constructive, something resembling the person she might have been if Michael had never occurred. She thought of him as a natural disaster, something which had hit her life without warning and wrecked it. Once in Florida she had passed a drive-in movie which had been hit by a tornado. The huge screen lay crumpled in the field like a giant handkerchief. That was the scale of her own devastation.

Nick was in the café one evening; she had met him a few times, the brother of one of her new colleagues, a virologist attached to a multinational research team. He mumbled and his wiry golden hair was thinning at the front. A big man, but his round blue eyes always seemed to be looking up at her in apology. She had liked him but felt no genuine attraction. He admitted openly that his first wife had left him, complaining that he was dull. The ritual of home thoughts in the café was boring Grace by that time, and the old news adrenaline was flowing less readily. Nick was another escape so she had drifted along with his unhurried courtship.

Her mind persistently argued that he was a good person and ought to be loved. Now they were married, and probably happy. Nick was happy, at least, it was his nature. They were waiting for a baby, something else she thought he deserved, that she owed him. Stress, they agreed, must be a factor. Below their joint reasonableness, they felt desperation. Neither was capable of buying a house for pleasure, but the baby was different, the deciding reason to buy the Alhambra.

Michael still appeared in her thoughts every day, but here he seemed less powerful than in Paris. At the Alhambra, Grace found it easier to reflect on the present, which meant thinking of her husband, whom she could not love, and their child, which she could not conceive. Lately the superstition had crept up on her that this was her punishment for the affair.

When the adults assembled for supper, Xanthe suddenly flipped into a screaming tantrum. It flayed Jane's nerves; tantrums had been Emma's speciality, Xanthe had never displayed a moment of temper in her life until now. Was her lovely little last-born to be as wretched as the rest? Michael was actually frightened by the sight of the pretty creature transformed into a gargoyle by her uncontrollable rage. Antony had the whisky out by the time Debbie took the child away for the fail-safe solution, a ride in the car.

Night slowly embraced the land. High in the old walls the birds roosted and were silent. The vault of the sky was black and at first stars glittered optimistically, but in a while clouds, invisible in the darkness, gathered and extinguished them, a handful at a time. Louisa held court over the meal, trying to fascinate both men. Michael's thoughts dissociated. He had drunk too much, and the surges of self-loathing which always accompanied re-integration into his family were strong. He needed release; everything else started to lose its meaning.

His body was hot with tension; Jane felt it across the room and it made her desperate to be bright, to stoke up the conversation and postpone the inevitable moment when they would be alone. His fingers were moving constantly, the nervous mannerism which betrayed his tension. When Michael had a new woman he went through some kind of internal agony that had only one resolution: sex. And he would choose to have sex to prove his innocence, and to try to quell her internal rebellion – which she knew he had sensed. If she let him into her body now, she would feel like killing herself.

The moment came in the end, a little after midnight. Louisa dragged Antony, now sentimentally drunk, away to their quarters. Jane saw that Michael, unusually for him, had drunk enough to be a little out of control. They began the measured ritual of washing and teeth-flossing and hanging up clothes which she prolonged in the hope that he would fall asleep before she came to bed.

'I think I'll just look in on Xanthe.' She put on a

nightshirt, a Doris Day cotton thing treated with some wonder compound which made its white ruffles ever-fresh.

'Why?' he said, already installed against his pillow. 'She's fine now. Debbie said she'd sleep in the girls' room, didn't she?'

'Oh, did she?'

'Yes, didn't you hear?'

There was no way out. She got into bed with him.

Around her chest there was a thin, fierce pain, as if someone were tightening a wire around her ribs. Michael was not an insensitive man; that was the problem. He was not a man who would be content with a body. He wanted your heart and mind as well. Perhaps that was why he was insistent about having the light on.

He was stroking her hair. 'Michael.' She had to clear her throat. 'I'm really tired tonight. Could we just snuggle up?'

'What's the matter?'

He had an erection, she could sense it across the cool sheet between them, although she was holding her lower body away from his. The pain in her chest was more intense. 'Nothing. Please . . .'

'No, there is something. I felt it when I came in. What is it? Tell me, my love.'

'There really isn't anything. I'm just tired, that's all.'

A silence, and then he said, 'Sixteen years we've been together – don't you think I know when there's something going on with you?'

She was struggling for words when her body betrayed

her, and the pain cut right into her chest and let out great screaming sobs, four or five of them, tearing open her mouth, bursting her lungs, leaving her gasping chaotically like a woman in the crisis of childbirth.

'My God, Jane, my love, whatever is it? There, there, now, come on, come on now, you must tell me, come on . . .' She had crawled away to the edge of the bed but he was leaning over, reaching out for her, his breath still smelling of whisky under the toothpaste.

'Don't touch me!'

Although her face was turned away she knew he had reacted. He knew. Horrible that their very intimacy blocked the way out of this hell.

'Oh, no. It's not that again, is it?' That voice. So many nuances of menace.

Thank God, she could not get control of her breath to answer him.

'It is, isn't it? This is another one of your . . . this is about one of your suspicions, isn't it? This idea you have that I've been unfaithful.' Absolutely rational, he was. Not the kind of man who dismissed his wife's feelings because he did not understand them. 'You're out here by yourself and I'm a long way away from you and you've been feeling insecure, getting tortured by imaginings, is that it?'

She was cold now, very cold. So cold she was shivering. Cold right to the core of her mind, freezing her disordered senses. She could sit up, and drag the quilt around her knees. When things were frozen, they were very clear. 'Michael, I know. I know. That's all.'

'You can't know. There isn't anything to know. Jane, please, how many times do I have to say this? I have never, *ever* been unfaithful to you.'

She kept silent. Nothing she could say would get through. He was such a snake, he would twist and slither and get himself out of any argument she raised, and besides, she had no argument, only her instinct. Better to save her strength.

'You put me in an impossible position, you know that, don't you? I can't prove that there isn't anyone else. There just isn't, that's all. There never has been. I wanted to make love to you – would I want that if I had another woman? But I can't make you believe me. It's about trust, isn't it? It has to be. If we love each other we trust each other. But . . .' A deep, traumatized sigh. 'You make me feel so guilty. And there's nothing I can do. Is there? I mean, is there? Because if there is, tell me. Tell me and I'll do it, whatever it is. Whatever I can do to make you trust me. I'll do it. I swear.' He lost control a little, towards the end; he did not quite manage to keep the anger out of his speech.

That old, sick, disorientated feeling. He would go on the same way until she gave in, until she agreed with him, let go of her own vision and found some way of distorting herself into the shape that fitted the hole left for her in his picture of his world.

'No.' It was the first word that offered itself. 'No. Michael, there is nothing for you to do here. I have this idea. You are right about that.'

'Thank you.' A sarcastic murmur.

'And I know you think I'm wrong.'

'But I know what the truth is – don't I?'

'Yes, you do. So you know that what I'm thinking is not true, but I know that it's all I can think. I can't change my mind about this.'

He was sitting up himself now, leaning forward, almost leaning over her.

'But that's crazy, Jane.'

'If you are right, yes it is. It's a delusion.'

'What *is* this?' He ran his hands through his hair, holding the side of his head as if the thought itself would not fit inside his skull. 'I just don't understand. Are you trying to humour me because you think I'm drunk, or something?' He had drunk too much, he could feel it, the flush of alcohol in his face. 'You're saying you're having delusions that I'm unfaithful? That you'd rather do that than just accept the truth and trust me?'

'Well, yes, Michael. I think that is what it comes down to.'

'But that doesn't make sense. Jane, I've always respected your mind, you're an intelligent woman . . .'

'I do accept that it doesn't make sense, Michael. But there isn't anything I can think of that you can do that will make me trust you.'

He was angry now, his fist hit the pillow and the whole bed shook. 'I can't stand this, this is like a nightmare. You're accusing me of something, refusing to hear any evidence and finding me guilty.' Then nothing for a while, one of his final moves, a pit of silence dug for her to fall into with explanations or apologies. Not this time.

She bit her lips, but the pit was yawning. At last she said, 'When we were married, I thought I'd be entering into the greatest happiness I'd ever know.' Then the road opened up in front of her, right to the end, and it was so direct, and the end so close, that she stopped speaking and felt afraid.

'I only wanted to make you happy, Jane,' he said. 'It's all I want now. Truly. You must believe me.' And then he got off the bed and walked to the door, reaching for his bathrobe as he went. 'I think you need some space now, I'm going downstairs for a while.' He went out.

She fell sideways and lay curled up, a few tears of relief running from her open eyes, remembering, reviewing. Against her bride's expectation, he had given her so few scraps of joy. One hour, two hours, never more, never so much as a whole afternoon. Always the work, the story, the filming, the editing, the meeting. Then the day when she was newly pregnant with Emma, and Andrea Moynihan had turned up on her doorstep, in tears on her behalf, blocking out the daylight with her bulk.

A lovely woman, Andy. Jane would never have managed Imogen without her mentor in stepmotherhood, scooping up the wretched child along with her own, initiating Jane into the mysteries, and when the problems began, night after night, assuring her from the base of her psychology degree and her warm heart that it was not her fault. Once her kids were in school, Andy had gone back to work, counselling at a big city hospital.

Every word she said came right back when Jane needed the memory. 'I should not be telling you this, but

I have to. I was called to see this woman today who they thought had tried to kill herself by driving her car into a wall. She said it was an accident, she was just upset. I don't care if I get struck off, I'm your friend, I can't be professional about this. What she was upset about was Michael. They're having an affair. Oh God, I wish we'd done more on ethics when we were training. Let me come in, Jane. I need to use your bathroom.'

The pain had been fearful, but she had done nothing then. A mistake perhaps, but she was afraid of Michael, and afraid for Andy's job. A few hours later he rang and she heard the shock in his voice when he told her that one of his producers had been injured in a road accident. She had sympathized and offered to organize the flowers. Andy came back with advice; men strayed when their wives were pregnant, it was a fact of life. A certain kind of immaturity made some of them unable to find a pregnant woman sexy. But it was just a phase.

It made her feel powerful to keep the secret. Perhaps the power was what he needed from his affairs, the power of deceiving another and keeping the truth for yourself.

After that day, and before it, there had been the distances and the false behaviour, the sneaking away for telephone calls, the calls to the house, dead lines, wrong numbers, bold women's voices asking for Michael. After that day there had been one or two letters, the sad looks other women gave her, the silent, patronizing approval of his male associates, the occasional courageous soul who solemnly passed on a rumour. Five secretaries he had had since then, and all of them must have known. Each one had her own strategy; Marianne was terribly soft, caring and conscientious, as if to make up for Michael's cruelty with her own kindness.

The bed was inviting now. Jane straightened her body out, found a pillow and got comfortable, feeling great tiredness. Something had shifted at last. Perhaps she would be able to sleep. Her throat was dry.

Michael went downstairs, struggling with panic. He needed his equilibrium back, his heart was hammering. Jane was acting out of character. Complaints he had endured, she often had a compulsion to make everything his fault – natural, perhaps, in anyone who under-achieved their ability. If she had stayed in the civil service she could have had the career she deserved but . . . her choice, he hadn't pressured her. This was a new thing, it was bizarre.

Out on the pool terrace the night air seemed heavy. The drink was still making him clumsy and he put a hand out to steady himself on the wall. At the far side of the terrace a figure sprawled low in a chair, faintly lit by the reflected light from the pool.

'Debbie, is that you?'

'Yes, this is me.'

He was annoyed once more and crossed to her side of the pool. 'What are you doing out here? What about the girls?'

'The girls are asleep. They're OK. I came out to watch the moon.' The hand which gestured at the sky held a can of drink, but it did not escape him that the arm was graceful. The moon was an unrecognizable thing, a huge blood-red disc hanging low over the horizon. He paused, considering what to say, longing to turn the tide of his violent discontent.

'I've never seen a moon that colour before.'

'Me neither.' Her defences seemed to be down.

'There's something I remember in the Bible: the sun shall turn to darkness and the moon to blood before the great and terrible day when the Lord shall come.'

'If we're expecting Jesus tomorrow he'd better like garlic.'

His harsh laugh flew out across the fields and echoed faintly from the hillside. 'Do you mind if I join you?'

'They're your chairs.' The length of her legs was remarkable, and their smooth straightness. Everything about her was like that, elongated and unblemished. Her hair was unclipped, and she was lying with her head thrown back so it hung like a curtain and the moonlight caught its sheen.

'I hope you don't mind me saying this, Debbie, but I sometimes get the impression that I've offended you in some way.'

A wisp of black cloud veiled the moon's upper edge. From his seat beside her she appeared in profile against the faint light of the sky, smooth forehead, vigorous brows, a tough, short nose, sharp chin and then the girlish swell under her T-shirt. He had never seen any evidence that she wore a bra.

'I don't mind you saying that at all, Mr Knight. I know I can be too much in people's faces sometimes. You haven't offended me; you would know for sure if you had.'

'There is something I wanted to ask you – about my wife. How's Jane been these last few days?'

'How's she been?' She seemed not to understand. He had expected her to sit up and pay attention, but she did not stir.

'Has anything upset her?'

'I don't think so. Nothing unusual, anyway. There's been no real pressure since she wrapped up her last series. The children make her tired. Their problems make her tired, I should say. They're nice kids in themselves.'

'I'm worried about her. The mood she's in – I've never seen it before. I suppose you've had a lot of experience with other families. How long have you been over here?'

'Three years now. Two years with one family, then I decided to stay on and take some temporary jobs and travel around Europe a bit.'

'Do you think she's feeling . . .'

'I can't speak for Jane, Mr Knight. I don't really like to get mixed up in a family's personal affairs, if you don't mind my saying so.' She was stretching out her arms and legs, yawning. To his inflamed reason, it was an invitation. Then suddenly she was standing. He stood up at once beside her. They were of equal height; had it been daytime, he would have been looking directly into her eyes.

'I wish you wouldn't always tie your hair back.' There was a thick lock of it which had fallen forward and lay dark against her white shirt, curling around one of her breasts. He had to touch it. 'It's beautiful.'

Planted firmly on her feet, the girl stuck her hands in

the back pockets of her jeans and said, 'You know what people used to believe the moon was made of? My grandfather told me this. They used to believe that everything which was useless on earth was precious on the moon, so it was just crammed full of everything totally worthless: things like wasted time and stupid ideas and broken promises.'

He was reaching for her face when she knocked his hand away. 'Let's not make the moon any bigger, eh?'

'Debbie, please . . .'

'You've had a fair bit to drink, Mr Knight. Why don't you go inside now?' His silhouette was swaying in the darkness, his head weaving from side to side. She tried to assess how drunk he was and what the chances were that he'd fall in the pool if she left him.

'Oh, don't say things like that. Don't be so cynical, you're too young. Come here . . .' In the darkness he stumbled over the empty drink can, lost his balance, lunged for her and fell with his whole body weight, dragging her to the ground with him. Something ripped, he heard it, but he had hold of one of her arms and could grab for the other. They were struggling and then all he knew was a fierce pain in his leg. She had kicked him under the kneecap and the pain screamed down the nerve all the way to his ankle.

Debbie was back on her feet standing over him, breathing hard. 'If you really want to know, you struck me as a sleaze right off. Don't try anything like this again or I'm out of here.'

He was writhing on the ground, clutching his leg like

a histrionic soccer star. Brushing herself down as she walked back to the house, she found one of the pockets was hanging off her jeans and tore it away. The lights were still on in the hall, and the door was open, and in the doorway stood Jane in her white nightshirt, holding a bottle of mineral water.

'Debbie – I'm so sorry . . . are you all right?'

'Shit, why should you be sorry? It wasn't what I guess it must have looked like. He's had too much to drink, that's all.'

'No he hasn't. Don't make excuses for him. Michael could drink Brendan Behan under the table with one hand tied behind his back. He always knows what he's doing. We had a row earlier and he was taking it out on you.'

'Still, nothing for you to be sorry about. I'm good, don't worry about me. That was nothing. I've had much worse happen travelling.'

Together they went in and without thinking closed the door on Michael. At the foot of the stairs they stopped and Debbie said, 'You look like a sleepwalker in that shirt.'

'I feel like a sleepwalker. I can't get in contact with anything tonight.' Jane had one foot on the lowest stair.

'I'm sleeping in with the girls tonight. Would you like me to make up one of the guest rooms for you?' It was said with no shadow of emotion on the open face; the plainness of the offer made Jane hesitate, and the simple morality which it implied gave her confidence. She said, 'That's very kind of you, Debbie, but,' then she remembered that there was a room in the children's wing already prepared for Imogen. 'I'll take Imogen's room, shall I?'

The bed was comforting in its narrowness. Lying awake, she heard Michael go upstairs slowly a few minutes later. The curtain was pulled back and she watched the moon through the window, still red as blood and low in the vaporous sky.

CHAPTER FIVE

Sunday: The Beginning

'This is hooking, isn't it? I'm the hooker and you're my driver, and Jane's a hooker and the john is my dear father. And his sicko thing is being the great family man, and he's paying us to act out this fantasy for him. He can't get it on without a whole fucking crew of us in fetish suits running around acting out his weird little scenario for hours. What do you think of my daughter outfit, Stephen?' She picked contemptuously at the skirt of her yellow flowered dress. 'It'll do things for him, you'll see. And the hat, eh?' Her hat was a steeple of straw, the colour of orange sherbet, fantastic in shape and proportion, a Mad Hatter creation that toppled crazily over one eye; she put it on and posed for herself, using the train window as a mirror.

'I love it,' he said. 'I love you for wearing things like that.'

'They'll hate it, though. And after the old man's

tortured us all day he'll have his pathetic little orgasm, feel like King Kong, hand over the wedge and tell us all to fuck off. Until he gets the urge again.'

'Do you want some of my Snickers?'

'No.' She took off the hat and scowled out of the train window.

Without concern, Stephen unwrapped the bar and began to eat it. 'D'you think there's a buffet on this train? I wish we'd got to the station in time for coffee.' They had hardly slept. After he had made dinner, and her rage at Michael had died down to a lethargic sulk, she had started talking and smoking, telling him about her life in Paris, her work and her new friends, showing a new personality, socialized and amusing. The conversation had been too good to stop for sleep. After a couple of hours of fitful dozing he had somehow got them both to the Gare Montparnasse.

The train passed a crossing, the distorted clanging of the automatic bell sounding faintly through the sealed window. Outside, the sun was bright but low clouds were moving fast over the earth, their shadows racing after them over the parched fields. Where the wheat was still standing the ears were bronze and ripe; here and there summer storms had punched holes in the crops.

Imi suddenly turned back to him and smiled. 'Oh, well, if you insist.' She held out her hand and he gave her the rest of the bar; she chewed it thoughtfully, her mouth too full. One of the easiest ways to get her to eat was to eat yourself and ignore her. Feline manipulation, he called it. Ask the animal to do anything and she wouldn't; pretend you didn't care what she did and she chose to do exactly what you wanted.

'This country isn't real, is it?' She sat back and pointed out of the window. Close to Paris the land was flat and the perspectives deceitful. It was a child's painting, with straight roads, tiny houses and round-headed single trees like lollipops. 'Eurodinky, that's where we are. Look – there are the plastic cows. What do you think it does to people's heads living in a picture like that?'

'The trees are taller than the houses.'

'Yeah.' For some time she was content to sit gazing out of the window, licking the last of the chocolate from her lips and furtively, awkwardly picking her teeth with the one fingernail she had left unchewed, on the little finger of her left hand.

He waited for her to speak. Her elliptical thought patterns were familiar to him, he knew there was a subject which was working its way to the surface. Last night's social conversation had been a smokescreen; she had raised the subject of her mother earlier and would return to it again. Stephen kept in the back of his mind an agenda of things to do to make Imi better; to make her talk about her mother was the top item. In a year she had said nothing about their visit until, in the café, she had made that passing allusion to the rain. There was no need to prompt. The journey took more than three hours and she would be a captive for that time.

'So we are going,' she said at last. 'I wasn't going to go, was I? But somehow Daddy got you to get me to do it, and here we are. But we're not staying, are we?'

'Come on, Imi – we agreed to stay the night. It's a long way to go just for the day.'

'Oh yeah, we've got our little bag, haven't we? You're looking forward to that, aren't you? Don't lie to me, you like all Jane's lovely food and clean white beds. Beats sitting on my skanky old floor all night, you're thinking.'

'I hate being there because it upsets you. But, I mean, Jane has made it into a beautiful house . . . what's wrong with that?'

'Nothing. Just a waste of life, nothing wrong with it.' The judgement was handed down in an ominously gracious tone. 'It always seems to me like it's a film set not a home, and Jane's in front of the camera playing Superwife, you know? She's acting all the time, Jane. My mother would never have been able to cope with all that, would she? Can you imagine my mother in a show like that?'

Stephen shook his head, trying to hide his satisfaction. She looked at him sharply and said nothing more.

'How do you think . . .' he prompted.

'It's no *use*, I don't want to Talk About Her, I haven't anything to Say About Her, OK?'

'I didn't . . .'

'You don't have to, I *know*, Stephen. I can see you coming ten miles down the road. Why don't you just give up on me?'

She turned back to the window again. The land was so dry, fucked out at the end of summer. The hay was all cut, shaved down to the root, elephant toilet rolls everywhere, made by one machine and waiting to be loaded on to another. Some of the fields were stubble, some of them were already ploughed. There was a haze of yellow over the woodlands. The vineyards were beginning, acres of tame, trimmed vines stretched out on wires swelling up their grapes on schedule. Her throat was dry; it was the chocolate.

Fuck Stephen, he was too clever sometimes. The thought was in her head now and the memories were coming up fast. Her mother was saying, 'It's green all year round up here, you get tired of everything always being green sometimes.' It rained so much; the rain dripped through the great forest trees, and the trees were so massive and so close together that the water was always dripping underneath them, whether it was raining or not. You couldn't tell one kind of wet from another, rain or dew or clouds or fog, the trees made them all come to the same thing. It was a rainforest, not the media cliché sort old rock'n'roll singers droned on about saving, but the cold North Pacific rainforest where the natives fought off the loggers by themselves.

She saw her mother with water all around her, so many different kinds and forms and colours of water. They had to take a boat to get there, an hour on the still grey water of the Sound; misty rain and the little green pines coming down to the water's edge. Even in the house you could hear the water all the time, trickling through the ferns, oozing into the spongy floor of the forest. They went to a lake, where the water was an unbelievable turquoise because it came from melted glaciers. Sometimes when the sun shone above the forest and light struck through the canopy, the rays got lost in the wet air and broke up into rainbow mist.

The trees were called hemlocks, but they were not what the poison was made from, that was another plant. Her mother had a husband who was much younger than her but not as tall, with blond hair in a hideous footballer's haircut, and he was right into the forest. When Jane told people things about nature she had this awful Miss Jean Brodie way of doing it, but with him it was more that he assumed everyone was interested and mumbling on about the trees was only polite. The frogs started in the evening and he tried to make her hear the difference between the tree frogs and the others but they all sounded the same, exactly like cartoon frogs: *gribbit, gribbit.* They had been there a day and a night, a green dream.

She could hardly remember anything that had been said, except when the husband caught a salamander for her, and some worms to feed to it. Wonderful animal, a little dragon with a crest, paddling angrily around in a plastic bucket. It had savage jaws to chomp the worms and when you picked it up its flesh felt solid, as if it had been boiled.

Fucking chocolate: her throat felt as if the sides were sticking together. Stephen was asleep. What's the betting if I go looking for a bar he'll wake up and freak out because I'm gone. So he's going to have to wake up now, either way. She kicked his feet and his eyes reluctantly opened.

'Are you going to let me die of thirst here or what?'

'You want a drink?'

'Yes. Please.'

Scrubbing his eyes and tousling his hair, he got to his feet slowly. She tugged at the corner of his shirt.

'I tell you what about my mother . . .'

'Uh?'

'My mother. You were asking, weren't you? I was thinking. She couldn't run a beautiful house and maybe she couldn't cook gourmet lunch for fifty people either, but I think she's a normal person. That's what I think about her, since you want to know. I mean, she was teaching music, teaching tiny children. They wouldn't have given her the job if she was mad, would they? Didn't you think that?'

'Yes, that's what I thought. It must have been quite a trip for her, you showing up just like that, but she handled it OK, didn't she?'

'Yeah. I don't think she was mad, like he always said. I mean, living with my father would drive anyone mad, anyone normal.'

'I thought she'd had a tough life, you could see that. She looked older than I expected.'

'I didn't think she was so into drugs, either. Or him, her husband.' Actually, that had annoyed her. Since her first joint she had been telling herself that wanting to do drugs must be something she got from her mother.

'There wasn't anything in the house.'

'How do you know?'

'I looked.' He was still half-asleep, for a few seconds not thinking of how she would react. All of a sudden, she was enraged. Her face had actually turned red, she was so angry.

'You went through my mother's house looking for drugs?'

'I did it so they wouldn't know. I just woke up early in the morning, nobody else was up, and . . . don't look so disgusted. I only wanted to know. After what your father always says about her.'

'You're disgusting. Go and get me a drink, I don't want to have another row with you.'

Disgusting lingered in her mind after he had swayed away out of the carriage and out of sight. It's me that's disgusting; Stephen's just a great soft bear. I kick shit out of him and he gets softer and bearier and thinks all I need is love. Going to find my mother was his idea, although he did this great elaborate dance around me to put it in my head. Because I'd said we could get married one day. He shouldn't be pissing away his cleverness trying to get me to impersonate a human being.

Something came back, a fragment of conversation, just her mother and herself in the kitchen. She had been so shy about it. 'It seems like you've had problems, Imogen. I wish I'd known. If I could have done anything – you know – to help, I would have.' And Imi had groped around for one of her special tough, nasty little answers and instead come out with a plain one, 'I never thought to tell you.' And she'd said, 'We didn't have much money or anything, not like Michael. He used to just write and tell me you'd changed schools or something.'

That was it, all that came back.

She thought about makeup and rummaged in her bag. The train was swaying too much to do more than slap on some foundation. The rest could be done in the station. In the bottom of her cosmetics purse was the tiny plastic envelope with the square of strawbs and her present – she had forgotten about it.

Licking her finger to make it stick, she pulled Marc's free sample out to look at it: very ordinary-looking, a grey dot like a full stop, which meant nothing. Wacky-looking stuff on coloured card with silly faces could turn out to be a complete waste of time. It was reassuring to know she had something for emergencies. Her intention was to be straight today, but if things got too heavy she could just leave the party. And she had the temazepam to bring her down if necessary, she'd popped it in while Stephen wasn't looking. Here he was, bringing the drinks.

Good smile, her mother had. Flat lips like women got when they were older, and her front teeth were not quite straight, but it was a good smile. Imi smiled at herself in the train window, wondering if when she was older and her lips flattened out she would be able to smile the same way. You probably needed crooked teeth for that sort of smile. She had rich kid's teeth, perfect white tombstones, although one of the lower ones seemed to be loose.

'Look,' she said to Stephen, rocking the tooth in its socket like a child.

He flinched. 'Don't do that, it looks horrible.' So she did it again.

*

The caterers arrived in two trucks at 8 a.m. and Jane was up to meet them. Waking early was a habit with her now; it had begun with Emma and her sleepless nights, and continued with the accumulating anxieties of her life. Businesslike in shirt and slacks, trying not to think about Michael or to feel her tiredness, she distributed copies of the final plan for the day. Always, at this moment, it seemed absolutely impossible that everything would be ready in time.

In the fresh morning air the work began. The skylark was up, relentlessly pouring song down on the scene from the cloudless turquoise heavens. Deep shadows still etched the shape of every clod and tussock, bringing the whole landscape into high relief.

This year there were so many guests that Jane had decided on two tables, and since the weather was obviously set fair she ordered them to be set up under the young oak trees. The first truck carrying canopies, flooring, tables and linen drove slowly down to the edge of the wood. Men set off to mark out the field behind the caretakers' cottage as a car park. The cooks, two young men and a woman, took over the kitchen. Thus scattered, the army kept in touch by portable telephone.

Michael also woke early; on his uneasy mind lay the long shadow of the chairman of Altmark, Alan Stern. Talking fluently, even glibly, to the media ownership committee had been a simple intellectual exercise; their concerns about the merger were so far from his own. At the moment when NewsConnect joined the Altmark group he would more than double his personal wealth but at the same time lose his autonomy. Ten years ago – he could only now admit it to himself – taking his destiny in his own hands had been terrifying. Without Grace to anchor him he would never have made the transition; he remembered calling her constantly, just to reassure himself that in a world which had suddenly become huge and alien there was one person by his side.

Now it seemed as frightening to merge into a larger group. He would need to move in fast and dominate his territory. Once more, he would be dealing with a hierarchy. He thought of the complex network of alliances in the Altmark group, of the relationships which needed constant monitoring and servicing if he was to prevail. Above all, he thought of Stern.

Michael became fully conscious, and aware of feeling lousy. He had drunk too much: mistake. Stern was famous for his Lutheran intolerance. Drinking, smoking, business entertaining and divorce were not encouraged at Altmark. In the courtship phase of their negotiations Stern had been amiable, as he might have been expected to be. His negotiators had been tough, as Michael had expected them to be. The honeymoon would shortly be over – then what?

With determination, Michael got to his feet and went into the bathroom, telling himself that he had laid strong foundations with Stern and all that was needed now was to raise a strong friendship upon them.

He shaved with great care and dressed without enjoyment; casual clothing always made him feel vulnerable.

Jane had brought out his new suit for the day, blue and black striped linen, cut loose, with a white shirt. Downstairs, the bustle in the kitchen irritated him and he disappeared into his study, where he sat over a cup of coffee, faced his memories of the previous night and worked through an hour of self-loathing. Then his attention flowed on to the day ahead, and he began to rationalize everything that troubled him; he had drunk too much, his actions would be forgotten. Jane was on edge before the party. He would go to her now and make amends. Essential that she should be smiling and content by the time Stern arrived. Important for the family portrait to be fully animated.

If he was questioned, Michael always affirmed his respect for his wife, for her intelligence, for her success and for being a good mother. This was the only one of the many liberties he took with actuality in order to maintain his marriage which he admitted to himself was a lie. He did not respect Jane, he despised her. She sacrificed too much for him. Thus apologizing to her was difficult.

He took a few more minutes to put himself in the right frame of mind, and before he left the room he found Serena's number on a scrap of paper in his wallet and called it.

'This is me,' he announced. 'How are you?'

'Where are you calling from?' Her voice was muffled and, he thought, annoyed.

'My office. My office in the house.'

'Oh. Look . . .'

'Have I picked a bad time?'

'Yes . . . I . . .' Confusion, maybe even panic in her voice.

'I'll try you again later.' He used a reassuring tone.

'Good. That would be fine. Take care now.' And she hung up. Evasive, but he could not spare the energy to speculate on her reasons just then.

Apart from the kitchen, the house seemed deserted. Debbie and the children kept to their quarters and the guests were not yet about. In Jane's office he found an elegant woman of about fifty with sleek chestnut-brown hair tied back in a blue velvet ribbon. She greeted him brightly and he remembered that she was the calligrapher. Sitting at Jane's desk with the final seating plan and an open bottle of dark red ink, she was preparing to write out the place cards and menu sheets.

'Even more guests than last year.' She dipped her head to one side with a smile to indicate that she was complimenting him. 'Would you like me to begin with the name cards? I remember you like to take a look at the *placement* yourself, and anyway it seems there are one or two queries on it still.'

'Sounds good to me,' he told her. 'Let me see the plan.' Nervously, Michael took up a pencil and began to look down the list of acceptances, needing to reassure himself that guests were expected. Even at his current level of eminence, he was not proof against the insecurity of a party-giver; he was afraid that no one would come, or that the Sterns would pull out at the eleventh hour.

'I haven't seen your wife,' the calligrapher remarked.

'Nor have I.' The acceptance list was gratifying.

'I will need to see her before I begin the seating plan.'

'When you're ready we'll find her together. I want to congratulate her myself.'

'This is always the great event of the year for us.' With delicate care, the woman folded each square of card after writing it, and arranged them in a line for the ink to dry. The card was hand-pressed, with tiny green leaves and pink carnation petals. 'We do bigger occasions, it's true, but Madame Knight has such good taste . . .'

Michael accepted the compliment.

In the wood, Jane was thankful to have a task to keep her away from the house. Her mood was bleak as she watched the tables and chairs being unloaded from the caterers' truck. Another battle lost to Michael, and yet as she turned the events of the night over she could not see where her victory could have been seized. He would be furious, and frustrated because they had pledged themselves to spend the day smiling together in public and so his anger would have to wait.

Added to that, Imogen was coming. Jane could picture her. She would wear something outlandish and draw everybody's eye as she drifted into the gathering. That knowing half-smile would be slow-burning across her face, her eyes would be too wide and too innocent, the idiotic look she had when she had her father at a disadvantage; it threw Michael into such an agony of apprehension that even if she behaved perfectly he would be drained by the anxiety.

'Coo-ee! Jane!' With a mug of coffee splashing in one hand, Louisa in her bathrobe was rolling across the grass in her direction, every movement large with dissatisfaction. 'I've been looking for you everywhere.' She appropriated a rush-seated, green Van Gogh chair as it was handed off the truck and traped herself over it with a groan.

'How did you sleep?' enquired Jane euphemistically.

'Oh God, *don't*.' The cranberry mouth pursed with distaste. 'Antony just fell over. Fell over. He has not moved for eight hours.' She sighed. 'Do you think that women who don't like sex have happier lives?'

Nervously, Jane glanced at the caterers' staff who were now unpacking tablecloths and cutlery. They were mostly students doing vacation work; she had asked for English-speakers, but fortunately their own conversation was absorbing and they were taking no interest in the client and her friend.

'He always has liked his drink, Antony.'

'Telling me. So, do you think they do? Would your life be easier if you didn't like sex?'

'It would be easier if I had a choice.' Was there any chance that Louisa could understand?

'What do you mean? That Michael's such a sensational lover . . .' Apologetically, someone explained that the chair was needed. Louisa flounced off it and lounged over the wheel arch of the truck. 'Is that thing on?' She pointed to the telephone in Jane's hand.

Smiling for the first time in twelve hours, Jane pressed the off button. 'I don't have so much to compare him with, but Michael's not a great lover. I mean, technically he is . . .'

Louisa raised her eyebrows. '*Technically?*'

'He does all the right things, he plays me like a violin, he makes me come . . .'

'And you're *complaining*? Jane, this is a revelation!' Fully awake at last, Louisa sat up and pushed back her hair as if to hear better. 'So what are you saying?'

'Well, I certainly wouldn't call it making love, although he's got all the dialogue. I wouldn't call it lust, or passion, or sensuality or desire or hunger – I honestly don't think he can feel those things.'

'Jane! So why on earth does he screw around the way he does?'

'Don't you see that if it was all just for sex it would be easy?' She dropped her voice and looked fearfully around, even up at the sky, as if retribution for publicizing the secrets of the marriage bed might strike from anywhere. 'For me, it would be easy. I could say off you go, dear, have your fun, we'll have separate bedrooms and a civilized arrangement. I wish to God he was a good old-fashioned lecher, then we could have a good old-fashioned marriage.'

Jane leaned closer to Louisa's ear, leaning on the hot metal and speaking in a whisper the words which were now seething in her head. 'What Michael does is the newest, most refined technique of modern sexual warfare. Michael isn't a new man, remember. Michael is a new hero. He's the founder of NewsConnect but his family comes first. Which is another way of saying he wants it all, including me, including the deepest, most private, most intimate parts of me, including my sexual satisfaction. Heart and mind, vagina and uterus. And talking about it. My God, does he talk about it. And about us. And he uses sex to fix everything. Like now, when he's got a new woman. Or if he's jealous because I've signed a new series – oh yes, he is jealous, but being Mr Perfect he can't act jealous, so he stages another epic fuck scene with champagne in the bath or whatever to show he's not jealous. And if I ever, *ever* even suggested that I didn't like sex – my God, I think we'd have to talk about it so much that I'd be having multiple orgasms until my pelvic floor blew out.'

She scanned Louisa's face for comprehension and did not quite find it. But there was sympathy. Louisa was at least distracted from her own problems. 'I had no idea you two were so – messed up,' she murmured.

'Neither did I. Until you asked.'

'Oh God. What a pair we are.' Louisa heaved herself upright and came forward to give Jane a hug. It was awkward, because Jane had never liked being mauled by emotional women, but she needed it.

'Hadn't you better get dressed? You'll be getting me a very interesting reputation with the waiters.' She pulled Louisa's robe decently about her.

'Hadn't you? It's past eleven already.'

They returned to the house through the pool garden, where a small bar had been set up under a candy-striped canopy and the white umbrellas shaded the terrace. The caretaker, a muscular, long-jawed ex-soldier who worked as a fitness instructor at Saint-Victor's police college, was sweeping the pool while his wife dead-headed the geraniums.

Michael was coming towards them with the calligrapher at his side. Her radiant animation suggested that he had given her the full benefit of his charm. Jane felt resentment at the sight of him, spruce and clear-eyed, behaving as if nothing of consequence had taken place the night before, but he immediately came forward and took her to one side, saying, 'Forgive me, J. I was drunk I know, and I'm on edge over this Altmark business, but there's no real excuse. I acted badly, I'm really sorry.'

For a moment, she could not respond. 'Don't look at me like that, I can't bear it,' he went on. 'If you can't say anything right now, that's fine. But I am sorry, really and truly. You must have been so angry.'

'Yes,' she managed, 'but don't say any more. That's all right, I heard you.'

'Really?' His eyes were searching hers intently but she had no intention of allowing him into her feelings, so she met his gaze blankly.

'Yes.'

'OK. That's very generous. I wanted to say what a wonderful thing you've done organizing today. I wanted to thank you.' He kissed her gently on the cheek and since they were being observed by strangers she felt obliged to accept it without flinching. 'The seating plan is almost finished – can you help us with one or two queries? Who are these two – Mr and Mrs Nicholas Nichols?'

The name immediately relieved her chill distaste. In an unnecessarily loving tone, she said, 'You remember Grace Evans, Michael. Wasn't she one of your producers?

She's married now; Nick's her husband, a friend of mine.' Then she looked him squarely in the eye.

'Wasn't Grace a producer when you were with the network?' To mask her interest in his response, Louisa found a plate of truffled canapés to sample.

Michael reacted only with an eager, approving smile. 'Grace Evans – good, *good.* That's so typical of you, J, you're so thoughtful. I'd love to see her again. It's been years.' All he did was make an alteration to the seating plan. 'And would you like him near you?'

'I don't mind. He's in AIDS research in Paris. Maybe he'd have a good conversation with Amina. Or Stuart. Or Morris.' She wanted to kick him, or hit him: anything to crack open the pretence, but somehow he had put himself beyond reach of her emotions in a place she dared not follow.

'I'll take care of it. Are you going up to change?'

Her self-control suddenly perilous, Jane was already walking towards the steps to the house. Louisa said, 'Happy birthday, Michael dear,' and kissed him on both cheeks. For an instant, he was surprised, having forgotten the cause of the celebration. Emma appeared from the house, with her tiny sister anxiously following, and Debbie at a distance behind. Between them the girls carried a long banner of lining paper daubed with birthday greetings. 'And Sam says he's doing you a picture on his computer but it will take longer,' his daughter added with jealous disdain.

'Great. Lovely. This is marvellous. Where are you going to put it?'

Debbie had resumed her withdrawn front, but she knew what was expected in this situation. 'Em, why don't we go and stick it up by the gate, so all the guests can see it?'

'Yes! Yes!' The child was jumping with excitement.

'Hey, chill out now, cool it down – you're going to tear the thing.'

Nick had named it Silence of the Lambs Corner. The communal abattoir stood at the junction of the Castillon road with the departmental highway. A complex of towers and ducts constructed of shining metal, it bore no name and operated all hours. Day or night, you could hear the pigs squealing from the road.

'So what's he like, this Michael Knight?' Nick asked at last. He put his foot down as they hit the wide highway.

'Michael? He's extraordinary.' It was a catechism Grace had said a thousand times; people always asked about Michael. 'He's a man who has everything. Mainly, he has vision – such vision. Whatever we were doing he had the concept in his head, perfect in every detail, and all he had to do was communicate it to us and it happened. He was inspiring, he really was.'

They were in the MGB, with the top up for the sake of Grace's hair. The road was empty and Nick, who considered that if a speedometer was marked in miles a speed limit in kilometres was inapplicable, had his foot on the floor and his eyes in the dusty distance. Poplar trees cast bars of shade over the tarmac, but hardly cooled the road or hid the garish warehouses and factories of the Saint-Victor industrial park.

'When he started NewsConnect there was a great opening party and he just stood up and said something like, "This is more than a news agency, this is an ideal. We are here, all of us, at the service of the truth in the world. All we are here to do is take the news and tell it the way it is." He has a magnificent voice, he should have been an actor. Then he said, "You may think that's a simple thing, but I believe that when the people of this planet understand each other then there will be a world-wide outbreak of peace." And then he quoted from the Bible, Isaiah, they shall beat their swords into ploughshares, he actually picked up the book, and then ran on to say, "And nation shall speak peace unto nation." And people cried. Even people who knew he'd misquoted – it was the old BBC motto, dreamed up by the Governors in the Twenties – had tears in their eyes. And four hundred people gladly worked their backsides off for peanuts and the occasional herogram, because they were working for world peace. That was ten years ago, and I can remember almost every word.'

There was no response from her husband. 'Are you listening?' she asked.

He looked at her from the corner of his eyes. 'Yes, but what's he *like*?' A tanker transporting unthinkable mega-litres of yoghurt was ahead of them, farting fumes, maintaining a stately pace in the centre of the road.

'Asshole!' he yelled suddenly. 'Get your stinking back-side outa my face!'

'Personally, what's he like? He's pleasing, compulsively pleasing – charming, terribly funny, the most caring man in the world when he wants to be . . .' She paused, recalling the exquisite illusion that she was Michael's whole world. He wove it from a thousand tender threads, calls and notes, jokes and remembrances, silly presents, and above all his total concentration upon her in the moments when they were together. It was years before she noticed that he gave everyone else the same exalted attention, for the same fragments of time.

The car lurched violently; Nick was trying to pull out, hazardous in a low, left-hand-drive sports car. The passenger's duty was to be the driver's eyes. 'I can't see the road,' she told him, 'there's a blind bend coming.'

He pulled back, but she could feel his irritation mounting. 'Go on, I'm listening. Pillock! Go suck cocks in hell!'

'I had no idea you knew such language.'

There was an ill-tempered pause, then he said, 'Just tell me when the road's clear.'

'No luck, there are three trucks coming down now.' He kept the car's nose dangerously close to the tanker's rear, ready to pull out as soon as he could. She went on, 'Michael does have great intelligence, but more than that, great concentration, that's his real gift, I suppose. He's insecure – much more than you'd imagine. He can't bear anyone to have a bad opinion of him. He was always asking what people are thinking, what they're saying . . .'

Again, Nick swerved violently, to avoid a double-rig cattle truck thundering past in the oncoming lane, a drool of manure trailing from its tailgate. 'Now, you fucking moron, let me out willya?' He pulled out again, slammed down a gear and screamed past the yoghurt tanker yelling, 'Eat shit and die, fuckface!'

Grace was frightened, and his language offended her, but she said nothing about it, certain that in talking about Michael with too much passion she had betrayed herself. This response was instinctive jealousy. She prayed that he would not ask her to confirm his suspicions – right now, she would have to lie again, neither of them would get through the day otherwise. Did a painful day mean more than her marriage, then? Dear God, she was still hung up on Michael's good opinion.

The car was cruising evenly, so she opened her eyes and reached over to touch Nick's arm. 'I do love you, Nick,' she said. It did feel true when she said it.

He was still glaring malevolently at the tanker in his mirror.

'You're so normal. Such a normal man. You forget our anniversaries, you can't say "I love you" except in bed and you turn into an animal in a car.' She felt weak and childish, almost out of control.

'I suppose you'd rather I was an animal in bed and said "I love you" in the car? What's so lovable about it? Sounds pathetic to me.'

'I don't know – something seems so right about you. You're just the way you have to be. I'm sorry, I'm not making sense . . . have you got a handkerchief?' He had real handkerchiefs, old-fashioned cotton squares that she found impossible to get clean in the wash; every Sunday he boiled seven of them in a saucepan. She pulled one from his trouser pocket, a crumpled item smelling faintly of lubricating oil, and dabbed her eyes. 'There's nothing to be nervous over,' she added, feeling that he needed reassurance.

'I'm not nervous.' This was said with a bitterness that she had never heard him use before. Guiltily, she waited for his accusation, but all he said was, 'Let go of my arm, I've got to change down.'

Despite her brave red dress, Grace knew she was overwrought. She made herself take deep breaths, trying to calm the tension that was eating into her mood like acid.

'Did you do your spit test this morning?' he asked without warning.

'Damn, no. I forgot. I'll do it when we get back.'

'You have to do it in the morning. Hormone levels are highest then.'

'Then I've missed a day. I'm sorry.'

'There's no need to apologize. You can just skip a day.' Now she was irritated. All through their infertility treatment he had been one move ahead of her, just because he knew more about medical procedures, and conscientiously cross-checked her treatment with his books or his colleagues.

'I wish you'd be my husband when we're talking about this, instead of being another doctor – you make me feel incompetent, and that I haven't got any privacy.'

'I'm sorry, I thought I was being helpful.' An icy tone. They were having a row, in as much as they had rows. He was afraid of confronting her. Nick hated aggression and certainly, with him, Grace checked her temper; she was afraid their connection was too fragile to survive a real fight.

In silence, they were approaching Saint-Victor's castellated battlements, which enclosed the crown of the highest hill for five hundred miles around. The road forked at the bottom, sweeping around the base of the fortifications. The old stone walls curtained with creepers looked inviting after the valley of commercial brutality below. Grace was never happy to be early for a party, so he chose to drive through the town.

They passed an imposing façade behind elaborate iron gates, with a tricolour hanging from a flagpole. It was a police college. Eager to sweeten the atmosphere, she was suddenly enchanted. 'This must be the prettiest town in France,' she exclaimed, craning out of the window as he turned up the main street. The buildings were all of white stone washed with pale gold, decorated with colonnades and porticos, the elegant townhouses visible through noble gateways under carved coats of arms. Humble doorknockers enchanted her, the lace curtains were adorable, the ironwork balconies were the finest she had ever seen and she marvelled that even the paving slabs were of the same yellow-veined rock.

'But it's too pretty, isn't it? It's almost artificial. Why . . .'

'The town burned down some time in the seventeenth century and they rebuilt it all at the same time and all in the same stone. The yellow tint comes from local deposits of chromium.'

'That's not in the Michelin.' She had already opened the guidebook.

'Jane Knight told me.' He turned off into the level, gravelled area at the top of the battlements, once a military parade ground, now a site for *fêtes* and dances, with a municipal bandstand and pink tamarisk trees shading the *boules* pitches. 'And here's the bar with the best view in Gascony.'

'Did she tell you that too?' He noticed that her mood deflated at the mention of Jane.

'No, I figured it out for myself.' He ordered coffee for himself and her preferred *kir aux mûres*, made with blackberry liqueur, but while they were waiting for the order to be executed he got to his feet and walked away from her to the edge of the flattened ground, where he leaned on the battlement wall and looked out over the misty patchwork of fields. She knew better than to follow. When they were troubled he would go away by himself for a while, then return, thinking he had avoided the storm. Sometimes he was right.

His coffee was tepid by the time he came back. After a while, he said, 'I thought there was something not quite right about Jane Knight.'

'I thought she was your heroine.'

'She was but she seemed – washed out, somehow. I see it in patients sometimes, when they've been suffering a long, long time, so long that the pain is almost their best friend. Then it becomes the most important thing in their lives, and they actually don't want you to get rid of it for them. It's one of the real mysteries in medicine, how people can love their pain, even while it's killing them.'

For a while she sipped her drink in silence, arranging her thoughts, remembering his innocence in the ways of her old world. 'Have you heard the stories about Michael? About women, I mean?'

He shook his head. 'Well, Michael has a lot of women. A lot of affairs. He always has had, all through their marriage. I don't know why she stays with him. He's a terrible husband. That's the kind of man he is, one woman is never enough, even the most wonderful in the world.'

'What is it, then? Sex?'

'I don't think he's a very sexual man. Not the way you are.' Careful, don't give too much away. 'He wants the big stuff, the love and the care and the worrying and the praise and the reassurance. I think it's part of his ambition.'

'You didn't say he was ambitious.'

'No, I didn't.' She shook her head, considering the power of Michael's persuasion, even after all these years. 'Because he hates people to think he's ambitious. He wants it all, you see. Absolutely everything, including everyone's love, everyone's admiration. And he must need something special from women, because he just eats women up, one after the other. Greed, that's what it is.'

'So that's how a man gets to have everything, then?'

'Just by being greedy for everything? Maybe.'

He reached across the table and squeezed her arm; she

was comforted and so was he. Somehow, they had told each other what they both needed to hear.

'We'd better go,' he said. The waiter came, and she stood up with reluctance, holding out her dress to let the breeze shake out the creases of the journey.

'Stephen, we have to find a *pharmacie*.'

'OK. We can ask to stop on the way to the house. There must be one in the town somewhere.'

Imogen favoured him with a warm, grateful smile; men were such suckers for female biology. Just hint that something to do with periods was coming down and they were so keen to get into deep empathy mode that you could get away with anything.

'Are you OK?' he asked.

'Oh, sure.' She tossed him the reply sarcastically. 'You know I love Daddy's parties.' That old familiar feeling was creeping up her throat. Standing there in the middle of all those people being asked moron questions about what she was studying and what she wanted to do, Jane's horrible brats festering around the place and those great dreary lumps, the Moynihan kids, sniggering behind their hands because she wasn't like them, she wasn't doing European Studies or a gap year teaching leper children in Somalia, and she didn't have twenty pounds of puppy fat and half a million zits to lose. And Daddy, exaggerating everything and trying to pretend he was proud of her, but really just storing up things to criticize her for afterwards. She felt as if she could start choking at any moment.

Between fields and orchards, the train was crawling

along the flat floor of the Garonne valley. They had travelled nearly three hundred miles and where the earth was exposed it showed rich southern colours, reds and ochres; against it the spiky onion tops gleamed almost blue and the young potatoes foamed emerald. The vines here were already golden. Stacks of fruit crates stood in the corners of the fields, waiting to be filled with melons, yellow peaches, white peaches, early apples and late strawberries.

They got out at Agen, where the full force of the summer heat beat up from the platform and the whole station shimmered in a haze. A young woman with long dark hair was looking out for them.

'Hi there, I'm Mrs Knight's nanny, my name is Debbie.' Imogen surrendered her bag. So many arrivals, so many strange young women introducing themselves in the same form. It was good to be adult at last, and no longer dependent on these hired personalities for the success of the summer vacation.

'We need to stop at a pharmacy,' Stephen explained.

'No problem,' she responded, 'There is one open somewhere all day today, for medicines. I wouldn't mind picking up some stuff for Emma at the same time. We're getting through her cream really fast, with them being in and out of the pool all day.'

Damn, the nanny was going to come in with her. They drove around the town looking for the Sunday dispensary, and when it was found Imogen bought tampons and Debbie bought skin cream. As they came back to the car, Imogen allowed Debbie to lead, and made sure she was in the driving seat before flouncing to a halt on the pavement. 'I've left my stuff,' she called out and went back into the shop. So simple. They didn't suspect a thing. Three disposable syringes into the bottom of the bag in thirty seconds, and out she came again. The girls in the dispensary never reacted, the French were so busy shooting themselves full of vitamins and collagen.

In the back of the car she sank down in the seat out of view of the driving mirror and began to freshen her makeup. The microdot was in the bottom of the purse, almost winking at her. Quite safe to take it now, because if it was too much to handle she had the T to bring her down. Some dope would have been nice; the ideal way was to mellow out first and then get going from that base. Especially with new stuff, that was the best, but Marc was reliable, she'd heard no bad word on microdots and if there had been any dope Stephen would have made her leave it behind. Dear man, he was talking to the nanny about the weather. It had been hot, but the forecast was stormy, she was saying.

Imogen uncapped a pot of lip balm and rubbed a spot in the centre of her lower lip, then licked her finger, picked up the dot and transferred it to her tongue with the same gesture. Excellent. Even if she was visible in the mirror, that girl would never have seen anything. She closed her makeup purse and put her feet up on the seat, waiting to go somewhere more interesting than down the Roman road and past the old watchtower to Les Palombières.

*

Children. As they emerged from the track between the sunflowers, and Les Palombières stood before them decorated for the celebration, Grace realized that there would be children. Respectful of her car's low suspension, Nick turned slowly into the field where cars were parked. There were six or seven little figures in bright-coloured clothes running up and down the terrace at the side of the house. Some of them must be Michael's. Everyone will be watching me and thinking how hopeless I am with them and how fortunate all round that I can't have any. I *will not* have this ridiculous thought in my head. She flipped down the vanity mirror and reached for her lipstick.

'This can't be worse than scuba-diving.' Nick came over and helped her out of the car. Unconsciously, she had been touching the scar on her forehead.

She shook her head, fluffing up her hair. 'You can't burst a lung leaving a party early. Let's plunge in.'

A large new Mercedes, a large old Mercedes, a classic BMW and a Mitsubishi Shogun already occupied the parking field. The route to the terrace was marked with posies of pink roses tied with green ribbon and fixed to the tree trunks.

A maid held a tray of cocktails, the Rapier Thrust, champagne and *pousse rapière* liqueur made from oranges and Armagnac. '*Un pour tous*,' Nick toasted her. '*Et tous pour un*,' she replied and drank. It was not right, they could not be one for all when they were only two.

Staff in green and white invited them to move down the terrace, and through the arch overhung with honeysuckle which led to the pool. At the top of the steps they paused involuntarily to appreciate the scene. The pool and its surrounding garden were nestled between two spurs of creamy white rock, and large boulders of it seemed to have tumbled haphazardly down the hillside. Between them, cypress spires and low bushes grew; there was no obvious colour scheme, but the planting favoured lavender bushes and strong pink and purple flowers. Here and there stood large earthenware pots.

'It's a bit *Marie Claire Maison.*' From Nick, this observation came hesitantly with the hint of a question, since he was unsure that he had the name of the magazine right, what Grace's feelings were about *Marie Claire Maison*, or if the vista was indeed typical of it; he was only sure that it was an intimidatingly expensive sight and he felt out of place.

Conscious of making her entrance, Grace walked slowly down the curved gravel path. The paving had been done with old dressed building stones of a light grey which was gentle on the eyes. The pool itself was a classic rectangle, with an iron lion's head fountain spouting quietly at the deep end; across the water the view down the shallow valley was interrupted only by a pair of immense terracotta pots from which geraniums trailed in abundance.

About twenty people were making eager conversation under the sunshades. Grace saw Michael at once, and was surprised to feel nothing particular. His face was more lined, he seemed bony rather than slender, his hair was still brown and needed cutting – as always. He did not see her. Alan Stern of Altmark dominated the gathering with no effort. 'Who's the Mount Rushmore face?' Nick whispered, and she told him.

Stern was built on a heroic scale, broad and muscular, blond hair swept back from a high forehead; he matched his host in height but beside his athletic solidity Michael looked fidgety. The wife, Berenice, was posed beside her husband, glancing warily up at the cypress trees as if she expected them to fall on her at any moment. She wore a yellow silk hat which hid most of her black hair, and a matching yellow linen dress with a strapless top and gilt snaps down the front. At the edge of the group a young man with slick dark hair, fashionable in collarless shirt and waistcoat, hovered at Michael's elbow, waiting for the moment to raid the conversation and make his mark.

'There's Jane, right over there behind the hippopotamus in the spinnaker.' Nick was half-whispering in her ear.

'It's Andy Moynihan. She's always been that big, she can't help it. They used to be good friends.' Now there was a stab of emotion. She had no recollection of her first meeting with Andy, after her accident; Michael had introduced them two years later, when Andy had made an offensive hash of explaining their connection. Now she could detect a formality between the two women which prompted her instinct that they were no longer friends.

'She could help that dress, though. We'll have to lash her to the deck if the wind gets up.' It was a garment typical of Andy, yards of splashy batik.

'They're the only people we know, we're going to have to talk to them.'

'Not necessarily.' He nudged her elbow and she saw Louisa undulating towards them, radiating social expectancy. For six tempestuous months, Grace's newspaper had retained Louisa as food editor, a role she interpreted as requiring monthly trips to Paris, to the severe detriment of the features budget and to the benefit of Grace, who had never dined so well in her life.

'*Grace!* My dear, *what* a surprise!' One cheek after the other, excessively made up for the climate and the occasion, was offered for kissing. 'And is this your *husband*?' Nobody pronounced the word 'husband' quite like Louisa, although some people had a similar breath-held way of saying 'Galapagos tortoise' or 'white rhinoceros'.

Jane's attention was attracted by the loud greeting. She was still disturbed by the events of the night, and playing cool was beyond her. She eyed her husband's sometime mistress with blatant fascination. Striking, definitely, taller than she had imagined, wonderful bones. Jane willed herself to approach, noticing that the couple were standing independently of each other. 'And this scarlet woman must be your wife?' she heard herself say brightly.

'We met years ago, when I worked with your husband.' Plainly delivered, with neither offence nor pretence, followed by a dry handshake; neither of us is quite the kissy-kissy type. How extraordinary, we are not at all alike. Grace found herself inspecting Jane; in fact, Jane was almost offering herself up for it, standing quietly with her hands by her sides as if to say, well – this is me, a neat figure in a cinnamon brown tunic, the dowdy mate of the showy male.

'How brave you are to wear red.'

'Not really – I feel brave once I've put it on. I think it's braver to be subtle.' A flush of pleasure, even under the tan. Relaxing, Grace noticed details of the terrace; the old foundations restored as ornamental arches, the blending of colours in the garden, the placing of each cypress so the eye was led in tantalizing steps past the shining water and out to the view beyond. 'How lovely you've made this house.'

'I didn't really make it, that woman over there did.' A little rabbit-twitch of a smile as she pointed out an angular, uncoordinated body under a panama hat.

'Tamara Aylesham – our design writer did a story on her my first year in France. Tamara Lady Aylesham, decorator extraordinary to the international Francophiles.'

'Extraordinary was the right word.'

'I always wondered how she got on with her clients.'

'At the time, she was good company.' Jane remembered long afternoons beside the pool at the local hotel, lounging under the sun with a hat on her pregnant belly to shade Sam's unborn eyes, while Tamara, well lubricated after lunch, lost swatches, dropped samples and let her calculator fall in the water.

'Aren't they farming wild boar now?'

'In a manner of speaking.'

'Not a success, then?'

'They're great rooters, the *sangliers.* They root up their

fences and then they charge out into the fields and root up the crops.'

'You're talking about my savage piggies!' The decorator extraordinary windmilled towards them. 'You've never heard such cheek – the mayor came to see me and said I had to give up, the farmers were furious with me. I told him they ought to hunt them, I wouldn't mind . . .'

'Great sport, boars. Dangerous, you know, you need the right dogs.' Tamara's fourth husband left conspiring with Anthony to ensure a supply of whisky and joined them. 'Rhodesian ridgebacks would do the job . . .'

'Darling, do you think we should breed them instead? Let the piggies breed themselves? Boar shooting at the Château . . .' The conversation crackled merrily around ways Tamara and her husband could redeploy their dwindling assets to provide an income sufficient to maintain a castle without needing to get up before lunchtime more than once a week.

Jane said, 'Did you ever meet Graham Moynihan? Michael's old partner? Interesting man?' and seeing Nick hugely amused Grace let herself be taken away from him, wondering why neither she nor Jane seemed to be feeling the antagonism that was expected of two women involved with the same man.

She was aware now that Michael was aware of her. How many times they had played this scene, both cool and social, she almost nauseous with the tension of pretence, he flawless in his timing. First the flash of greeting containing the silent promise of a semi-private conversation later. He would choose the time. Useless to cut across his will in that, she had tried it once and his bubbling spring of amusing conversation had dried at once, leaving them high and dry as strangers until someone else approached.

The terrace was becoming crowded. So many familiar faces, just a little more lined after five years. Moynihan was stoop-shouldered with a dry, lopsided smile; his wife, for all her weight, would be a girl forever, with bright, naïve brown eyes. She talked to their kids, a blond boy and a brown-haired girl who towered bashfully over most of the adults, politely answering questions about their exams. 'I know this is a gruesome thing to say, but I haven't seen you since you were little moppets waiting for the tooth fairy.'

'That's OK, just don't go on about how much we've grown, all right?'

She let the gathering crowd take her where it would, talking to a French lawyer, the neighbouring Belgians, two jolly gay writers from the far side of Castillon, and Berenice Stern, who she decided was living proof that a woman could be too rich and too thin but still be too Versace and blow the lot. Morris Donaldson appeared, the most changed of them all, his pleasant rounded face lost in the bloating of his cheeks and neck. Perspiration already stained his shirt, and with him came a dark-haired woman Grace did not recognize but presumed to be his former researcher and second wife. She looked uncomfortable balancing a large baby on one hip and holding a shy older boy by the hand, out of place in her short, tight-skirted suit.

A fresh-faced boy in green breeches appeared and conferred with Jane. Under his arm was a hunting horn glinting in the sun. Nobody could look at their watch as slyly as Michael. It was past one. Unobtrusively, he pulled Jane away from the crowd.

'Where's Imogen?'

'I don't know, isn't she here?' She was irritated. He had made no move himself to check on his daughter's arrival.

'Has she rung?'

'You know if she wasn't coming she wouldn't bother telling us. Yes, Stephen called, from the train. They were expecting to be here on time.'

'Stephen . . .'

'Why must you always be down on that boy – you know he's been the saving of Imi's life.'

'That's your opinion.'

'It's the general opinion. I've sent Debbie to meet them.'

'Then where are they?' he demanded immediately, brazen-faced. Evidently he believed that he had apologized enough that the night before could now become a fading memory.

'I don't know. Maybe I overestimated Debbie's capacity to get over attempted rape.'

'Jane, what is the matter with you? That's an unkind thing to say, it's not like you . . . why are you trying to undermine me today?'

'Please don't use that tone of voice to me.' Amazing that he could be bursting with rage and the only sign was the darkening of his eyes and the compression of his brows which made him glare like an eagle. He left her abruptly. She found herself pleased to have succeeded in making him angry.

The Moynihans had goaded her; they had arrived first, bringing with them bitter memories. 'How are you?' Andy had enquired, implying that she knew the answer, and it was not good, but she had no intention of hearing any conversation on the subject. Graham had given her his hearty handshake and said the same thing, 'How are you, Jane?'

What a fool she had been to presume that because Andy had brought her the bad news, and been the first confidante of her unhappiness, their friendship was to endure. She had learned immediately how defenceless the wife of a powerful man becomes when she chooses to oppose her husband. Her mistake had been to assume that because Andy sympathized with her, Graham would do the same. Over a kitchen supper at their house, with Emma, six months old, asleep in her Moses basket, she had dissolved into tears because on Michael's desk at home she had found a notebook with Grace Evans's name on it and a recent date. 'There's no significance in that,' Graham had asserted immediately from the head of the table. 'It's ridiculous to assume anything because Michael's picked up a producer's notes. He probably needs them.' Andy, at the stove behind her husband, made an alarmed face but Jane ignored it. 'It's not ridiculous, I know they're having an affair.' 'You can't possibly claim that kind of knowledge,' he had told her, and then allowed an uncomfortable silence to fall, making her feel that she had been unpardonably rude to question the character of his friend under his roof.

She was never invited to their house without Michael again. Within a year Andy distanced herself, pleading her workload and her family, and Jane realized that without it being asked Graham had disciplined his wife into loyalty to Michael. Masculine *force majeure* prevailed, and cut her off. Even when Michael ousted him from the NewsConnect board, Graham apparently did not consider it proper to allow his wife to associate with her.

Standing by herself at the end of the gathering party, Jane reflected that most of the couples in the room would behave the same way. Beside Michael's influence, her poached salmon and handwritten place cards counted for nothing. No wonder Berenice Stern was so vinegary. Jane shook off her cynicism and decided that lunch should wait no longer. Imogen was late as usual.

Thinking that Grace was still tense, Nick leaned towards her and said quietly, 'Are you all right? You look all right. You know all these people, don't you? It's not an ordeal after all.'

He himself was glowing with enjoyment. Grace poked him gently in the stomach, knowing how much he would be looking forward to the meal. 'You really can enjoy other people's good fortune as much as if it was your own, can't you?'

'Of course. That's the best way, isn't it? How much nicer it is to enjoy all this than to have to organize it, eh?' He noticed that she had not really answered him.

A second youth bearing a hunting horn appeared and the pair took up positions either side of the terrace steps. At a nod from Jane they raised their instruments and blew a long, merry fanfare to indicate the commencement of lunch.

For Berenice's sake Jane had ordered a temporary board walkway under a striped canopy across the meadow. It led to a wide dais in the shade of the young oaks, where green chairs decorated with roses were ranged around the long white tables. Further into the wood, in the deep shade of the old trees, two white fringed hammocks were tied, and the small children were tumbling in and out of them. A small pink and white striped pavilion with a pennant on top hid the caterers' equipment. The salmon was enthroned in splendour at the apex of the serving table.

Dropping their pretence of dignity, the horn players sprinted boyishly past the procession to join the rest of their quintet a short distance away from the diners, where they applied themselves immediately to Mozart.

'That must be your husband.' Michael was at Grace's side, seizing his moment while Nick was deep in conversation with Andy Moynihan.

'Yes, that's the poor fool who took me on.' She looked at him calmly, willing him not to start scanning her face with his old, searching expression. It was no good, already Michael was standing too close and examining her with too much intimacy, and he had hold of her arm so she could not move away. Andy was screening her. She could hear Nick getting a lecture on one of her favourite subjects, toxic shame as an element of the addictive personality.

'A lucky man, not a fool. In medicine, isn't he? A surgeon?' Luscious was the right word for her, Michael decided. She looked luscious. The sheen on her golden skin, those magnificent shoulders.

Unconsciously, he was caressing her with his eyes. Grace smiled inwardly, flattered against her will, recognizing the extent of the man's greed. He was insisting even that his ex-lover's husband should reflect his glory.

'Nick's a virologist. He's attached to a team studying the HIV virus in mothers and babies, and does some general practice as well.'

'Good, good.'

'It's very interesting, because some babies born with the virus manage to overcome it; his team want to find out how they do it and if adults can do the same. I'm simplifying, of course.'

'But that's fascinating.'

'I'm glad you approve.'

'I always approved of you, whatever you did. You know that. And which of these children are yours?'

'None of them. That's been a problem for us.' Now which way was he going to jump?

He was making his I-could-kick-myself face. 'Oh God, was that insensitive. It was, wasn't it? Sorry. Sorry.' Her memory retrieved a sad moment when she had told him that he was so fond of that word she would not be surprised when he died if it was found engraved on his heart.

Screaming came from the little ones; a thin girl with a cream smock flapping about her legs detached herself from the group and sprinted towards them. 'Daddy! You've got to come and sort Sam out. He wants to kill our frogs.'

'This is Emma.'

The child who almost killed me. In spite of her expensive embroidered sun frock Grace's instinct was that the little girl was a mess. She looked messy, not at all the chocolate-box angel portrait which Michael had always painted of her.

'*Daddy*, you must *come*.'

'I'm sure Sam isn't doing anything he shouldn't.'

'He *is*, he *is*.'

'Don't be silly, Emma. Go and tell the others to come and sit down.' The genial father was not Michael's best role. He was looking around for his wife while Emma's eyes were growing huge with distress.

'You're always on Sam's side. You never say I'm right, and I always am.'

Michael simply turned away and ignored her. Grace was distressed; the child's sense of grievance moved her so much she forgot her inhibitions. 'I'll come and see, shall I?' she offered. 'It's all right, Emma, I'll come – you show me . . .'

The child regarded her in a cautious silence. Then Grace found her hand taken and she was led away across the meadow and on into the ancient trees, trying to fit this odd little girl into Michael's endless accounts of her precious charm and adorable cleverness. The eczema was ugly, but the sunken eyes, the lifeless thin hair, the shadowy face had nothing of childhood in it, and the little mouth was pursed as if it was used to demanding what was needed but seldom received. There was something inconsolable about Emma, she felt that nothing would make the child content. But what are my instincts worth, since nature doesn't find me fit to be a mother?

In a shady area Morris Donaldson was already on his knees by the hammock investigating the threatened frogs. He had put on weight, she had seen that from occasional photographs in the paper, but now that she was close she could see that he had aged too; his face was almost grotesque and his hair was grey and thinning.

'All a big fuss over nothing.' He rose clumsily as she approached. 'The wee girls haven't caught a frog yet, so this talk of amphibicide is all exaggeration. Grace. Good to see you.'

'How are you, Morris?'

'I'm going to catch my own frogs.' The announcement was made by the biggest child, a fleshy boy with glasses.

'You can't, piggy. You're too fat.' This taunt came from a white-blonde sprite whose sweet oval face was splashed with large freckles. Grace placed her as the eldest of Morris's children.

'That isn't kind,' her father admonished her.

'No, but it's right.' Emma rolled herself sulkily into the hammock.

'I'm not unkind. You have to be really quick to catch these frogs and Sam's much too fat. He can't bend over . . .'

'That's enough. Come along, everyone's sitting down for lunch.'

'He can't, though.' Emma was swinging the hammock from side to side, a malicious smile on her face. Grace felt an atmosphere among the children; whatever squabble there had been had obviously been disturbing. Sidelong, so he would not feel observed, she looked at Sam in wonder. Stolid and self-important. She would never have imagined Michael's son like that; nor would Michael, she was sure. He had spoken with touchingly unoriginal enthusiasm about skateboards and football.

'Come on, everyone.' Sam was pompous behind his glasses. 'My father wants us to sit down now.' None of the smaller children moved. 'Come on,' he urged, 'it's lunchtime.'

'We know, Sam.' Emma did not move. 'You go on. We'll come later.'

'No,' he insisted, 'we must all go now.' The two Donaldson children took Morris's hands and began to drift towards the table, with Sam marching behind them. A very small child with a red topknot remained, sitting placidly on the grass watching Emma in the hammock.

'That's my baby sister. She's not too bad, but my brother's disgusting.' Emma had extended her arms and was squinting at the trees through her fingers. 'He is a pig. And don't tell me that's not nice, because it's true.' She rolled out of the hammock, ran over to Grace and pulled her skirt. 'Will you sit with me? I think he's frightened of you so he'll behave.'

The toddler suddenly put up her arms, demanding to

be carried, and Grace timidly picked her up, expecting a howl of protest at any second. The infant seemed content, however, and poked her cheek experimentally with one tiny finger.

'How are you, Grace?' Donaldson asked again as they caught up with each other. 'I haven't seen you here before.'

'I'm a foreign correspondent now; my husband and I live in Paris, but we've a summer place about fifty miles south of here. Jane asked us, actually.' His question, of course, was about herself and Michael; her answer seemed largely satisfactory.

The little girl was lying content and wide-eyed against Grace's shoulder. As they approached the dining table with the troop of children, Jane came quickly forward to take the child, her eyes apologizing. 'She wasn't upset?'

'She wanted to be carried, that's all,' Emma informed her mother, then took the little one by the hand and led her down to the seats allocated to the children. Looking over Jane's head, Grace saw an odd expression of benevolence on Michael's face. He's getting off on this, she thought; he wants to keep us like some kind of harem, all his women and children living happily together under his roof. And his eunuchs. She saw that Graham Moynihan had been seated with the Belgians.

She found her name card opposite Michael at the middle of the table, a long way from Nick who was with Jane and Andy near the children. There were three empty seats next to the young Moynihans. She had Alan Stern on her right and the young black-haired man on her left. It must have been Michael's doing; he was trying to tell her she was important to him. Michael had Amina Bhatia, his evening news presenter, on one side, and Berenice Stern on the other. Beyond her was Stuart Devlin, another old network face who looked almost unchanged, in a short-sleeved khaki shirt with a new scar just visible in his hairline.

'Great report from Gaza,' she complimented him.

'Glad you saw it,' he muttered.

Her dark-haired neighbour leaned over. 'Stewart Molfetto.' His handshake was fierce. 'With NewsConnect. I gather you're a former employee?'

'Not quite, I was a network news producer.'

'Oh, I see.' Having made one misjudgement, he was almost too wary to speak again. Wild mushroom salad was served.

She turned to Stern and said flattering things about his recent profile in *Vanity Fair*, watching him relax as she assured him of the distinction of both the writer and photographer employed.

'I thought it was rather bitchy, myself.' Stern was listening intently, his blue eyes narrowed to triangles.

'*Vanity Fair* is bitchy. That's its function, I think people allow for that. I thought the piece was excellent for Altmark. Aren't your people pleased?'

'Oh yes. My wife – less so.' A very gentle smile. Berenice had merited half a paragraph, mentioning her commitment to couture clothes.

'I haven't seen this article.' Michael sounded

aggrieved, as if he had been the victim of a conspiracy. 'How long was it?'

'Six pages, maybe – I don't remember.' Stern applied himself to his food. Michael's plate was already empty. He always disposed of food immediately, as if afraid of missing the opportunity to say something important while his mouth was full.

'I think it was eight pages.' After so many years of dutifully reflecting her lover at twice his natural size, Grace found the temptation to cut him down a little quite irresistible. 'And a full-page portrait.'

'They've done you, surely?' asked Stern.

'No, never.' He was looking at Grace now as if she had been worryingly irrational.

'Well, your day will come, I'm sure. These chanterelles are magnificent. A clever man to marry a professional cook.'

Louisa embarked on a gracious tribute to Jane and the bounty of Les Palombières. There was a sniff from Berenice, who had half-heartedly mangled a leaf of rocket with her fork for ten minutes. Clumsily, Molfetto broke in with a question about Altmark's recent acquisition of a Russian news film library, and Grace, knowing she had staked her claim, let the men have the field. Two senior waiters reverently served the salmon, each portion deposited in a pool of sorrel sauce.

Soothed and pleasured by their food, the guests became mellow. The tempo of their talk slowed, the volume lowered, the diligent plying of cutlery was audible. Jane was rejoicing in their happiness. Like this her bright prettiness shone through, but Grace could still identify in her as well the keynote of all Michael's women, the undertow of grief in all her animation.

All the old faces around her had aspects of character which had suddenly petrified. As a child she had been scared to make her eyes cross, in case the wind changed and she stayed like that forever; in that way maturity had caught her old associates unawares, freezing ugly faces on them. Moynihan showed pedantry, Donaldson disappointment. They had been men of extraordinary promise, but Michael did not keep men like that about him. He bust their balls in the relentless process of imposing his own vision; now he could use younger men, like Molfetto, the process would seem more natural. Of his old team, the best served their apprenticeship quickly and left him. Moynihan and Donaldson had never been deficient in ability; their weakness had been their loyalty. It was a handicap in Michael's world. Loyalty had been her weakness also.

Three figures were walking across the meadow in the sun. When they gained the shade of the trees a young woman in white shorts peeled away from the other two and went to talk to Jane. A dark man and a dark woman who carried a huge fantastically sculptured straw hat walked on towards the centre of the table, watched by the whole company. At a distance the woman was beautiful, tall and slender, wearing a long fluttering dress; there was a peculiar mechanical element in her gait.

Closer, she was extraordinarily pale, with thick white foundation and heavy black eye makeup. She seemed subdued and withdrawn, and allowed the man to guide her to the table; he was tense, his black eyebrows contracted almost to a line.

'Daddy, darling.' Languid and histrionic, she draped her arms around Michael's neck. An expression of annoyance flitted across his face. 'Oh God, we're late. How stupid, stupid, *stupid* of me. Ugh, stupid! I just had to stop for a loo, I forgot to go on the train. How *are* you? Have we missed everything?'

So this was Imogen. The child for whom I endured it all, the justification for eight years of my misery, and the untold agony of an unknown number of other women. He was right to worry about her, she looked like a fucked-up kid. Michael was introducing her with every pretence of paternal pride, and Grace watched Stern, flawlessly polite but unable to hide his disapproval. Molfetto was aggressively welcoming, Louisa delighted to be shocked; Berenice began her social smile, but a flicker of amusement took it further than she intended.

'Stephen Bendorf.' The young man introduced himself, friendly and unfazed that Michael had overlooked him. Then the newcomers made their way to their seats, and the staff started forward to remove empty plates. The next course was quail with a grape salsa and a sauce of verjuice and pink peppercorns.

Louisa lectured on verjuice. '*Unripe* grapes, so they aren't pressed but pureed and strained, and then when it's *cooked* the acidity becomes wonderfully refreshing so it actually *stimulates* the palate . . .'

Yells came from the children's end of the table. There were missiles in the air. Sam marched to his father's side and said, 'Imi's throwing food, Daddy.' Michael seemed not to have heard him, although he leaned forward and tried to catch Jane's eye – unsuccessfully, because Nick seemed to have her total attention. With Andy, they were absorbed in a deep conversation.

'The sourness is caused by tartaric acid, which some people think actually has a lemon flavour . . .' Louisa was in full flood. Confronted by a stony lack of response, the boy walked away. Molfetto again diverted the conversation to Altmark's affairs, although Stern was responding with less and less interest.

A few minutes later Grace saw Sam returning, and the smaller children around him in an excited group. Imogen got up, knocking over her chair and almost falling, she had a splash of sorrel sauce on her dress. She urged the boy forward. 'Go and show Daddy,' she was urging him. 'Go on.'

This time Michael was obliged to pay attention. Sam's hands were clasped together and held out in front of him. 'I've got a frog, Daddy. All by myself, he's mine. Look!'

'Not now, Sam. Imogen, can't you . . .'

Deliberately, the boy pushed forward, held his hands over the table and parted his fat fingers one by one. In his palm sat a small bright green frog. For a split second it was still, then it jumped. Berenice Stern screamed. The expression on her face was indescribable.

'Revolting thing!' She flung up her arms, splay-fingered in horror. Her fork fell and smashed her glass. 'For God's sake, do something!'

'Where's it gone?' Adult eyes had been too slow to follow the tiny thing. Stern got to his feet, but the width of the table barred him from his frantic wife. Two waiters ran forward, then halted, uncertain of the right etiquette for this emergency.

'It's down her front,' Sam said with satisfaction. 'It'll probably die there. They can't get hot, it kills them.'

'Oh, poor little creature! Here, I can save it.' With the distaste of one about to clear a drain, Imogen plunged her hand down the front of Berenice's bustier. She nearly fell over doing it. Then she giggled, and began groping clumsily. 'I can't find it, there's so much room in here.'

'Imogen, for God's sake!' Michael got to his feet, prepared, if necessary, to pull his daughter away by force.

'Here he is, dear little thing.' She extracted her closed fist, her knuckles scraping Berenice's slack skin in a way that looked painful, although the face still registered nothing but extreme distaste. 'He really wouldn't have hurt you, you know. Nothing in nature harms you if you treat it right.'

'Imogen, please . . .'

The young woman looked at her father with a mild expression of fear. She stepped backwards away from him, whispering into her cupped hands. 'Come on, little one, that's enough adventures for today. What a pretty colour you are. It's OK, Daddy. I'll just put him back in the long grass.' Unsteadily, she strolled away. Sam was about to follow until Michael ordered him to apologize and then return to his seat.

Berenice wiped her face clear of any expression and calmly tugged the top of her dress up, restoring the flesh beneath to its proper position. She patted her throat, stood up, caught her husband's eye and with a gracious but frozen smile said, 'I think I need to find a bathroom.'

Michael began his own apologies, this time with flourishes fit for a matador, and left the table to accompany her to the house. Louisa followed, euphoric with fun.

The guests remaining at the table were naturally unable to laugh until Stern himself chuckled, pulled his napkin from his shirt front and said, without any detectable humour, 'My poor wife. She's had very little experience of reptiles.'

CHAPTER SIX

Sunday Continued

The leaves were turning colours. Very beautiful. Must let the frog go before he cooks in my hand. Wow, what a kickback. Bye-bye froggie. Tell the pond about your great expedition in search of Berenice Stern's tits. They won't believe you, but you can tell them anyway.

It's nice, this microdot. Clears all the rubbish out of your head, so you can really connect. Trips like this you know you're a few more atoms in the universe, the energy's flowing all through you, you can get in touch with the real powerful forces. I wish I had paint, even a pencil, piece of charcoal or something. I could really draw things now. Or write. Poetry. Ages since I did any poetry.

This wood is so beautiful. Old trees have all this wisdom and it comes out in their leaves, and just drops on you when you stand underneath. Wisdom and goodness. Hundreds of years growing in this beautiful earth, summer after winter, sun after rain. What bliss to lie down on the earth under the old trees and feel their goodness. And the sunlight pouring through, brilliant brilliant rays, particles of light exploding in the air.

Someone was coming, the earth was shaking with footfalls. Daddy. Whoops, that wasn't too good. A vicious little face or something in the corner of my mind. Don't look at it. It's only Stephen. I love Stephen. Musn't realize I'm tripping, he'll get freaked. Pretend I'm just sleepy.

'Imi, are you OK?' She was sitting under a tree, a cross-legged Ophelia gazing at a leaf she held in one hand. He thought she looked withdrawn, and oddly detached, but every time she was forced into proximity with her family there was a different reaction and this seemed a promising improvement on her usual black sulk.

'Oh sure. I'm fine, I'm just tired. Last night's catching up with me. It's nice here, I'm just having a little rest.' Bother. He was going to hang around. Don't say too much or he'll suss.

'Are you sure you're OK?'

'Really. Is Berenice upset? I was worried about her, I think I really freaked her.' That's great, he'll definitely think I'm OK if I'm saying nice polite things. Nice polite Stephen, it would never occur to him that for some people being nice and polite is totally abnormal.

'She's gone into the house to have a shower. It was an accident, after all. Sam fooling around. She took it very well.' He's going to sit down beside me. Damn, damn. This is not going to be easy.

'Oh great. She was really frightened, wasn't she?'

'Her husband seems to be cool too, or maybe he's just not reacting to be polite. Either way, there can't be much harm done. If you're really all right I'll go back now. Do you think it'll be OK to talk to him?'

'What, that Stern guy? What do you want to talk to him for?'

'I read about him in the *Architectural Quarterly.* He funded a housing project in South Africa, or one of his companies did. Resettling people from the townships.'

'I don't get it – why shouldn't you talk to him?'

'Oh, you know. Your father might think . . .'

'Oh no, Keith, I don't think you ought to upset my father. That wouldn't be nice, would it? I mean, it is his birthday, poor man.' This is going really well. I'm doing a brilliant job of being me. Old Stephen hasn't a clue. I'll give him a good long stare just to underline it all.

'So you think he would . . .'

'Fuck it – what does he know? The guy'll probably be knocked out to have somebody actually interested in him. Go on Stephen, I'm OK, really I am. I just can't handle too much family, that's all. I just want to chill out over here for a while. That doctor going on and on about eczema and acupuncture and stuff and Jane pretending she cares. Makes me feel sick.'

'You're sure?'

'Go on, for fuck's sake. I'll just rest here and then I'll be back.'

'OK then. Catch you later.'

He was walking away. Excellent. Was old Stephen going to turn into a suit? Maybe all men were suits, some of them just pretended. Now, come on leaves, let's hear you. Nothing. Her hand was sticky where the frog had been. Maybe she should wash it. The colours had stopped, everything was beautiful.

Michael was really, really angry. He was sending some people to get rid of her, they were looking for her now. They were coming up all around her, trapping her. Could she hide in the split in the tree trunk? No, she was too fat. Try harder. Oh shit, this was going wrong. She was going to get paranoid. Time to get out of the wood. Faster, faster, they would find her soon.

Fuck, what is this stuff? This is not a good trip. Better be quick and take the sleepers. Good thing I brought them. Sensible. I'll never get into bother, I can look after myself. Quick shot of Mr T and I'll be cool, that's all it takes. Get to the house now, quickly, quickly.

Under the trees the party was relaxing. All the small children got down from the table and scattered to play. The adults fell into deep, well-lubricated conversations. Only Nick noticed the tall figure moving erratically towards the house. Periodically, she covered her head with her arms as if she was frightened of something above her in the air. Her hat was still sitting at her place at table. He thought it had considerable personality.

What was Michael thinking? Did Michael think, in the way most human beings did? After fourteen years with him, Jane was ready to describe her husband's mental process as a huge, elaborate, multilayered system constantly acquiring and arranging information to support his own omnipotence. Because in all practical senses, he did believe he was God. He was a churchgoer of a kind, Michael. He did better than Easter and Christmas; if Sunday found him at home he would take off for the politician's church, and it was more than habit or networking. Perhaps he needed to keep in touch with God because otherwise he would have to believe he himself was God, seeing as he created the world, he commanded the world, and no sparrow fell without making the NewsConnect agenda. Anything which did not confirm this was only a faulty communication.

It was impossible to challenge such a mind. Your reality became a delusion; you yourself were something which upset the natural order, a mutation doomed to swift extinction.

The celebration continued around her and Jane looked on as if from a distance. It was not tiredness, nor the burden of organizing the day that had numbed her senses. An emotional process of some kind was under way, and all her energy was being diverted to it. Parts of her mind were almost closed down; Nick had asked her questions about the salad and she could not retrieve simple names she had known for years. It was an effort to tell him that she grew her own rocket and all the rest of the herbs in the garden behind the staff cottage.

They had begun by discussing Emma, a conversation of a kind which, she realized, she had longed to have for many years. She found him extraordinarily receptive; he was distant, a cool scientist of course. In that coolness there was no judgement, and she found herself describing the progress of her child's condition, the effects of climate or food or emotional factors, so freely that insights she had overlooked were suddenly obvious. He was fascinating on complementary medicine, one of Andy's favourite subjects. Above all, it was almost intoxicating to find a man so interested in her child's health.

Jane noticed that events which ought to have caused pain had simply flowed past her like river water. None of the children had eaten anything except Sam, who must have stuffed the equivalent of two whole loaves into his face before Andy admonished him. Her seating plan had placed Grace and Nick together near her, and Michael had changed it, so now Grace was opposite him. And Imogen, of course, had found a new excuse for an outrage.

As a hostess, she had duties and carried them out automatically, surprised within herself at what was accomplished. With Louisa absent, she had to make the little speech about Gascony not being a great cheese region, in fact some of the best cheese being made by émigré German hippies; this introduced a board featuring their fresh goat cheese, local soft-rinded ewe's milk rounds, creamy Roquefort and wedges of hard black-skinned Pyreneen (which she considered inedible, banal and fit for the inescapable faint-hearts who would never outgrow Kraft sandwich slices).

The hired staff were conferring anxiously. Next came

the most challenging course, given the heat: three sorbets, dark red cassis, delicate green *Izarra*, and pale pink cantaloupe, decorated with frosted red currants and melon flowers. The caterer had frozen the plates overnight to ensure that nothing melted until it was in the mouth. The small children hopefully left their game and returned to the table.

Clarinet notes bubbled through the convivial air; the musicians had mellowed into Schubert. With empty chairs, people began to move about; Stephen hesitantly took Louisa's seat, his eye upon Stern. Sadly curious about the man obviously in love with Michael's neurotic daughter, Grace made an opening in the conversation for him.

'Mr Stern, I was wondering . . .' A timid pause, engaging in such a large young man. Stern inclined his head, encouraging. 'About the Jansendorp project. I'm studying architecture and I was hoping to do my thesis on the development of workforce housing from Bournville to the present day . . .'

'What can I do for you?' Now, for the first time, the great stone face grew radiant with interest. Stern hardly drew breath before launching into the longest speech he had made all day. 'Of course, Bournville was one of the developments we studied when we were planning Jansendorp. We realized it was going to be a lot more than a matter of putting roofs over people's heads; we were going to have to create a community, and doing that was going to be a matter of actually building an integrated social structure into the village . . .'

Grace was enraptured. In all her career of interviewing she had found nothing more thrilling than a true passion expounded; the dullest person on the most abstruse topic became mesmeric. Stern was transformed, he was glowing. Questioned by Stephen, he responded with no condescension, quite casually unfurling the majestic intellect he had declined to exhibit when the conversation was only of the media business.

Around them, lesser conversations dwindled. Head on one side, listening intently, Amina Bhatia filed information for future programmes. Devlin followed the exchanges with surprised, unblinking eyes. Scenting their fascination, Moynihan moved up to take an abandoned chair. Molfetto's wife materialized in time to hear her husband make an ill-advised attempt to get a toehold in the dialogue; they did not hear him, and he was forced to fall back and pretend interest in silence.

Michael returned, and the scene momentarily threw him. Two centres of power had appeared in the group. His wife was the closest of several people listening to the man who was married to Grace; his guest of honour was almost holding court in a larger gathering, with the irritating Stephen prompting him. Grace was also in the centre of that group, with that fathomless, admiring expression her face acquired when she was fascinated. Michael's first alarmed assumption was that the young man had made some typically maladroit approach to Stern which was being politely evaded. Then he took in the intense rapport between the two, and the rapt attitudes of their listeners.

Stern was now aware of his audience, and addressing his answers generally. 'We had to take account of the culture that the people had developed in the townships. Apart from the struggle against the whites, that was what had unified them. So our aim was give the positive things in that culture the space to flourish. At the same time we had to make it difficult for the negative aspects to persist. And with a good amount of flexibility so people had no feeling that a way of life was being imposed . . .'

'What did you identify as the negative aspects?' A good interviewer would have picked up that point earlier; Michael frowned, reluctant to concede that Stephen was doing well. Amina Bhatia became aware of his presence and moved aside from his respectfully unoccupied chair.

'Clever young man,' she whispered. 'He's discovered what's close to the boss's heart.'

'A township is typically very volatile, a place where it is easy for a riot to start. We decided to look at the factors in that which our buildings could address, the way that most of the time most of the people were out on the street, for example . . .'

Grace watched Michael hesitate, guessing that he was anxious for Stern's approval, positively annoyed, concerned to disguise it and reluctant to give Stephen the tribute of his attention. Waiters distributing coffee and *petits-fours* saved him, disturbing the company enough to break the spell.

Stern took his memo pad from his shirt pocket and

made notes. 'I think you should come out and talk to the people working on Jansendorp – what kind of funding do you have for this thesis?'

'Funding? I haven't considered that aspect yet . . .'

'Why don't you put a proposal together for me? Let me get someone in touch with you.'

Almost incoherent with gratitude, Stephen withdrew to his own place and Michael prepared to reoccupy his territory, where further discomfort was in store.

'That's a very worthwhile young man,' pronounced Stern. 'Tell me about him. He came with your daughter.'

'They've been close for years. In fact, last year they were talking about marriage. We thought they were too young, really, but you have to let children go their own way in the end.'

There it was, deadly and precise as the *coup de grâce*; Michael had annexed Stephen to his own glory. Inwardly Grace sighed with frustration. But Stern was not persuaded.

'In the end, maybe, but that's a long way off. They are both young, and it's an important decision. Actually, I think it's the most important decision a man can make, the woman he marries. There are very few choices in life which you can't reconsider, but that is one of them. At least, that was how I was brought up. I hope he takes his time.' He nodded, and devoted himself to the coffee, his face reverting to a graven mask.

Michael defensive was a rare phenomenon, and not an inspiring one. In too loud a voice he started talking about his daughter's determination to study in Paris.

Stern shifted uncomfortably. This time Amina Bhatia mounted the rescue mission, recounting the negotiations before her own marriage, a good story delightfully delivered. Grace looked around for Nick, and saw that he was still in deep conversation with Jane and Andy Moynihan.

Presently Berenice Stern picked her way back to the party, and after her followed Michael's final disgrace.

'Daddy, have I missed the ice cream?' Imogen was drifting towards her father. 'Say I haven't, say you saved some for me.' Her frock hung loosely from her bony shoulders, the ends of the belt dangling untied. Her necklace was missing. She had smudges of mud on her skirt and a brown smear down one of her bare arms, but more than her dishevelled dress her manner was alarming. Her eyes were huge and she was obviously having difficulty in coordinating her limbs enough to walk.

Guilty because he had left her alone so long, Stephen intercepted her and pulled her down to a seat beside him.

'I'm so hungry, Stephen. Find me something to eat.' She leaned imploringly on his shoulder.

'Do you think you could find my daughter some dessert?' Having commanded a waiter, Michael stood up and held a chair for Berenice, freshly scented and lipsticked, rigidly composed as if she could make the embarrassing creature vanish by sheer force of will.

A sorbet plate was found for Imogen, who gulped the exquisite composition down as if she had not eaten for a week. All the remaining *petit-fours* within reach of her long arms followed. Then she threw up, the first time quite quietly into her lap, the second time noisily and copiously as she was lurching to her feet with her hand over her mouth. Most of the company were watching the third time she spewed, with such force that the mess splattered Stephen, the table in front of her and the polished knees of the Moynihan kids, who scrambled back with faces that said oh-not-again as loudly as voices.

She staggered a few steps away, spitting and heaving, then Stephen was by her side, holding her waist as she began to retch uncontrollably.

After a short exchange with Jane, whose face was scarlet, Nick patted her arm and nodded, then left his seat to help. 'Let's take her into the house,' he said, stooping to put his sturdy arm around Imogen's body. She was able to take the napkin from him and wipe her mouth; her stomach was empty but she was still bringing up bile and mucus. In the mellow afternoon sunlight the two men half-carried her across the meadow, followed by the young Moynihans pointing disgustedly at each other's soiled legs.

Jane watched her step-daughter's departure with resignation. She knew it would be better not to follow, that there was nothing she could do for the miserable girl. In fact, there never had been anything she could have done for her. She had become a mother-substitute for a child damaged beyond the power of love to restore. Perhaps Imogen had been born as she was; perhaps a secure home would have made no difference. She had never acquired the inner strength to survive her life. For all she could give herself good counsel, Jane felt the girl's wretched existence as a constant reproach.

Michael wanted her help with damage limitation. 'Oh dear,' he said, as if nothing significant had taken place. 'My poor girl. Too much champagne, I suppose.'

'Not at all,' Berenice Stern corrected him. Her timing was spot-on. 'I don't think she drank very much, and it was mostly water. But she was shooting up in the bathroom a few minutes ago.'

The faces. The whole circle frozen with shock. Most of all Amina, good clean-living woman that she was. Stern's frown projected four hundred and fifty years of Calvinist disapproval.

Michael took care not to speak too soon. 'Are you sure?' he demanded, an outraged parent to the core.

Berenice was taking no prisoners. 'Of course I'm sure, Michael. I saw her. She had the goddamn needle hanging out of her arm.'

'Surely not.'

'Do you know what it was?' Grace interjected in her most down-to-earth voice. She was shocked at Michael's lack of concern and wanted to get away from him, immediately, before she had to listen to one more polished, self-serving speech. 'My husband is a doctor, he'll be able to take care of her, but it would help if we knew what she's using.'

'Well, no, I'm afraid I didn't stop to enquire.'

'Which bathroom was it?'

'The one in the pool house. She didn't bother shutting the door.'

'Do excuse me, everybody, won't you?'

Grace ran. Her long strides swallowed up the distance at a speed she hadn't reached for years. She was too full of outrage to look at the entire picture of Jane and Michael going about their businesses while the wretched creature they had raised collapsed in front of them. More, she was appalled by the reality of Michael's family. Eight years of her life she had laid on their altar, believing the sun-kissed picture he had projected of his home life. Night after night she had wrenched her imagination away from the vision of the man she loved reentering the family which excluded her. Now here was the reality, and here he was among them, a manipulative stranger.

Once she gained the terrace, there were urgent, practical tasks to be done. On the floor by the lavatory in the pool house she found a glass, some empty green gelatine capsule cases and Imogen's long necklace of silver discs joined by leather thongs. She collected them carefully and went to find Nick. As she entered the hallway of the house she heard the Sterns' driver being called to bring their car to the door in ten minutes.

'Almost everything, at one time or another,' Stephen was saying as Grace found them in an upstairs bathroom. 'What I mean is, she was never an addict or anything like that. It's when she's stressed sometimes she'll just take whatever she can get her hands on. I didn't know she had anything, I went through her place yesterday and there was nothing.'

As he spoke he was dabbing at Imogen's upturned

face with a towel, supporting her with an arm around her shoulders. Eyes closed and clean of heavy makeup, she had a look of dreamy innocence. An angelic smile played around her slack lips. Sitting swaying on the edge of the bath, wearing a vest and old shapeless knickers discoloured from much careless washing, she seemed to be a child who had mysteriously outgrown her strength, bolting away into a long, pale, odd-shaped adult. In spite of the fleshless condition of her arms and legs her body carried some fat; she still had breasts, wide and flat with sharp nipples, and a distinct mound of belly looking almost like a pot because of her collapsed posture. The dress was a heap under the running shower.

Nick, kneeling at her side, was holding one of her wrists, taking the pulse.

In the act of releasing her arm he noticed something, and took the other hand to examine it as well. Stephen was talking on. 'There was nothing in her place. Nothing. No tabs or E or anything, not that I could find and I know the places. She had a bottle of aspirins and some vitamins, that was all.'

'She was taking vitamins.' In the most unobtrusive and neutral way, Nick was prompting. Grace recognized the technique; it drove her mad when he used it on her when she was trying not to burden his good nature with the piffling evils of a newspaper day just because he was there.

'Oh, Imogen really takes care of her nutrition. She's been vegetarian for years and she knows she has to make sure she gets Vitamin B and iron and things. Actually, there were just a couple of them, loose in a little box.'

'Capsules or tablets?'

'Capsules.'

'Any idea of the colour?'

'Oh God, no. They were all one colour, not blue and white. I'm sorry, I should have remembered . . .'

'Were these the ones?' Grace held out her hand with the evidence. 'After you left, Berenice said she'd seen her in the pool house with a syringe, but this was all I could find.'

'Oh yes. At least, I think so. But . . .' Stephen mumbled into silence, using a corner of the towel to clean the last of the smudged mascara from Imi's eyelids. The evidence told him that she must have used a needle; in fact, her insistence on stopping at a pharmacy must have been in order to buy the syringe.

Taking the upper arm between his careful thumb and finger, Nick massaged a particular spot, trying to feel what he could not see in the dim room. 'There was a mark here earlier, wasn't there? Can you put the light on?' Grace reached for the switch and he peered closely at the white skin. 'Yes, she made a real mess of it, look at these marks. When you arrived together, was she like she is usually?'

'Well, not quite. Seeing the family always stirs up a lot of feelings, you know. We were together all the time on the train, but while we were driving here she said her period was starting and insisted we stop at the chemists and then a café on the way so she could use the lavatory.

And she put on all that makeup. By the time we got here I thought she was withdrawn, a bit out of it. I suppose she could have taken something back at the café.' He had wrapped the towel around Imogen's shoulders, and kept pulling it up as it slipped.

'Her pulse is slow but it's quite strong and regular so I'm not concerned on that score. The capsules are temazepam. It's a major tranquillizer which she could have had on prescription. Seems to be quite a fashionable thing to inject it at the moment, and that's obviously what she's done – not very efficiently because there are several punctures here, quite ragged, she bled a bit. You didn't find the syringe?' This was a question to Grace. He was getting heavily to his feet, satisfied with his diagnosis.

'No, but I didn't look for long.'

'There's so many little kids about, we ought to find it before they do. Needles . . . it can be tricky stuff. There's a risk of embolism, I read a paper on it just recently. Injected, temazepam acts fast but wears off quickly. Probably feels pleasantly swimmy, like a valium drip at the dentist. The danger is that it can solidify in a vein, stop the circulation. Anywhere in the body. Could cause a stroke, pulmonary embolism. There've been cases of gangrene, mostly with multiple users who perhaps weren't very aware of pain or numbness in their limbs. And there's a bad reaction with alcohol, fatal in fact.'

'She only drank water.' Hope flickered pathetically across Stephen's eyes.

Briefly, Nick put a hand on the younger man's arm.

'Good. But my guess is that she did take something else earlier. I remember noticing when you both arrived, she had that look of being withdrawn. It was obviously difficult for her to get the needle into her arm. You said she sometimes used psychedelics? You can never predict a bad trip. People use temazepam to cool things out if they don't like what starts coming down.' Out of his mouth, street language sounded as bland as a weather forecast. Grace listened in fascination. This was the man she seldom met, Dr Nichols, who sat in his Friday clinic and opened a file on a new tragedy every fifteen minutes. He was at home here; she felt proud of him.

'I thought she didn't have anything with her.'

'Those little tabs are so small. Easy to miss.'

Stephen felt that he had failed. He had so much wanted Imogen to carry off the day successfully. 'I suppose she seems pretty messed up to you?'

Nick considered this as if it were an interesting but not very sound academic proposition. 'Well, yes,' he conceded, 'but I see a lot of messed up people and compared . . . Put it this way, from what you say, she has a pattern of using drugs, but at present it's more at the level of attention-seeking. It's dangerous of course, there are dangers obviously inherent in that lifestyle, but it's a phase a lot of people go through and if she leaves it behind her then it won't amount to more than a sort of mild neurosis of growing up in this crazy world.'

Since this was his own opinion, Stephen was gratified. 'Do you think she could . . .'

'Anybody can do anything, can't they?' Bothered by

the young man's assumption of responsibility for the girl's future, Nick glanced in the mirror. His shirt was speckled with sauce and crumbs. He was letting Grace down in this grand gathering. He looked back at Stephen with a spark of mischief in his eyes. 'Do you know how many psychotherapists it takes to change a lightbulb?'

Bewildered, Stephen answered, 'No . . .'

'Only one, but the lightbulb must *really want* to change.'

'Oh. Yeah, I get it. But she . . . no, forget it, nothing.' The joke had disappointed him. 'So what should I do now, try to keep her awake?'

'No, I think she could sleep quite safely now, but while she's like this there's a danger of the Jimi Hendrix thing, breathing in your own vomit.'

'So I should stay with her?'

'Somebody should, all the time. And she may still be tripping when she wakes up, of course. The embolism thing is quite rare, but if it did happen, it could be any time in the next few days. Pain and swelling where the blockage is perhaps, but they can be symptomless.' He paused to think. 'In Paris, I'd send her for ultrasound. I know there's a clinic in Toulouse – let me make some telephone calls later. For now, we'll put her to bed and I'll stay here with her.'

Stephen went to fetch a bathrobe. He knew which rooms Jane usually assigned to himself and Imogen – Michael would have balked at them sleeping together under his roof; in hers was a huge mahogany wardrobe, a traditional *armoire* from a much more ostentatious style of home. It contained a few of her clothes, items left behind rather than actually kept there, and a fresh white towelling bathrobe folded up and tied with mauve ribbon and lavender bags.

Imogen sighed softly as she was picked up. They carried her easily to the room, where she lay flat under a sheet. The afternoon sun had not yet reached the windows, but the air was already close. Grace opened the window and saw departing guests in the car park; crucifying for Michael, but she banished the first shadow of sympathy and reproached herself. Was she merely in the habit of feeling sorry for people, whether or not they deserved it?

'Perhaps you should let her parents know what the situation is?' Nick was pulling a chair to the side of the bed, hinting to Stephen that there was no place for him there at present. 'And if you would be kind enough – there's a case in the back of our car, square and black. It's the old red MGB, it's not locked.'

'Yes, of course.' Stephen hesitated at the bedside, looking down at the sleeping face; against her ivory skin, to which the day's sun had not added any colour at all, her black eyelashes lay so flat they could have been drawn on with a pen.

There was an awkward hiatus in which none of them moved, then Stephen turned back and continued as if he had been asked another question. 'It's just . . . well, we've been together a long time, you know, and I've seen what goes on in her life. There's no one she can be really close with, not in the family. She's got this terrible sense of being on her own. Michael has always been away, and when he is around he frightens her with his expectations. And Jane's sort of washed her hands, now she's got children of her own. I really think Imi only does this stuff to get attention from Michael and Jane. I mean, I'm sorry to be a sort of drawing-room psychiatrist . . .'

'Don't be. It could be a fair analysis. I saw some scarring on one of her wrists.'

'She cut herself at Christmas, just at the beginning of lunch.'

'But that was the only time?'

'Yes.' He was thinking that in all their months of separation she could have been doing anything. Certainly, she had made something of a life for herself, full of secrets she kept from him, like the silver things in her rucksack. 'As far as I know.'

'There are women who cut themselves habitually, but of course the scarring is much more extensive. Anorexia can be part of the same syndrome.'

'Imi's never been anorexic; I mean, she doesn't eat a lot but she does eat.'

'You care a great deal for her, don't you?'

'Yes. So much. There's so much potential with her. When nothing's happening to upset her she can be so sweet and gentle, and there are so many things she can do, she's got so much talent. She's absolutely instinctive – she can draw and paint, she writes extraordinary poetry. It's only having the confidence. She just won't believe she's any good.'

'The parents must be very glad she's got you in her life.'

It was liberating to hear this neutral description of Michael and Jane; as merely 'the parents', not awesome figures cloaked in public glamour, they shrank in Stephen's mental scheme. He was not as intimidated as he had been. 'Well, not always. They didn't like it when I took her to see her mother.'

'Oh yes, I was told. Second marriage . . .'

'There's no reason you should . . . it wasn't anything I planned, we were just travelling together the year after I left school and it happened. And it was what Imi wanted, it was her idea. Michael and Jane acted like it was some kind of betrayal. I'm not keen to bring the bad news again, I've got shot before.' Feeling almost interrogated, he had been walking to and fro at the end of the bed, but now he halted. 'I thought you . . . how do you know so much about all this?' It was a defensive question. The broad, open face had clouded and he was pushing around a corner of the rug with one foot.

'I see quite a lot of addictive or abusive behaviour. A lot of my patients are users, the adults that is. It's about half and half. It's not really my field, I'm interested in the virus itself, but the team I work with at my clinic take a holistic approach. And when you're looking at patients' histories, compared to most of them, this' – he glanced at the thin, restless body now wound up in the white sheet – 'is kindergarten stuff. You read therapists' notes; pretty soon you pick up on the fact that there's more than one way to abuse a child. And most of them are legal.'

'I think – well, I can understand that.'

'You like looking after her, don't you?'

'It's almost a habit.' The last word reverberated in a silence precisely engineered by the older man. 'You're saying she's my addiction, is that it? No, you're not saying anything, are you? I am, I'm saying it.' He snapped back his shoulders and brushed his hair off his forehead with the palms of his hands. 'OK. You could be right.' Turning away from them, he put one hand over his eyes, trying to hide the tears. 'You are right. But what can I do? I care for her so much. I love her. That's it, that's the whole thing. I love her.' Now he had retreated to the corner of the room, and was looking from one face to the other as if he felt they hemmed him in. 'I'm sorry,' he said, 'I'll get your bag anyway.' And abruptly he left, almost blundering into the door frame as he went.

At the bedside Nick fell into his typical posture of thought, a still slump with elbows resting on his knees, eyes fixed on his clasped hands.

The sun suddenly struck through the open window and Grace went to close the shutters. In the distance she saw the guests' cars bumping slowly away up the hill in a purposeful exodus. 'The party's breaking up,' she said.

'Come here a minute?' Grace went to stroke the back of his neck. He pressed his face against her belly.

'Neurotic. Erotic. For some people it's almost the same thing. Men especially. You know he reminds me of myself?'

It was comforting to feel his voice vibrating through her body. She said, 'He's only young.'

'I was older when I met my first wife, but it was the

same old voodoo. You think all she needs is taking care of, and you're the only one who can do it. Totally seductive. But you're wrong. You can't make her well, no one can until she decides to heal herself. She won't do that while you're running around after her picking up and covering up. And you won't start your own journey while you're wrapped up in her.'

'You're saying he's got to get out?' Before, he had never talked about his first marriage in any but the most trivial terms.

'Absolutely. Only hope for both of them.' He sat up, trying to shake off introspection. 'This is a very interesting family. Did you see neither of them responded to her? Both the other kids are in trouble, the little girl and the boy.'

Grace thought of the beaming, round-eyed infants whose photographs were so proudly framed on the wall by Michael's desk, and the wonderful detailed anecdotes of their childish triumphs that had cut her to the heart. He had told them with a radiant pride; pride not in his children, she now understood, but in his own ability to act out fatherhood. 'They're nothing like I imagined,' was all she said.

'And Jane. She's completely different, I can't believe it. All through lunch I thought she was going to start crying. I found myself talking on and on to try to hold her together. Last week, when we met, she was a different person, totally different. Confident – how I'd imagined her to be. A sturdy Scots lass with floury hands, bright and sparky and full of good advice. Now it's like someone pressed her mute button. What goes on in this house?'

'I don't know.' Grace glanced at the sleeping girl, wondering if she could hear their conversation.

'Well, if this is a modern family, I'm glad we haven't got one.' He wrapped his arms around her and hugged her to him, while she recorded his voice in her mind and played it back, straining to hear the notes of regret.

'You need a clean shirt,' she said at last. One of her more fruitful habits was never to travel without throwing together an overnight bag.

'Sure do.'

'There's one in the car, I'll fetch it.'

'Kiss me before you go.'

High clouds like a band of smoke had gathered at the zenith of the sky. There was blazing blue still to either side of them, but at the western horizon, above the burning yellow of the sunflowers, puffs of white and grey were piling lightly upon each other, feathers from a celestial pillow-fight. The breeze had died down and the heat was suffocating.

It was five in the afternoon; never before had the party ended so early. In previous years Michael's inner circle had regrouped around the pool, to watch their children cooling off in the water and talk over old times. The last guests had often lingered until nightfall. It was always the most satisfying part of the ceremony. The glow he got from the admiration of old friends was very precious; he had come so far in life, he was afraid that his integrity had been damaged on the journey, and only his old friends could confirm that he was still intact.

A sour atmosphere had settled on the table after Imogen's removal and he recognized that it was of his own making. He had attached her to himself completely, taken all the decisions on her life, and there she was, a disastrous ruin of a human being, his creation, his monster. His own parents would have been deeply ashamed to have raised such a child.

Amina Bhatia, exquisitely well-mannered to the end, was the last to leave. He walked her to her car and accepted two cool social kisses with her emollient assurances that the day had been a success. He gave her good wishes for her husband, who was at NewsConnect editing the weekend bulletins, then closed her door, she twitching her sari away before it was caught, and waved as she eased the unfamiliar hire car up the road. It was over. The little crowd which had come together so gaily four hours ago had dispersed, the festive camp was being struck, and he was by himself.

It annoyed him that Jane was not with him. It would mitigate the disaster a little if she was at his side to say goodbye. All day she had been remote from him, contained within herself, a peculiar mood he had never felt before. Now her absence emphasized his responsibility for the failure of the event; he had actually asked her to come with him, but she had refused sweetly, for some reason wanting to supervise the caterers as they cleared away.

Solitude was intolerable to him. Since the terrifying

melancholy of his adolescence, his life had seemed like a walk in the shadow of a hungry despair. Each year, as his achievements piled up and the world awarded him higher status, the shadow behind him was deeper, and the temptation to give up, stop running and let that darkness swallow him became stronger. All the time, he needed to feel that he was advancing, staying ahead of the shadow, and when he had no work distraction was the only way to feel safe. People, ideas and above all action were what kept him ahead. At that moment, they were all unavailable.

Rapidly, he reviewed his options. Jane, in her present bizarre mood, could be dangerous. His secretary might be at home, he could discuss his schedule for the next day with her. At NewsConnect, the editor of the day could update him. And he could call Serena. Her distraction this morning was only one of the reverses of the past twenty-four hours, but it was a thorn in his side. She was deserting him – he thought of it in those terms, having already painted her into his picture.

In the house, at least, it was cooler. His office, which he seldom used, was reached through the drawing room. An immense window, framed in a stone arch which had once been a barn doorway, brought into the room the spectacular view over the pool to the wood and the valley. This window had a single red curtain draped from a high pole and held back with red and gold ropes. The arrangement was so elaborate and the view so good that the curtain was seldom released, but someone had boldly loosened it and half the room was in shadow.

As he walked past, there was a disturbance in the depth of a sofa. 'Michael! I must have dozed off! Oh, what a heavenly day!' A pair of deep red Chesterfields stood either side of the colossal stone fireplace, the nearest one with its back to him. Louisa reared up from its seat, her jacket slithering around her curves, stretching extravagantly. Today she was in a dusty pink cocktail suit with a gold double-heart choker. He found adult women wearing little-girl outfits unattractive.

'I have had *such* a wonderful time. What about you? You looked so relaxed. I can never enjoy my own parties, I worry too much.'

The nectar of praise drew him towards her, stepping around her stiletto sandals, which she had discarded some distance away across the dark floorboards. She swept her legs off the cushions and patted a place for him to sit. 'You're not worrying about Berenice, are you?'

'That was – embarrassing. I don't know what came over Imogen . . .'

'Oh, Berenice was laughing about the whole thing by the time we got inside. Everyone understands about problem children, don't they? Haven't the Sterns got some of their own? Little moments of comedy like that are part of a great occasion, they lift the whole atmosphere, don't you think?' Somehow every question cued a flirtatious flash of her eyes. Louisa was lolling back, fluffing up her hair and pulling pins from it, letting her breasts strain against her tight jacket while she considered where her duty to Jane might lie in this situation.

People described Louisa variously as aggressive,

demanding or courageous. Something in her upbringing had clearly left her with the impression that she was not tied by the good manners which, as she saw it, restrained other people ridiculously. No thought was too unpalatable for Louisa to voice, no argument too intrusive for her to advance – particularly in the cause of a friend. And for once she had captured Michael's interest.

'Berenice really was laughing?'

'Oh yes. She's quite an amusing woman, isn't she?'

'Is she?' Michael seldom registered the qualities of his associates' wives. As a consort, he rated Berenice as impressive if somewhat low on integrity for a man of Stern's muscular morals.

'Oh *yes.* I've known Berenice forever, we were at school together – just. She's older, of course. She can be quite witty when she's not clamped on to Alan like a barnacle. I'm surprised she hasn't sparkled in your direction before. She's got a great eye for the men, has Berenice.'

There was a sudden contraction of distaste from Michael – not the reaction she had envisaged. 'Don't tell me you don't know women find you attractive.' On the pretext of putting the hairpins on the table, she leaned towards him and in sitting up again, needed to put her hand on his knee.

'I don't really think about things like that.'

'Oh come *on*, everybody thinks about things like that. Especially with you. Although – forgive me for saying this, Michael, but I am an old friend – I would have thought that a man in your position would want to take perhaps a *little* more care. Isn't it funny, nowadays it's almost easier for a man to get a bad reputation than a woman?'

'Louisa, I'm sorry, you've lost me.' Was this a roundabout way of making a pass? Women could be maddeningly indirect.

'What I mean is, people are so sensitive about things like sexual harassment nowadays, and there are so many of these new puritans – like Stern, for example – it must be rather undesirable for a man in your position to have so many affairs.'

'What on earth are you talking about?' He spoke quite lightly, relieved to discover a familiar agenda. He prepared once more to brush off the challenge. 'I don't have affairs.'

It was at this point that Grace, coming downstairs, heard his voice through the half-open door and hesitated.

'Michael, everybody *knows*.' Louisa put her hand on his arm, partly to emphasize her argument, partly because he was looking rumpled and vulnerable and, unexpectedly, she found him attractive.

'They can't possibly know, because there is nothing to know. In my business there is a world of difference between gossip and reality.' His tone was chilling. Had Jane confided in this woman? A very unwise choice. She was a loose cannon, liable to cause damage with her bizarre ideas.

'How can you possibly say that?' Louisa's inflection was almost operatic. 'You've been unfaithful to Jane ever since I've known you, ever since you were married almost. There must have been at least three women here today who you've had affairs with.' Frozen at the bottom of the staircase, Grace dismissed the immorality of eaves-dropping in the face of a greater evil. Through the half-open door she could see nothing but the unoccupied corner of the sofa.

'That is the most absurd assertion I have ever heard. Louisa, is this some kind of seduction routine? Because it isn't working. If you thought I'd be flattered by . . .'

A rich chuckle rose from her throat. 'You *are*, though, aren't you? Flattered? Eh? Just a tiny bit? Go on, you can admit it . . .'

Michael felt himself running out of control. She was correct, he was flattered by his reputation; in fact, he was not nearly as discreet as he ought to be, because he revelled in the knowing glances and the envious snipes of his associates. In cold fact, he thought he was a hell of a guy – only it was essential that no one else knew that. He searched for the argument that would end the conversation.

'I'm not *condemning* it,' Louisa continued in a contented tone. 'I'm just remarking on it, if you like. And wondering why, when in every other way you're so anxious to present a really *contemporary* image, you don't clean your act up a little. Infidelity is for men who're still wearing flared trousers, didn't you know that? Of course, power is an aphrodisiac, and people do condone extraordinary behaviour in a man in your position in the world . . .'

'Then they're wrong.' Michael stood up and Grace soundlessly retreated a few steps up the stairs, out of his sight. 'Look, let me explain how it is for a man in my position in the world, as you call it.' He took up a position in front of the fireplace and delivered his speech. 'You're the subject of all kinds of speculation. That's only natural. Sometimes it's accurate. Sometimes it's not. This time, it's not. I am very much a married man, Louisa. And married to Jane, who I know counts you as one of her closest friends. At times I've been quite envious of what you share with her, you know? But you really are mistaken here. I have never, ever been unfaithful to Jane. And I never intend to be.'

Grace felt weak. Michael had negated her in a few easy words, delivered in the resonant, authoritative tone he used to announce global disasters. Afraid of falling, she sat on the steps and found herself covering her heart with her hands as if to protect it from another blow. Her heartbeat was wild and irregular.

Below, in the drawing room, the sofa creaked as Louisa quit it. She was annoyed now, and determined to be revenged, and also intrigued by the erotic mastery which Jane had described to her. She advanced on him, brushing down her skirt with gestures that were intended to be sensuous. 'And anyway, this would hardly be infidelity. Since I am so close to Jane. Almost a family affair, I think.'

The reply came in a harsh and lofty tone which Grace had never heard him use before. 'How dare you use that word? My family, to me, is the most precious, the most important, the most sacred thing in my life. The idea that betraying my wife with you could have anything whatever to do with family is absolutely obscene. My God, what kind of woman are you?'

Louisa was magnanimous in defeat. Without haste or shame, she collected her hairpins from the table and her shoes from the floor. 'Not your kind of woman, obviously,' she said, making for the terrace on swaggering hips. 'Such a *pity*.'

CHAPTER SEVEN

Clearing Away

Nick went back to the bathroom to use the lavatory. As he raised the seat, he saw something at the bottom of the pan, a tiny patch of cream against the white porcelain. It was a tooth, a lower incisor, natural enamel not a broken crown.

As he sat down again at Imogen's bedside, a tremor crossed her eyelids, and the long black lashes lifted a little, then fell back against her cheek. Another spasm seized her throat, but she was too sedated to do more than give a weak cough, then curl more tightly in a ball. Thoughtfully, Nick looked at her long body; the sheet was still pulled around her, she was clutching the pillow in her arms. He considered the contrast between her limbs and her abdomen. At her age, perhaps, it was not unusual.

Diagnosis, the most important aspect of medicine. They had dinned it into him, and he saw himself in his turn boring the students at the clinic with the same lecture, getting pompous with the authority of his experience. Lastly, once you've made your diagnosis, don't get so obsessed with it that you ignore information which doesn't fit. Keep checking your observations. A patient may be presenting symptoms of more than one condition. And – you may be wrong.

Here was a young woman, with a history of random drug abuse and eating disorders, severely underweight and, for all the fashionable rig, showing signs of chronic self-neglect; hence the lost tooth, which she probably spat out with the last mouthful of bile. He would have liked to open her mouth to make sure the tooth was hers, but experience added to inhibition had made him wary of invasive procedures without a witness.

Was she spewing because of the drug, or in spite of it? The vomiting centre in the brain was affected by stimulation from the stomach, and by emotions. The body's own chemicals could produce vomiting, so could toxic reactions, but they affected a different part of the brain. Drugs to relieve vomiting fell into three groups, according to which brain area they targeted. Prozac prescribed to treat bulimia produced nausea. The boy had not mentioned any prescribed drugs, but he'd been wrong, she'd deceived him. And emotion was part of this – but what else?

The boy had protested too much, trying to defend her. An eating disorder seemed likely: her arms were like sticks and her ribs like park railings, although she had full breasts and an unexpected ripeness in her abdomen.

An examination would probably confirm it, but again it was a procedure that was out of the question in this situation. The most persuasive thing was the condition of her skin; it was rich and smooth, almost like cream. He had seen the papery complexion and harsh, thin hair of anorexics persist years after the disorder was past, but this woman was blooming, even with her pallor and smudged makeup. Over her chest the distended blood vessels were obvious. Put all that together with the vomiting and you could get more than a shot of temazepam.

Then there was the boy. He was transparently honest, so in all probability he knew nothing. How to raise the subject with him? The mere idea made Nick squirm. He was so pitifully clumsy with words; sometimes he considered that staying in clinical medicine at all was just a form of masochism. This was where Grace saved him so often, she would happily invade his mind and pull out his thoughts for him in flowing declarations. But he could not involve her here.

Stephen returned with the case and keys; it was obvious he had kept many vigils like this with Imogen. He was restless because someone had taken his chosen seat beside her at the head of the bed. Gentle, conversational, Nick decided on a few questions about the relationship, and then began to advance his suspicions. 'What does she do about contraception?'

He was very ready to answer. 'Nothing. I do it. When we need to.'

'When you need to?'

We agreed last year we were so close that sex wasn't

adding anything. In fact, it was taking away, for her, because she doesn't enjoy it. So contraception isn't an issue for us at the moment.'

'Uh-huh. But when you were having sex, it was necessary? I'm wondering about her menstrual cycle.'

'It's always been very erratic. She started her periods very late, years after the rest of her class, and there were always long gaps. That was another reason. There was certainly less risk for her with a condom than for someone with regular periods. And less risk than pills or something. She hates interfering with nature.'

Looking at the malnourished body now restless in its chemical sleep, Nick could not help saying, 'Isn't it strange how people think of nature?'

OK, so there's nothing very natural about sticking a needle in your arm. OK, so I indulge her. OK, you've taken my role away and I resent it. Stephen said nothing but walked about the shadowy room again, glaring into the corners, avoiding Nick's gaze.

There was an ugly noise from the bed. With eyes half-open, Imogen pushed herself up on one elbow. She started to retch again, a little mucus dripping from her open mouth.

'Imogen, can you hear me talking to you?'

She heaved and swallowed, the painful force of the convulsion bringing her round, although all she could do was moan in reply.

'Take it easy. You've been out for a while. Do you remember me? I was at lunch, talking to your – to Jane. I am a doctor. Can you hear me talking?'

'Yeah.' It was only a whisper. Her eyelids fell again; she swayed in the bed, then fell sideways in the grip of another spasm.

'I think you're vomiting because you shot up some stuff, is that possible?'

The streaked face half-buried in the pillow wore a silly but cynical smile. 'Oh yeah. Def.'

Even with her eyes open, Stephen was not in her sight. He was holding back uncertainly, still at the edge of the room camouflaged by the bars of shadow from the shutters. Nick continued, 'I can give you something to stop you being sick, but I need to know if it'll be safe for you. Are you allergic to anything at all?'

'No. Not really.' She raised herself again; the shot was wearing off.

'Not allergic to any drugs?'

'No.' An uncoordinated shake of the head.

He looked up over the bed and fixed Stephen with a stare, keeping his voice even. 'And is there any chance that you could be pregnant?'

'No *chance.*' Another shake, a dreamier smile. Stephen's face was a mask of indignation. 'Don't take chances, me. I had the test.'

'You mean, you took the test to see if you were pregnant?'

'Uhnh.' Weakly, she raised her free arm and wiped her mouth with the back of her hand.

'A test at home you did yourself, or did someone else do it, a pharmacist? Maybe a doctor.'

'Man at the pharmacy.'

'And what result did you get?' With a stern look, he was still pinning Stephen back away from her; suddenly the younger man understood that she would not tell the truth if she knew he was there. He leaned back against the wall with folded arms, his face set.

'Yes.'

'What do you mean?'

'Yes, I am. Positive. 'Sokay. Don't matter. I can deal with it. You can give me whatever you like.' Even at a distance, Stephen's shock could be felt in the air.

'Okay. But I'll give you something safe anyway.' Nick opened his case and ran his eye over the lines of plastic bottles. 'One last question – did you drink any alcohol today?'

'Don't know. Can't remember.'

The vomit had not smelt of alcohol. Stephen was shaking his head. Nick made his choice. 'This may make you sleepy again, though probably not so much. But there'll be someone with you. It'll be another needle because you won't keep anything down now. Just lie back and let me have your arm.' In a few quiet movements, it was done and she was lying looking at him with a peaceful smile, her elbow bent to hold a swab against the puncture. Within a minute her eyes closed again.

Now, the boy. Nick got up and walked to the door, inviting him outside the room with an inclination of his head. Stephen said, 'She lies constantly, you know.'

'Sense of hearing is the last to go, first to come back.' Nick pulled the door almost closed without a sound. 'You don't believe she was telling the truth?'

'I could hardly hear what she was saying.'

'You heard, though. I needed to ask, I'm sorry.'

'It's a routine question, I suppose.'

'Yes, but I had a positive reason. How do you think she's looking at the moment?'

He was leaning against the corridor wall, hostile and suspicious, fiddling with the rolled sleeve of his shirt. 'Great. I hadn't seen her for a while until yesterday and she looked good.'

'Healthy?'

'For her, yes.'

'But she's underweight, isn't she? Undernourished, really.'

'Yes, she always is. She likes to be thin. I thought she had a sort of glow, all the same.'

'So did I.' Nick was pleased with himself. He was getting through. 'My line of thinking was this: vomiting after injecting a benzodiazepine isn't typical. You want to inject a narcotic for that. Vomiting in early pregnancy, of course, is very common. And you're right, she has got a sort of glow. In pregnancy the amount of blood in a woman's body increases by a third, and the process gets under way as soon as the pregnancy is established. Hence that blooming look.'

'You're telling me you think she really is pregnant?'

'Yes.'

'Oh God. She won't be able to cope . . .'

'She seems to have taken care of herself so far – up to a certain point.'

Stephen turned around and walked a few steps down

the corridor, his hands in his black hair. Then he came back, bracing his shoulders and looking Nick directly in the eye. 'I suppose I should say thank you.' He reached out a hand, then thought better of it. 'You did that very well. I'm sorry I was hostile.'

'I don't call people hostile until they pull a knife on me.'

'I care for her so much.' Now it was said unsteadily, but he was not going to cry. 'Can I stay with her for a while?'

'Of course. She won't make much sense and I expect you realize that the acid or whatever it was may not have worn off. The thing to watch for is . . .'

'Inhaling the vomit, I know . . .'

'So it's best if she lies on her side, as she is now, rather than her back. Keeps the airway clear.'

'OK.'

'I'll go and find my wife.' He indicated his messed-up shirt. 'I'll come back in an hour.'

At the end of the corridor a misgiving prompted Nick to turn and look back; there was no one there, the boy had immediately retreated to the bedside.

Another part of his lecture on diagnosis dealt with instinct; it was the passage his experience had added to the standard text, an observation which made all the students nod in agreement. Respect your instinct, he would tell them. If necessary, make the silence for its voice to be heard. There are ways of gathering information outside your conscious intelligence, ways of knowing things which can't be noted on a chart or entered on a file. If you have an irrational feeling, don't act on it without good reason, but don't dismiss it. Let it guide you.

The voice of his instinct was distinctly advising him that the sad, angry girl in the bedroom had come to her father's house with an intention which was not yet discharged. She intended to do something more here.

Michael can pull the truth out from under your feet like a rug. Grace grabbed at the thought, the first piece of the jigsaw. The rest of her mind was a meaningless jumble. Hardly aware of her actions, she had walked out of the side door of the house, through the garden and across to the trees, heading in the direction of her car.

The party was over. The canopied path across the meadow had gone, leaving a trampled causeway through the long grass. The tracks of the caterers' truck led to the edge of the trees, where it stood with the long grass up to its axles while sections of dais were loaded on to it. There was activity and noise, but to Grace everything was muted. She was absorbed in the tumult of her feelings, not in the concrete world outside. At least it was a familiar state. Only Michael, with his passion and his disorienting certainty, could blend all her emotions into a primordial soup.

At times like this, her talent for the *mot juste* took care of quite a bit. Putting the right word to her feelings was the beginning of mastery. When she knew what her experience was, she could analyse it, and then control it. Name it and you could tame it, the Rumpelstiltskin effect. Right now she felt cheated, but the word wasn't big enough; this was a giant's cheat, a cheat worth eight years of her life. She had heard Michael deny her, and himself; she had seen the reality instead of the picture he projected of his family and himself as a father.

Automatically, she found Nick's clean shirt as she had packed it, folded into a box in their bag in the car. As she turned she remembered that she had promised – what were Nick's words? To let the parents know. Had he avoided saying Michael's name?

'Have you seen Mrs Knight?' She had to ask several people. Under the young oaks, the circus was packing up. The food had been cleared, the utensils crated, the tables folded, the chairs stacked. While she watched the striped pavilion collapsed, flapping canvas and tinkling tent-pegs.

At the far edge of the melancholy scene was the Knights' nanny, a surreal figure straddling a solitary chair, her chin resting on her folded arms. The two little girls were nearby, wandering separately among wreckage.

'How's Imogen?' Debbie asked as Grace approached. She was tired; the vigour had drained from her body, she looked ungainly and pale.

'She's asleep now and my husband is staying with her. I was looking for Jane, to let her know.'

Nothing was said, but they held the same opinion; Michael and Jane were not concerned enough. Even tacitly, that was as far as the two women would go, being by character discreet and slow to condemn. Debbie did not ask for more information; all she said was, 'Jane went back to the house. She'll probably be in her office, just off the kitchen. We'll be coming back in a few minutes ourselves. I like to get the kids in the pool before bed-time, it relaxes them a bit.'

'Train.' The little one, rubbing her eyes, was tugging her sister's skirt, which the older child pulled away with a cross exclamation.

'Be gentle, Em, she's only little.' Wearily, Debbie held out her hand to the toddler. 'Yes, Xanthe, we'll go see the train and then it's time for a swim.' To Grace she said: 'The train's at six, so we'd better be making tracks. You go into the kitchen from the hall, then straight through to the office.'

She left the chair and set off with the children, three pale figures meandering separately into the shade of the wood. Grace retraced her path across the meadow. What did she feel for Michael now? Nothing so passionate as hatred. On this point she interrogated herself, suspicious that she was seeing merely the dark side of love. Contempt. Disgust, perhaps. Shock, more than anything. His words repeated themselves in her mind. Evangelical family-values speeches were nothing new from him, she had heard him make them a thousand times, for her alone and for a public audience.

Now she was seeing him standing at the edge of his own family, a sham, a stranger, inhibited and inauthentic. She had Nick's evaluation, which was sterner than that. 'He seems to have an overwhelming compulsion to prove that his family is a good family, that it really works. A competitive thing, it must be.'

Jane's office was almost as large as the kitchen, cool, with only one small, deep-set window; the embrasure caught the rich gold rays of the late sun. Books were shelved along the long interior wall, and more books were stacked untidily on the large table which took up the centre of the room. Jane was sitting at her desk near the door putting a folder of bills away in the filing drawer; as Grace entered, she turned towards her with an expectant expression.

'Imogen . . .' Confusion distorted the delicate face; Jane had been expecting her to say something else. 'Imogen's asleep upstairs. Nick thought you ought to know – he's staying with her for a while.' Tactfully, having learned to tread carefully around the subject of drugs, she passed on Nick's diagnosis.

'Tranquillizers? Is that all she's taken? What did Stephen say? He usually knows what she's been up to.' In speaking she bit her top lip. She muttered 'Damn' under her breath. A little blood oozed from the corner of her mouth and she licked it away.

'Stephen wasn't sure; Nick thinks she was tripping, so she may still be affected by that when she comes round.'

'Well, I'm glad you warned me. It's very kind of him to stay.'

'He's like that. He wouldn't dream of doing anything else.'

'Yes.' Jane rubbed her eyes, feeling that she wanted to clear her sight. Events were still passing by in a dream. Then she saw distress in the other woman's face. 'Are you all right, Grace? Has this upset you? I'm sorry, I'm so used to Imogen acting out . . . Why don't you sit down? Shall we have some tea?'

Her voice was soothing. What sweet relief to accept its comfort, to sit down in the cool quietness and be looked after. She took the shabby wing chair beside the desk, automatically murmuring compliments on the party while they waited for one of the staff to bring in the tray. Jane was comforted in her turn. When they were settled with the tea, she suddenly said, 'You must think I'm very cold, but Imogen's been the same for so long. I have to cut off. I wish I could do something, but now there's nothing anyone can do for her.'

'How old was she when you were married?'

'Not much more than a baby. And Michael – well, he had his work, you know.'

'Yes.'

A curious bond was materializing between them. As with old friends, they knew the landmarks of each other's lives. The pretences they put on for other people were unnecessary. 'Michael just abandoned her for me to cope with.' Jane sighed, a sigh of relief because at last she had made a confession which was normally silenced by loyalty. 'I tried to love her, but she would never respond and then the trouble began. We did it all, the therapy, everything. I'm sorry, I'm out of order here – I shouldn't be telling you this . . .'

'You can tell me.' Strange that she really wanted to know, she had real sympathy for her lover's wife.

'At first I thought it was my fault, that I didn't know how to be a mother because I hadn't got any kids of my own. You always blame yourself first.'

'I know that one. I feel it's my fault that I can't have

any – unworthy to care for children, not even a real woman.'

'I didn't know. Grace, do forgive me, that must . . .'

'No, no. I've accepted it. What else can I do?'

In the quiet, cool room the connection had been made, the first gossamer threads of recognition. Each had the same impression. I know this woman, I know how soft she is, how tender, how self-denying, honourable. She is a woman like me. How good to be with.

The insulation between Jane and the world thinned a little. She became aware of the small birds squabbling in the cherry trees outside the window, the faint aroma of the hot grass.

An instinct was pressing her to speak. It was very strong. She resisted, then asked herself why she had invited this woman to her house if it was not for this? She had no perverse bent for revenge, no masochistic curiosity about one of Michael's lovers. What she wanted was to get out of the cage of Michael's reality. She wanted a good look at the truth, it would give her strength.

'There's something we have to get in the open, Grace. I don't really know you and – I suppose I want to. You must be wondering . . .'

'Did you ask us on purpose, then?' For Nick's sake, Grace was protective.

'Yes. When I realized it was you who Nick was married to. It seemed – I don't believe in fate or any rubbish like that but it seemed such a coincidence.' What are you afraid of? Jane asked herself. Her eyes flew open wide with effort. 'You know I know about you and Michael, don't you?'

It sounded like something Grace had been expecting to hear for a long time. It felt like a blow in the stomach. She put down her tea in case she spilt it. 'I didn't know, no,' was all she could say, but her face was showing panic.

'I'm sorry.' Jane leaned forward to touch her arm.

'Aren't I the one who should be sorry?'

'Only if you insist.' A hard, humorous shrewdness suddenly settled in the child–woman face; she leaned closer, as if proposing a sneaky deal. 'I mean, we both know what we're talking about here, don't we? Michael isn't a normal erring husband.'

'I suppose not.'

'I don't think he's a normal man, or a normal human being even. He's a serial adulterer. If he's picked you as his next victim, you have no hope, you will not escape. I do know about the guilt – he was having an affair with me when he was married to Pia, don't forget.'

'When . . .?' Was it a cruel question? There were no Miss Manners conventions for this conversation.

'I found out when you had your accident. Andy Moynihan told me; she wasn't as immaculate about confidentiality then as she is now. Michael denied it, of course.'

A flash of outrage illuminated Grace's eyes. 'I had no idea,' she said slowly. 'He told me you didn't know, that he was terrified you'd find out.'

'He's not a normal liar, either, is he? Even when I had one woman's brother on the doorstep ready to beat him up, he just lied his way out of it.'

They stared at each other, realizing that here at last was a witness, that here was an end to their solitary confinement. 'What . . .' Jane hesitated. 'This isn't just curiosity, or masochism or anything – so simple. I need . . . I've lived in this swamp of his lies so long, I don't know who I am any more. Will you tell me what he said about me? Then at least I'll know who I'm supposed to be.'

Delicately at first, neither wanting to hurt the other, they retraced the steps of their dance. One by one, they pulled memories of those years out of the shadows of Michael's interpretation and held them up to be compared. Again and again, they agreed. Soon, like very old friends, there was no need to fill in details or finish sentences. Taking courage, they pulled out the deepest and darkest of their lonely miseries. The single thread connecting them became a web.

The tea turned cold. Jane fetched a bottle of velvety red wine, and then they began to share their suspicions, and tried the names of other women on each other, and found again that they agreed. Finally, Grace dared to relate the scene with Louisa in the library, feeling she and Jane were bound together, two people suddenly in possession of a secret history. 'My God,' was all Jane could say. 'My God.'

'She's an old friend of yours, isn't she?'

'Not much of a friend, you mean? No, I know Louisa. She knew somewhere she was doing me a favour.'

Outside, the sunlight was fading. 'You left him,' Jane said. 'That's more than I've achieved.'

'But the children . . .'

'That's not it. Oh, I say it is. You've seen my children. They're the real victims. I do everything I can, I do my best, I over-compensate, but they've grown up in a world that isn't real, with a father who's just pretending. I can't make that better for them. And people say I like the status and the money, and I let them think that because it's easy. But that's not it. I believed him for years, tried to live in this world he conjures up. It's so *right*, just how you feel a family should be. All his beautiful statements, great speeches. You know it's a lie, I know it's all a lie, but everybody else believes him.'

'Of course they do – he's in business to make people believe him. Communications czar, chief executive of NewsConnect . . .'

'I *want* to leave. I want to live in the real world, not this sick fantasy of his. Then I get scared and I lose faith. Maybe I can't make it, maybe the real world won't work for me, I've lost the skills, I don't know how to make it work. I'm just a coward. He's the one with guts, he'll always win over me.'

'That's why you asked me.'

'Yes. Yes it is. I met Nick, I liked him, I realized it was you he was married to. I thought, this is the proof, life after Michael. Maybe she'll give me the courage.'

They were elated now, and the wine had played little part in it. Grace fell back into the depths of the chair, her big white teeth flashing in an ironic laugh. 'I was nearly too scared to come. God, the shame and the guilt – I was imagining some neurotic-bitch conspiracy.

Then I thought about you and realized you couldn't.'

'Michael doesn't pick neurotic bitches. He turned Louisa down, didn't he?'

'No, he likes women like us. Kind and decent and moral and self-sacrificing, guaranteed never to give him any trouble. That's the sickest, isn't it? Your own goodness kills you.'

Jane poured out the last of the bottle. 'I didn't plan us talking like this – but I hoped. Who else could share it, what we've been through?'

'You can't talk about him, nobody understands, nobody believes it. I've tried to tell Nick, he's as honest as a dog, he can't begin to understand.'

'Yes.' Jane looked into her empty glass and for an instant it seemed as if her mood was crashing and she was going to cry.

'He is an honest man, isn't he? You're lucky.'

Grace didn't know what to say. Other women had made the same observation in the past, and she had found it easy to confess that there was some vital spark missing in her marriage. Now the words would not come. She thought of Nick with an intensity she had never felt before. His shirt was still in its box on her lap; he was waiting for it.

'But now . . .' Jane was looking at her, bright-eyed, over the edge of her glass. 'We've done it. We've broken through. We're not on our own with this madness any more.'

'It was like madness,' Grace agreed.

There was a knock at the door. It was Debbie. She

came in quickly, tense and anxious, and asked, 'Is Xanthe with you in here? We can't find her.' Then she sensed the atmosphere in the room and hesitated.

'Never a dull moment.' Jane collected herself with reluctance. 'Have we lost the little one?'

'I'm so sorry, I thought she was with Emma. We watched the train and then we came back to the house, and I went to get her night clothes and when I came back Emma was out of the pool and it was a few minutes before I realized little Xanthe wasn't with her. It'll be getting dark soon . . .' Her normally placid face was tense with anxiety.

'All right. She can't be far away. If we all look we're sure to find her.' Automatically Jane had turned to Grace, not wanting to leave her.

'I'm coming. I must just go upstairs and give my husband his shirt. He'll be wondering what has happened to me.' And I can't tell him, she finished to herself, pricked with disloyalty like a hundred needles.

The smothering air of a late summer afternoon filled the room. Sitting on the floor, watching the bed, his back against the wall, Stephen sighed for breath, and for grief. How had she got pregnant? Another of her defiant acts of self-destruction, falling under another body, too out of it to care? Or was there some middle-aged idiot around, stupid enough to see only her beauty and selfish enough to want to possess it?

Imogen was the kind of woman who took great moral pleasure in exploiting the lechery of men twenty years older than herself. 'Watch that sleaze over there watch me,' she would say, stalking across a room in a tiny skirt, pouting and preening. She enjoyed looking wild and condemning men who took her at face value. The whole sex thing was nothing to her, except a way of evening the score with old men; the most enjoyment she got from it was playing this malicious game.

How it had happened didn't mean anything. What was unendurable was what she would become. He saw her determined to seize the experience and harm herself with it. It was a knife she was holding to her arm. She wanted another terrible scar across her life, another crippling of her heart. Something more of her would die, physically and spiritually. She would turn another loop in the spiral down, and there was nothing he could do to help her. At times when he analysed her actions everything she did was just a great dare with destruction.

It was his fault, in a way. If he had been with her she would never have got into whatever madness had hold of her now. He thought again of the silver under the bed in her room, her manic outburst when he had confronted her. Madness was always at the end of her lane, holding out its arms in welcome, and without him to turn her away she was running full tilt towards it. She said it sometimes. 'Why don't you just leave me alone and let me go crazy? It's in my genes, Stephen, you can't do anything about it.'

Alone for the first time in her life, away in Paris – how fearful he had been for her, when she announced her intention. Her father had been so full of phoney approval, making all those speeches about how marvellous that she had found a direction, wanted to strike out on her own, do her own thing. The truth of it was that she was desperate to get away from him and he was thrilled to get rid of her. So was Jane, but Jane was one of Michael's prisoners, he never blamed her. There was no place for Imi under her father's roof, there never had been.

She was muttering something in a soft child's voice. He got to his feet and went to kneel at the bedside.

'Keith? That you Keith?' She meant to giggle, but it became a spluttering cough. Eyelids opened hesitantly, the eyes dark, not focused yet.

'Yeah, it's me.'

'You all right then?' She was struggling to get an arm free of the sheet.

'Uh-huh.' What state of mind was she in?

'Has he gone? The doctor bloke, has he gone?'

'Yeah. There's nobody else here.'

She reached for his hand and pulled it to her cheek, appealing with eyes which could look at him now but were brimming with remorse. A hot pain seized his throat. 'Are you mad at me, Keith? Don't be, don't be angry, say you aren't . . .'

'No, no. Of course I'm not . . .'

'You should be, shouldn't you?' It was a mere echo of her old, scornful, teasing voice. 'You should be saying, "Never darken my doors again," or something, shouldn't you?'

'I'd never say that. I'm not angry. I'm just afraid for you – I love you.'

'Yeah, but . . . fuck it.' Abruptly, she released his hand and started struggling to sit up. 'You shouldn't do that either.'

'Yeah, well – don't you tell me what I ought to do, OK? I'm not going to get angry with you and fuck off just because that's what I ought to do, right?'

That extracted another humorous splutter and again she wiped her mouth with the back of her hand, pulling herself further upright. There was a spare pillow on the floor and he put it behind her head. 'Are you still tripping?'

'Don't think so. I feel good, maybe I am. But you make me feel good. Feel safe. If I could actually have this baby, we'd be safe with you.'

'Don't talk about it now.'

'Well, we're going to have to talk anyway, aren't we? Might as well get started now.'

'But why . . .'

'Don't be daft. I'm not fit to look after a cockroach, am I?'

'But . . .'

'Don't hassle me. Just be nice, OK?' Abruptly, she pulled his tenderly placed pillow around to the front of her body and hugged it to her stomach as if to smother everything within. 'Do you suppose the baby was tripping too? Inside there, out of its tiny, tiny box? How big do you think it has to be before it's got a brain?' Then she put her hands over her ears, twisting her neck around as if she could squeeze the thought out of her head. 'Stop me thinking this stuff. Stop it. I can't believe there's anything still inside there, I chucked up so much. If that doctor had stuck around we could ask him, couldn't we?'

'He's coming back. Can I get you anything?'

She moved her lips around, monkey-like, as if trying to decide what she would like to taste. 'Water. My mouth feels disgusting.'

There was no glass in the bathroom, or in the next bathroom along the corridor. 'I'll go down to the kitchen,' he told her.

'No.' She was getting up, looking much more together and moving energetically. 'I'll go. I feel all right now.'

'No, let me . . .'

'I want to walk around a bit, get my head clear.' She went over to the *armoire* and pulled it open, looking for clothes.

'I think you've got some jeans in there,' he advised.

'Jeans make my bum look huge.' It was a reassuringly normal reply.

'Nothing could make your bum look huge.'

'What do you know about it?' He was annoyed at her rudeness and sat down on the chair again, declining to help while she rummaged through the cupboard. Jeans and a white shirt were the only things in it that were not too hot for summer, so she dressed with bad grace and made for the door. She paused in the doorway, said nothing but looked at him, the look that told him he was boring.

While he waited, he reflected on his dullness and how it infuriated her. Once she had thrown a total witch-out on the crest of the South Downs, screaming into the wind and hurling chalk rocks at him because, she said, he could not go for a walk happily without knowing how he was going to get back. He had always felt pitifully ordinary, beside her.

Away from her for the past few months, it had been different. Since he went to university, they had been parted three times now for almost three months. The first half he had been utterly lost, passively looking on while the other freshers scrambled for whatever they wanted, the tutor, the partner, the extra-curricular enhancement to the CV. It had been a genuine shock when a lecturer made a formal point of telling him he was by far the most interesting student of his year, perhaps of his decade.

By the second term, he seemed suddenly to have friends. At school, Imi had taken up his company all the time. There had been a lot of people who disliked her. He was surprised to find the space she left filling with new friends who enjoyed him, praised him and had open ears for his confidences. He had defended himself, unaccustomed to such closeness, but they persisted; one in particular, a nice girl. She knew about Imi, of course, he'd made it clear in the beginning, and she respected the situation. There wasn't any chemistry there, but it had been a new experience to eat in a restaurant with a woman who just ordered food, ate it and enjoyed it, instead of making a five-act opera out of getting a plate of vegetables cooked without animal fat.

So much had happened this year. Now there were two

Stephens, the old one and the one who dared and won, who had dared to go up to Alan Stern.

It was even new to think about himself. He felt guilty when Imogen needed so much care, but he was looking at her now from a different angle, feeling resentment that she took so much from him. And Nick had made him feel guilty in another way. Had he been caught out in using her, with her talent for trauma, just to insulate himself from his own thoughts?

'What's going on?' Michael came out of his office, wearing his dark blue jacket and his public air of consequence. He was up again, in control. His secretary had been at home, able to take some letters and restore him with an extended conference, preparing the week ahead. Considerable as it was, the sense of his own identity always began to leach away when he entered his home circle; he needed contact with the bigger world to keep himself strong.

He saw Jane approaching the small group gathered on the pool terrace; her voice was high with concern. There was a general air of distraction. A domestic crisis, probably a missing child. Privately, he felt that his wife had no idea what a real crisis was. People ran about like chickens with their heads cut off, manufacturing drama to spice their own lives; these mundane anxieties were nothing in comparison with the business of a newsroom.

By coincidence, Grace came out of the house after him, also looking distracted; he saw that she had something odd in her hand, a shirt in an individual laundry box. She was obliged to pass him. Delighted to find that not all his guests had fled, Michael took her arm fondly, saying, 'Don't go yet – you're not leaving too, are you? There's something I wanted to talk to you about.'

'I was looking for Nick,' she said, without the interest he had anticipated.

'What's that you're carrying?'

'A clean shirt for my husband.' She emphasized the last two words. 'Have you seen him?' Would he register that the shirt was needed on account of his daughter? Not a hope. He just looked her over in a benevolent, proprietorial manner, a look which assured her that he understood she would have cared for him just as well if things had worked out differently.

Before Michael could reply she saw Nick down on the pool terrace, and an agitated group gathering around Jane. The sight of him suddenly opened a small bud of happiness in her inner turmoil. Beside Michael, she descended through the garden and went to Nick's side, grateful for his substantial presence.

'Where were you?' he muttered, taking the shirt.

'I got caught up,' was all she could give him in explanation.

They watched Michael assume command of a situation in which he was clearly at a loss to know what to do. 'Now what's this all about?' he demanded.

'We've lost Xanthe, or rather I've lost Xanthe.' While the rest of the company stood, Louisa was still sitting on her sun-lounger. She had changed for swimming into a masterpiece of structural and chemical engineering, white in colour, Grace Kelly in inspiration. Her tone implied that only ill-mannered children got lost. 'She was in the pool with Emma a moment ago and now she's disappeared.'

'Debbie . . .'

'I was fetching their night things.' The suntanned face was devoid of apology.

'Ah.' Michael's manner implied that a woman employed in childcare had no right to delegate her responsibilities, even for a minute. 'You've searched the house?'

'Just downstairs so far. It takes her ages to manage the stairs.'

'Tell me exactly what happened. What was she wearing?'

The last time anyone had seen her, Xanthe had been wearing her white swimming costume printed with red ladybirds and she had been in the pool with Emma, floating happily, wearing her pink armbands.

'She must have made off as soon as I left, because there weren't even any little wet footprints. Nobody who was about saw her either.'

A few of the staff had been clearing away the last traces of the party, but they had not seen her. Antony had staggered back to the house but he was asleep and snoring in the chair he had adopted under the honeysuckle, a suspicion of whisky in a glass beside him on the ground.

'No point asking *him*.' Louisa kicked one of his feet disdainfully, provoking only a grunt.

With a superstitious dread, Jane turned on the pool

lights and they peered into the water, thankful to find nothing but a dead mouse.

With an effort, Michael brought his mind to bear on his infant daughter's motivations. 'What would have attracted her interest? The frogs in the wood, do you suppose?'

'Or the *train*.' Courteously, Louisa sucked in a yawn. The problem for her was that she found children hopelessly irritating. 'She kept saying she wanted to see it come back. She threw a fit because nobody would take her.'

There was a toddler gate to close the exit to the meadow from the pool terrace, but no one had shut it. Jane felt a cobweb of guilt that she had been so deeply caught up with Grace, so attracted by the notion of breaking taboos and tipping the balance of power with her husband, that she had forgotten this simple precaution.

It was that moment in a late summer evening when the twilight seems to fall like fine rain. The birds were roosting and in the utter quietness the only noise was from the caterers' truck, driving slowly up the trampled meadow. Soft grey clouds were gathering in the western sky and below them, in a band of clear pale blue, the sun was sinking to the horizon, its light fading through layers of vapour. It was not going to be a gaudy sunset, nor one to delight shepherds. The colour had bled from the landscape, green turning to grey, yellow fading to ash. The oak wood was already nothing but a shadow in the middle distance.

'Go and ask them to turn the truck round and put on the headlights.' Michael gave orders as he strode towards the house. 'I'll be down there in a minute with a flash-light.' The staff obeyed him immediately, but the four women held back in misanthropic unison. You go on dear, Jane's face said. Land on the beaches, take the bridge too far, shoot it out at the OK Corral. We'll just stay here and keep the world turning round.

Nick cleared his throat, anxious that he might be intruding. 'Could she have put herself to bed?'

'It wouldn't be typical. She made a fuss about going down last night.' Jane sighed, recalling that first tantrum. 'But we'd better look.'

In the fading light they saw Michael's dark figure stride past the terrace and away to the trees, the flash-light beam raking the grass. 'Someone ought to go with him,' she added, looking regretfully at Debbie, who muttered a grim 'OK,' and left them.

In panicky haste, Jane set off for the children's wing, with Grace and Nick following, united in wanting to be with her. Charming and low-roofed, this outbuilding had been the tumbledown barn used for fattening ducks. Tamara Aylesham had raved over its cottage proportions and insisted it should be restored, brushing aside Jane's misgivings about walls which for centuries had witnessed the annual imprisonment of hundreds of birds, who would then be force-fed with cracked maize until they were too dazed to clean themselves and too bloated to stand; the barn would stink of their slimy green droppings and the grain fermenting in their stomachs. In their last days some of the birds would collapse and lie wretched and bedraggled on the pallets which kept them from the worst of the filth, choking on their precious fat livers and waiting for the knife. Another universal quirk of husbandry; poultry were the woman's job on a farm. Jane had been happy to agree with her new editor that *foie gras* was too contentious a subject for a modern readership.

Now these horrors were unimaginable. The building had little white windows wreathed in roses and fresh white walls adorned with nursery friezes.

They went first to the room the girls shared, where Emma was desultorily applying cream to her arms. Jane was about to criticize her for not helping when she realized that the child was exhausted. Her little face was grey and puffy, more like the face of middle-age than of an eleven-year-old.

'I'll look in Sam's room, if you two can check in here.' Jane left them with a distracted air; slightly timid in a strange house, Grace and Nick began to look under the beds and inside the cupboards.

'Maybe she found something interesting to play with.' One arm finished, Emma carefully squeezed more cream from the tube and began on the other.

'You're sure you didn't see her get out of the water, Emma?'

The child shook her head.

'Did you see her at all – do you think she's with Sam?'

'She won't be. Sam gets furious if she goes in his room. She interrupts his games. He said he'd pull her head off if she ever went in there again.'

In Sam's room, the unearthly light of the computer screen threw shadows on the white walls; the rest of the room was dark. Jane saw her son's rounded figure sitting motionless at the desk, his lenses reflecting the screen. 'Turn that off,' he commanded when she put on the light.

'You turn *that* off,' she snapped back at once, pulling the plug from the socket. 'Your sister's disappeared. Come and help us look for her.'

'Good. I hope she drowned.' He got off the stool and tried to grab the plug from Jane's hand.

'Sam!' To her amazement, Jane felt a flash of fear; he would soon be as tall as she was, and he was already heavier. When Michael was at home, Sam had begun to swagger about the house in imitation of his father, living in his own world and expecting to be able to move his sisters around as easily as the gibbering images on the screen. When anyone crossed him he withdrew to the games. When the games were threatened, or unavailable, a sort of panic possessed him.

'Stop it, Sam. We've lost Xanthe – this is serious.'

'Interrupting me is serious. Give me that . . .' He made another grab for the plug. She checked herself; finding Xanthe was the most important thing. She could search his room without his cooperation; this little power struggle was not the immediate priority. She let the plug drop to the floor and began to open cupboards, while her son, to her relief, reconnected his machine and settled down again with nothing more hostile than an irritated remark about having lost his game points.

'You're sure you haven't seen her?'

'No.' He was intent on the screen. Conscious of valuable time passing, Jane left him and began opening the cupboards outside. Then she noticed the bathroom door at the end of the corridor move a few inches.

In the girls' room, Grace sat down on the nearest bed watching Emma flicking at her snarled hair with a brush. What the child had said reminded her of the curious thing people did in interviews, when they felt interrogated by their own consciences, and so answered a question which had not been put to them.

'Your hair gets tangled easily, doesn't it?'

'I like it messy. It looks really wild.'

'Certainly does.' And when people held out that way they were really trying to make you probe, so they couldn't be blamed when the truth came out.

'Debbie says it's the pool water makes it tangle. She puts conditioner on it sometimes, but I like to leave it.' Grace found it delightful, the way the little girl had sat down to make conversation, with a prim inflection and bright eyes and legs neatly crossed at the knee.

'So Xanthe might have found something interesting to play with?' Nick was wandering around the room with a contemplative face, obviously deep in thought. He was still holding his clean shirt. 'Darling, why don't you just put that on?'

'Uh?'

'The shirt.'

'Which you kindly fetched from the car for me. I'm so sorry, yes, I'll do that right now. Is there . . .'

'We have a bathroom at the end of the corridor,'

Emma graciously announced, then continued her line of thought. 'I mean, OK, Xanthe is a pest but you can just get away from her. Sam's always on his computer, he's obsessed with it. Actually he's better when Daddy's not here. Sometimes, do you know, he gets up out of bed, after Debbie's put the lights out, and plays with it all night sometimes?'

'Did Xanthe find something to play with?'

The girl looked at her, obviously weighing the advisability of passing on sensitive information. 'One of those needle things,' she said at last. 'Like doctors have. I did ask her to give it me, but she wouldn't.'

'Oh God.'

'She went into the bathroom,' Emma went on, obviously reassured that nobody was angry.

They reached the door just as Jane pushed it open, and the three of them entered at the same time. The bathroom, like all the others in the house, was plain white with tiled walls. Xanthe was leaning over the edge of the bath, a syringe held firmly in one tiny fist, the needle upmost, a few inches away from her rosy face.

'Darling.' Jane made a great effort to appear calm and friendly. 'What have you got there?'

Xanthe said something, a happy but unintelligible reply.

'Give it to me, darling. Please.' It was not going to work. A shadow of suspicion darkened the round blue eyes and the plump little hand clutched the syringe more tightly. 'It's dangerous, Xanthe. You must give it to me.' The tiny figure turned defensively away. Then the child looked at the needle and appeared to make a decision; the little arm was raised and the syringe thrown crossly into the bath. Xanthe paused for an instant, burst into tears and held up her arms, wanting to be picked up.

'Thank God.' Jane snatched her into her arms and kissed her. 'There's a good girl, you threw it away. Good girl. There, it's all right now.' The tears became sobs, then developed into a scream, then began to subside to a fussy snuffle. In a few minutes Xanthe was calm, and obviously tired, lolling in her mother's embrace with unfocused eyes. Emma appeared with the baby's particular blanket, which had been draped over the side of her cot.

As Jane left the bathroom, Nick went in and retrieved the syringe. 'Where can I put this for safety?' he asked her. 'They're a menace, these things. The kitchen might be the best place, if I can find something to wrap it in. I have to give them out at the clinic, and I hate doing it, I know perfectly well that twelve hours later they'll be lying around on a building site or a back alley . . .'

'You don't have to be responsible for everything your patients do,' Grace teased him.

'Yes I do,' he replied, only half in jest. 'I certainly ought to have been responsible for getting this found before now.'

'There's a dustbin in the kitchen, the staff will help you. Can I ask you to do one more thing for me?' Tenderly, Jane tucked the blanket under the sleepy infant's head. 'Let Michael know everything's OK now? I'm afraid he'll be getting a search party out from Saint-Victor soon.'

'Of course, of course. Right away. Right. Can I just borrow this?' From a basket of toys, he pulled a torn sheet of a comic and carefully wrapped the syringe in it, before setting off on his mission. Grace smiled after him.

'You're so lucky,' Jane said again. Restlessly, the baby turned her head, her eyes still wide. 'I'm going to walk with this one for a little while, to help her drift off. Are you OK for a while, Em? We'll just go into the orchard. I'll come back and say goodnight.'

Out in the soft, humid air, Jane and Grace wandered side by side, listening to Xanthe snuffle sleepily. Among the young trees the scent of apples mingled with lavender. 'This one is my last hope, you know.' Jane looked across her daughter's copper curls. 'Emma was a problem the first minute, never slept, wouldn't feed. They keep saying the eczema will clear up as she gets older, but it isn't happening. It's like I've been found out, you know. I was pretending I was happy, and then I gave birth to all the pain I was trying to hide and there it was, screaming at me. The same with Sam; I look at him now and all he's doing is running away, just like me. He's got his computer and I've got my work.

'I even wonder if I love them sometimes,' she said with resignation. 'I do love them, I *care* about them, in a dutiful sort of way, but it isn't a feeling. I'm all out of feelings, have been for years.'

There was a pause, and then the young man in charge of the caterers came to say a respectful goodbye, adding his personal pleasure that the little one had been found safe and sound. They went out to see the lorry away, its lights flaring on the sunflowers as it climbed the hill.

'Did you envy me, when you were with Michael? I suppose you must have done.'

'Yes, in the beginning. Then I felt the same, out of feelings. I'm not sure I've ever got them back.'

'You adore Nick now, don't you? I can see it. You just light up when he's with you.' It had cut her to the heart to see the two of them fly together like magnets.

Grace was surprised, but there was no mistaking Jane's sincerity. There was a note of genuine envy in the observation, although it had been sympathetically delivered. 'Yes,' she said, to be polite. 'I suppose I do.' The idea sat comfortably with her.

Where the fuck was everybody? The house was empty, there was no one on the terrace. She could hear car engines, a few people were still leaving. Shitbags, all of them. All Daddy's so-called friends were crap. They hung about because he was powerful, no other reason, and he was such a fucking egomaniac he'd never see it.

Far off on the ground floor there were noises of people working in the house, but a claustrophobic hush lay unbroken in the drawing room. The light through the window was fading and she didn't like the long shadows. Everything in the room looked menacing. Fucking microdot, whatever it was. Never, never again. Forget it, it was evil.

Daddy was really, really angry with her. In the middle of throwing up, she had caught sight of his face with that vicious, fierce compression of all his features that signified absolute rage. And by now, of course, he knew she was pregnant. That doctor had told him. That's why he hadn't come back; what else would you expect from the filth Michael and Jane collected round them. Where was Stephen? He always took care of her, where was he now? Michael was coming now to look for her, sending people to blow her right off the planet. He didn't need a daughter causing scandal all the time, not in his life. He'd decided, she had to go. Time to get away, get out, fast, now.

The white shirt would show up in the dark, make her too obvious, but at least she had bare feet, she could move around without making any noise. That was cool, no one would hear her.

Outside the house she felt better. This was paranoia, it was the stuff. Mr T hadn't taken care of everything, the trip wasn't over. There was a rich red light over the sunflower fields, and shadows dancing under the trees. The water in the pool was a sizzling turquoise. Pop Art colours. Hyper-realism. Even at a distance she could see every seed in the flower heads, every hovering beetle. No art history tutor she'd ever heard had mentioned psychotropic drugs and colour values but it was a really important connection. They were all on something. And not just the moderns. Even Michaelangelo – it was so obvious, the whole beauty of the Sistine Chapel was that sublime sense of universal connection drugs released in your mind. Maybe that would be her thesis, her contribution. Must get it written down.

People made a lot of fuss about trips but they didn't understand. If you were sensible you could control things. When the paranoias started the thing to do was hook your mind on to something beautiful, get some positive input. Then all those feelings of wonder and oneness would come back, and the nasties wouldn't be able to take hold. So now all she had to do was take care of herself that way and sit it through. Already the illusions were fading in and out; it was nearly over.

Restless energy made her ready to run. She decided to go back to the old trees. Ever since meeting her mother and staying in that forest trees had seemed protective. Stephen would be able to find her there; he could find her anywhere. They had this heavy psychic connection, he always knew where she was.

There were still a lot of people about, which was good. If she really needed help there'd be someone to ask. Bunch of creeps though they were. Looking at her in that patronizing way, sliming her with their eyes. All her life she had been surrounded by people in mindless awe of Daddy, people who even worshipped him, intelligent people absolutely zapped who said shit like, 'You must be so proud of your father,' or 'You're so lucky, your father's such a wonderful man.' Then Jane had got started on her thing and it had been the same with her, everyone at school being stupid, saying, 'Can I come home with you – I bet you get really good meals at home.'

They never asked any questions, they just bought the family photograph. Michael Knight, media czar, at home with his wife Jane and their children, Imogen, Emma,

Sam and their new baby, Xanthe. Everybody smiling, everybody happy. What is wrong with this picture?

She was slowly drifting over the grass, avoiding the young trees, a graceful figure with a fixed, lazy smile and tentative, barefoot steps who drew the eyes of the caterers' men as they searched for the missing child. Creeps. To avoid their interest she feigned nonchalance and veered deep into the wood.

Her tree was waiting for her, the big oak with a split trunk and the flattened root that was almost like a seat. It was large enough to hide her from the creeps. She really wanted to hide herself. Everything was shadowy now; the early evening light was too weak to shine through the leaves. Close by was the little spring, the tiny trickling noises of water were distinct to her enhanced hearing.

In this condition, emotion was like the weather down in Texas, pretty extreme but at least you could see it coming. Next was going to be some sort of pain. The sorrow clouds were gathering rapidly, bowling towards her faster and faster. Oh fuck, this thing wasn't dying down, she was in for another round.

She tried to focus on the leaves but her mind obstinately refused to obey. Visions welled up from her memory. She saw her mother's face, very lined and pale-skinned like her own, but delicate. Very lovely, she was, a comforting angel. The dry, fine lines criss-crossing her cheeks were like cobwebs. There was that tiny trace of an accent when she spoke. She was slim in a stringy way, in her arms and legs you could see all her muscles. Her clothes looked as if they had been washed a lot and she spoke quietly all the time as if her feelings were all washed out as well.

The house was cluttered with objects, pottery, driftwood, seashells, old plates, little paintings, stones, everything worn or damaged. Her mother's house was like a celebration of damage.

A huge wave of sadness broke over her. All those years alone, all those years when her mother's face was still fresh and silky and she never saw it, never touched it. The pain was like a single vibration holding her entire being. Surely she was going to die of it, her soul shatter like glass. It was unbearable, she would never survive. She could hear screaming, a sound from her own throat joining all the anguish of the world in a great howl.

The tumultuous grief retreated as violently as it had come, leaving a bitter melancholy in which fragments of their conversation echoed. 'I had to do what your father said, he had everything on his side.' 'Not having you with me was like having my arms torn off.' 'Of course, when I wasn't married any more there was a question about my citizenship. For a while I thought I would be forced to go back to Sweden.' 'I want you to know I think of you every single day of my life. All day, sometimes.' 'I wish I had known how you looked. He never sent me a photograph, I did ask. You are a beautiful girl, Imogen.'

Thank God, the sadness was going, dwindling down to sentimental poignancy, a breath of regret, blowing away. She was cool again, at least for a moment. The light was going fast now, it was hard to find anything to focus on. Stephen would be along soon, not to worry, and in the white shirt she would be easy to see.

Her eyes roamed over the floor of the wood, looking for an object to hold her attention. No flowers. Close to her feet was a maidenhair fern, uncurling a new, vivid, leathery leaf. Concentrating, absorbing its spiral beauty, she grew irritated by a form behind it, something angular and artificial which seemed to cut across the helix of life.

It was a kitchen knife.

Scrambling forward from her seat in the tree roots, she retrieved it and held it by its point, swinging it like a pendulum in front of her eyes. The blade was dull but its edge was keen, a thread of silver in the dim light. Really, she was much less sick now than even six months ago. Here was this exquisitely sharp knife – and obviously belonging to Jane – and she had no compulsion at all to cut herself with it. If she had, it would do a beautiful job, it probably was as sharp as a razor. But she had no desire even to try the blade. She really was in control now.

The gathering twilight was becoming spooky. It was full of noise, dry noises, crackling and crunching, sweeping branches, brushing leaves. And she was alone. No Stephen. Probably still blundering about looking for her. Or maybe Daddy had stopped him. How they hated each other. Stephen was the one person who had never bought the picture, so Michael hated him.

She'd seen him for years, fixing his laser killer stare on Stephen. All the smiley smarmy stuff he did, all his chat and bonhomie and handshaking, all that high-toned talk about the ethics of broadcasting, it was a disguise, a cloak of illusion. All the time he was sucking the life from everyone around him. A vampire; dead himself, feeding on the essence of living people. She was almost dead now, he'd had so much from her, but he was coming now to finish her, empty her veins. He knew where she was hiding. The tree was no longer safe. A growing terror sent her off at random, with the intention of getting back to the house, to Stephen.

She was walking faster and faster. Her feet hurt. It was only paranoia, no one was after her, least of all Daddy. Come on, when had he ever been concerned enough to come and actually find her? Be cool. Keep moving, keep the terrors handled.

As she picked her way between the trees, the leaves loud under her feet, the fear refused to die down. In her hand, the knife was a significant burden. Idly, she bent down and swiped at a plantain stem, slicing off the flower head. The way it fell cleanly to the ground was very satisfying. A little drop of the fear was released.

On her knees, she cut some more stems, enthralled at the miraculous way the knife toppled each small, dark inflorescence. It was a poetic weapon, a samurai sword in miniature. It had been put in her path to protect her.

'Imogen. Imogen. *Imogen.*' That was somebody calling her name. Something was clawing at her shoulders. She dared not look round. She dared not stop cutting. Was it Stephen? Please God it was Stephen, he'd make everything OK. She was terrified now, resisting the pulling hand. He was going to kill her. Knives everywhere so he could kill her. Please God it wasn't Stephen, what might she do to him?

Michael turned off his flashlight and let his eyes grow accustomed to the gathering darkness. 'That's great news,' he said to Grace's husband. 'Great news.'

'She was in their bathroom, playing by herself. No harm done.'

'Good, good. Excellent.' He turned and called out to the handful of catering staff who were scattered across the meadow. 'It's all right, everybody, she's fine, she's been found.'

The two men looked at each other, awkward with unspoken antagonism. Nick was quite ashamed of his opinion that Michael was a smooth, hypocritical asshole. The source of his hostility was not quite clear to him, and so he felt it was unreasonable and, given that the man was his host, ungracious. Michael was once more feeling that his importance was being diminished, and that this man was something to do with it.

'I'll – um – get back,' Nick said at last.

'Yes. Yes, thank you, thanks again. I'll be right up in a minute.' Michael reached out and squeezed Nick's arm briefly, then turned away again, feeling embarrassed.

Above the oak trees one bright star was already shining. The mystery of the wood beckoned him. The ability to surrender to nature was something he knew he lacked, one of the many paths to repose and contemplation which he had hesitated to follow for fear of finding himself along the way. Work was justified, and everything that supported it, but he saw that other people gave their energy to distractions, arts or football or the leisurely expression of love, and felt he must be judged incomplete unless he did the same. So periodically he would attempt such behaviour, and now he stood and listened attentively to the night noises on his own land, and felt stupid because he had no notion of what or where the creatures were who churred and chirruped in concert all around him.

The spectral figures of the staff were gravitating towards the truck. One by one they climbed aboard and the vehicle ground slowly up towards the car park. Out of the corner of one eye, Michael caught a movement on the far side of him, and turned towards it. One person was left, he saw a white shirt. The etiolated proportions of the body were quite unmistakable.

'Imogen,' he called out. 'Imogen? Where are you going? Come back, they've found Xanthe.' She seemed to be alarmed at his voice, and stumbled away. He thought she was probably drunk. The notion flashed into his mind that the railway track might also have attracted her. After the episode at Christmas, Jane had suggested to him, in her annoyingly soft way, that it might be sensible to put a fence along the cutting, for the safety of all the children. He had the builder's quotation for the work in his office.

She was floundering away from him, the white shirt flashing between the trees as she gained the depth of the wood. He followed; the ground was treacherous with briars and undergrowth. When he reached a clearing where a few pine trees grew the light was stronger, but in walking forward confidently he tripped over an unseen root and half-fell, putting his hands down to save himself.

With a wry smile to himself, he admitted that this was not his lucky day. He had met failure at every turn since his arrival in France, and the sense of chaos was building steadily. The need to recoup the disaster of the party was chewing at his mind. The fact that he could take no action until the morning, that he was marooned here in his wife's world, was an added frustration.

After the roasting heat of the day, the air was cool and full of scents, the pleasant smells of crushed plants and the rich aroma breathed out by the earth itself. There was a primitive excitement in walking among the trees in the almost-dark, hearing twigs crunch under his feet, having to feel the way as much as see it. For a few minutes his imagination took flight, suggesting how, among these dim, deceptive vistas of leaves and branches, simple people came to believe in wood-gods, Pan and Herne the Hunter, attended by dancing fauns and dryads.

'Imogen!' He could see her quite clearly now, on the ground about fifty feet ahead of him, cowering against a tree trunk. A few more steps and his shoe was almost sucked from his foot in a patch of mud, an accident which grounded his mind in annoyance. 'Imogen, do come on. Come back with me.'

She crawled away around the base of the tree, and he halted, wondering why she was behaving so strangely.

It was Imogen's way to attack, he was accustomed to it. Now she was acting as if she was terrified. The dark, perhaps? She had always been hyper-sensitive. Had he been unwise to talk graphically about her mother's breakdown? Since that wretched boy had taken her over there, she had started making sarcastic references to her bad blood. Was she staging some copycat scene now?

Warily, at a distance, he followed her towards the railway cutting. The pine trees mingled with the oaks meant that there was more light at this edge of the wood. She got down on the ground again and seemed to be absorbed in looking at the plants.

Approaching as quietly as he could, he saw that she was cutting the tops off grasses with a kitchen knife. Better the plants than her own arm, but a knife was a knife.

'Imogen,' he said gently.

She was talking to herself. 'I want you to know,' was all he could hear. 'I want you to know.' Another stem decapitated. Her feet were bare and muddy.

'Imogen. *Imogen*.'

He took hold of her free arm and tried to pull her to her feet. 'Stop this, Imogen. Stop it.' She was limp but resistant, pulling towards the ground, still whispering fearfully to herself. 'You don't know what you're doing,' he said. 'Give me the knife. Don't be afraid.'

'No!' All of a sudden her long limbs were infused with strength and she bounded upright, snarling incomprehensibly. He had forgotten how tall she was, how difficult to restrain. Her arms were whipping wildly around his head.

'Give me the knife,' he repeated, grabbing at the blade as it flashed briefly into his field of vision. 'Give it to me. Come on now.'

'No, no!' She tore her arm out of his grasp. Her teeth were shining white in the darkness. She was trying to hit him. He felt her hit him at the back of his neck. She struggled away from him, pushing him from her. For an instant he stood still. Imogen was standing about three feet away, looking at him in absolute terror, her eyes staring. He wanted to go to her and reassure her, but when he moved the ground rushed up towards him. Then it was dark.

CHAPTER EIGHT

Harvest Supper

'I never felt so loved.' Jane and Grace were sitting at the kitchen table now, face to face across the oak plank which gleamed with the grease of ten thousand dinners and the polishing of a hundred hands. Xanthe was sleeping soundly in bed, and the rest of the household was dispersed. Grace had pinned up her hair, feeling that it hampered her; this long exchange was a conference, not a conversation. There was work to be done here. 'All that sensitivity, that intelligence, all poured into loving me. *Knowing* me. I couldn't believe anyone would ever know me so deeply and love me so much.'

'Yes. But . . .' With one finger, Jane was tracing the edge of her table, needing a task to settle her restless mind. 'He doesn't, does he? He doesn't love. Any of us. He can't.' Could she make the final confession? She looked up, reading compassion on Grace's open face. To her surprise, she was coldly angry that this woman too had been betrayed. 'I feel terrible for you,' she said.

'But that's wrong – I feel terrible for you, for what I did to you. That's how it should be . . .'

'You never wanted to take him away from me, did you? I know you didn't, you aren't like that. You didn't want him for yourself.'

'No, I didn't. There was a sort of beauty in the hopelessness of it But I was doing you wrong, Jane.'

'No, that's not how I feel about it. I know whatever happened between you was his initiative, his persistence, his creation.' She stopped short, seeing that the pride in Grace had been goaded by her words. That's what saved her in the end, she had enough pride to run away. That's what I need. 'I can't tell you how good it is to talk like this. So many years I've been alone with it . . .' Jane sighed, for her loneliness and her children, and for the pity of her weakness. 'Love is giving yourself, isn't it? It's self-sacrifice. He can't do that. Michael's god is himself. So he acts it out, love – and we, all of us, all his women, give ourselves, but he can't do it. And – I think that's why he goes on and on, eating up one woman after another. I've asked him, of course, a hundred times. Why can't you just screw around like other husbands? Serial monogamy's quite normal nowadays, so why can't you leave me, marry the next one. I'm sorry, that was unkind.'

'Be my guest.'

'Why do you have to keep me here, married alive? Then he says he loves me, that there isn't anyone else. And if he gets angry he says I don't have to stay, which of course I don't, but . . .'

She stopped, hearing sudden footsteps in the hall outside. The door did not open. 'Who's there?' Jane demanded, alarmed to think that they might have been overheard.

There was no answer, so she opened the door. In the hallway Imogen was sitting on the floor, her long thin legs buckled as if she had collapsed there. 'Help me?' Her voice was almost a whisper.

'She's covered in mud. She's been outside.' Grace left the table, intending to help, but the girl managed to get to her feet and come into the kitchen, bowing her head as she went through the doorway.

'What's the matter? Imi, what is it?'

'I have taken this thing.' Standing against the wall, Imogen was making a supreme effort to be coherent. 'And it's turned really bad on me, Jane. Really bad. Evil. It is coming and going, but it's really bad. I'm sorry. I'm so sorry. I know I've spoiled everything for you . . .'

'Hush, that's not so. Not at all.' Jane felt helpless. 'But I don't know what to do.'

Imogen's jeans were blotched with mud. Her white shirt was covered with pieces of twig and leaf. There was a grass stain on one arm and some round, dark spots on the embroidered shirt front.

'Have you cut yourself?' Jane asked her.

'Have I cut myself?' She looked puzzled. 'No. I left the knife behind. I did really well, you'd have been proud of me. I was having this great paranoid thing about Daddy, but I just – left it.'

'Let's go and find Nick, he's only in the drawing room,

he'll take care of you.' Grace was surprised at her own optimism, but it was justified. Stephen was with him; evidently it was the hour for confidential conversations. They had started a fire, and the cheerful light of the flames flickered over their faces and the white walls.

Seeing Stephen, Imogen collected herself for a final effort of crossing the room and falling into his arms. Tenderly he installed her beside him on the sofa.

'Vitamin C,' Nick recommended. 'Orange juice or the stuff you give people for colds.' He was still running on high energy, his face redder than ever from the day's sun. 'And best not leave her until we're sure it's over.'

'You poor man – what on earth must you think of us? You're practically running a hospital here and I invited you as a guest to have a lovely day and taste the Adour salmon.' To disguise her discomfort, Jane went over to the window and closed the curtain.

'And a marvellous experience it was. Imogen's no trouble, don't think that. She'll be OK.' She smiled pathetically at him and sank further into Stephen's embrace.

'Will she remember her – experiences?' The subject was so emotionally charged for her that Jane found it difficult to talk about drugs in a normal voice.

'The trip? Some people remember everything . . .' He looked enquiringly at Stephen.

'Imi doesn't usually remember much.'

'I don't wanna remember this one, that's for sure.' Imogen gave a weak laugh, burying her face in her hands. When she took her arms away, Jane noticed that the stains on her shirt front were spreading; at the edges they were raspberry red.

'I hardly dare ask, but . . .' Jane set about turning on lamps and plumping cushions, trying to evade her dark unease. 'I don't know how to deal with this. Nick, will you stay a while longer? Stay for supper.'

Nick looked at his wife, who apart from her misgivings about this particular house had always said there was nothing worse in the world than being trapped in a house party which had turned sour, but she nodded quickly. 'Of course,' he said amiably. 'Delighted. Imogen will be fine, though.'

But will I? Jane wondered. Grace said, 'Let me help you,' and they went back to the kitchen.

'Shall we open a nice bottle of Pacherenc for them?' Jane disappeared into a side room and returned with a bottle, then looked abstractedly for glasses. 'Isn't it pathetic – I actually feel bad about talking to you about Michael. He surrounds himself with . . .' She paused, groping for the right words.

'I'd call it a climate of confidentiality.' A pompous piece of journalese when actually spoken, but Grace had used the term in her own mind often.

'Yes.'

'Where is he? Nick said he was following them when he came back to the house.'

'Imogen said something about him, didn't she?' Jane was busying herself with a tray, reluctant to acknowledge that they were sharing a growing misgiving. 'He's probably upstairs. I'll take a look.'

'Could he have gone for a walk?'

'No. He doesn't do walks, much. He's probably found some work to get on with.'

She took the tray with wine and glasses into the sitting room, then looked into Michael's office, and their bedroom, which were empty. In the children's wing, she found Emma and Sam watching a video with Debbie, but no Michael.

'I'm wondering if something has happened.' Grace was waiting for her in the kitchen; she raised her eyebrows at the words chosen. 'All right, I'm sure something's wrong. Those spots on her shirt looked like blood.'

'How did she get so muddy? It looks as if it hasn't rained much for days round here, the ground is bone dry.'

'Ah, but there's one place on our land that's always muddy, there's a tiny spring in the wood. Tiny in the summer, anyway. It's a bog in winter. But when it's bone dry everywhere, there's always mud there.'

'Do you want to go and have a look?'

'Yes.'

They tramped across the grass without speaking for a while. Jane took a flashlight, but did not use it; a huge brilliant moon had risen above the gathering clouds. Preparing for the deep night, the land was cool and quiet, except for the rustling of dry crops in a fitful breeze.

'I don't have a good feeling about this,' Jane said at last. 'It's nothing rational, it's just . . .'

'It's not like Michael, somehow. A charmed life, he's got.'

Later Grace asked, 'Is that a full moon?'

'Yes. Don't worry, Gascony is not noted for its werewolves.'

They were not really in the mood for humour. Jane led the way confidently into the trees, retracing her route on the mushroom hunt. There was a bright patch of moonlight by the spring, and the ground had been thoroughly trampled, but there was no evidence of Michael.

'I feel stupid,' Jane said at last. 'I don't know what ridiculous idea I had . . . Imogen's always blamed him for everything. Especially her mother. I couldn't make her out when she was tiny, maybe it's having children of my own that's helped me to understand. She's just been in a fury with him all the time I've known her, but because she's a powerless child she never has been able to hurt him, except by spending his money or letting him down somehow, or hurting herself.'

Aimlessly, they walked on, with the vague objective of reaching the railway line before they turned back. Apart from the surreal two-dimensional planes of moonlight, it was almost as bright as day towards the edge of the wood. The long dark shape on the bank was clearly visible.

Afterwards, they admitted that they had known immediately, by instinct, that Michael was dead. At the time, they nerved themselves to go sensibly forward, kneel down by the body, touch it, search for a pulse in a wrist and then in the neck, and systematically verify that his limbs were utterly cold, he was not breathing, there was no pulse and no reaction from his half-open eyes.

Afterwards, they admitted that in this process they had both recalled touching his body in the early ardour of love, and felt a piercing visceral regret for a joy long lost but still treasured, and not completely despaired of, even in the coldest agony of their hatred.

To keep their courage up, they talked as they knelt beside him, their legs getting lacerated by the butcher's broom. While her reason told her that Michael was dead, Jane could not comprehend it; the struggle against this man's monstrous intelligence was her whole life.

'Do you think – did he have . . . a heart attack? Could Imogen – what happened?' Grace felt herself shiver.

'He never took care of his health.' Jane turned on the flashlight and used the beam to probe the deep shadows around the body. She raked the litter of dead leaves with her fingers to see if by any chance there was a stone big enough to fracture a skull buried underneath. The flashlight which he had carried was still gripped in one hand.

'What's that?' Hesitantly, Grace touched something half in shadow at the base of the neck. In full light, it was a wooden handle bound with twine, sticking out of the hollow of the collarbone. The shirt around it was bloody.

'I know what that is. It's the knife I use for mushrooms. I've been looking for it in the kitchen all weekend.'

Grace said, before she could stop herself: 'He's been killed then.'

'It looks like it. I know – natural causes would have

been nice.' That was it, the instant of conspiracy from which everything they did afterwards flowed inevitably. A fatal accident was ideal, that was the verdict of them both. Then they thought of Imogen.

'I can't believe she did this.' Jane regained her feet and walked away from the body, wanting to be away from it and keep her mind under control. 'Look at the position of it, too. This is the most awkward place to reach if they were both standing – she's not taller than he is, after all?'

'He can't have fallen on it. And she will be the prime suspect.'

'Yes. Poor wretched child. All she needs.' There was suddenly no breath in her lungs; she gulped the air. 'Let's go where it's light and think about this.'

On the shoulder of the railway embankment the moon was clear and bright. Feeling the approach of an extraordinary moment, they sat down on the ground and Grace asked, 'So where was the knife the last time you saw it?'

'So much has happened today. And yesterday. Let me think back. It wasn't there when the salmon came. I can remember having it when I went out with Louisa for the mushrooms a couple of days ago.'

'What happened?'

'Why are we so calm?'

'I don't know.' Grace could have answered the question. They were calm because they had been chosen for it; Michael's women did not panic. For what they had to endure, good nerves were essential.

Jane ran through the now distant memory of Friday morning until the episode of the wallowing deer.

'Ah! That's it! Louisa had the knife – she dropped it when she fell over, and in all the drama, while she was carrying on the way she does, I forgot it and left it out here. In the same place, where the stream is.'

'It was just lying around and Imi found it?'

'She must have done.'

'But to have actually killed him . . .'

'I know.' An idea was forming in front of Jane's eyes, a perfect idea, pleading for her attention, so thrilling that she had flinched from acknowledging it, feeling that as soon as she admitted it into her mind it would compel and control her.

Grace looked vacantly across the track to the bank opposite, her eye temporarily fascinated by the gleam of the moonlight on the rails and the white clinker below them. 'It feels like we made it happen. We were sitting there in the kitchen talking about him, getting out all the things we'd suffered and at exactly that moment . . . exactly . . .'

She stretched out her bare legs and observed the marble sheen of her skin under the moon, while her mind turned over the options they had. None of them had anything approaching the majestic sense of justice aroused by Michael's death. A macabre peace was settling over her, against her will; she wanted to feel disturbed, at the least, but could not.

'I didn't finish what I was saying.' Should she trust this woman now? All that sisterly intimacy, that comradeship of suffering, it could be nothing, an emotional illusion born of wishing for comfort. Forcefully, instinct prompted Jane to speak. 'I was going to say I hated him. I'd put it off a long time, facing that. But I do. Or I did. I hate him. Don't you?'

In her new state of calm, Grace examined her heart. 'No, I don't think so. He wasn't standing over my life the way he was over yours. Objectively, yes, I think he was – evil. But it's not a feeling, just an opinion.'

'Well, for me right now, I'd say it was a passion. Do you know what I can't forgive him? It's not just that he betrayed you and me. It's everything he said about love. He talked about it being so important to him, but really . . . he was just using the word. It didn't mean anything to him.' She turned towards Grace, her voice low and rough, her pale hair in the surreal light seeming incandescent. 'I thought we believed the same thing about it: love is everything to me. It's what life's for, it's how life's made, it *is* life. And he trashed it. He pissed on it. I hate him, and I'm glad he's dead.' She sat back upright, looking down at her hands. 'The question is, what are we going to do? Because if he's found like this, Imogen will go to jail for killing him.'

'In a place like this they won't be able to pin it on a wandering psycho. These sleepy little villages, people know every blade of grass.' They were silent, listening to the gathering wind stirring the tree branches, then Grace asked, 'Did you ever meet his first wife?'

'Pia? You mean that story he tells – told – about her cracking up. It's a lie, it was all lies, of course it was. He took care we never met. Stephen and Imi went all the way up to Seattle last year and stayed a few days. She's perfectly fine, normal. She just couldn't take it. Can you blame her?'

'I used to wonder if that was how it was.'

'And he frightened her off for years, gave her propaganda about it being best for Imi to stay away. I trust Stephen, he tells the truth and he cares for Imi. I should have done it, because I'd figured the whole thing out years ago. I never did enough for Imogen. I failed her. The least I ought to have done was fought Michael harder for her.'

She leaned over and covered one of Grace's hands with her own. 'Look, I can't let her suffer for this. She can't have known what she was doing. There is one way though. Will you trust me?'

Astonished at her own self-possession, Grace said, 'Probably. Tell me what you want to do.'

'We can make it look like an accident. It's really simple and we can do it; there'll be no evidence.'

'How?'

'In a few hours the train will be thundering along this track pulling ten tons of wheat behind it. If he's on the line, it will look like an accident. He will be crushed.' When it came to the last word, Jane could not quite say it.

Then Grace felt the irresistible perfection of it, and it took hold of her imagination as it had possessed Jane. She said nothing, thinking through every angle, while Jane continued in an urgent tone: 'No one will ever know. When the train comes through here it's been running downhill in the cutting for half a mile already. I promise you, I've watched it with the children. It'll be going too fast for anyone to see anything, much too fast to stop.'

Deliberately, neither of them spoke of the train driver. This was no time to be undone again by their own decency and compassion. They set about the task quietly, not liking to discuss any more than necessary in case their courage failed. There was an impression of flying above everything, looking down on themselves. Michael's body was large and heavy and awkward and they were ill-matched in strength, but as soon as they lifted it that definite sense that it was not him, only a discarded husk, gave them the power they needed to carry it down the breakneck slope and across the rough clinker.

In silent, careful unison, like two craftsmen who have long toiled side by side, they laid him with his neck on the rail to be certain that the wound itself would be obliterated. No memories rose in their minds to undermine their resolve. Jane took the knife by the handle, sensed its lie and pulled it out in one clean movement.

By the time they left the wood the moon was disappearing behind a hard-edged black cloud. They returned by the side of the house. 'Tell me what to expect now,' Jane asked, suddenly beginning to feel her fear. 'What's the legal procedure for something like this?'

Calming herself as well as the other woman, Grace related her experience of French inquests. 'You will never tell,' Jane asked suddenly. 'Even after I'm dead, if one of the children . . .'

'No. Of course not.'

'I'm sorry, I shouldn't have asked . . .'

'Or you, you won't . . .'

'Never. Of course not.' They made for the building standing some yards off the courtyard gate, which had been the pigsties and was now garages. There was a tap in the wall with a hose connected to it, and towels drying on the washing line. They took off their shoes and washed the mud and dust from their legs, and the small smear of blood from the knife, prudently letting the water run a while to flush the drain through. Then they waited by the gates until they felt calm enough to go inside the house.

'We must do everything as normally as we can.' Grace was dealing with an awkward, unexpected emotion. 'So we'll be away soon, but . . . Jane, I will be around. If you need me. Not just – what we've done – you . . . well, today was a sort of setting free for me.'

'And for me. I will need you. Don't you think we'll need each other?'

Someone had reached up to the shelf over the fireplace and taken down the two wooden candelabra. They had lit candles and placed them down the centre of the table; the electric lights were still on and the scene was richly illuminated. As Jane opened the door, she thought of a Victorian genre painting, a picture sentimentally gilded with virtue. The scene in the kitchen was close to her cherished imaginings of an abundant family celebration around the hearth.

Needing to get a better grip on their emotions, the two women waited unnoticed in the doorway. Sam, in his night-clothes, was passing knives and forks to Debbie, who was laying places at the table. Stephen occupied the carver chair at the far end and Antony leaned over his shoulder, filling his glass with red wine. At his elbow, on the corner of the table, was a checkerboard; Emma, with a wicked expression suggesting she had won at least the last game, was setting out the counters. At the work table Imogen was in the process of cutting a loaf and was stealing a mouthful of the soft, fragrant centre. The distant, in-turned look which she had worn all day was gone, and her face was clear and open.

Beside her, Louisa and Nick were arguing about salad dressing. She had about her the flouncing animation which Jane recognized as an indication that for once she had enjoyed a satisfactory erotic experience; a second glance at Antony detected a certain cat-like satisfaction on his face.

'Garlic crushed in salt is always sweeter,' Louisa was saying. She was clutching a wooden salad bowl protectively in her arms. 'The salt takes off that eye-watering edge.'

'But I *like* the eye-watering edge,' and he closed the crusher defiantly over the bowl. Louisa pouted in annoyance. Grace wanted to kiss him. It must be true what Jane had said, at the sight of him she had felt herself illuminated. But first, she had a final responsibility.

'Crushed garlic turns bitter in cooking.'

'But we aren't cooking it.' How could anyone be annoyed with the dear man?

'Suit yourself.' Louisa gave him the bowl. In sashaying

away from her disobedient new apprentice, she was the first to see them. 'There you are. We've been wondering about you two . . .'

'We went for a walk.' The power of lying. It was sinister, but Jane felt it. Grace followed her into the room, her hands in her pockets, concealing the knife. There was such an atmosphere of harmony in the kitchen that her fear was melting away. She could see the knife block on the work table; it was quite natural to walk towards it.

'We didn't know what you wanted to do about *dinner*? And where's Michael? Everybody's starving.' Jane felt accused, but did not react; dear Louisa, last in the queue when restraint was handed out.

'Well, we don't need to wait if people are hungry. Let's see what there is to eat.' Jane strode to the refrigerator and pulled open both doors, confident of the bounty within. 'Bayonne ham, cooked ham done with hay . . .'

'Oooh!' Emma forgot her game and came over, eager to carry dishes. 'How do you cook ham with hay, Mummy?'

'Marinated artichokes, broad beans with savory . . .'

'Nobody does veggies as well as you, Jane.' Miraculously, it was Imogen, speaking with her mouth full.

'Pâté from Tamara's darling savage piggies . . .'

'Hooray!' Louisa forgot her ill-temper. 'I've been longing to try them.'

'Well, everybody . . .'

Jane was exhausted. On her pale face the shadows of

tiredness were almost mauve; her dress had crumpled and her hair, although neat as ever, hung lifelessly against her cheeks. All the same, Grace noticed, she looked pretty and girlish in the light from the interior of the refrigerator. The heavy etching of strain had disappeared and her eyes no longer had a darkening of pain in them.

In the eager commotion and the carrying of dishes to the table, Grace walked unnoticed across the room and, as Jane had directed, slipped the knife back into its home in the lowest hole of the block. At the sink she ran water over her fingers, then she felt hands on her hips and a kiss on the back of her neck. Of course it was Nick. 'I missed you, you were gone for hours. Do you know it's nearly ten? I hope you're driving. That Pacherenc de Vic Bilh goes down a treat.'

'I like that shirt on you.' It was a dark forest green, a colour she did not remember him wearing before.

'Do you realize we forgot something?'

For a fearful second she thought that he had guessed everything, but then he showed her the present she had carefully wrapped for Jane the previous evening, the old butcher's labels from Castillon market. 'I found them when I took my case back to the car.'

'Oh my goodness.' She felt almost likely to hiccup with relief. 'Shall we give them to her now? It is a good time, isn't it?'

'If you're sure?'

'Yes, yes, of course I'm sure. Much better now than when we arrived.'

Clumsily, because Nick was still uncertain that these

odd little bygones were a suitable present, he made a little ceremony of the presentation. Grace saw Jane's pale face colour with the first genuine pleasure in being a hostess that she had shown all day.

'Oh! Absolutely divine! Look at this ridiculous chicken – wherever did you find them?' Louisa seized the labels with rapture. Emma insisted they should decorate the dishes on the table immediately and Antony, whose mood was positively skittish, picked out 'beautiful breast, 3 francs a kilo' and tucked it into the straining neckline of Louisa's blouse.

The feast commenced with enthusiasm. The cooked ham was massacred, the Bayonne ham mutilated. 'Now you see why I'm not a surgeon,' Nick said, dealing out shreds and corners with a generous hand.

The entire party was inspired. Sam ate salad, at which Emma caught her mother's astonished eye and put her finger to her lips.

'I mustn't drink.' Grace covered her glass. 'I'm chauffeur tonight.'

'Suppose she asks us to stay over?' Her husband was under the impression that he was whispering.

'I want to go home tonight.' He kissed her fingers; he had misunderstood her, and she was glad of it.

The whole party was absorbed in eating. Conversation was fragmentary and punctuated with expressions of relish. Jane sat at the end of the table and smiled at the compliments, urging people to try her pickled lemon chutney and prompting the children to pass dishes, while a growing sense of detachment settled upon her. She was numb, she recognized. It was the same eerie isolation that came upon her after childbirth, a mixture of physical exhaustion and mental trauma. She experienced it always as a protected state, when the primitive survival instincts of the body kicked in and took over its hour-to-hour operation until her conscious self was fit to rule again.

She reached for a bottle of water but missed her grasp, a failure which confirmed the theory. Her sense of distance had disappeared. One of her bitterest memories was driving home from hospital after Sam's birth; Michael had been absent, and never thought to send her help. Her car was in the car park, she had already driven herself when her waters broke. In a fit of rebellious independence she had decided to drive home with her son in his carry-cot, and the road then, like the table now, became an interesting scheme of objects whose precise relation to each other she was unable to estimate.

No one had asked about Michael. The household was so accustomed to his absence that it was natural to be without him. Natural and, it seemed, better; people's natures seemed to flower more freely without his dominating presence. Even Antony, she noticed, was drinking in moderation and being an entertaining guest. He was giving an imitation of a yuppie wine snob complaining about an order which was hilarious, even to Louisa.

'Mummy.' Emma climbed on the arm of her chair and put her arms around her neck. 'You look sad, Mummy.'

'Do I?'

'Are you tired? If you are, why don't you slip off and go to bed? Nobody will mind and we can clear up.' Her daughter was talking to her in the same soothing voice she used herself. Jane laughed.

'I'm OK, Em. I'll be fine, don't worry.'

'But we love you and we want you to take care of yourself. Let me run you a nice bath . . .'

'Not now, darling. It's a very kind thought – maybe tomorrow.'

Xanthe's fretful voice came over the baby alarm, she was fetched and sat on Stephen's lap while the ice cream was dispensed. A chocolate tart was remembered and as Jane was installing it at the centre of the table a huge crack of thunder shook the glass in the open windows. Rain hissed and pattered outside a few seconds later. People got up to watch the lightning. Someone threw the switches, leaving the room to the flickering candle-light. When the lightning came it was spectacular, great triple forks stabbing the horizon.

The storm was in no hurry, and after a while the attraction of it palled and the wind began to gust, so that they had to shut the windows. Seeing the children shrieking for further excitement, Nick said, 'Now, in our house, we have a custom on nights like this. We read to each other, like people did before television.'

'When was before television?' It seemed that Sam doubted such an era had ever existed.

'Oh, a long time ago.'

'Before dinosaurs?'

'After dinosaurs. When my father was about your age, I should think.'

'Don't you have one, then?'

'I dropped it when we brought our stuff down from Paris,' Grace confessed. 'And we never got around to getting another one.'

'What's your best book to read?' Emma was looking at Nick with eyes made enormous by tiredness, as well as adoration.

'My favourite is the book about the musketeers, at the beginning, where D'Artagnan sets off from just around the corner from our house to ride all the way to Paris on his father's poor old yellow horse which everybody laughs at . . .'

He got no further before Louisa whisked the book off the mantelshelf and slapped it down in front of him. It was opened, and passed around the table, and held up to the candles as they read. While Emma was stumbling through the secret recipe for Madame D'Artagnan's special ointment which healed every wound except wounds of the heart, a new note was added to the drumming of the rain. Jane looked up at the clock. The train was on time. Grace had not heard it. She was looking at her husband with wet eyes, feeling poignantly miserable at the sight of him sitting around a long table with another woman's children.

A few minutes later, Nick was asking Antony about brandy, and he began to hold forth on the subject, beginning cautiously by saying, 'The taste of Armagnac is a difficult thing to describe, even for a connoisseur. The men who make it describe it as like a dancing fire followed by a velvet flame, which is extraordinary but it doesn't say very much . . .'

Jane put the bottle on the table, came around to where Grace was sitting and leaned on the back of her chair.

'It is a more powerful brandy than Cognac. Like its country,' he waved his glass to embrace the entire province, 'and its people, it is exciting and given to excess.' He frowned at Louisa. 'And they say that while Cognac is like a pretty young girl in a cotton dress, Armagnac is a tempestuous older woman, who excites the blood and scandalizes your mother . . .'

'Do you realize,' Jane whispered, 'what your husband has done? Years I've dreamed of this table like this, a whole family around it sharing a meal – not just eating in the same place, but *sharing.* Now he's made it happen.'

'Are you all right?' Grace was physically tired, and feeble after the high emotion of the day, but underneath that she felt oddly disconnected. Jane looked very pale. Her skin by the light of the candles was shadowy and her eyes seemed hollow and fearful.

'Why, because I'm being emotional?'

'No, just are you?'

'No. I'm in shock, I guess. I feel I could sleep for a month.'

'Me too. It'll be a while before we can believe what's happened today, I think.'

They looked at each other without speaking for a few moments, feeling the strength of the bond which had formed between them so quickly and then been put to such an unthinkable test. So many secrets bound them together, secrets of Michael's conjuring and of their own creation.

Jane broke the silence, wanting to make it easy for Grace to do what she must; in a voice that was suddenly pleasant and social, she asked, 'Will you be going soon?'

'Yes, but . . .' Surprise brightened Grace's tired eyes.

'I know you won't be strangers. Don't forget, I need you.' There was a slim, cool hand on her shoulder and Grace pressed it.

In spite of the late hour, the three children were bright and wakeful, particularly Xanthe, who began running around the table, laughing and inviting the others to chase her. Debbie persuaded them outside into the corridor to work off their energy, and in the temporary lull Louisa suddenly demanded, 'What on earth has happened to Michael? He's missed all the fun.'

Jane would have liked to have said nothing, but she saw everyone except Grace looking to her for an answer. 'Perhaps he's sneaked away to his office,' she suggested.

'Who cares?' Defiantly unconcerned, Imogen picked up the last crumbs of pastry from the tart. 'If he wanted to be here with us, we would know.'

In the face of the author of the outrage, no one cared to put forward the suggestion that Michael's mood might have been affected by the disastrous events of the day. All the men suddenly looked embarrassed. Jane said, 'Maybe I should go and see if he's all right.'

'I'll come with you,' Louisa offered, standing up and hoisting the unfastened waistband of her skirt back into its proper position. 'Maybe he's not feeling well, or something.'

From the empty office they went upstairs to the

bedroom, then descended and looked around the covered terrace. The rain was still falling heavily; the terrace had no gutter and water ran off the roof tiles in streams. Louisa felt cold, shrugged her shoulders and said, 'Oh, come on. Imogen's right, he'd be here if he wanted to be. He's probably got out of the rain somewhere, or gone off to the bar in Saint-Victor to drown his sorrows. Let's go back inside.' Jane followed her without another word, curious that she felt nothing that would have been appropriate, no guilt, alarm or anxiety, only exhaustion and a persistent sense that everything was happening in another dimension.

It was 2 a.m. by the time Grace slid behind the wheel of the MGB and negotiated the track to the main road. It was still raining heavily; visibility was hardly twenty yards. She drove slowly, finding pools of water unexpectedly at bends in the road. The gargoyles on Saint-Victor's church spouted noisily into the street and the water drummed on the car bonnet.

She poured all her concentration into the task of driving, relieved to have the events of the day temporarily wiped from her mind. Beside her, Nick fell asleep. In the garish light from the factories she saw the rain gusting across the road like a storm on a film set, curtains of water blown by the wind. A file of container trucks passed in the opposite direction, spraying waves of water over the low MGB, forcing splashes through the small holes in the soft top. She reached into the back of the car for a coat to protect her husband from the drips.

Some miles further on and the rain began to fall steadily and less hard. Towards the end of the highway it eased off to a few drops, and she switched off the windscreen wipers. The pilgrim road zigzagged across the hilltops, with cascades of water coursing down each side of it and puddles in all the potholes. The fresh light of dawn was gathering, throwing the far-off hills into silhouette. An occasional bird swooped low over the dripping crops.

As they approached their village in the half-dark the car disturbed a field of geese and she smiled to herself to hear the ghostly white birds honking in alarm and scrambling away from the hedge. The tyres scrunched on the gravelly surface; here there had not been so much rain. The centre of the road looked completely dry, a silver-white ribbon leading up to their square church tower.

Nick stirred beside her and asked if they were home. He sat up and rubbed his face, scratching behind his ears to wake himself up, yawned and reached over to pat her thigh. Water had splashed over her lap, and her red skirt was stained. 'Well driven,' he said.

Gently, she ran the car across the empty village square and stopped in front of the Alhambra.

In the cool kitchen the white cat was waiting reproachfully, accompanied by two black and white kittens. Grace put down two helpings of milk and they watched the tiny ones dive into the dish and withdraw in surprise, shaking their heads and licking their noses.

For a while they trailed restlessly around their house,

reassuring themselves that they were home and they were together. Grace was tired, but not ready for sleep. There was a tension between them, something new she could not identify. As she watched her husband idly picking up utensils as he reconnected with the kitchen she became aware of a peculiar dual emotion, both trust and fear; trust in his goodness, as immovable as the earth itself, and fear of her own frailty beside it.

Outside, the sky was a faint turquoise colour. She walked out into the garden, enjoying the scents of the flowers in the damp air, watching the raindrops shivering on the rose petals. Nick made tea in the British brown teapot which all their French friends found so amusing. They went upstairs and she took a shower. He asked her to leave the water running for him.

There were fresh white cotton sheets on the bed; some instinct had instructed her to change the linen before they left, all those extraordinary hours ago. Destiny was not a concept she enjoyed, but she felt that what had happened had all been inevitable, that to have tried to act in another way would have been to refuse her part in a natural drama.

She began to brush out her hair. He came out of the bathroom with a towel around his waist and another in his hands, drying his arms. He sat on the bed beside her.

'You look different.' The blue eyes were examining her face.

'Do I?'

'You looked unhappy earlier. Now you look – I don't know . . .' She had the lucid, direct gaze of a small child, but he was reluctant to try to describe it. Words were her business.

'You've caught the sun,' she said, touching the soft skin by his eyes.

'That was an awful day. I'm sorry we went.'

'No, I think we had to do it, don't you?' Of course, in the deep, instinctive level of his mind, he knew everything. There had never been any secrets between them, that had only been another illusion of her conscience. The invisible barrier which had kept them apart against their will had dissolved. She said, 'Your breath smells of ginger,' and reached up to kiss him.

His skin felt new and his mouth fresh. This time their desire was directed by a mystical sense of harmony. They wanted to be simple, and affectionate; all the most ordinary acts had the dazzling glamour of new love. The touch of skin to skin was thrilling, the movement of lying down together was exquisite. All technique was forgotten. The first instant of joining their bodies passed like a flash of light. They threw themselves into their love as if into a river where they would dissolve into each other, and into a new life.

The morning over Les Palombières brought a misty precipitation that was not quite rain. The entire sky was packed with fluffy, light grey clouds, lying in ridges like a ploughed field.

Jane woke late to find that Emma had made coffee for her; regretfully, she sent the child away to play while she prepared herself for the day ahead. It was already ten o'clock. She had been sunk in an exhausted sleep. The first emotion of which she grew aware was a gentle satisfaction connected to Imogen. From the day Michael had entered her life his daughter had haunted them, an unquiet spirit who would not be consoled. Jane had denied the guilt, but it had never left her. Part of her blamed herself, part of her argued that in becoming Michael's lover she had expelled Pia from her daughter's life just as much as he had.

Now that burden on her conscience was lighter. She had done something for Imogen at last, something of much more significance than the daily chores of parenthood. She had taken a great risk for the girl's sake as well as her own. At the same time Imogen herself, after the worst of her vengeful outrages, had felt regret for the first time. There would be more suffering for her, but perhaps after it the time for healing would come at last.

In her numb, automatic state, Jane slowly recalled the plan she had discussed with Grace in the bad dream of the evening. She was preparing to drive into Saint-Victor to report Michael missing, and was backing the car out of the garage, when she saw another vehicle coming down the track, a police car. The mayor of Saint-Victor got out of it, followed by the young officer who this year had been stationed on the roundabout on market days.

The mayor, a substantial man in a dark suit with short black hair flecked all over with grey, was subdued by his solemn purpose. He was anxious that his choice of phrases should be appropriately delicate; it was a few minutes before Jane could discern the facts among the extreme regrets and the unfortunate necessities.

At the railway yard at Bordeaux, where the communal train had stopped for fuel, routine checks were made and remains, perhaps human, had been discovered at the front of the engine. A search had been made immediately, although after first light progress had been much faster. It was at the edge of their land that a discovery had been made.

Stephen came out to join her and, steadied by his solid innocence at her side, Jane delivered her account of Michael's movements the day before. Soon Louisa and Antony joined them and the mayor, reassured to find that the lady had the support of her friends and family, continued with the suggestion to which he had given greatest thought; the scene of such an accident was difficult to speak of. By the afternoon the police surgeon would have supervised the removal to his laboratory. It was unfortunately necessary to make a formal identification, and possible for the family to do so then.

When the time came, they accomplished the affair with due formality and undue tact. She chose to go alone. She was shown an unmarked shoe and a few fragments of Michael's wallet and the papers in it. It was enough.

The hardest task was to tell the children, but they had few words, death being too large for their understanding to grasp at once. Imogen was ready to be tough, but stopped herself. It was of course Stephen who was distressed. The years of antagonism between Michael and himself immediately weighed on his conscience; he wanted to talk over their last encounter, concerned that his hostility, however well checked, had been a factor affecting Michael's actions afterwards. The others listened and reassured him. Jane went out to the terrace and stood looking over the drenched land, hearing the night's rainfall still dripping from stems. Her mind was washed out now. There would be an inquest, of course, but she contemplated that without alarm.

That was wrong. She strained to find the correct emotions. Where were they – her grief, her remorse, her guilt? Had she perhaps lost the ability to feel what was natural in all those years of collaboration with Michael's deceptions? A great man was dead – and she acknowledged Michael had been a great man, in the world if not in his home. His children were fatherless, and would never know the circumstances of his death. Try as she might to goad her instincts into life, they did not respond; she wanted to weep but her eyes were dry and she wanted to reproach herself but her heart was unmoved. In hatred, in a foolish conspiracy with a stranger, she had committed a crime – at the very least she should be afraid.

Instead, an unearthly tranquillity possessed her. It was beyond her at that moment to be more than anxious or fearful for the future. Perhaps soon her conscience would rear up and destroy this new peace; if it did, could that be worse than what she had endured before?